THE GUARDIAN

THE GUARDIAN

Julie Baranson's young husband left her two unexpected gifts before he died—a puppy named Singer and the promise he would always be watching over her. Now, four years later, twenty-nine-year-old Julie is far too young to have given up on love. She may be ready to risk caring for someone again. But who?

Should it be Richard Franklin, the sophisticated, handsome engineer who treats her like a queen? Or Mike Hardt, the down-to-earth nice guy who was her husband's best friend? Choosing one of them should bring her more happiness than she's had in years. Instead, Julie is soon fighting for her life in a nightmare spawned by a chilling deception and a jealousy so poisonous that it has become murderous desire.

Dear Jules,

I know that if you're reading this letter, I've already passed away. I don't know how long I've been gone, but I hope you've been able to begin healing. I know that if I were in your position, it would be hard for me, but you know I've always believed you were the stronger of the two of us.

I bought you a dog, as you can see. Harold Kuphaldt was a friend of my father's, and he's been raising Great Danes since I was a kid. I always wanted one when I was little, but since the house was so small, Mom always said no. They are big dogs, granted, but according to Harold, they're also just about the sweetest dogs in the world. I hope you enjoy him (or her).

I guess I always knew in the back of my mind that I wasn't going to make it. I didn't want to think about it, though, because I knew that you didn't have anyone to help you get through something like this. Family, I mean. It broke my heart to think that you would be all alone. Not knowing what else to do, I made arrangements to get you this dog.

If you don't like it, you don't have to keep it, of course. Harold said he'd take it back, no problem. (His number should be included.)

I hope you're doing all right. Since I got sick, I've worried non-stop about that. I love you, Jules, I really do. I was the luckiest guy in the world when you came into my life. It would break my heart if I thought you'd never be happy again. So please do that for me. Be happy again. Find someone who makes you happy. It might be hard, you might not think it's possible, but I'd like you to try. The world is a better place when you smile.

And don't worry. From wherever I am, I'll watch out for you. I'll be your guardian angel, sweetheart. You can count on me to keep you safe.

I love you,

Jim

THE GUARDIAN

Nicholas Sparks

WINDSOR
PARAGON

First published 2003
by
Time Warner Books
This Large Print edition published 2004
by arrangement with Time Warner Books

ISBN 0 7540 9520 7 (Windsor Hardcover)
ISBN 0 7540 9411 1 (Paragon Softcover)

British Library Cataloguing in Publication Data available

Printed and bound in Great Britain by
Antony Rowe Ltd., Chippenham, Wiltshire

For Larry Kirshbaum and Maureen Egen
Wonderful people, wonderful friends

Acknowledgments

It would be impossible to begin any acknowledgments without thanking Cathy, my wife of nearly fourteen years. You're the sweetest person I know, and I love you more than you could ever imagine.

And, of course, no book would be complete without thanking the kiddies. Miles, Ryan, Landon, Lexie, and Savannah can be a handful, but are nonetheless a source of endless joy. My days would be incomplete without you.

Theresa Park of Sanford Greenburger Associates also deserves my thanks. Theresa, you're my agent and manager, but also a genius and a sympathetic ear. You're also one of my dearest friends. It's hard to believe we've been through seven novels so far, and I look forward to many more in the future.

Jamie Raab, my editor, is quite simply the best editor in the business, and this book, more than any other, needed her patient guidance. Jamie, I couldn't have completed this novel without you, and it's my honor to work with someone as wise and kind as you are.

Denise DiNovi, the producer of *Message in a Bottle* and *A Walk to Remember*, has become one of the most special people in my life. Denise, thank you so much for changing my life for the better. I don't know if there will ever be a way I can repay you.

Julie Barer, an agent at Sanford Greenburger, was gracious enough to read and offer suggestions for the manuscript while on vacation. Julie, I can't thank you enough for what you did, and I hope you're pleased with the main character.

Howie Sanders and Richard Green, my film agents at UTA, also deserve my thanks for their work not only on this project, but on all of my novels. They are the best at what they do.

Scott Schwimer, my entertainment attorney, is not only fabulous at what he does, but also a friend who makes my job a lot easier. Thanks for always sticking by me.

Dave Park, my television agent at UTA, has patiently guided me through the intricacies of the television world, and deserves my thanks for all the work involved with *The Rescue*.

Lorenzo De Bonaventura and Courtenay Valenti of Warner Brothers, Lynn Harris of New Line Cinema, Mark Johnson, Hunt Lowry, and Ed Gaylord II have all been tremendous to work with and deserve my thanks.

Jennifer Romanello, Emi Battaglia, Edna Farley in publicity, editor John Aherne, and Flag have all helped to make my career what it is. Thanks all.

And finally, thanks to Todd Robinson for working so diligently on the television series. I'm fortunate to have been able to team up with you.

Prologue

Christmas Eve 1998

Exactly forty days after she'd last held the hand of her husband, Julie Barenson sat looking through her window toward the quiet streets of Swansboro. It was cold; the sky had been angry for a week, and the rain made gentle tapping sounds against the window. Trees were barren, their cragged limbs curling in the frigid air like arthritic fingers.

She knew Jim would have wanted her to listen to music tonight; she could hear Bing Crosby singing 'White Christmas' in the background. She'd put up the tree for him as well, though by the time she'd made that decision, the only trees left were dried out and sparse, free for the taking outside the supermarket. It didn't matter. Even when she finished decorating it, she couldn't summon the energy to care. It had been hard to feel anything at all since the tumor in Jim's brain finally took his life.

At twenty-five, she was a widow and she hated everything about the word: how it sounded, what it implied, the way her mouth moved when she formed the word. She avoided it completely. If people asked how she was doing, she simply shrugged. But sometimes, just sometimes, she had the urge to answer. *You want to know what it was like to lose my husband?* she wanted to ask. *Here's what it's like.*

Jim's dead, and now that he's gone, I feel like I'm dead, too.

Is that, Julie wondered, what people wanted to

1

hear? Or did they want platitudes? *I'll be okay. It's hard, but I'll make it through this. Thank you for asking.* She could do the brave soldier routine, she supposed, but she never had. It was both easier and more honest to simply shrug and say nothing.

After all, she didn't feel as if she were going to be okay. Half the time, she didn't think she was going to make it through the day without breaking down. Especially on nights like tonight.

In the reflected glow of the Christmas tree lights, Julie put her hand to the window, feeling the cold press of glass against her skin.

Mabel had asked if she'd wanted to have dinner tonight, but Julie had declined. So had Mike and Henry and Emma, but she'd turned them down as well. All of them understood. Or, rather, they pretended to understand, since it was obvious that none of them thought she should be alone. And maybe they were right. Everything in the house, everything she saw and smelled and touched, reminded her of Jim. His clothes took up half the closet, his razor still sat next to the soap dish in the bathroom, the subscription to *Sports Illustrated* had come in the mail the day before. There were still two bottles of Heineken, his favorite, in the refrigerator. Earlier that evening, when she'd seen them on the shelf, she'd whispered to herself, 'Jim is never going to drink those,' and she'd closed the door and leaned against it, crying in the kitchen for an hour.

The scene outside her window was out of focus; lost in her thoughts, Julie gradually registered the faint sound of a branch thumping against the wall. The thumping was persistent, steady, and it was a moment before she realized she'd been mistaken about the branch.

2

Someone was knocking at the door.

Julie stood, her movements lethargic. At the door, she paused to run her hands through her hair, hoping to compose herself. If it was her friends checking in on her, she didn't want them to think she needed them to stay for a while. When she opened the door, however, she was surprised to see a young man in a yellow slicker. In his hands was a large, wrapped box.

'Mrs Barenson?' he asked.

'Yes?'

The stranger took a hesitant step forward. 'I'm supposed to deliver this to you. My dad said it was important.'

'Your dad?'

'He wanted to make sure you got this tonight.'

'Do I know him?'

'I don't know. But he was pretty insistent about it. It's a gift from someone.'

'Who?'

'My father said you'd understand as soon as you opened it. Don't shake it, though – and keep this end up.'

The young man pushed the box into Julie's arms before she could stop him, then turned to leave.

'Wait,' she said, 'I don't understand . . .'

The young man glanced over his shoulder. 'Merry Christmas,' he said.

Julie stood in the doorway, watching as he climbed into his truck. Then, back inside, she set the box on the floor in front of the tree and knelt beside it. A quick peek confirmed the absence of a card, and there were no other clues about the sender. She loosened the ribbon, then lifted the separately wrapped lid and found herself staring

1

wordlessly at what she'd been given.

It was matted with fuzz and dwarflike, no more than a few pounds, and it was sitting on its haunches in the corner of the box, looking just about as ugly as she'd ever seen a puppy look. Its head was large, out of proportion to the rest of its body. Whimpering, it looked up at her, a glob of muck in its eyes.

Someone, she thought, bought me a puppy. An ugly puppy.

Taped to the inside of the box was an envelope. As she reached for it, it dawned on her that she recognized the handwriting, and she paused. No, she thought, it can't be . . .

She had seen that handwriting on the love letters he'd written to her on their anniversaries, on hastily scrawled messages by the phone, on paperwork he'd piled on the desk. She held the envelope in front of her, reading her name over and over. Then, with trembling hands, she took the letter out. Her eyes traveled to the words written in the upper left corner.

Dear Jules,

It was Jim's nickname for her, and Julie closed her eyes, feeling as if her body were suddenly growing smaller. She forced herself to take a deep breath and started again.

Dear Jules,
    I know that if you're reading this letter, I've already passed away. I don't know how long I've been gone, but I hope you've been able to begin healing. I know that if I were in your position, it

2

would be hard for me, but you know I've always believed you were the stronger of the two of us.

I bought you a dog, as you can see. Harold Kuphaldt was a friend of my father's, and he's been raising Great Danes since I was a kid. I always wanted one when I was little, but since the house was so small, Mom always said no. They are big dogs, granted, but according to Harold, they're also just about the sweetest dogs in the world. I hope you enjoy him (or her).

I guess I always knew in the back of my mind that I wasn't going to make it. I didn't want to think about it, though, because I knew that you didn't have anyone to help you get through something like this. Family, I mean. It broke my heart to think that you would be all alone. Not knowing what else to do, I made arrangements to get you this dog.

If you don't like it, you don't have to keep it, of course. Harold said he'd take it back, no problem. (His number should be included.)

I hope you're doing all right. Since I got sick, I've worried non-stop about that. I love you, Jules, I really do. I was the luckiest guy in the world when you came into my life. It would break my heart if I thought you'd never be happy again. So please do that for me. Be happy again. Find someone who makes you happy. It might be hard, you might not think it's possible, but I'd like you to try. The world is a better place when you smile.

And don't worry. From wherever I am, I'll watch out for you. I'll be your guardian angel, sweetheart. You can count on me to keep you safe.
I love you,
Jim

Through her tears, Julie peeked over the lid of the box and reached in. The puppy curled into her hand. She lifted him out, holding him close to her face. He was tiny, and she could feel the bones in his ribs as he trembled.

He really was an ugly thing, she thought. And he'd grow up to be the size of a small horse. What on earth would she do with a dog like this?

Why, she wondered, couldn't Jim have gotten her a miniature schnauzer with little gray whiskers or a cocker spaniel with sad, round eyes? Something manageable? Something cute, that might curl up in her lap now and then?

The puppy, a male, started to whine, a high-pitched cry that rose and fell like the echo of far-off train whistles.

'Shh . . . you'll be okay,' she whispered. 'I won't hurt you . . .'

She continued to talk to the puppy in low tones, letting him get used to her, still getting used to the idea that Jim had done this for her. The puppy continued to cry, almost as if accompanying the tune on the stereo, and Julie scratched beneath his chin.

'You singing to me?' she asked, smiling softly for the first time. 'That's what it sounds like, you know.'

For a moment, the dog stopped crying and looked up at her, holding her gaze. Then he started to whine again, though this time he didn't seem as frightened.

'Singer,' she whispered. 'I'll think I'll call you Singer.'

One

Four Years Later

In the years since Jim had died, Julie Barenson had somehow found a way to start living again. It hadn't happened right away. The first couple of years after his death had been difficult and lonely, but time had eventually worked its magic on Julie, changing her loss into something softer. Though she loved Jim and knew that part of her would *always* love Jim, the pain wasn't as sharp as it had once been. She could remember her tears and the total vacuum her life had become in the aftermath of his death, but the searing ache of those days was behind her. Now when she thought of Jim, she remembered him with a smile, thankful that he'd been part of her life.

She was thankful for Singer, too. Jim had done the right thing by getting her the dog. In a way, Singer had made it possible for her to go on.

But at this moment, while lying in bed on a cool spring morning in Swansboro, North Carolina, Julie wasn't thinking about what a wonderful support Singer had been during the past four years. Instead, she was mentally cursing his very existence while gasping for breath, thinking, I can't believe that this is the way I'm going to die.

Squashed in bed by my very own dog.

With Singer splayed across her, pinning her to the mattress, she imagined her lips turning blue from oxygen deprivation.

'Get up, you lazy dog,' she wheezed. 'You're

killing me here.'

Snoring soundly, Singer didn't hear her, and Julie began squirming, trying to bounce him from his slumber. Suffocating beneath the weight, she felt as if she'd been wrapped in a blanket and tossed in a lake, Mafia style.

'I'm serious,' she forced out, 'I can't breathe.'

Singer finally lifted his massive head and blinked at her groggily. *What's all the racket about?* he seemed to be asking. *Can't you see I'm trying to rest here?*

'Get off!' Julie rasped out.

Singer yawned, pushing his cold nose against her cheek.

'Yeah, yeah, good morning,' she gasped. 'Now scoot.'

With that, Singer snorted and found his legs, further squashing various parts of her as he got up. And up. And up. And up. A moment later, towering over her with just a smudge of drool on his lips, he looked like something from a low-budget horror movie. Good Lord, she thought, he is *huge*. You'd think that I'd be used to it by now. She took a deep breath and looked up at him, frowning.

'Did I say you could get into bed with me?' she asked.

Singer usually slept in the corner of her room at night. The past two nights, however, he'd crawled in with her. Or, more accurately, on top of her. Crazy dog.

Singer lowered his head and licked her face.

'No, you're not forgiven,' she said, pushing him away. 'Don't even bother trying to get out of this. You could have killed me. You're almost twice as heavy as I am, you know. Now get off the bed.'

Singer whined like a pouting child before hopping down to the floor. Julie sat up, ribs aching, and looked at the clock, thinking, Already? She and Singer stretched at the same time before she pushed aside the covers.

'C'mon,' she said, 'I'll let you out before I get in the shower. But don't go sniffing around the neighbors' garbage cans again. They left a nasty message on the machine.'

Singer looked at her.

'I know, I know,' she said, 'it's only garbage. But some people are funny that way.'

Singer left the bedroom, heading toward the front door. Julie rolled her shoulders as she followed him, her eyes closed for just a moment. Big mistake. On the way out of the bedroom, she slammed her toe against the dresser. The pain shot from her toe up through her lower leg. After the initial scream, she began to curse, combining profanity in all sorts of marvelous permutations. Hopping on one foot in her pink pajamas, she was sure she looked like some sort of deranged Energizer Bunny. Singer merely gave her a look that seemed to imply, *What's the holdup? You got me up, remember, so let's get going here. I've got things to do outside.*

She groaned. 'Can't you see I'm wounded here?'

Singer yawned again, and Julie rubbed her toe before limping after him.

'Thanks for coming to my rescue. You're worthless in an emergency.'

A moment later, after Singer stepped on Julie's sore toe on his way out the door—Julie *knew* he'd done it on purpose—he was outside. Instead of

7

heading toward the garbage cans, Singer wandered over to the vacant wooded lots that bordered one side of her house. She watched as he swung his massive head from side to side, as if making sure that no one had planted any new trees or bushes during the preceding day. All dogs liked to mark their territory, but Singer seemed to believe that somehow, if he found enough places to relieve himself, he'd be anointed King Dog in all the World. At least it got him out of her hair for a while.

Thank heaven for small favors, Julie thought. Singer had been driving her crazy for the last couple of days. He'd followed her everywhere, refusing to let her out of his sight for even a few minutes, except when she put him outside. She hadn't even been able to put the dishes away without bumping into him a dozen times. He was even worse at night. Last night, he'd had a growling fit for an hour, which he'd thoughtfully interspersed with an occasional bark, and the whole thing had left her fantasizing about buying either a soundproof kennel or an elephant gun.

Not that Singer's behavior had ever been . . . well, ordinary. Except for the peeing thing, the dog had always acted as if he thought he were human. He refused to eat out of a dog bowl, he'd never needed a leash, and when Julie watched television, he would crawl up on the couch and stare at the screen. And when she talked to him—whenever anyone talked to him, for that matter—Singer would stare intently, his head tilted to the side, as if he were following the conversation. And half the time, it did seem as if he understood what she was telling him. No matter what she told him to do, no matter how ridiculous the command, Singer would carry it out. *Could you go get my purse from the bedroom?* Singer would come trotting out with it a moment later. *Will you turn off the bedroom light?* He'd balance on two legs and flick it with his nose. *Put this can of soup in the pantry, okay?* He'd carry it in his mouth and set it on the shelf. Sure, other dogs were well trained, but not like this. Besides, Singer hadn't needed training. Not real training, anyway. All she'd had to do was show him something once and that was it. To others it seemed downright eerie, but since it made Julie feel like a modern-day Dr Dolittle, she kind of liked it.

Even if it did mean she talked to her dog in complete sentences, had arguments with him, and asked for his advice now and then.

But hey, she told herself, that wasn't so odd, was it? They'd been together since Jim had died, just the two of them, and for the most part, Singer was pretty good company.

Singer, though, had been acting strangely ever since she started dating again, and he hadn't liked any of the guys who'd shown up at the door in the last couple of months. Julie had expected that part. Since he'd been a puppy, Singer tended to growl at men when he first met them. She used to think that Singer had a sixth sense that enabled him to tell the good guys from the ones she should avoid, but lately she'd changed her mind. Now, she couldn't help but think that he was just a big, furry version of a jealous boyfriend.

It was getting to be a problem, she decided. They were going to have to have a serious talk. Singer didn't want her to be alone, did he? No, of course not. It might take him a little while to get used to having someone else around, but he'd understand eventually. Hell, in time, he'd probably even be happy for her. But how, she wondered, was the best way to explain all this to him?

She halted for a moment, considering the question, before realizing the implications of what she was thinking.

Explain all this to him? Good Lord, she thought, I'm going insane.

Julie limped to the bathroom to start getting ready for work, slipping off her pajamas as she went. Standing over the sink, she grimaced at her reflection. Look at me, she thought, I'm twenty-nine and falling apart at the seams here. Her ribs hurt when she breathed, her big toe throbbed, and the mirror, she realized, wasn't helping things. During the day, her brown hair was long and straight, but after a night in bed, it looked as if it had been attacked by comb-teasing pillow gnomes. It was frazzled and puffed out, 'under siege,' as Jim so kindly used to put it. Mascara was smeared down her cheek. The tip of her nose was red, and her green eyes were swollen from the springtime pollen. But a shower would help with those things, wouldn't it?

Well, maybe not with the allergies. She opened the medicine cabinet and took a Claritin before glancing up again, as if hoping for a sudden improvement.

Ugh.

Maybe, she thought, she wouldn't have to work so hard at discouraging Bob's interest after all. She'd been cutting Bob's hair, or rather what was left of it, for a year now. Two months ago, Bob had

10

finally worked up the nerve to ask her out. He wasn't exactly the best-looking guy in the world—balding, with a round face, eyes set too close together, and the beginnings of a paunch—but he was single and successful, and Julie hadn't been on a date since Jim had died. She figured it would be a good way to get her feet wet in the world of dating again. Wrong. There was a reason Bob was single. Bob wasn't only a triple bogey in the looks department, he'd been so boring on their date that even people at nearby tables in the restaurant had glanced her way in pity. His preferred topic of conversation on their date had been accounting. He'd showed no interest in anything else: not her, not the menu, not the weather, not sports, not the little black dress she was wearing. Only accounting. For three hours, she'd listened to Bob drone on and on about itemized deductions and capital gains distributions, depreciation and 401(k) rollovers. By the end of the dinner, when he'd leaned over the table and confided that he 'knew important people at the IRS,' Julie's eyes were so glazed that they could have flavored a dozen doughnuts.

It went without saying, of course, that Bob had had a wonderful time. He'd been calling three times a week since then, asking 'if they could get together for a second consultation, hee hee hee.' He was persistent, that was for sure. Annoying as hell, but persistent.

Then there was Ross, the second guy she dated. Ross the doctor. Ross the good-looking guy. Ross the pervert. One date with him was enough, thank you very much.

And can't forget good old Adam. He worked for the county, he said. He enjoyed his work, he said.

11

Just a regular guy, he said.

Adam, she found out, worked in the sewers.

He didn't smell, he didn't have unknown substances growing under his fingernails, his hair didn't carry a greasy shine, but she knew that as long as she lived, she'd never get used to the idea that one day, he might show up at the front door looking that way. *Had an accident at the plant, dear. Sorry to come home like this*. The very thought gave her the shivers. Nor could she imagine handling his clothes to put them in the laundry after something like that. The relationship was doomed from the start.

Just when she was beginning to wonder whether normal people like Jim even existed anymore, just when she was beginning to wonder what it was about her that seemed to attract oddballs like a neon sign flashing 'I'm Available—Normalcy Not Required,' Richard had come strolling into the picture.

And miracle of miracles, even after a first date last Saturday, he still seemed . . . *normal*. A consultant with J. D. Blanchard Engineering out of Cleveland—the firm repairing the bridge over the Intracoastal Waterway—he had made her acquaintance when he came into the salon for a haircut. On their date, he'd opened doors for her, smiled at the right moments in the conversation, given the waiter her order for dinner, and not so much as tried to kiss her when he'd dropped her off. Best of all, he was good-looking in an artistic sort of way, with sculpted cheekbones, emerald eyes, black hair, and a mustache. After he'd dropped her off, she'd felt like screaming, *Hallelujah! I have seen the light!*

12

Singer hadn't seemed quite as impressed. After she'd said good night to Richard, Singer had put on one of his 'I'm the boss around here' acts. He'd growled until Julie had opened the front door.

'Oh, stop it,' she'd said. 'Don't be so hard on him.'

Singer did as he was told, but he'd retreated to the bedroom, where he'd pouted the rest of the night.

If my dog was any more bizarre, she thought, we could team up and work for a carnival, right next to the guy who eats light bulbs. But then, my life hasn't exactly been normal, either.

Julie turned on the faucet and stepped into the shower, trying to stem the tide of memories. What was the use of replaying hard times? Her mother, she often mused, had been fatally attracted to two things: booze and toxic men. Either one without the other would have been bad, but the combination had been intolerable for Julie. Her mom went through boyfriends the way kids go through paper towels, and some of them made Julie feel less than comfortable once she hit adolescence. The last one had actually tried to have his way with her, and when Julie had told her mother, her mother, in a drunken, teary rage, had blamed *her* for coming on to *him*. It wasn't long before Julie found herself without a home.

Living on the street had been terrifying even for the six months or so before Jim came along. Most everyone she met used drugs and panhandled or stole . . . or worse. Scared of becoming like the haunted runaways she saw every night at the shelters and in the doorways, she searched frantically for odd jobs that would keep her fed and

13

out of sight. She worked every menial job she saw offered and kept her head down. When she first met Jim at a diner in Daytona, she was nursing a cup of coffee with the last of her pocket change. Jim bought her breakfast and on the way out the door said he'd do the same thing the following day if she returned. Hungry, she did, and when she challenged him about his motives (she assumed she knew his reasons and could remember gearing up for quite the embarrassing public tirade about cradle robbers and jail time), Jim denied any improper interest in her. And at the end of the week, when he was getting ready to head for home, he made her a proposal: If she moved to Swansboro, North Carolina, he would help her get a full-time job and a place to stay.

She remembered staring at him as though he had bugs crawling out of his ears.

But a month later, considering she didn't have much scheduled on the old social calendar, she showed up in Swansboro, thinking as she got off the bus, *What in the world am I doing in this nowhere town?* Nonetheless, she looked up Jim, who—despite her persistent skepticism—brought her over to the salon to meet his aunt Mabel. And sure enough, she found herself sweeping floors for an hourly wage and living in the room upstairs from the salon.

At first, Julie was relieved by Jim's lack of apparent interest. Then curious. Then annoyed. Finally, after running into Jim repeatedly and dropping what seemed to her quite shameless hints, she broke down and asked Mabel if she thought Jim found her unattractive. Only then did he seem to get the message. They went on a date,

14

then another, and the hormones were surging after a month together. Real love came a short time later. He proposed, they walked the aisle in the church where Jim had been baptized, and Julie spent the first few years of their marriage drawing smiley faces every time she doodled by the phone. What more, she wondered when considering her life, could anyone want?

A lot, she soon realized. A few weeks after their fourth anniversary, Jim had a seizure on the way home from church and was rushed to the hospital. Two years later, the brain tumor took his life, and at the age of twenty-five, Julie found herself starting over once more. Add in Singer's unexpected appearance and she'd reached the point in her life where nothing surprised her anymore.

Nowadays, she thought, it was the little things in life that mattered. If the highlights in her past set the tone, it was the day-by-day events that now defined who she was. Mabel, God bless her, had been an angel. She'd helped Julie get her license so she could cut hair and earn a decent, if not extravagant, living. Henry and Emma, two good friends of Jim's, not only had helped her fit into town when she'd first moved here, but had remained close even after Jim had passed away. And then there was Mike, Henry's younger brother and Jim's best friend growing up.

In the shower, Julie smiled. Mike.

Now there was a guy who would make some woman happy one day, even if he seemed a little lost sometimes.

A few minutes later, after toweling off, Julie brushed her teeth and hair, put on some makeup, and slipped into her clothes. Since her car was in

15

the shop, she'd have to walk to work—it was about a mile up the street—and she put on a pair of comfortable shoes. She called Singer just as she was locking the door on her way out, nearly missing what had been left for her.

Out of the corner of her eye, she spied a card wedged between the mailbox and the lid, right next to the front door.

Curious, Julie opened it, reading it on the porch as Singer burst from the woods and trotted up to her.

Dear Julie,
I had a wonderful time on Saturday. I can't stop thinking about you.

Richard

So that was the reason Singer went bonkers last night.

'See,' she said, holding out the card so Singer could see it, 'I told you he was a nice guy.'

Singer turned away.

'Don't give me that. You can admit you were wrong, you know. I think you're just jealous.'

Singer nuzzled against her.

'Is that it? Are you jealous?' Unlike with other dogs, Julie didn't have to bend down to run her hand down his back. He was bigger than she had been when she'd entered high school.

'Don't be jealous, okay? Be happy for me.'

Singer circled to the other side and looked up at her.

'Now c'mon. We have to walk because Mike's still fixing the Jeep.'

At Mike's name, Singer's tail wagged.

16

Two

Mike Harris's song lyrics left a lot to be desired, and his singing voice didn't exactly make recording executives beat a path to his door in Swansboro. He did, however, play the guitar and he practiced daily, hoping his big break was just around the corner. In ten years, he'd worked with a dozen different bands, ranging from the big-haired noise of eighties rock and roll to the mamas-trains-and-pickup-truck style of country music. On stage, he'd worn everything from leather pants and boa constrictors to chaps and a cowboy hat, and though he played with obvious enthusiasm and the band members couldn't help but like him, he was usually pulled aside after a few weeks and told that for some reason it just wasn't working out. It had happened enough times for even Mike to know that maybe it wasn't just a personality conflict, though he still couldn't bring himself to admit that he might not be any good.

Mike kept a notebook, too, and scribbled down his thoughts in his spare time with the idea of using these impressions in a future novel, but the writing process was more difficult than he'd first imagined it would be. It wasn't that he didn't have ideas, it was that he had too many ideas and couldn't figure out what should and shouldn't go in the story. Last year, he'd tried to write a murder mystery set on a cruise ship, something Agatha Christie might have written, and it included the usual dozen suspects. But the plot, he thought, wasn't quite exciting enough, so he'd tried to jazz it up using every idea

17

he'd ever had, including a nuclear warhead hidden in San Francisco, a crooked cop who was witness to the JFK assassination, an Irish terrorist, the Mafia, a boy and his dog, an evil venture capitalist, and a time-traveling scientist who'd escaped the persecution of the Holy Roman Empire. By the end, the prologue had run to a hundred pages and the main suspects hadn't even arrived on the scene yet. Needless to say, he didn't get any further on it.

In the past, he'd also tried drawing, painting, working in stained glass, ceramics, wood carving, and macramé and actually assembled some free-form art pieces in a burst of inspiration that kept him away from work for a week. He welded and wired scraps from old car parts into three towering, off-balance structures, and when he was finished, he sat on his front steps, staring with pride at what he'd done, knowing in his heart that he'd finally found his calling. That feeling lasted for a week, until the town council passed a 'no junk in the yard' ordinance at a hastily called meeting. Like many people, Mike Harris had the dream and desire to be an artist; he just didn't have the talent.

Mike could, however, fix practically anything. He was the consummate handyman, a veritable knight in shining armor when puddles formed beneath kitchen sinks or when garbage disposals went on the blink. But if he was a good handyman, he was a modern-day Merlin when it came to anything with four wheels and an engine. He and Henry co-owned the busiest garage in town, and while Henry handled the paperwork, Mike was in charge of the actual work. Foreign cars or domestic, four-cylinder Ford Escorts or turbocharged 911 Porsches, he could repair them all. He could listen to an engine, hear pings and clicks where others couldn't, and figure out what was wrong, usually in less than a couple of minutes. He knew manifolds and intake valves, shocks, struts and pistons, radiators and wheel base adjustments, and he could set from memory the timing on practically every car that had rolled in the shop. He could rebuild engines without having to look at a manual. His fingertips were stained permanently black, and though he knew it was a good way to make a living, he sometimes wished he could take a fraction of that talent and apply it to other areas of his life.

The traditional ladies' man reputation associated with mechanics and musicians had passed Mike by. He'd had two serious girlfriends in his life, and since one of those relationships had been in high school and the other with Sarah had ended three years ago, a case could be made that Mike wasn't looking for a long-term commitment, or even a commitment that might last through the summer. Even Mike wondered about it sometimes, but these days, no matter how much he wished otherwise, it seemed as if most of his dates ended with a kiss on the cheek while the woman thanked him for being such a good friend. At thirty-four, Mike Harris was remarkably well versed in the tender art of embracing women in brotherly hugs while they cried on his shoulder about what a jerk their previous boyfriend had been. It wasn't that he was unattractive. With light brown hair and blue eyes and an easy smile to go with his trim build, he was good-looking in an all-American kind of way. Nor was it that women didn't enjoy his company, because they did. His lack of luck had more to do with the fact that women who dated Mike sensed that a relationship with them wasn't what Mike was really looking for.

His brother, Henry, knew why they felt that way; so did Mike's sister-in-law, Emma. Mabel knew the reason as well, as did practically everyone who knew Mike Harris.

Mike, they all knew, was already in love with someone else.

* * *

'Hey, Julie—wait up.'

Having just reached the outskirts of Swanboro's old-fashioned business district, Julie turned when she heard Mike calling. Singer looked up at her and she nodded.

'Go ahead,' she said.

Singer galloped off, meeting Mike halfway. Mike stroked his head and back as they walked, then scratched behind his ears. When Mike stopped moving his hand, Singer bobbed his head up and down, wanting more.

'That's all for now, big guy,' Mike said. 'Let me talk to Julie.'

A moment later, he reached Julie as Singer sat beside him, still going after the hand.

'Hey, Mike,' Julie said, smiling. 'What's going on?'

'Not much. I just wanted to let you know your Jeep is done.'

'What was wrong with it?'

'The alternator.'

Exactly what he'd said the problem was on Friday when she'd dropped it off, she remembered. 'Did you have to replace it?'

'Yeah. Yours was dead. No big deal—the dealer had plenty in stock. I also fixed the oil leak, too, by the way. I had to replace a seal near the filter.'

'There was an oil leak?'

'Didn't you notice the stains in your driveway?'

'Not really, but then I wasn't looking.'

Mike smiled. 'Well, like I said, that's fixed, too. Do you want me to grab your keys and bring them by?'

'No, I'll get 'em after work. I don't need 'em until later. I've got appointments all day. You know how Mondays are.' She smiled. 'So how'd it go at the Clipper, by the way? I'm sorry I couldn't make it.'

Mike had spent the weekend playing grunge rock with a group of high school dropouts who dreamed of nothing more than meeting babes, drinking beer, and filling their days with MTV. Mike was at least a dozen years older than any of them, and when he'd showed Julie the baggy pants and ratty T-shirt he would wear for the show last week, she had nodded and said, 'Oh, that's nice,' which really meant, *You're going to look absolutely ridiculous up there.*

'Okay, I guess,' he said.

'Just okay?'

He shrugged. 'It wasn't my type of music anyway.'

She nodded. As much as she liked *him*, even she didn't like his singing voice all that much. Singer, though, seemed to love it. Whenever Mike sang for friends, Singer howled along with him. It was a toss-up, according to local opinion, as to who would be the first to make it to the big time.

'So how much were the repairs?' she asked.

Mike seemed to debate the question as he scratched his chin absently. 'Two haircuts should

21

do it.'

'Come on. Let me pay this time. At least for the parts. I do have money, you know.'

In the past year, the Jeep, an older-model CJ7, had been in the shop three times. Mike, however, was somehow able to keep it running smoothly between visits.

'You are paying,' Mike protested. 'Even though my hair's getting a little thinner, it does need to be cut now and then.'

'Well, two haircuts doesn't sound like a fair trade.'

'It didn't take all that long to fix. And the parts weren't that much. The guy owed me a favor.'

Julie raised her chin slightly. 'Does Henry know you're doing this?'

Mike spread his arms, looking innocent. 'Of course he knows. I'm his partner. And besides, it was his idea.'

Sure it was, she thought.

'Well, thanks,' she finally said. 'I appreciate it.'

'My pleasure.' Mike paused. Wanting to talk a little longer but not knowing exactly what to say, he glanced toward Singer. Singer was watching him closely, his head tilted to the side, as if urging: *Well, get on with it, Romeo. Both of us know the real reason you're talking to her.* Mike swallowed.

'So how'd it go with . . . um . . .' He tried to sound as casual as he could.

'Richard?'

'Yeah. Richard.'

'It was nice.'

'Oh.'

Mike nodded, feeling beads of perspiration forming on his brow. He wondered how it could

22

possibly be so hot this early in the morning.

'So . . . um . . . where'd you go?' he asked.

'The Slocum House.'

'Pretty fancy for a first date,' he offered.

'It was either that or Pizza Hut. He let me pick.'

Mike shifted from one foot to the other, waiting to see if she would add anything else. She didn't.

Not good, he thought. Richard was definitely different from Bob, the romantic number cruncher. Or Ross, the sex maniac. Or Adam from the bowels of Swansboro. With guys like that as the competition, Mike thought he stood a chance. But Richard? The Slocum House? *It was nice?*

'So . . . you had a good time?' he asked.

'Yeah. We had fun.'

Fun? How much fun? This, he thought, was not good at all.

'I'm glad,' he lied, doing his best to fake enthusiasm.

Julie reached for his arm. 'Don't worry, Mike. You know I'll always love you the most, right?'

Mike pushed his hands in his pockets. 'That's just because I fix your car,' he said.

'Don't sell yourself short,' she said. 'You helped patch my roof, too.'

'And repaired your washing machine.'

She leaned over and kissed him on the cheek, then gave his arm a squeeze.

'What can I say, Mike? You're just a good guy.'

*　　　*　　　*

Julie could feel Mike's eyes on her as she walked to the salon, though unlike the way she felt about some men's attention, she wasn't bothered at all.

23

He was a good friend, she thought, then quickly changed her mind. No, Mike was a *really* good friend, someone she wouldn't hesitate to call in an emergency; the kind of friend who made life in Swansboro a whole lot easier simply because she knew he'd always be there for her. Friends like him were rare, and that's why she felt bad for keeping some of the more private aspects of her life—like her most recent date—off-limits.

She didn't have the heart to go into detail about it, because Mike . . . well, Mike wasn't exactly Mr Mysterious when it came to how he felt about her, and she didn't want to hurt his feelings. What was she supposed to have said? *Compared to my other dates, Richard was* great! *Sure, I'd go out with him again!* She knew Mike wanted to date her; she'd known that for a couple of years now. But her feelings for Mike—aside from regarding him as her best friend—were complicated. How could they not be? Jim and Mike had been best friends growing up, Mike had been best man at their wedding, and Mike had been the one she'd turned to for comfort after Jim had died. He was more like a brother, and it wasn't as if she could flip a switch and suddenly change the way she felt.

But it was more than just that. Because Jim and Mike were so close, because Mike had been part of both their lives, even imagining a date with him always left her with a vague feeling of betrayal. If she agreed to go out with him, did that mean that deep down, she'd always wanted to? What would Jim think about it? And would she ever be able to look at Mike without thinking of Jim and those times in the past that they were all together? She didn't know. And what would happen if they did go

24

out, but for whatever reason it didn't work out? Things would change between them, and she couldn't bear losing him as a friend. It was easier if things just stayed the way they were.

She suspected that Mike knew all of this and it was probably the reason he'd never so much as asked her out, despite the fact that it was obvious he wanted to.

Sometimes, though—like when they were on the boat last summer waterskiing with Henry and Emma—she got the feeling that he was working up the nerve to do it, and Mike was a little comical when those moods seemed to strike him. Instead of being Mr Happy-Go-Lucky—the first to laugh at jokes, even those made at his expense, the guy you'd ask to go pick up some more beer from the convenience store because everyone knew he wouldn't mind—Mike would suddenly get quiet, as if he suspected his whole problem with Julie arose from the fact that she didn't think he was being quite cool enough. Instead of laughing at what the others were saying, he'd wink or roll his eyes or study his fingernails, and when he'd grinned at her on the boat that time, it had looked as if he were trying to say, *Hey, baby, how about we blow this joint and have some real fun?* His older brother, Henry, was ruthless when Mike got in those moods. Spotting his brother's sudden attitude shift, Henry had asked Mike if he'd had too many beans for lunch because he didn't look all that well.

Mike's ego had deflated right there.

She smiled, thinking back on it. Poor Mike.

The next day he was back to his old self. And Julie liked that version of Mike a whole lot better anyway. Guys who thought that any woman was lucky to have them, guys who acted tough and cool or picked fights in bars to show the world that they couldn't be pushed around, bored her. On the other hand, guys like Mike were pretty much a catch, no matter how she looked at it. He was both good-hearted and nice looking; she liked the way his eyes crinkled at the corners when he smiled, and she adored his dimples. She had come to treasure the way bad news seemed to slide off him with a simple shrug. She liked guys who laughed, and Mike laughed a lot.

And she really, really liked the sound of his laugh.

As always, though, when she began thinking along these lines, she heard a voice inside her immediately pipe up, *Don't go there. Mike's your friend, your best friend, and you don't want to ruin things, do you?*

As she mulled this over, Singer nudged against her, freeing her from her thoughts. He looked up at her.

'Yeah—go on, you big mooch,' she said.

Singer trotted ahead, past the bakery, then turned at the propped-open door of Mabel's salon. Mabel had a biscuit for him every day.

* * *

'So how'd her date go?' Henry leaned against the door frame next to the coffeemaker, talking over the rim of a Styrofoam cup.

'I didn't ask her about that,' Mike answered, his tone implying the very thought was ridiculous. He stepped into his coveralls and pulled them up over

26

his jeans.

'Why didn't you ask?'

'I didn't think about it.'

'Mmm,' Henry said.

At thirty-eight, Henry was four years older than Mike and in many ways Mike's alter, more mature, ego. Henry was taller and heavier and coasting into middle age with a waistline that expanded at the same rate his hair was receding; with a twelve-year marriage to Emma and three young girls and a house instead of an apartment, he had a bit more stability in his life. Unlike Mike, he'd never had artistic dreams of any sort. In college, Henry had majored in business finance. And like most older brothers, he couldn't escape the feeling that he had to watch out for his younger sibling, to make sure he was okay, that he wasn't doing things he'd later regret. That his brotherly support included teasing, insults, and the occasional zinger to bring Mike back down to earth might have struck some as heartless, but how else was he supposed to do it? Henry smiled. Somebody had to watch out for Mike.

Mike had worked the grease-stained coveralls up to his waist.

'I just wanted to tell her that her car was finished.'

'Already? I thought you said it had an oil leak.'

'It did.'

'And it's already done?'

'It only took a few hours.'

'Mmm . . .' Henry nodded, thinking, *If you were any more whipped, little brother, they'd serve you on ice cream.*

Instead of saying that, Henry cleared his throat.

'So that's what you did this weekend? Worked on her car?'

'Not the whole time. I also played at the Clipper, but I guess you forgot about that, huh?'

Henry raised his hands in defense. 'You know I'm more of a Garth Brooks and Tim McGraw fan. I don't like that new stuff. And besides, Emma's parents came by for dinner.'

'They could have come, too.'

Henry laughed, nearly spilling his coffee. 'Yeah, right. Can you imagine me bringing those two to the Clipper? They think the stuff you hear in elevators is too loud and that rock music is Satan's form of mind control. They'd bleed from their ears if they went to the Clipper.'

'I'll tell Emma you said that.'

'She'd agree with me,' he said. 'Those were her words, not mine. So how'd it go? At the Clipper, I mean?'

'Okay.'

Henry nodded, understanding completely. 'Sorry to hear that.'

Mike shrugged as he zipped up the coveralls.

'So what did you charge Julie for her car this time? Three pencils and a sandwich?'

'No.'

'A shiny rock?'

'Ha, ha.'

'Seriously. I'm just curious.'

'The usual.'

Henry whistled. 'It's a good thing I run the books around here.'

Mike tossed him an impatient glance. 'You know you would have given her a deal, too.'

'I know that.'

'So why are you bringing it up?'

'Because I want to know how her date went.'

'How does what I charge her to fix her car have to do with her date?'

Henry smiled. 'I'm not sure, little brother. What do you think?'

'I think you had too much coffee this morning and you're not thinking straight.'

Henry finished his cup. 'You know, you're probably right. I'm sure you don't care at all about Julie's date.'

'Exactly.'

Henry reached for the coffeepot and poured another cup. 'Then you probably don't care what Mabel thinks, either.'

Mike looked up. 'Mabel?'

Henry nonchalantly added cream and sugar. 'Yeah, Mabel. She saw them out on Saturday night.'

'How do you know?'

'Because I talked to her after church yesterday and she told me about it.'

'She did?'

Henry turned his back to Mike and headed for the office, breaking into a grin. 'But like you said, you don't care, so I'll just drop it.'

Henry knew from experience that Mike was still standing outside the door, frozen in place, long after he'd taken his seat at the desk.

Three

Though Andrea Radley had earned her cosmetology license a year ago and had been working for Mabel for nine months, she wasn't the best of employees. Not only did she have a tendency to take 'personal days' without warning—usually without bothering to call—but on the days she did manage to arrive at work, she was rarely punctual. Nor was she particularly adept at styling and cutting hair, at least according to the directions her customers gave her. It didn't make a difference if her customers brought in a picture or explained slowly and clearly exactly what they wanted; Andrea cut everyone's hair exactly the same way. Not that it mattered. Andrea already had nearly the same number of clients that Julie did, though not surprisingly, every one of them was a man.

Andrea was twenty-three, a long-legged blonde with a perpetual tan who looked as if she'd come straight from the beaches of California rather than the small mountain town of Boone, North Carolina, where she'd been raised. She did her best to dress the part, too—no matter how cold the weather, she wore miniskirts to the salon. In the summer, she augmented that with skimpy halter tops; in the winter, tall leather boots. She called every client 'sugar,' batted her long, mascara-enhanced lashes, and chewed gum incessantly. Julie and Mabel used to giggle at the dreamy looks men gave Andrea as they stared at her reflection in the mirror. Andrea, they thought, could have accidentally shaved a client's head and still kept

30

him coming back for more.

Despite her outward appearance, Andrea was a bit naive about men. Oh, she thought she knew what men wanted, and for the most part she was right about that. What Andrea didn't understand was how to keep a man afterward. It never occurred to her that her appearance might attract a certain type of man at the expense of another. Andrea had no trouble getting dates with tattooed men who drove Harleys, or drunks who hung out at the Clipper, or guys on parole, but she was never able to get a date with men who had steady jobs. At least that's what she told herself when she was in one of her self-pitying moods. In reality, Andrea did get asked out regularly by reliable workingmen, but she seemed to lose interest in them quickly, then promptly forget they'd even asked.

In the past three months, she'd been out with seven different men, thirty-one tattoos, six Harleys, two parole violations, and zero jobs, and right now she was feeling a little sorry for herself. On Saturday, she'd had to pay for dinner and the movie because her date didn't have any money, but had he called this morning? No. Of course not. He wouldn't think of calling her today. Her dates never called, unless they needed money or were 'feeling a little lonely,' as so many of them liked to put it.

But Richard had called the shop this morning, asking for Julie.

Even worse, Julie probably didn't have to buy him dinner to get him to do it. Why, she wondered, did Julie get all the good guys? It wasn't as if she dressed well. Half the time she looked downright plain, what with her jeans and baggy sweaters and— let's be frank here—ugly shoes. She didn't exactly go out of the way to flatter her figure, her nails weren't manicured, and she wasn't tan at all, except in the summer, and anyone could do that. So why had Richard been so taken with Julie? They had both been here when Richard walked into the salon for a haircut last week, they both had a break in their appointments, and they both looked up and said hi at the same time. But Richard had asked Julie to cut his hair instead of her, and somehow that had led to a date. Andrea frowned just thinking about it.

'Ouch!'

Brought back to the present by the yelp, Andrea glanced at her customer's reflection in the mirror. He was a lawyer, in his early thirties. He was also rubbing his head. Andrea pulled her hands back.

'What happened, sugar?'

'You jabbed my head with the scissors.'

'I did?'

'Yeah. It hurt.'

Andrea's lashes fluttered. 'I'm sorry, sugar. I didn't mean to hurt you. You're not mad at me, are you?'

'No . . . not really,' he said finally, pulling his hand away. Looking in the mirror again, he studied the job she was doing. 'Don't you think my hair looks a little lopsided?'

'Where?'

'Here.' He pointed with his finger. 'You cut this sideburn way too short.'

Andrea blinked twice, then slowly tilted her head from one side to the other. 'I think the mirror's crooked.'

'The mirror?' he repeated.

She put one hand on his shoulder and smiled.

32

'Well, I think you look handsome, sugar.'

'You do?'

Across the room, near the window, Mabel looked up from her magazine. The man, she noticed, was practically melting into the chair. She shook her head as Andrea started cutting again. After a moment, feeling reassured, the man sat up a little straighter.

'Listen, I've got tickets to see Faith Hill in Raleigh in a couple of weeks,' he said. 'I was just wondering if you'd like to go.'

Unfortunately, Andrea's mind was back on Richard and Julie again. Mabel had told her that they'd gone to the Slocum House. The Slocum House! She knew, though she'd never been there before, that the Slocum House was a fancy restaurant, the kind of place where there were candles on the table. And they hung your coat for you, if you needed it, in its own special room. And there were cloth tablecloths, not those cheap plastic ones with the red-and-white checkerboard pattern. Her dates had never taken her to a place like that. They probably couldn't even *find* places like that.

'I'm sorry, but I can't,' she answered automatically.

Knowing Richard (though, of course, she didn't know Richard at all), he'd probably send flowers, too. Maybe even roses. Red roses! In her mind, she could see it clearly. Why did Julie get all the good ones?

'Oh,' the man said.

The way he said it brought Andrea back again. 'Excuse me?' she asked.

'Nothing. I just said, oh.'

33

Andrea had no idea what he was talking about. When in doubt, she thought, smile. And she did. After a moment, the man began melting again.

In the corner, Mabel stifled a laugh.

*   *   *

Mabel saw Julie come through the door a minute after Singer had entered. She was about to say hello when Andrea spoke up.

'Richard called,' Andrea said, not bothering to hide her disgust. She was filing her perfectly manicured nails with vigor, as if trying to scrape a bug off the tips.

'He did?' Julie asked. 'What did he want?'

'I didn't bother asking,' Andrea snapped. 'I'm not your secretary, you know.'

Mabel shook her head, as if telling Julie not to worry about it.

At sixty-three, Mabel was one of Julie's closest friends—that she had been Jim's aunt was almost beside the fact. Mabel had given Julie a job and a place to stay eleven years earlier and Julie would never forget that, but eleven years was long enough for Julie to know she would have enjoyed Mabel's company had none of those things happened.

It didn't matter to Julie that Mabel was a little eccentric, to put it mildly. In her time here, Julie had learned that practically everyone in town had rather colorful aspects to their personality. But Mabel put the capital *E* in eccentric, especially in this small, conservative southern town, and it wasn't simply because she had a couple of harmless quirks. Mabel *was* different compared to others in town, and she, along with everyone else, knew it.

Despite three proposals she'd never been married, and this alone disqualified her from the various clubs and groups of people her own age. But even if you ignored her other idiosyncrasies—the fact that she drove a moped to the salon unless it was raining, favored clothing with polka dots, and viewed her Elvis collectibles as 'fine art'—Mabel would still be regarded as positively odd for something she'd done over a quarter century ago. When she was thirty-six, after living in Swansboro her entire life, she moved away without telling anyone where she was going or even that she was leaving at all. For the next eight years, she sent postcards to her family from around the world; Ayers Rock in Australia, Mt Kilimanjaro in Africa, the fjords in Norway, Hong Kong Harbor, the Wawel in Poland. When she finally returned to Swansboro—showing up as unexpectedly as she'd left in the first place—she took up right where she'd left off, moving back into the same house and going to work in the salon again. No one knew why she did it or where she got the money to travel or buy the shop a year later, nor did she ever answer questions about it when asked. 'It's a mystery,' she'd say with a wink, and this only added to the whispered speculations of the townspeople not only that Mabel's past was a bit unsavory, but that she had more than a couple of broken cups in the china cabinet.

Mabel didn't care what people thought, and to Julie this was part of her charm. Mabel dressed the way she wanted, associated with whom she wanted, and did the things she wanted. More than once, Julie wondered whether Mabel's quirks were real or whether she simply played them up to keep people wondering about her. Either way, Julie adored everything about her. Even her tendency to pry.

'So how'd it go with Richard?' Mabel asked.

'Well, to be honest, I was a little worried about you the whole time,' Julie said. 'I thought you might pull a neck muscle if you craned your head any farther trying to listen in.'

'Oh, don't worry about that,' Mabel said. 'A little Tylenol and I was good as new the next day. But stop changing the subject. Did it go okay?'

'It went well, considering I just met him.'

'From where I was sitting, it almost looked like he knew you from somewhere.'

'Why do you say that?'

'I don't know. His expression, I guess, or maybe it was the way he kept staring at you all night. For a second there, I thought his eyes were attached to you by an invisible string.'

'It wasn't that obvious, was it?'

'Honey, he looked like a sailor on shore leave, watching a girlie show.'

Julie laughed as she slipped into her smock. 'I guess I must have dazzled him.'

'I suppose.'

Something in her tone made Julie look up. 'What? You didn't like him?'

'I'm not saying that. I haven't even met him yet, remember? I was out when he came into the shop, and you didn't exactly introduce us on Saturday. You were too busy staring back.' Mabel winked. 'And besides, I'm an old romantic at heart. As long as a man listens and is interested in what you say, his appearance isn't all that important.'

'You didn't think he was good-looking?'

'Oh, you know me—I'm more partial to the guys who come in looking for Andrea. I think tattoos that cover the arms are sexy.'

Julie laughed. 'Don't let Andrea hear you say that. She might get offended.'

'No, she won't. Unless I drew pictures, she wouldn't know who we were talking about.'

Just then, the door swung open and a woman stepped in. Julie's first appointment for the day. Mabel's appointment, another woman, followed her a moment later.

'So . . . are you going to go out with him again?' Mabel asked.

'I don't know if he'll ask, but I probably would.'

'Do you want him to?'

'Yeah,' she admitted, 'I think I do.'

Mabel's eyes twinkled. 'Well . . . what's your sweetie Bob going to say? He'll be heartbroken.'

'If he calls again, maybe I'll just tell him you're interested.'

'Oh, please do—I need some help with my taxes. Unfortunately, though, he might think I'm a little too adventurous for him.' She paused. 'So how'd Mike take it?'

From her seat by the window, Mabel had seen them talking.

Julie shrugged. She'd known Mabel would ask. 'Okay.'

'He's a good guy, you know.'

'Yeah, he is.'

Mabel didn't press any further, knowing it wouldn't do any good. She'd already tried a few times without results. But, in her mind, it was a shame that things hadn't worked out between them so far. Mike and Julie, she thought, would make a good couple. And despite what either of them imagined, she was sure that Jim wouldn't have minded at all.

She should know. After all, she was his aunt.

*   *   *

As the morning sun fed an early-season heat wave, Mike's wrench got stuck on a bolt in the inner reaches of the engine. Struggling to free it, he pulled a little too hard, nicking the back of his hand. After disinfecting the wound and putting on a bandage, he tried to free the wrench a second time with exactly the same result. Cursing to himself, he pushed away from the car in frustration and stared at it, his expression cold, as if trying to intimidate the car into doing what he wanted. All morning long he'd made one stupid mistake after another on a repair that was second nature to him, and now he couldn't even get the stupid wrench free. Not that it was entirely his fault, of course. If anything, Mike thought, it was Julie's fault. How was he supposed to concentrate on his work when he couldn't stop thinking about her date with Richard?

Her *nice* date. Her *fun* date.

What, he wondered, had been so *nice* about it? And what had she meant by *fun*?

Only one way to find out, he knew, though he dreaded the very thought of it. But what other choice did he have? It wasn't as if Julie had been all that forthcoming with him, and he couldn't exactly head over to the salon and ask Mabel in person, not with Julie standing right there. That left Henry as his only option.

Henry, the good, kind, older brother.

Yeah, right, Mike thought.

Henry could have told him earlier, but *nooooo*, he had to set him up. Henry knew exactly what he was doing when he left the conversation hanging like that. He wanted Mike to come begging for information. To come crawling. To toss a few zingers.

Yeah, well, not this time, pal, Mike decided. Not this time.

Mike approached the car again and began working his hand toward the wrench. Still stuck. Looking over his shoulder, he wondered if using a screwdriver would give him the leverage he needed to pry the wrench free. Deciding to give it a try, he reached in, but just when he had it where it needed to be, he heard Julie's voice again and the screwdriver slipped from his grip.

It was nice, Julie had said. *We had fun*.

As he reached for the screwdriver, it slid further, rattling downward like a Pachinko ball and finally vanishing from sight. He leaned over, and despite the fact that he knew everything about this particular engine, he had no idea where it had gone.

Mike stared, blinking back his disbelief.

Great, he thought, just great. The wrench is stuck, the screwdriver was absorbed in a mechanical black hole, and I'm not getting a single thing done here. I've been working for an hour, and if it keeps going like this, I'm going to have to place a new order with Blaine Sutter, the Snap-on tool representative.

He had to talk to Henry. It was the only way he could put this behind him.

Crap.

Mike reached for a rag and began wiping his hands on his way through the garage, hating the fact that it had come to this and trying to figure out the best way to ask. The challenge, he knew, was to not let Henry know why he was so interested. It would be best if the topic came up naturally, or Henry would end up rubbing his nose in it. His brother lived for moments like this. He'd probably spent the whole morning preparing zingers. With people like that, there was only one thing to do, and that was to use the fine art of deception. After taking a moment to formulate his plan, Mike poked his head into Henry's office.

Henry was sitting behind his cluttered desk, placing an order on the phone. Directly in front of him was a packet of miniature doughnuts sitting next to a can of Pepsi. Henry always kept a stash of junk food hidden in his drawer, to make up for the healthy lunches Emma made him. Henry waved him in, and Mike took a seat in the chair across from the desk just as he hung up.

'That was the dealer down in Jacksonville,' Henry said. 'They won't have the switch you need for the Volvo for another week. Remind me to call Evelyn, will you?'

'Sure,' Mike said.

'So what's on your mind, little brother?'

Of course, Henry already knew what Mike needed to talk about. The look on his brother's face made the topic plain, and though he could have come straight out with what Mabel had told him, he didn't. There was something about seeing Mike squirm that always left him feeling gleeful the rest of the day.

'Well,' Mike said, 'I was thinking . . .' He

trailed off.

'Yes?' Henry asked.

'Well, I was thinking that maybe I should start going to church with you and the family again.'

Henry brought his finger to his chin, thinking, *That's an original way to begin. Won't do you any good, but it's definitely original.*

'Oh, really?' he said, hiding his smile.

'Yeah, you know. I haven't been in a while, but it would be good for me.'

Henry nodded. 'Mmm . . . you might be right. You want to meet there, or do you want us to pick you up?'

Mike shifted in his seat. 'Before we get to that—I just want to know what the new reverend is like. I mean, do people like what he says in his sermons? Do they talk about it after the services?'

'Sometimes.'

'But people do talk. After church, I mean.'

'Sure. But you'll find out this Sunday. We go at nine.'

'Nine. Okay. Good.' Mike nodded, pausing for a moment. 'Well, just for example, what did people say after last Sunday?'

'Oh, well, let's see . . .' Henry tapped his finger in feigned concentration. 'Come to think of it, I don't really know. I was talking to Mabel.'

Bingo, Mike thought, smiling inwardly. *Just like I planned. I am a master of deception.*

'Mabel, huh?' he asked.

Henry reached for the doughnuts. Taking a bite, he waved a hand and leaned back in his chair, talking as he chewed. 'Yeah. Usually she goes to the earlier service, but I guess she was running late. We talked for a good long time, and boy, did she

41

tell me some interesting stuff.' He took a moment to look upward, began counting the little holes in the ceiling tiles for effect, then rocked his seat forward again, shaking his head. 'But you don't want to hear about that. We were just talking about Julie's date, and you've already told me you're not interested. So should we pick you up on Sunday or what?'

Realizing his plan had just gone up in smoke, Mike just sat there, trying vainly to recover.

'Uh . . . well . . .'

Henry glanced his way, challenge lighting in his eyes. 'Unless, of course, you've changed your mind.'

Mike paled. 'Uh . . .'

Henry laughed. He'd had his fun, and as much as he'd enjoyed it, he knew it was time to stop. 'Answer me a question, Mike,' he said, leaning forward. 'Why do you keep pretending you don't want to go out with Julie?'

Mike blinked. 'We're just friends,' he said, the answer coming automatically.

Henry ignored his answer. 'Is it because of Jim?'

When Mike didn't respond, Henry put down the doughnut. 'He's been gone for a long time now. It's not like you're trying to steal his wife.'

'Then why have you been acting like I shouldn't go out with her? Like last summer on the boat?'

'Because she needed time, Mike. You know that. She wasn't ready to start seeing people last year, or even six months ago. But she's ready now.'

Put on the spot, Mike wasn't sure what to say. Nor did he understand how Henry seemed to know so much.

'It's not that easy,' he finally answered.

42

'Of course it's not easy. Do you think that asking Emma out the first time was easy for me? There were a lot of guys who wanted to go out with her, but I figured the worst that could happen was that she would say no.'

'Come on—Emma told me she had eyes for you even before you asked her out. You two were meant for each other.'

'But I didn't know that. Not then, anyway. All I knew was that I had to give it a shot.'

Mike met Henry's eyes. 'But she wasn't married to your best friend.'

'No,' Henry said, 'she wasn't. But then, we weren't friends beforehand like you and Julie, either.'

'That's what makes it so hard. What if things change between us?'

'They already are changing, little brother.'

'Not really.'

'Sure they are,' he said. 'Otherwise you wouldn't have had to ask me about the date, would you? Julie would have told you herself. She told you about Bob, didn't she?'

Mike had no answer to that, but when he left the office a minute later, he knew that Henry was right.

Four

Singer's head rose from the blanket as soon as Richard entered the salon, and though he growled, the sound was muted, as if he thought Julie might scold him again.

'Hey, sugar? Here for another haircut?' Andrea

43

asked, smiling. He was wearing jeans, and his denim shirt was unbuttoned at the top, leaving just enough room to see the curly hair on his chest. And those eyes. 'I'll be done here in a couple of minutes.'

Richard shook his head. 'No, thank you,' he said. 'Is Julie around?'

Andrea's smile faded. She snapped her chewing gum and nodded toward the rear of the salon. 'Yeah, she's here,' she said, pouting. 'She's in the back.'

Mabel had heard the bell on the door jingle, and she stepped out from behind the partition.

'Oh . . . Richard, right? How are you?' she inquired.

Richard brought his hands together in front of him. He recognized her from the other night in the restaurant, and though her expression seemed pleasant enough, he knew she was still evaluating him. Small towns were the same everywhere he'd been.

'Fine, ma'am, thanks. How are you?'

'Good. Julie will be out in a minute. She's setting someone up under the hair dryer, but I'll tell her you're here.'

'Thank you.'

Though he didn't turn toward her, Richard knew that Andrea was still watching him. A knockout, that's what most people would say about her, but he wasn't all that impressed. She struck him as a forced beauty, as if she were trying too hard. He liked women who looked wholesome, the way Julie did.

'Richard?' Julie asked a moment later. She smiled at him, struck again by his good looks.

Singer stood from the blanket and nearly followed her, but she held up a hand to stop him. He froze and stopped growling.

'Hey there,' Richard answered. 'I guess he's getting used to me, huh?'

Julie glanced toward Singer. 'Him? Oh, we had a talk. I think he's fine now.'

'A talk?'

'He gets jealous.'

'Jealous?'

She shrugged. 'You'd have to live with him to understand.'

Richard raised an eyebrow, but he let the comment pass.

'So what are you doing here?' she asked.

'I thought I'd see how you were doing.'

'I'm fine, but I'm kind of busy right now. I've been swamped all morning. Why aren't you at work?'

'I am. Kind of, anyway. Being a consultant gives me a bit of freedom, and I decided to pop into town.'

'Just to see me?'

'I couldn't think of anything I'd rather do.'

She smiled. 'I had a good time on Saturday night,' she offered.

'So did I.' Richard's eyes darted from Mabel to Andrea, and though they both appeared to be occupied with other things, he knew they were listening. 'Do you think you could take a quick break so we can talk outside? I called earlier, but you weren't in.'

'I'd love to, but I've got someone in the back.'

'It won't take long.'

Julie hesitated, glancing toward the clock.

'I promise,' Richard added. 'I know you're working.'

A quick estimate said she had maybe a few minutes.

'I guess that's okay,' she said, 'but it can't be long. Otherwise I'll have to spend the rest of the day trying to fix the color and you're going to find yourself in the doghouse. Give me a second to check on her, though, okay?'

'Sure.'

Julie went to see her customer again. The woman was having highlights put in, and her head was covered in a perforated plastic cap. Assorted strands of hair, sticking through the holes in the cap, were coated in purple slime. Julie checked the color, turned the dryer on low, buying an extra couple of minutes, and went out front again.

'All right,' she said, walking toward the door, 'I'm ready.'

Richard followed her outside. The door swung shut behind them, the bell jingling again.

'So what did you want to talk about?'

Richard shrugged. 'Nothing important, really. I just wanted to have you all to myself for a minute.'

'You're kidding.'

'Not at all.'

'But why?'

'Gee,' he said, playing innocent, 'I'm not really sure.'

'I found your card,' she said. 'You didn't have to do that.'

'I know I didn't. But I wanted to.'

'Is that why you called the salon this morning? To see if I got it?'

'No. I just wanted to hear your voice. Good

memories, you know?'

'Already?'

'I was charmed.'

Julie looked up at him, thinking, Flattery is such a *nice* way to start the day. After a moment, Richard began to tug at his watchband.

'But actually, besides wanting to see you, there is another reason I came by.'

'Oh, I get it. Now that I'm all buttered up, the truth comes out, huh?'

He laughed. 'Sort of. The truth is I wanted to see if you'd like to go out again this Saturday.'

Saturday, Julie remembered with a pang, was supposed to be dinner at Emma's with Henry and Mike.

'I'd love to, but I can't. A couple of friends invited me over to their house. Can we go on Friday instead? Or maybe sometime during the week?'

Richard shook his head. 'I wish I could, but I'm going to Cleveland this evening and I won't be back until Saturday. And I just found out today that I might be out of town again the following weekend. It's not set in stone, but odds are I'll have to go.' He paused. 'Are you sure you can't make it?'

'I really can't,' she said, playing out the words, wishing she didn't have to say them. 'They're good friends. I can't blow them off at the last minute.'

For an instant, an unreadable expression crossed Richard's face, but just as quickly as it had come, it was gone. 'Okay,' he said.

'I'm sorry,' she said, hoping he knew she meant it.

'Don't worry about it.' He seemed to look into the distance before focusing on Julie again. 'Look, these things happen. It's no big deal. But you won't mind if I give you a call in a couple of weeks? When I get back, I mean? Maybe we could arrange something then.'

A couple of weeks?

'Well, hold on,' Julie said. 'You could always come to the dinner with me. I'm sure my friends wouldn't mind.'

Richard shook his head. 'No. They're your friends, and I'm not real good at meeting new people. I never have been—shy, I guess—and I don't want you to have to change your plans.' He smiled before nodding toward the salon. 'Listen, you made me promise not to keep you, and I'm the kind of guy who keeps his word. Besides, I've got to get back to work, too.' He smiled again. 'You look great, by the way.'

As he turned to leave and before she could stop herself, Julie called out, 'Wait!'

Richard stopped. 'Yes?'

They'd understand, wouldn't they? she thought.

'Well, if you're not going to be in town next week, maybe I can change my plans. I'll talk to Emma. I'm sure she won't mind.'

'I don't want you to have to break your date.'

'It's not that big of a deal . . . We get together all the time.'

'You sure?' he asked.

'Yeah, I'm sure.'

He met her eyes, staring as if he were seeing her for the first time. 'That's great . . . ,' he said, and before she realized what was happening, he leaned in and kissed her.

Not hard, not too long, but a kiss nonetheless.

'Thank you,' he murmured.

Before Julie could think of anything to say,

48

Richard turned and started down the sidewalk. All she could do was watch him go.

*　　　*　　　*

'Did he just kiss her?' Mike asked, his mouth hanging open.

Earlier, he'd been standing near the open bay of the garage when he'd seen Richard walking up the street. He'd watched Richard walk in alone, he'd watched Julie and Richard walk out together, and Henry had walked up just as Richard was leaning in to kiss Julie.

'That's what it looked like to me,' Henry answered.

'They don't even know each other.'

'They do now.'

'Thanks, Henry. You're making me feel a whole lot better.'

'Do you want me to lie to you instead?'

'Right now, I think I would,' Mike mumbled.

'All right,' Henry said, thinking about it. 'That fella sure is ugly.'

At Henry's comment, Mike put his head in his hands.

*　　　*　　　*

Once inside, Julie went back to her client.

'I thought you'd forgotten about me,' the woman complained as she lowered her magazine.

Julie checked the color on a few strands of hair. 'Sorry about that, but I was watching the clock. It looks like you've still got a couple of minutes. Unless you want it this dark.'

49

'I think it should be lighter, don't you?'

'I think so.'

The woman went on about the exact color she desired. Though Julie knew she was speaking, she wasn't concentrating on what the woman was saying. Instead, she was thinking about Richard and what had just happened outside the door.

He'd kissed her.

It wasn't a big deal, of course, not in the grand scheme of things. Yet for some reason, she couldn't stop thinking about it, nor did she know exactly how she felt. The way it happened had been so . . . so . . . so *what?*

Forward? Surprising?

Julie went to the sink in search of the right shampoo, still trying to figure it out, when Mabel walked up.

'Did I just see what I thought I saw?' she asked. 'Did you just kiss him?'

'Actually, he kissed me.'

'You don't look too happy about it.'

'I'm not sure whether "happy" is the word to describe it.'

'Why?'

'I don't know,' Julie said. 'It just seemed . . .' She trailed off, still looking for the right word.

'Unexpected?' Mabel offered.

Julie thought about that. Though it *was* forward, it wasn't as if he'd gone too far with it. And she *did* find him attractive, she *did* agree to go out with him, so she wasn't sure if 'surprise' was the right word. At the same time, she also knew that if he'd done it after their date next Saturday, she probably wouldn't have been questioning it at all. Next Saturday, she might have been insulted if he *hadn't* tried to kiss her.

So why did it feel as if he'd just crossed a barrier without asking her permission first?

Julie shrugged. 'I guess that's it.'

Mabel studied her for a moment. 'Well, I'd say that means he had just as good of a time as you did,' she said. 'Though I'm not really all that surprised. He's obviously giving you the full-court press.'

Julie nodded slowly. 'I guess.'

'You guess?'

'He also left a card on my porch. I found it this morning.'

Mabel raised her eyebrows.

'You think it's too much?' Julie asked. 'Considering I just met him?'

'Not necessarily.'

'But it might be?'

'Oh, I don't know. He might be the kind of guy who knows what he wants, and when he finds it, he goes after it with gusto. I've met lots of men like that. They have their appeal. And you are quite the catch, you know.'

Julie smiled.

'Or then again,' Mabel said with an elaborate shrug, 'he might be bonkers.'

'Thanks a lot.'

'No problem. But either way, all I can say is welcome back to the wonderful world of dating. Like I tell everyone, it's never boring, is it?'

*   *   *

It had been a long time since Richard laughed aloud, and in the confines of his car, the sound

51

seemed louder than it was.

He gets jealous, Julie had said about her dog. As if she honestly believed he was human. Cute.

Their evening together had been wonderful. He'd enjoyed her company, of course, but what he'd come to admire most was her resilience. Her life had been hard, and most people would have been marked by bitterness or anger, but he'd seen no traces of that on their date.

She was also lovely. The way she'd smiled at him with almost childlike excitement and the look of struggle as she'd debated whether to break her plans with her friends . . . he felt as if he could watch her for hours and never grow tired of it.

I had a good time on Saturday night, she had said.

He was almost certain that she had, but he'd had to see her today to make sure. The mind can do funny things on the day after a date, he knew. The questions, the worries, the concerns . . . Should he have done this, should he have said that? Yesterday, he'd recalled the date in detail, remembering Julie's expressions and trying to discern any hidden subtexts in her statements suggesting that he'd done something wrong. He'd stayed awake, unable to sleep, until he'd finally had to write a note and drop it off for her to find in the morning.

But he need not have worried. They'd both had a good time—no, a great time. Ridiculous to have even considered that he might have been wrong about it.

His cell phone rang, and he checked the caller ID.

Blansen from work. The foreman, no doubt offering more bad news about the schedule, about falling behind, about cost overruns. Delays. Blansen always had bad news. The bearer of bad tidings. Depressing, that one. Said he cared about his men, but what he really meant was that he didn't want them to work hard.

Instead of answering, he summoned Julie's image again. It had to have been fate, he thought, meeting her the way he had. There were a thousand other places he could have been that morning. He wasn't due for another haircut for a couple of weeks, but he'd pushed through the door of the salon as if guided by an unknown force. *Fate*.

The cell phone rang again.

Yes, the date had gone well, but there was one thing. Today, toward the end . . .

Maybe he shouldn't have kissed her. It wasn't as if he'd planned to kiss her, but he'd been so elated when she broke her plans in order to see him again . . . it just *happened*. A surprise for both of them. But was it too much, too soon?

Yes, he decided, it probably was, and he regretted it. There wasn't any rush here. It would be better to take it easy the next time he saw her. Give her a little space, let her come to her own conclusions about him, without pressure. Naturally.

The cell phone rang a third time, but he continued to ignore it. In the back of his mind, he replayed the scene again.

Very cute.

Five

On Saturday night over dinner, Richard stared across the table at Julie, a faint smile playing over his lips.

'What are you smiling at?' Julie asked.

Richard seemed to come back to her, a sheepish look on his face. 'I'm sorry. I was just daydreaming there for a second.'

'Am I that boring?'

'Not at all. I'm just glad you were able to come out with me tonight.' Bringing up his napkin to dab at the corner of his mouth, he met her eyes. 'Have I told you how lovely you look this evening?'

'About a dozen times.'

'Do you want me to stop?'

'No. Call me strange, but I sort of like life on the pedestal.'

Richard laughed. 'I'll do my best to keep you there.'

They were at Pagini's, a cozy restaurant in Morehead City that smelled of fresh spice and drawn butter, the kind of place where the servers wore black and white and dinner was often cooked tableside. A bottle of Chardonnay sat in an ice bucket next to the table; the waiter had poured two glasses, and they glowed yellow in the soft light. He'd shown up at the door dressed in a linen jacket, holding a bouquet of roses and smelling faintly of cologne.

'So tell me about your week,' he said. 'What exciting things happened while I was gone?'

'You mean at work?'

'Work, life, whatever. I want to know it all.'

'I should probably be asking you that question.'

'Why?'

'Because,' she said, 'my life's not all that exciting. I work in a beauty salon in a small southern town, remember?' She spoke with good, brisk humor, as if to ward off sympathy. 'Besides, I just realized that I don't know much about you.'

'Sure you do.'

'Not really. You haven't told me much about yourself yet. I don't even know what you do exactly.'

'I think I told you I'm a consultant, didn't I?'

'Yeah, but you didn't go into a lot of detail.'

'That's because my job is boring.'

She pretended to look skeptical, and Richard thought for a moment. 'Okay . . . what I do . . .' He paused. 'Well, just think of me as the guy who, working behind the scenes, makes sure the bridge doesn't collapse.'

'That's not boring.'

'That's just a fancy way of saying I work with numbers all day. When it gets right down to it, I'm what most people would consider a nerd.'

She ran her eyes over him, thinking, I doubt that. 'Is that what the meeting was about?'

'What meeting?'

'The one in Cleveland.'

'Oh . . . no,' he said, shaking his head. 'There's another project the company is getting ready to bid on in Florida, and there's a lot of research to do— cost projections, traffic projections, expected loads, things like that. They have their own people, of course, but they bring in consultants like me to make sure everything will go through the

55

government bidding system without a hitch. You'd be amazed at the amount of work it takes before you can start a project. I'm single-handedly responsible for destroying vast tracts of timber, just for the paperwork required by the government, and right now I'm a little short staffed.'

Julie observed him in the dim light of the restaurant. His angular face, at once rugged and boyish, reminded her of men who made their living posing in cigarette advertisements. She tried, and failed, to picture what he might have looked like as a child.

'What do you do in your spare time? Hobbies, I mean.'

'Not too much, really. Between work and trying to stay in shape, I don't have much time for anything else. I used to do a little photography, though. I took a few courses in college, and for a short time there, I actually considered making it my career. Even bought some equipment. But it's a tough way to pay the bills, unless you want to open a studio, and I had no desire to spend my weekends photographing weddings and bar mitzvahs, or kids whose parents dragged them in.'

'So you became an engineer instead.'

He nodded. For a moment the conversation hit a lull, and Julie reached for her wineglass.

'And you're originally from Cleveland?' she asked.

'No. I haven't been in Cleveland all that long. Just a year or so. Actually, I grew up in Denver and spent most of my life there.'

'What did your parents do?'

'Dad worked at a chemical plant. And Mom was just a mom. In the beginning, anyway. You know, stay home, cook supper, keep the house clean, *Leave It to Beaver* kind of stuff. But after my dad died, she had to take a job as a maid. It didn't pay much, but she was somehow able to keep us going. To be honest, I don't know how she did it.'

'She sounds remarkable.'

'She was.'

'Was?'

'Is.' He looked down, swirling the wine in his glass. 'She had a stroke a few years ago and . . . well, it's not good. She's barely cognizant of what's going on around her, and she doesn't remember me at all. Doesn't remember much of anything, in fact. I had to send her to a place in Salt Lake City that specializes in her condition.'

Julie winced. Seeing her expression, Richard shook his head.

'It's okay. You didn't know. But to be honest, it's not something I usually talk about. Kind of brings conversations to an uncomfortable stop, especially when people hear my father died, too. Makes them wonder what it must be like to be without family. But you don't need me to explain that, I suppose.'

No, she thought, I don't. I know that territory well.

'So that's why you left Denver? Because of your mom?'

'That was only part of it.' He glanced at the table before looking up again. 'I guess now's the time to tell you that I was married once. To a woman named Jessica. I left because of her, too.'

Though a little surprised he hadn't mentioned it before, Julie said nothing. She could feel him debating whether he should go on, but finally he did, his voice flat.

'I don't know what went wrong. I could spend all night talking about it and trying to make sense of it, but to be honest, I still haven't figured it out. In the end, it just didn't work out.'

'How long were you married?'

'Four years.' He met her eyes across the table. 'Do you really want to hear about this?'

'Not if you don't want to tell me.'

'Thank you,' he said, exhaling with a laugh. 'You have no idea how glad I am that you said that.'

She smiled. 'So Cleveland, huh? Do you like it there?'

'It's all right, but I'm not there all that much. Usually I'm on-site like I am now. After this project finishes up, I have no idea where I'll go next.'

'I'll bet that's hard sometimes.'

'Yeah, sometimes it is, especially when I'm stuck in hotels. This project is nice because I'll be here for a while and I was able to find a place to rent. And, of course, I got the chance to meet you.'

As he was talking, Julie was struck by how much their lives seemed to have in common, from being only children raised by single mothers to their decisions to start over in someplace new. And though their marriages had ended differently, something in his tone suggested he'd been the one left behind, that he'd struggled with real feelings of loss in the aftermath. In her time in Swansboro, Julie hadn't met anyone who could understand how lonely she sometimes felt, especially around the holidays, when Mike and Henry would mention that they were going to visit their parents or Mabel headed off to Charleston to spend time with her sister.

But Richard knew what it was like, and she felt

an emerging kinship with him, the kind visitors to a strange country might feel upon discovering that the people at the next table come from a town in their home state.

The evening wore on and the sky deepened in color, unveiling the stars. Neither Julie nor Richard rushed through dinner. They ordered coffee at the end of the meal and split a piece of key lime pie, eating their way in from opposite sides until only a sliver was left that neither would claim.

It was still warm when they finally left. Expecting him to offer his hand or arm, she was surprised when he did neither. Part of her wondered whether he was holding back because he sensed that she'd been caught off guard by his kiss earlier that week; another part wondered if he had surprised himself with all he'd told her about his past. There was, she thought, a lot to digest there. The little tidbit about being married in the past had come out of the blue, and she wondered why he hadn't mentioned it on the first date, when she'd first told him about Jim.

That was okay, though. She reminded herself that people were different when it came to talking about the past. And anyway, now that they were more comfortable with each other, she realized she was enjoying this date at least as much as the first one. It was nice—not earth-shattering, but definitely nice. When they stopped at the crosswalk, Julie glanced at Richard. I like him, she thought. I'm not crazy about him yet, I'll be ready to say good-bye later, but I like him. And that's enough for me right now.

'Do you like dancing?' she asked.

'Why? Do you want to go?'

'If you're up for it.'

'Oh, I don't know. I'm not all that good.'

'C'mon,' she said, 'I know a great place.'

'You sure you don't want to stay around here for a while? We could probably find a place to get a drink.'

'We've been sitting for hours. I think I'm ready for some fun.'

'You don't think the night's been fun so far?' he asked, pretending to be hurt. 'And here I was, having a great time.'

'You know what I mean. But if it makes you feel any better, I'm not a very good dancer, either, so I promise I won't say a thing if you step on my feet. I'll even try not to wince.'

'Suffer and smile?'

'It's the woman's plight, you know.'

'Okay,' he said, 'but I'll hold you to your promise.'

She laughed and nodded toward his car. 'Come on.'

Richard warmed to the sound of her laughter, the first time he'd heard it this evening.

She's a cautious one, he observed. Kiss her once, and she seemed to question it all. But allow her to lead, and the caution seemed to fade. He knew she was trying to figure him out, trying to match his story to the man she saw sitting across from her. But there was no mistaking the sympathy on her face the moment she realized how similar they were.

Six

The Sailing Clipper was a bar typical of small coastal towns: Dimly lit and smelling of mildew, cigarettes, and stale booze, it was popular with blue-collar workers, who crowded around the bar ordering Budweisers in volume. Along the far wall, the stage overlooked a slightly warped dance floor that seldom emptied when bands were playing. A few dozen tables, carved with the initials of most everyone who'd walked through the door, were arranged haphazardly, unmatching chairs circling them.

The group on stage, Ocracoke Inlet, was something of a regular at the Clipper. The owner, a one-legged man people called Leaning Joe, liked the group because it played songs that put people in a good mood, which made them want to stay, which in turn was good for business as they ordered booze in quantity. They played nothing original, nothing daring, nothing that couldn't be found in juke-boxes around the country, which was exactly the reason why, Mike thought, everyone liked them so much. *Really* liked them. When they played people came in *droves*, which wasn't the case with the bands he played with. Never once, however, had they asked Mike to fill in, even though he was on a first-name basis with most of the group. Second-rate band or not, the thought was depressing.

But then, the whole evening had been depressing. Hell, the whole week had been depressing, for that matter. Ever since Monday, when Julie came by to pick up her keys and casually *(casually!)* mentioned that she'd be going out with Richard on Saturday instead of spending tonight with them, Mike had been in a funk. He'd been mumbling to himself about the unfairness of it all with such regularity that a couple of customers had even commented on it to Henry. Worse, Mike couldn't summon the courage to talk to Julie the rest of the week, knowing that if he did, she'd press him on what seemed to be bothering him. He wasn't ready to tell her the truth, but seeing her walk by the shop every day reminded him that he had no idea what to do about the whole situation.

Sure, Henry and Emma were great, and he liked spending time with them. But let's be honest here—on a night like this, Mike knew he was a third wheel in this little group. They had each other to go home to. Mike, on the other hand, had zip, unless he counted the occasional mouse that scurried through his kitchen. They had each other to dance with; Mike had to sit at the table alone half the time, reading beer labels as he peeled them off the bottles. And when Emma did ask him to dance, which she'd done regularly tonight, Mike would head to the floor, his head hung low, hoping to God that no one would see him dancing with his sister.

Sister. Sister-in-law. Whatever. Technicalities weren't important at a time like this. When she asked, it still made him feel as if his mother had offered to go with him to the prom because he couldn't get a date.

This was not the way things were supposed to be tonight. Julie was supposed to be here. Julie was supposed to be the fourth wheel. Julie was

62

supposed to be the one dancing with him, smiling over a drink, laughing and flirting. And she would have been if it wasn't for Richard.

Richard.

He hated that guy.

Didn't know him. Didn't want to know him. Didn't matter. Simply thinking the name caused him to scowl, and he'd been scowling a lot, all evening long.

Watching his brother carefully, Henry finished the last of his Coors and set the bottle off to the side.

'I think maybe you ought to cut back on that cheap beer you're drinking,' Henry commented. 'Looks like it's giving you gas.'

Mike looked up. Henry was smirking as he reached for Emma's bottle of beer. She'd gone off to the bathroom, and considering the ever-present lines in a crowd this size, Henry knew she might be a while. He'd already ordered another to replace it.

'I'm drinking the same stuff you are.'

'True,' Henry said, 'but you have to realize that some men can handle it better than others.'

'Yeah, yeah . . . keep talking.'

'My, aren't we in a mood this evening,' Henry said.

'You've been riding me all night.'

'Considering the way you've been acting lately, you deserve it. We had a great dinner, I've been engaging you with my sparkling wit all night long, and Emma's been making sure that you're not always sitting alone at the table like some loser whose date just stood him up.'

'That's not funny.'

'It's not meant to be. I'm simply speaking the

truth. Think of me as your very own burning bush. When in doubt, when you need answers, you come to me. For instance—you need to lighten up about this. You're letting it ruin the whole night.'

'Look—I'm doing my best, okay?'

'Oh,' Henry said, cocking an eyebrow, 'I see. Sorry. I guess I'm just imagining all the deep sighs.'

Mike pulled the rest of the label off his bottle and crumpled it into a ball. 'Yeah, yeah. You're a funny guy, Henry. You should head to Vegas with your act. Believe me, I'd be the first to pack your bags.'

Henry leaned back in his seat. 'Aw, c'mon. I'm just having a little fun.'

'Yeah—at my expense.'

Henry held up his hands, looking innocent. 'You're the only one here. Who else can I pick on?'

Mike glared at him before turning away.

'All right, all right . . . I'm sorry already,' Henry said. 'But listen—I'll say it again. Just because she's out with Richard doesn't mean that you've lost your chance forever. Instead of moping around, use it as a challenge. Maybe this should inspire you to ask her out.'

'I was planning on that.'

'You were?'

'Yeah. After we talked on Monday, I decided to do exactly what you said. Tonight was supposed to be the night.'

Henry studied him. 'Good,' he finally said, 'I'm proud of you.'

Mike waited for more, but Henry stayed silent.

'What? No jokes this time?'

'No reason to make jokes.'

'Because you don't believe me?'

'No, I believe you. I have to, I guess.'

'Why?'

'Because I'll get to see you do it.'

'Huh?'

'The gods are with you, little brother.'

'What the hell are you talking about?'

Henry raised his chin, nodding in the direction of the door.

'Guess who just walked in?'

*   *   *

Richard stood beside Julie just inside the door as she craned her neck, looking for a place to sit.

'I didn't realize it would be so crowded,' Richard shouted over the noise. 'Are you sure you want to stay?'

'C'mon—it'll be fun. You'll see.'

Though he flashed a quick smile of agreement, Richard was doubtful. This place struck him as a refuge for those who drank to escape their problems, people who were desperate for the companionship of a stranger. It was, he thought, the kind of atmosphere that promoted the notion that everyone here, whether with someone or not, was up for grabs. Julie didn't belong in a place like this any more than he did.

On stage, the band had started up again and people were trading places on the floor, some heading in, others taking a break. He leaned in close to Julie's ear, and she could feel his breath against her. 'Let's get something to drink,' he said, 'before we find a place to sit down.'

Julie nodded. 'Sure. You lead the way. The bar's straight ahead.'

As Richard began squeezing between people, he

reached back, offering his hand to Julie. Without hesitation, she took it. When they reached the bar, he held on to it as he raised his other hand to get the bartender's attention.

*   *   *

'So that's him, huh?' Emma said.

Emma, thirty-eight, was a green-eyed blonde with a sunny disposition, which more than offset the fact that she wasn't all that pretty in the classic sense. Short and round faced, she dieted constantly with no success, though neither Mike nor Henry knew why she bothered. People responded to Emma not for superficial reasons, but for who she was and the things she did. She volunteered regularly at her children's school, and at three o'clock every afternoon, she propped open the front door with a brick so that kids in the neighborhood would have a place to congregate. And they did—her house was a beehive of activity for hours as children trampled in and out—drawn by the homemade pizzas she cooked almost daily.

But if the children loved her, Henry adored her and considered himself fortunate to have her by his side. Emma was good for Henry and vice versa; as they often told others, they were too busy laughing together to have any time to argue. Like Henry, Emma loved to tease, and when they got going, they seemed to feed off each other. And after a couple of drinks? Watch out, Mike thought. They were deadly, like sharks who fed on their young.

Unfortunately for Mike, he knew that right now he was nothing but a baby shark, swimming ahead of Mommy's open jaws. One look at the hungry gleam in their eyes made him want to dive for cover.

Henry nodded. 'That's him.'

Emma continued to stare. 'He's really something, isn't he?'

'I think Mabel used the word . . . sexy,' Henry offered.

Emma raised a finger, as if Henry were an attorney who'd made a valid point in court. 'Yes . . . sexy. Very sexy. In a handsome stranger kind of way, I mean.'

Mike crossed his arms and sank lower in his seat, wondering if the evening could get any worse.

'My sentiments exactly,' Henry said. Still waiting for drinks, Richard and Julie were standing at the bar, their faces in profile. 'They do make a lovely couple,' he added.

'They certainly stand out in a crowd,' Emma agreed.

'It's like one of those *People* magazine articles about the world's most glamorous couples.'

'Like they should be starring in a movie together.'

'Knock it off, you guys,' Mike finally cut in. 'I get it. He's perfect, he's wonderful, he's Mr Everything.'

Henry and Emma faced Mike, their eyes bright with amusement.

'We're not saying that, Mike,' Henry offered, 'we're just saying he *looks* like he is.'

Emma reached across the table and patted Mike on the shoulder. 'Besides,' she said, 'there's no reason to lose hope. Looks aren't the only thing that matter.'

Mike glared at them.

Henry leaned toward Emma. 'I guess you should

know my little brother's been having a hard time with all this. And from his expression, I don't think we're helping.'

'Oh, really?' Emma asked innocently.

'I'd be fine if you two would quit picking on me. You've been at it all night.'

'But you're such an easy target when you're this way.' Emma giggled. 'Pouting does that, you know.'

'Henry and I have already been through this.'

'And it's not attractive at all,' Emma said, ignoring his comment. 'Take it from a woman who knows. Unless you want to lose out to a guy like that, you'd better change your tune before it's too late. If you keep acting the way you've been acting all night, you might as well say good-bye right now.'

Mike blinked at the honesty. 'So I should act like I don't care?'

'No, Mike. Act like you do care, like you want what's best for her.'

'How do I do that?'

'Be her friend.'

'I am her friend.'

'Not right now, you're not. If you were her friend, you'd be happy for her.'

'Why should I be happy she's with him?'

'Because,' Emma said as if the answer were obvious, 'it means she's ready to start looking for the guy who's right for her, and everyone knows who that is. In the end, I honestly doubt if it'll be the guy over there.' She smiled and touched his shoulder again. 'Do you really think we'd be giving you such a hard time if we didn't believe this was all going to work out for you two in the end?'

As much as she teased him, Mike knew at that moment why Henry loved her so much. And why he loved her, too.

In a sisterly kind of way, of course.

*   *   *

Julie and Richard's drinks finally arrived—bourbon for him, a Diet Coke for her—and after paying, Richard put his wallet away, then glanced off to the side, toward the man sitting at the end of the bar.

The man was stirring his drink, seemingly minding his own business. But Richard waited, and sure enough, a moment later the man's eyes drifted over to Julie. The whole time he and Julie waited for their drinks, the man had been doing just that, though he'd tried not to be obvious. This time, however, Richard caught his gaze and watched him with unblinking eyes until the man finally turned away.

'Who are you looking at?' Julie asked.

Richard shook his head. 'No one,' he said. 'Just thinking about something else for a second there.' He smiled.

'You up for hitting the dance floor yet?' she asked.

'Not quite yet. I think I need to finish my drink first.'

*   *   *

Andrea, dressed in a tight black miniskirt, stiletto heels, and a halter top, had stretched the chewing gum from her mouth to her finger and was twirling it around in boredom as Cobra downed his sixth shot of tequila and chased it with a squeeze of lime. Wiping the pulp from his mouth with the back of

69

his hand, he grinned at Andrea, his gold incisor catching the light of the neon sign behind them.

Cobra had rolled up in front of the salon on his Harley on Thursday morning—though Andrea didn't know it, her name was frequently mentioned at biker bars as far away as Louisiana—and by the time he'd left, Andrea had given him her phone number and spent the rest of the day strutting around the shop, feeling downright pleased with herself. In her rapture, she hadn't noticed the pitying glances Mabel had cast her way, nor had she realized that Cobra was, like all the men she dated, basically a loser.

He'd called her earlier that evening after a couple of beers and suggested that she meet him and his friends at the Clipper. Though not technically a date—he hadn't offered to pick her up, nor had it occurred to either of them that he might suggest getting something to eat first—Andrea had been thrilled by the time she hung up the phone, thinking it was close enough to at least feel like a date. She'd spent an hour figuring out what she wanted to wear—first impressions were important—before she'd left to find Cobra at the Clipper.

The first thing he'd done was put his arms around her, resting both hands on her bottom while kissing her on the neck.

It hadn't bothered her. After all, Cobra wasn't bad looking, especially when compared to some of the other guys she'd gone out with. Though he wore a black T-shirt with the picture of a bloody skull emblazoned on the front and leather chaps over a crusty pair of jeans, he wasn't fat or hairy. And the tattoo of the mermaid on his arm, she had to admit, was relatively tasteful when compared to others she'd seen. She wasn't too keen on the gold-tooth thing, but he looked and smelled clean enough, which you couldn't always bargain on.

Nonetheless, she'd finally come to the realization that the evening had been a complete waste and that she'd made a mistake by giving him her phone number. For one thing, after the first couple of shots, when things were just beginning to get interesting, a few of his friends had shown up and one of them had informed her that Cobra wasn't the guy's real name, just the one he used with friends. His real name was Ed DeBoner.

That was when the interest began to fade. For the life of her, she couldn't imagine having to admit that to anyone. Unlike Cobra (or Snake, or Rat, or even Dean), Ed wasn't the name of someone who drove a Harley, someone one step ahead of the law and living the free life. Ed wasn't even the name of a real man. Ed was the name of a talking horse, for God's sake. And let's not even mention the last name.

DeBoner.

When he'd said it, she'd nearly spat her drink out.

'You wanna go back to your place, baby?' Cobra asked, slurring the words.

Andrea slid the gum back into her mouth. 'No.'

'Then let's get another drink.'

'You don't have any money.'

'So buy me a drink and I'll make it up to you later, baby.'

Though she'd liked being called 'baby' earlier in the evening, thinking it made her seem sultry, that was when Cobra was doing it. Not some guy named Ed DeBoner. Andrea snapped her gum.

Cobra seemed oblivious to her scorn. He reached under the table and ran his hand over her thigh, and she stood up, pushing away from the table, needing another drink.

It was when she neared the bar that she recognized Richard.

*　　　*　　　*

Julie's face lit up as soon as she saw Mike, Henry, and Emma at a table near the dance floor. She reached for Richard's hand.

'C'mon,' she said, 'I think I see someplace we can sit.'

They pushed their way through the crowd, crossed the edge of the dance floor, and reached the table.

'Hey, guys. I didn't expect to see you here,' Julie said. 'How are you?'

'We're doing well,' Henry said. 'We just thought we'd come by after dinner to see what was going on.'

Richard was standing behind her, and Julie tugged on his hand. 'I want you to meet someone. Richard—this is Henry and Emma. And this is my best friend, Mike.'

Henry held out his hand. 'Hey there,' he said.

Richard hesitated before grasping it. 'Hello,' he said simply.

Mike and Emma came next. When Julie glanced at Mike, he smiled pleasantly, though doing so practically killed him. In the warm air of the bar, her face was slightly flushed. She was, he thought, particularly beautiful tonight.

'Do you want to sit down?' Henry offered. 'We've

72

got a couple of extra chairs.'

'No—we don't want to bother you,' Richard said.

'It's no bother. C'mon. Join us,' Emma chimed in.

'You sure you don't mind?' Julie asked.

'Don't be silly,' Emma said. 'We're all friends here.'

Julie smiled and moved around the table to take her seat; Richard followed and did the same. Once they were comfortable, Emma leaned across the table.

'So, Richard,' she said, 'tell us about yourself.'

*　　　*　　　*

The conversation was stilted, almost uncomfortable at first, because Richard didn't volunteer much more than was asked directly. Occasionally, Julie supplied additional information for him, other times she elbowed him playfully, as if chiding him until he went on.

As he spoke, Mike did his best to appear interested.

And he was, at least in a self-interested way, if only to see what he was up against. But as the minutes rolled on, he began to feel as if his future were that of a salmon swimming upstream. Even he could see why Julie was interested in Richard. He was intelligent (and yes, good-looking, he conceded, but only if one like rugged, athletic types), and unlike Mike, he was both college educated and well traveled. Though he didn't laugh or joke much—or appreciate Emma or Henry when they did—it seemed that his discomfort stemmed more from shyness than arrogance. And the way he felt about Julie was obvious. Whenever

73

she spoke, Richard's eyes never left her face; he acted like a husband waking up on the first morning of his honeymoon.

Through it all, Mike kept smiling and nodding, hating Richard's guts.

A little later on, as Emma and Julie caught up on some of the latest news around town, Richard finished his drink. After asking if Julie wanted anything else, he excused himself to head back to the bar. When Henry asked him if he wouldn't mind grabbing another couple of beers, Mike stood as well, volunteering to go with Richard.

'I'll help you carry them back.'

They reached the bar, and the bartender signaled that he'd get there as soon as he could. Richard reached for his wallet, and though Mike was right beside him, he stayed silent.

'She's a great lady,' Mike finally offered.

Richard turned and seemed to study him before turning away again.

'Yes, she is,' he said simply.

Neither of them said another word to each other.

Once they were back at the table, Richard asked Julie if she'd like to dance, and after saying good-bye, they were gone.

*　　*　　*

'Now that wasn't so hard, was it?' Emma asked.

Mike shrugged, not wanting to answer.

'And he seemed nice enough,' Henry added. 'Kind of quiet, but polite.'

Mike reached for his beer. 'I didn't like him,' he said.

'Oh, now there's a surprise,' Henry said,

laughing.

'I'm not sure I trust him.'

Henry kept smirking. 'Well, since you missed your opportunity, I guess we'll have to hang around for a while.'

'What opportunity?'

'You said tonight was the night you were going to ask her out.'

'Shut up, Henry.'

*   *   *

A little while later, Mike sat drumming his fingers on the table. Henry and Emma had gone to say hello to another couple they knew, and now that he was alone, Mike tried to figure out what it was exactly that he didn't like about Richard Franklin.

Besides the obvious.

No, there was more to it than just that. No matter what Henry had said or what Julie seemed to think, Richard didn't strike Mike as a particularly *nice* guy. What happened at the bar made that plain. Once he'd said what he had about Julie, Richard had looked at him as if already recognizing Mike's feelings for her, and his face clearly expressed what he thought about that: *You lose, so stay away.*

Not exactly the hallmark of a *nice* guy.

So why didn't Julie seem to see the side of Richard that he did? And why didn't Henry or Emma? Or was the whole thing just a figment of his imagination?

Mike ran through the scenario again. No, he finally decided, I didn't imagine it. I know what I saw. And I don't like him.

He leaned back in his chair, taking a deep breath

as he scanned the room. His eyes found Richard and Julie, and he watched them for a moment before he forced himself to turn away.

During the band's break, Julie and Richard had left the dance floor and found a smaller table on the far side of the bar, and Mike had been glancing their way ever since. He couldn't help it. Though he tried to pretend that he was still trying to figure Richard out, he knew his compulsion to watch had more in common with what people feel when they come across the scene of a grisly accident. Or even more accurately, he thought, watching them together was like watching a car plunging off a monstrous cliff, with a bird's-eye view through the windshield.

That's how it seemed, anyway. As the night wore on, he couldn't escape the conclusion that his chance with Julie was suddenly going the way of Atlantis. While Mike was sitting by himself, Julie and Richard were staring into each other's eyes with goofy grins on their faces. They were leaning in to whisper and laugh, obviously enjoying each other's company.

Disgusting.

At least the last time he'd looked, just a few seconds ago.

But what, he wondered, were they doing *now?*

Slowly, ever so subtly, Mike's eyes began to travel their way again. Julie was facing the other direction, so thankfully she wouldn't see him watching her. If she caught him staring, she might wave at him, or nod and smile, or worse, ignore him. The first two would make him feel like an idiot, the last one would break his heart.

As he turned, he saw Julie rummaging through

her purse for something, her eyes focused in her lap.

Richard's eyes, though, locked on his in a cool, almost confident appraisal. *Yes, Mike, I know you're staring.*

Mike froze, a kid caught pulling a twenty from his mother's wallet.

He wanted to turn away but couldn't seem to summon the energy to move until he heard a voice behind him. He glanced over his shoulder and saw Drew, the lead singer from the band, standing near the table.

'Hey, Mike,' Drew said, 'got a minute? I wanted to talk to you about something.'

*　　　*　　　*

An hour later, with Cobra completely inebriated, Andrea headed to the bathroom. As she'd done since she'd first spotted Richard earlier, she scanned the room looking for him as she stood in line. He and Julie were walking off the dance floor. Richard leaned over to whisper something in her ear, then headed toward the men's room.

Knowing he'd pass right by her, Andrea quickly ran her hand through her hair and adjusted her skirt and halter. She stepped out of the line, heading him off.

'Hey, Richard,' she said brightly, 'how are you?'

'Fine, thanks,' he said. Though it took a moment, she saw the recognition in his face. 'Andrea, right?'

She smiled, thinking, I knew he'd remember. 'I haven't seen you here before,' she said.

'It's my first time here.'

'Don't you think it's great?'

'Not really.'

'Oh, well, neither do I, but there's not that many other places to go around here. Small-town life, you know?'

'I'm learning,' he said.

'Friday nights are usually better, though.'

'Oh?'

'Yeah. That's when I usually come. In fact, I'm almost always here then.'

He paused, looking directly at her and holding her gaze, before finally nodding in Julie's direction.

'Listen—I'd love to stay and talk, but I really can't.'

'Because you're with Julie?'

He shrugged. 'She is my date.'

'Yeah, I know,' Andrea said.

'Well, listen—it was nice seeing you again,' he said.

'Thanks. You too.'

A moment later he pushed on the door, letting it close behind him. While Andrea was staring at the door, Cobra staggered up behind her, mumbling something crude about bodily functions.

As soon as he followed Richard through the door, she decided it was time to leave.

Seeing Cobra one more time, she thought, would ruin the feeling she'd had when her eyes met Richard's.

*   *   *

Just past midnight, with the world glowing silver, Julie stood with Richard on the porch. Frogs and crickets were singing, a light breeze was moving the leaves, and even Singer seemed to be more accepting of Richard. Though his face was poking through the curtains and he was eyeing them carefully, he hadn't made a sound.

'Thanks for tonight,' she said.

'You're welcome. I had a wonderful time.'

'Even at the Clipper?'

'As long as you had fun, then I'm glad we went.'

'Not your kind of place, huh?'

He shrugged. 'To be honest, I probably would have preferred something a bit more private. So you and I could be alone.'

'We were alone.'

'Not the whole time.'

She looked at him, a quizzical expression on her face.

'Are you talking about when we sat with my friends for a while?' she asked. 'Did you think I did that because I wasn't having fun?'

'I wasn't sure what to think. Sometimes women use that as a kind of escape, when the date isn't going well. As in, "Help! I need rescuing!"'

She smiled. 'Oh, that wasn't it at all. They were the ones I was supposed to go to dinner with tonight, and when I saw them, I wanted to say hi.'

Richard's eyes drifted to the porch light, then back to Julie. 'Hey . . . listen, I know I was kind of quiet with your friends. I'm sorry about that. I never seem to know what to say.'

'You were fine. I'm sure they liked you.'

'I'm not too sure that Mike did.'

'Mike?'

'He was watching us.'

Though she hadn't noticed, she realized she should have expected something like that. 'Mike and I have known each other for years,' she said.

'He watches out for me. That's all.'

Richard seemed to evaluate that. Finally, a small smile flickered across his face. 'Okay,' he said. For a long moment, neither of them said anything else. Then Richard moved toward her.

This time, though she expected the kiss and though she wanted him to do it—or at least *thought* she wanted him to do it—she couldn't deny the slight feeling of relief when he turned to leave a minute later.

No need to rush into anything, she thought. If it's right, I'll know.

Seven

'There he goes,' Henry said, 'right on time.'

It was Tuesday morning, a few days after their evening at the Clipper. Henry was drinking Dr Pepper and watching Richard as he made his way down the street toward the salon. Richard was carrying a gift—a small box—but that wasn't the reason Henry was curious.

Because he'd told Richard where he worked when they met on Saturday, he'd expected Richard to at least glance toward the garage. The day before, Henry had even waved, but Richard either didn't see him or pretended not to. Instead, he'd kept his eyes forward and walked right on past. Just like today.

Hearing his brother, Mike emerged from beneath the hood of a car. After removing a rag tucked into his belt, he started wiping his hands.

'Must be nice being a consultant,' Mike said.

'Doesn't that guy ever have to work?'

'Don't get upset now. You used up your yearly quota of pouting last week. Besides, you'd rather have him go see her when she's working than when she's at home, right?'

One look told Henry that Mike hadn't thought of that. Then, almost immediately, Mike's face took on a startled expression.

'Is he bringing her a gift?' he asked.

'Yep.'

'What's the special occasion?'

'Maybe he wants to impress her.'

Mike wiped his hands again. 'Well, if that's the case, maybe I'll just swing by there a little later with a gift of my own.'

'Now you're talking,' Henry said, slapping his brother on the back. 'That's exactly what I wanted to hear you say. A little less whining, a little more action. We Harrises have always been men who rise to the occasion.'

'Thanks, Henry.'

'But before you head off with guns blazing, let me give you some advice.'

'Sure.'

'Scrap the gift.'

'But I thought you just said—'

'That's *his* thing. It won't work for you.'

'But—'

'Trust me on this. It'll make you look desperate.'

'I am desperate.'

'You may be,' Henry agreed. 'But you can't let her know that. She'll think you're pathetic.'

*   *   *

81

'Richard . . . ,' Julie said, staring down at the open jewelry case in her hand. Inside was an ornate, heart-shaped locket supported by a gold chain. 'It's beautiful.'

They were standing outside the door, unaware that Mike and Henry were watching from across the street and Mabel and Singer were peeking through the window behind them. 'But . . . why? I mean, what's the occasion?'

'No occasion. I just saw it and, well . . . I liked it. Or rather, I thought of you and knew you should have it.'

Julie's eyes flashed to the locket. It was obviously expensive and, consequently, carried added expectations.

As if reading her mind, Richard held up his hands. 'Please—I want you to have it. If you have to, think of it as a birthday present.'

'My birthday's not until August.'

'So I'm a little early.' He paused. 'Please.'

Still . . .

'Richard . . . it's sweet, but I really shouldn't.'

'It's just a locket, not an engagement ring.'

Still a bit unsure, she finally gave in and kissed him. 'Thank you,' she murmured.

Richard motioned toward the locket. 'Try it on.'

Julie unhooked the clasp and slipped it around her neck. 'How does it look?'

He stared at the locket, an odd smile on his face, as if he were thinking of something else. He kept his eyes on it as he answered.

'Perfect. It's exactly the way I remember it.'

'Remember?'

'From the jewelry store,' he said. 'But it looks better on you.'

'Oh. Well, you shouldn't have.'

'You're wrong there. It was exactly what I should have done.'

Julie put one hand on her hip. 'You're spoiling me, you know. People don't usually go around buying me gifts for no reason at all.'

'Then it's a good thing that I do. And do you really believe there always has to be a reason? Haven't you ever seen something that you thought was perfect for someone else, and bought it?'

'Of course. But not like this. And I don't want you to feel like I expect you to do these things, because I don't.'

'I know you don't. But that's part of the reason why I like to do it. Everyone needs a surprise now and then.' He paused. 'So, are you up for doing something this Friday night?'

'I thought you were leaving town for a meeting.'

'I was. But it turns out the meeting got canceled. Or rather, my part of it got canceled. I'm free all weekend.'

'What did you have in mind?' she asked.

'Something very special. I'd like to keep it a surprise, though.'

Julie didn't answer right away, and as if sensing her uncertainty, Richard reached for her hand. 'You'll love it, Julie. Trust me on this. But you'll have to get off a little early. I'd have to pick you up at your place around four o'clock.'

'Why so early?'

'It takes a while to get where we're going. Do you think you can make it?'

She smiled. 'I'll have to shuffle my schedule a bit, but I think I can make it. Should I wear something dressy or casual?'

It was a polite way of asking if she should pack a bag. If he said both, it meant a weekend away, and she couldn't see them doing that just yet.

'I'll be wearing a jacket and tie, if that helps.'

It certainly sounded like a legitimate date. 'I guess I'll have to do some shopping,' she finally said.

'I'm sure you'll be beautiful no matter what you wear.'

With that he kissed her again, and when he finally left, Julie's fingers traveled to the locket. It opened with a click, and she saw she was right in assuming small photos could be placed inside. She was surprised to see that he'd already had it engraved with her initials, one on each side.

*   *   *

'This is not looking good, little brother,' Henry admitted. 'I don't care what Emma said the other night. This is not looking good.'

'Thanks for the update, Einstein,' Mike grumbled.

'Let me give you some advice.'

'More advice?'

Henry nodded, as if telling Mike there was no reason to thank him. 'Before you do anything, you're going to have to come up with some sort of plan.'

'What kind of plan?'

'I don't know. But if I were you, I'd make it a good one.'

*   *   *

'It's lovely,' Mabel said, eyeing the locket. 'I guess he's really taken with you, huh? It looks like it cost a small fortune.' She motioned toward the locket. 'Do you mind?'

'No, go ahead,' Julie said, leaning forward.

Mabel looked it over. 'And it's definitely not from one of the jewelers in town. This looks handmade.'

'Do you think so?'

'I'm sure of it. Not only that, you've learned something important about Richard Franklin.'

'What's that?'

'He's got good taste.'

Mabel let go of the locket, and Julie felt it tap gently against her chest. She looked at it again. 'Now I just have to find a couple of pictures to go inside.'

Mabel's eyes twinkled. 'Oh, honey—if you're beating around the bush, don't worry about it. I'd be more than happy to give you a picture of me to carry with you. I'd be honored, in fact.'

Julie laughed. 'Thanks. You were the first one I thought of, you know.'

'I'm sure. So—you gonna put a picture of Singer in there?'

At the mention of his name, Singer looked up. He'd been standing beside Julie since she'd come back into the salon, and Julie ran her hand along his back.

'With this bozo, I'd probably have to stand a hundred yards away to get one of him that would fit.'

'True,' Mabel said. 'What's going on with him, anyway? He's been so clingy lately.'

'I have no idea. But you're right—he's been driving me crazy. I keep stumbling over him every time I turn around.'

'How is he with Richard? At home, I mean?'

'Like he is here,' she said. 'He stares, but at least he doesn't growl like he did the first time.'

Singer whined, a low squeak emerging from his throat, sounding almost too small to be coming from him.

Quit complaining, it seemed to mean. *We both know you love me no matter how I act*.

* * *

A plan, Mike thought, I need a plan.

Mike rubbed his chin, unaware that he was leaving grease along his jaw. Henry was right, he thought. For once, the guy had actually said something important, something that made sense. A plan was *definitely* what he needed.

But the problem, Mike soon realized, was that it was a lot easier to say that he needed a plan than to actually come up with one. Mike wasn't much of a planner and never had been. Things just sort of happened and he went along with the flow, like a cork bobbing atop the waves. Usually that wasn't such a bad thing. For the most part, he was happy; for the most part, he felt pretty good about himself, even if the whole artist and musician thing hadn't worked out so far.

But now the stakes were a little higher. The chips were down, and it was time to lay the cards on the table. Put up or shut up. The going was rough, and it was time to get going. There was no time like the present, because the early bird catches the worm.

It was time to 'Just do it.'

But even though all the clichés seemed

appropriate, he still wasn't sure what to do.

A *plan.*

The whole problem was that he didn't know where he should start. In the past, he'd been the good guy, the friend, the one she could always count on. The one who fixed her car and played Frisbee with Singer, the one who spent the first two years after Jim's death holding her as she cried. None of those things had seemed to matter; all they'd done was lead to the first two dates with Richard. Then, changing everything last week, he'd avoided her. He hadn't talked to her, hadn't called her at home, hadn't stopped by just to say hi. And the net result? She hadn't called, either, she hadn't stopped by, and in the end, based on what he'd seen on the street, all that had done was lead to a *third* date with Richard.

So what was he supposed to do? He couldn't just stroll over there and ask her out. Odds were she was going out with Richard, and what was he supposed to say to that? *Oh, you're busy Saturday? How about Friday? Or next week, maybe? How about breakfast, then?* That, he thought, would make him look desperate, which according to Henry was something he had to avoid at all costs.

A plan.

Mike shook his head. The worst part about this whole thing was plan or no plan, he was lonely.

Yeah, the whole situation with Richard was a royal bummer of the worst kind, but over the last couple of years, he'd grown used to talking to Julie at least once a day. Sometimes more than that.

He'd be heartbroken if Julie and Richard ended up together. But if that happened, it happened. In time, he *might* be able to accept something

87

like that.

But what he couldn't bear to face was the possibility of feeling the way he'd been feeling this last week or so. It wasn't simply frustration, or fear, or even jealousy. It wasn't depression, either. More than anything, he missed Julie.

He missed talking to her, seeing her smile, hearing the sound of her laughter. Watching the way her eyes, in the late afternoon when the sun was just right, seemed to change from green to turquoise. Listening to the quick intakes of breath whenever she was getting close to the end of a funny story. Even the way she punched him in the arm sometimes.

Maybe he should just head over later and talk to her, the same way he always had, as though nothing had changed between them. Maybe he'd even tell her that he was glad she'd had a good time the other night, the way Mabel or Henry or Emma would.

No, he thought, suddenly changing his mind. I won't go that far. No reason to get carried away. Take it one step at a time.

But I *will* talk to her.

He knew it wasn't much of a plan, but it was all he could come up with.

Eight

'Hey, Julie,' Mike called, 'wait up!'

Julie turned to see Mike jogging toward her as she was heading to her car. Singer loped off in his direction, reaching him first. Lifting first one paw and then the other, he looked as if he were trying to grab Mike in preparation for a series of sloppy, friendly licks. Mike avoided that—as much as he liked Singer, it was a little disgusting to be drenched with dog saliva—but he did pet him. Like Julie, he also talked to Singer as if he were a person.

'Did you miss me, big guy? Yeah, yeah, I missed you, too. We should do something together.'

Singer's ears went up, looking interested, and Mike shook his head.

'No Frisbee today—sorry. I meant later.'

It didn't seem to matter to Singer. As Mike started toward Julie again, Singer spun and walked beside him, nudging him playfully. Of course, playful was a relative term. The dog nearly sent Mike careening into the mailbox before he caught his balance.

'I think you need to take your dog for a few more walks,' he said. 'He's all wound up.'

'He's just excited to see you. How are you? I haven't seen too much of you lately.'

'I'm good. Just busy, that's all.'

As he answered, he couldn't help but notice that her eyes were very green today. Like jade.

'Me too,' she said. 'How was it with Henry and Emma the other night?'

'It was fun. Wish you could have made it, but . . .'

He shrugged as if it didn't matter, though Julie knew—from what Richard had told her—that it probably did. He surprised her, however, by immediately changing the subject. 'I did get some good news, though,' he said. 'The band that was playing? Ocracoke Inlet? On my way out the other night, Drew asked me if I'd fill in for their guitarist.

Their regular guy's got to go to a wedding in Chicago the next time they're supposed to be at the Clipper.'

'Wow—that's great. When is that?'

'In a couple of weeks. I know it's just a onetime thing, but it should be fun.'

'Playing for a full house, you mean?'

'Sure,' he said. 'I mean, why not? I know most of the songs, and the band's not all *that* bad.'

'That's not what you told me before.'

'They never asked me to play before.'

'Oh—jealous, were you?'

As soon as she said the word she regretted it, but Mike didn't seem to notice.

'No, not jealous. Miffed, yes, but jealous, no. And who knows where it might lead? Could end up being exactly what I need to get something more regular.'

'Well,' Julie said, not wanting to dim his enthusiasm, 'I'm glad it worked out.'

For a moment neither of them said anything, and Mike shuffled his feet.

'So what have you been up to? I mean—I know you've been seeing Richard, but I haven't talked to you much. Anything exciting going on?'

'No, not much. Singer's been driving me nuts, but that's about it.'

'Singer? What's he been doing?'

Julie filled him in on Singer's recent behavior, and Mike laughed. 'Maybe he needs some Prozac or something.'

'Who knows. But if he doesn't stop, I'm going to buy an outdoor doghouse.'

'Listen—I'd be glad to take him off your hands anytime. I'll take him to the beach, and by the time

90

he gets home, he'll be exhausted. He won't have the energy to growl or bark or follow you around for the rest of the day.'

'I might just take you up on that.'

'I hope so. I love the big guy.' He reached out to Singer. 'Don't I?'

Singer received Mike's affection with a friendly bark.

'So any good Andrea stories lately?' Mike asked. Andrea was a frequent topic of conversation between them.

'She told me about her date on Saturday.'

Mike's nose wrinkled. 'The guy she was with at the Clipper?'

'You saw him?'

'Yeah. He was one ugly dude. Had a gold tooth and everything. I thought she'd hit the low mark with that guy with the patch, but I guess I was wrong.'

Julie laughed. 'I wish I'd seen him. Mabel said exactly the same thing.'

She then launched into a description of the things Andrea had said about Cobra. Mike particularly enjoyed the whole Ed DeBoner thing, though why *that* part bothered Andrea and his other flaws didn't was beyond him. By the end, Julie was laughing, too.

'What's with her, anyway?' Mike asked. 'Can't she see what everyone else does? I almost feel sorry for her.'

'At least you don't have to work with her. Although, to be honest, it does keep things entertaining around the salon.'

'I'll bet. Oh—by the way, Emma wanted me to tell you to give her a call. At least, that's what

Henry said.'

'Will do. Do you know what it's about?'

'No, not really. Probably wants to give you a new recipe or whatever it is you two talk about.'

'We don't talk about recipes. We talk about *good* stuff.'

'In other words, you gossip.'

'It's not gossip,' she protested. 'It's called keeping in touch.'

'Well, listen, if you hear anything good, give me a ring, okay? I'll be in all night. And maybe we can set something up so I could get Singer off your hands, at least for a little while. Maybe this weekend?'

Julie smiled. 'You got it.'

* * *

I'm glad I did that, Mike thought, feeling rather pleased with himself.

Okay, so it wasn't exactly the most highbrow or intimate conversation, but it did reassure him that Julie still enjoyed talking to him. They'd joked around, they'd laughed together, and that counted for something, didn't it? Of course it did!

He'd played it just right—kept the conversation light, avoided anything touchy, and best of all, he felt confident that they'd probably talk again later, after she'd spoken to Emma. Emma always said something worth repeating, and if on the odd chance she didn't, the whole 'I'd be glad to help with Singer' thing was practically a guarantee that Julie would call.

He refused to think about Richard. Every time his image—or that of Richard and Julie together, or even the stupid locket—popped into his head, he forced the thought away. Richard might have the inside track, but Mike wasn't about to let that spoil his thoughts of Julie right now.

And for the most part, his strategy worked fairly well. Mike's good mood lasted through the rest of his work, the trip home, and even dinner. In fact, it lasted right up until he was lying in bed, watching the evening news.

The phone, he realized sadly, hadn't rung at all.

*   *   *

For Mike, the rest of the week passed torturously.

Julie didn't call, nor did she swing by the garage to say hello.

Though he could have called her, though he'd never hesitated picking up the phone to talk to her in the past, he just wasn't up to it. For all he knew, she hadn't called because she was with Richard, and he couldn't face the prospect of reaching her at home only to have her explain that she couldn't talk right now because she 'had company.' Or because she was 'getting ready to head out.' Or because she was 'right in the middle of something.' And if by chance she wasn't in, he knew he'd spend the rest of the night wondering where she'd gone and wouldn't sleep a wink.

Not only didn't Julie call that week, not only did Richard show up *every single* day (and probably at night, too!), but on Friday, Mike saw Julie leave the salon in midafternoon. Though he didn't know where she was going, he was pretty certain he knew why she was leaving early.

Richard, he thought.

He tried not to care; he told himself there was no reason to care. Why should he care what they were doing? His night was already planned; he had beer in the fridge, a video store around the corner, and a Domino's pizza just thirty minutes away. He would have himself a good time. No, a *great* time. Kick back on the couch and unwind from the week, maybe play a few tunes before popping the video in, stay up all night if he wanted.

For a moment he imagined how it would go, and then his shoulders sagged. I'm pathetic, he thought. My life could send healthy people into comas.

But what really toppled the wedding cake, so to speak, was that despite his determination *not to care*, he found out where Richard and Julie had gone. Not from her. Instead, he found out about it from people he barely knew, in bits and pieces overheard here and there around town: at the grocery store, at the diner, and even while working in the garage. Suddenly, it seemed that even casual acquaintances of Julie's, people she'd happened to visit with for a few minutes on Sunday afternoon, knew a lot more than he did. By Monday morning, it took him almost twenty minutes to summon the energy to get out of bed.

Richard, it seemed, had picked Julie up in a limousine that had been stocked with champagne; they'd gone to Raleigh for dinner. Afterward, at the civic center in front-row seats, they'd watched a live performance of *Phantom of the Opera*.

If that wasn't enough, if that wasn't quite *special* enough to *impress* her, it turned out that Richard and Julie had spent Saturday together as well, down near Wilmington.

There they'd taken a hot-air balloon ride before

94

picnicking at the beach.

How the hell was he supposed to compete with a guy who did things like that?

Nine

Now that was a weekend, Julie thought to herself. Richard, she decided, could give Bob a few pointers on how to impress a lady. Hell, Richard could give *seminars* on the subject.

Staring at her reflection in the mirror on Sunday morning, she still found it hard to believe. She hadn't spent a weekend like that in . . . well, she'd never spent a weekend like that. The theater was a new experience for her, and when he'd finally told her in the limousine where they were going, she figured she'd probably enjoy it but wasn't absolutely sure. Her concept of musicals was rooted in those that had been adapted into films a generation ago, like *The Music Man* and *Oklahoma!*; somewhere in the back of her mind, she supposed that seeing a performance in Raleigh as opposed to New York City would be something akin to watching a pretty good high school play.

Boy, was she ever wrong.

She was entranced by it all: couples dressed in evening wear as they sipped wine in the courtyard before the play started; the silencing of the crowd as the lights began to dim; the orchestra's first energetic notes, which made her jump in her seat; the romance and tragedy of the story; the virtuoso performances and the songs, some of which were so beautiful that they'd brought tears to her eyes. And

95

the colors! The props and wildly hued costumes, the use of gleaming spotlights and haunting shadows, had all combined to create a world on stage both strangely surreal and vividly alive.

The whole evening had seemed like a fantasy, she decided. None of it was familiar, and for a few hours she'd felt as if she'd suddenly slipped into an alternate universe in which she wasn't a hairdresser in a small southern town, the kind of gal whose highlight of the week was usually something as mundane as removing a stubborn ring from around the tub. No, this was another world, a place occupied by inhabitants of exclusive, gated communities who studied the stock quotes in the morning newspaper while the nanny got the kids ready for school. Afterward, when she and Richard had stepped outside and looked upward, she wouldn't have felt any stranger had she seen two moons hovering in the downtown sky.

But hey, she wasn't complaining. In the limousine on the way home, while inhaling the musky smell of leather as champagne bubbles tickled her nose, she remembered thinking. So this is how the other half lives. I can see exactly how people can get used to this.

The next day, too, had been a surprise. Not just because of the entertainment, but because it stood in such stark contrast with the evening before: day instead of night, a hot-air balloon ride instead of a show, a walk along carnival-like streets instead of a limousine ride, a picnic on the beach instead of dinner at a restaurant. An entire repertoire of dates in just a couple of days, like newlyweds squeezing everything they could into the last hours of their honeymoon.

Though the balloon ride was fun—scary when the wind gusted, but fun—of all they did, from holding hands as they walked to posing playfully as Richard took a number of photographs of her, she enjoyed the picnic the most. Now that, she thought, was more along the lines of something she was used to. She'd gone on lots of picnics in her life—Jim had been fond of them—and for a moment she felt like herself again. That feeling didn't last long. In the picnic basket was a bottle of Merlot and a cheese-and-fruit plate, and after they'd finished with the food, Richard had offered to give her a foot rub. It sounded corny when he said it, and she'd initially laughed and said no, but when he'd gently reached for her foot, slipped off her sandal, and begun his massage, she couldn't help but give in, imagining that Cleopatra must have felt much the same way as she relaxed under the gently swaying palm fronds.

Strangely, at that moment, she thought of her mother.

Though she'd long since decided her mother was pretty unreliable as a mother or a role model, she couldn't help but remember something her mother had said once when Julie had asked her why she'd stopped seeing a recent boyfriend.

'He didn't rock my boat,' her mother had informed her matter-of-factly. 'Sometimes it's like that.'

Julie, eight years old at the time, nodded, wondering where they kept the boat and why she'd never seen it.

Years later, she finally realized what her mother had meant, and while staring at Richard, her foot in his hands, the expression came back to her.

Did Richard rock her boat?

He should, she knew. Lord knew she probably wouldn't find anyone better, not in Swansboro, anyway. He was the full package as far as eligible men went, but even now, after four romantic dates and a lot of time spent together, she suddenly knew that he didn't. The realization left her feeling as if she were weighted down in a swimming pool, but she couldn't deny that whatever it was that brought couples together—whether it was chemistry or magic or some combination of both—simply wasn't there. She just didn't feel the little tingles on her neck that she had when Jim first took her hand. She didn't feel like closing her eyes and dreaming of a future together, and she knew with certainty that she wouldn't spend the following day wandering around in a romance-induced daze. The dates he planned were fabulous; it was just that, as much as she wished otherwise, she wasn't so sure about Richard, other than that he seemed like a nice guy . . . the kind of guy who'd be perfect for someone else.

Sometimes, as her mother had said, it's like that.

She wondered if part of the problem was that she was trying to rush her feelings. They might need some more time before things were comfortable and easy. Her relationship with Jim had taken time to develop, after all. After a few more dates, she might look back and wonder why she'd been so skittish. Right?

While brushing her hair in front of the mirror, she considered it. Maybe. Then, laying down her brush, she thought, Yes, that's got to be it. We just need to get to know each other better. Besides, it's partly my fault. I'm the one who's holding back.

Though she had talked for hours with Richard, most of their conversations had hovered over the surface. Yes, he knew the obvious things about her, and yes, she knew the obvious things about him. But she didn't volunteer much more than that. Whenever the past had come up, she'd found a way to avoid it. She hadn't revealed how difficult her relationship with her mother had really been, how unnerving it was to see men wandering in and out of her house at all hours, how desolate she felt leaving home before graduating high school. Or how scared she'd been when living on the streets, especially late at night. Or what it felt like when Jim had died, when she wondered how she would ever find the strength to go on. Those were the hard memories, the ones that left a bitter taste when she spoke them. Part of her was tempted to share them with him, so he could really know who she was.

But she didn't. For some reason, she couldn't. And he didn't tell her much about himself, either, she noticed. He had a way of avoiding the past as well.

But wasn't that what it came down to in the end? The ability to communicate, to open up, to trust? She and Jim had had that, but like 'the chicken or the egg' dilemma, she couldn't remember which part had come first, the little tingles on the back of her neck or all those other things.

The ringing of the phone interrupted her musings. Singer followed her to the living room as Julie picked up the receiver.

'Hello?'

'So what happened?' Emma demanded. 'I want to hear all about it. And don't leave anything out.'

'A foot massage?' Mike asked, not bothering to hide his disbelief. It was the one part he hadn't heard about from strangers.

'That's what she told Emma yesterday.'

'But . . . a foot massage?'

'I'll admit he does have a flair about him.'

'That's not what I mean.' Mike paused, pushing his hands into his pockets. His face took on a distracted look.

Henry leaned forward. 'Listen, I hate to offer you more bad news, but Benny's called to say he's coming in today.'

Mike winced. Benny, he thought. Good God, Benny.

Oh, this day was turning out grand, wasn't it?

'And Blansen still needs his truck,' Henry went on. 'You'll have it done, right? It's part of the contract I worked out with the bridge people, so it's important.'

'Yeah, I'll be finished.'

*   *   *

Andrea couldn't believe it, didn't want to believe it. The whole thing made her practically sick to her stomach, especially with Julie's oh-so-nonchalant attitude about the whole thing. A limousine? Champagne? The play . . . *Phantom of the Soap Opera* or whatever it was called? Hot-air balloon ride? Picnic at the beach?

Andrea didn't want to hear it. She didn't even want to overhear it by accident, but that wasn't

100

possible in a small place like this.

Her weekened hadn't been anything like Julie's. No, her weekend was just like all the others she'd spent lately, just another in a long line of forgettable weekends. On Friday, she'd spent the evening at the Clipper, fighting off Cobra's advances for the second time. Even though she hadn't planned on meeting him there, he'd spotted her right off and had been all over her the whole evening like a bug on roadkill. And Saturday? How about spending hours mending the stupid fingernail tips she'd lost the night before? *How's that for a weekend, honey?* she wanted to shout. *I'll bet that just makes your blood bubble with jealousy, huh?*

But of course, no one had even asked about her weekend. No, all Mabel and Julie cared about was what Julie did. *Then what happened? I'll bet you were surprised, huh? Sounds wonderful.* Julie, Julie, Julie. It was always all about Julie. And Julie shrugging and going on like the whole thing was no big deal at all.

In the corner, Andrea filed her nails like a human belt sander. This, she thought, wasn't the way things were supposed to be.

*   *   *

Richard pushed open the door of the salon and held it as Julie's client made her way out.

'Oh, hey, Richard,' Julie said. 'Good timing. I just finished up.'

Though she wasn't any closer to sorting through her emotions, she was still glad he'd come by, if only to understand whether seeing him would make them any clearer.

'You look beautiful,' he said, leaning in to kiss her.

Despite the brevity, for Julie it was an almost analytical undertaking when their lips met. No fireworks, she thought, but no sense of dread, either. Just . . . a kiss.

And if I keep going on like this, she immediately thought, I'll end up as crazy as my mother.

'Do you have a few minutes to grab a cup of coffee?' he asked.

Mabel had gone to the bank. Andrea was flipping through the *National Enquirer* in the corner— 'reading the paper,' she called it—but Julie knew she was listening in.

'Yeah,' Julie said. 'I've got a little time. My next appointment is in half an hour.'

As she answered, Richard's eyes focused on the soft triangle of flesh beneath her chin.

'Where's the locket?' he asked.

Julie's hand traveled automatically to her chest. 'Oh—I didn't wear it today. It kept getting snagged on my clothes when I was working, and I've got a couple of perms this afternoon.'

'Why didn't you just tuck it inside?'

'I tried, but it kept falling out.' She took a step toward the door. 'C'mon,' she said. 'Let's get out of here. I haven't been outside all morning.'

'Should I get you a shorter chain?'

'Don't be ridiculous. It's perfect just the way it is.'

'But you're not wearing it,' he persisted.

Julie didn't respond, and in the long silence that followed, she looked at him carefully. Though he was smiling, there was something almost plastic about his expression.

'Does it bother you that much that I didn't wear it?' she asked.

'It's just that I thought you liked it.'

'I do like it. I just don't want to wear it while I'm working.'

Again, his bland expression seemed forced, but before she could dwell on it, Richard seemed to snap out of the spell he'd been under and his smile suddenly became natural again, as if the whole thing had been an illusion.

'I'll get you a shorter chain,' he said. 'That way you'll have two and you can wear it whenever you want.'

'You don't have to do that.'

'I know,' he said, dropping his gaze for a moment, then meeting hers again. 'But I want to.'

She stared at him, suddenly feeling . . . what?

*　　　*　　　*

Andrea set down the *Enquirer* in disgust as soon as they left the salon. Julie, she thought, was just about the biggest idiot on the face of the planet.

After a weekend like she'd just spent, what was Julie thinking?

She had to know that Richard would be coming in. He'd been coming in every single day, and she could understand exactly why Richard was hurt by her lack of consideration. Who wouldn't be? It's not every day that a guy like Richard comes along, handing out gifts like a politician spending Christmas Eve at the orphanage. But did Julie appreciate the things he did? Did she ever stop to think that maybe, just maybe, she should think of what might make Richard happy, instead of

103

herself? Did she ever stop to consider that maybe Richard had bought her the locket because he wanted her to wear the stupid thing? Because wearing it would show that she appreciated all the things he was doing for her?

The problem was, Julie didn't know how good she had it. No doubt she thought all guys were like Richard. She probably thought all guys spent gobs of money on gifts and dates and took women out in limousines. But that wasn't the way things were. Not in this small town, anyway. There wasn't, as far as Andrea could tell, a single decent guy in the whole town. Hell, the limo alone probably cost more than all of her dates in the last year combined. It probably cost more than most of her dates *earned* in a year.

Andrea shook her head. Julie didn't deserve a guy like him.

It was just lucky for her that Richard was such a great guy. And let's not, of course, forget the way he looked. Richard, she was beginning to think, was just about the sexiest man she'd ever seen.

*   *   *

Manipulated.

That's how Julie was feeling now that Richard had gone back to work.

Manipulated. As though he'd wanted her to promise that she'd start wearing the locket at work again. As though she should feel guilty that she hadn't.

As though she should wear it *all the time*.

She didn't like that feeling, and she was trying to reconcile it with the man who'd taken her out over

104

the weekend. Why was he so upset about something so . . . insignificant? Was it really that big a deal to him?

Unless, of course, he was wondering if it was some sort of subconscious statement as to how she was feeling toward him.

Julie froze momentarily, wondering if that might be true, especially given the way she'd been feeling on Sunday. She'd worn the locket since he'd given it to her, she'd worn it on the weekend. And the locket wasn't impossible to work with, just inconvenient. But this morning, she'd decided to leave it at home, so maybe . . .

No, Julie thought, shaking her head, that wasn't it. She'd known exactly what she was doing. The locket *did* get in the way. She'd almost cut the chain twice last week, and it had gotten snagged in people's hair more times than that. She hadn't worn it because she didn't want it to get ruined.

Besides, that wasn't the point. This wasn't about her and why she did or didn't wear it, this was about Richard and the way he'd reacted. And not only *that* it happened, but *how* it happened. The way he'd said it, the look on his face, the feeling it gave her . . . all of it bothered her.

Jim had never been like that. When Jim got mad—which wasn't all that often, she had to admit—he didn't try to manipulate her. Nor did he try to hide his anger behind a smile. Nor did Jim ever leave her with the impression that Richard had left her with, one she didn't like at all.

As long as we do it my way, everything will be fine, Richard seemed to imply. *We won't have this problem again.*

What, she wondered, was that all about?

Ten

Mike was standing in the garage, nodding thoughtfully, doing his best not to wring his customer's neck.

And Henry's as well, for foisting this particular customer on him. As soon as Benny Dickens had entered, Henry had suddenly remembered an important call he'd forgotten to make and scampered out of sight.

'You don't mind taking care of him, do you, Mike?'

Benny was twenty-one years old, and his family owned the phosphorus mine just outside town; the company had more than three hundred people on its payroll, making it Swansboro's largest employer. Benny had dropped out of school in the tenth grade, but he owned a monstrous home on the river, purchased with Daddy's money. Benny didn't work, Benny had never so much as contemplated going to work, and there were at least two little Bennys living in town, by two different women. But the Dickens family was far and away the largest account at the garage, the kind of customer that small businesses couldn't afford to lose. And Daddy loved his son. Daddy believed his son walked on water. Daddy, Mike had long ago decided, was an idiot.

'Louder,' Benny said, his cheeks beginning to flush, his voice rising to a whine. 'I told you that I wanted it *loud!*'

He was talking about the engine of his recently purchased Callaway Corvette. He'd brought it into the garage so that Mike could 'make the engine loud.' Mike supposed he wanted it that way so it would match the flames he'd had painted on the hood last week and the custom stereo system he'd had installed. Though he didn't attend college, Benny was taking the car to Ft Lauderdale for spring break next week in the hopes of seducing as many young ladies as he could. Such an impressive young man.

'It is loud,' Mike said. 'If I made it any louder, it would be illegal.'

'It's not illegal.'

'You'll get pulled over,' Mike said, 'I guarantee it.'

Benny blinked, as if trying to understand what Mike had just said.

'You don't know what you're talking about, you stupid grease monkey. It's not illegal, you hear me?'

'Stupid grease monkey,' Mike said, nodding. 'Got it.'

Two hands around his neck, thumbs on his Adam's apple. Squeeze and shake.

Benny put his hands on his hips. As usual, he was wearing his Rolex.

'Doesn't my dad get all his trucks serviced here?'

'Yes.'

'And haven't I been a good customer, too?'

'Yes.'

'Wasn't this the place that I brought my Porsche *and* my Jaguar?'

'Yes.'

'Don't I always pay on time?'

'Yes.'

Benny waved his arms in exasperation, his voice

growing louder.

'Then why didn't you make the engine *loud!* I remember coming in here and explaining this very clearly just a couple of days ago. I said I wanted it *loud! For cruising the strip! Chicks dig loud! And I'm not going down there for the sun! You hear me?'*

'Chicks, not sun,' Mike said. 'Got it.'

'So make it loud!'

'Loud.'

'Right! And I want it done by tomorrow!'

'Tomorrow.'

'Loud! You can understand that, right? *Loud!'*

'Right.'

* * *

Henry was rubbing his jaw in contemplation as he stood behind Mike. As soon as Benny had screeched off in his Jaguar, he'd re-entered the garage. Mike was still seething, mumbling to himself as he tinkered with the engine, unaware of Henry's presence.

'Maybe you should have made it louder,' Henry offered. 'The engine, I mean.'

Mike looked up. 'Shut up, Henry.'

Henry raised his hands, as if playing innocent. 'I'm just trying to be helpful.'

'Yeah, sure. Like the guy flipping the switch on the electric chair. Why did you make me deal with that guy?'

'You know I can't stand him.'

'Oh, and I can?'

'Maybe not. But you're much better at taking abuse than I am. You handle it so well, and you know we can't afford to lose his dad's company as

108

a client.'

'I almost strangled him.'

'But you didn't. And just think, now we can probably charge him extra.'

'It's still not worth it.'

'Ah, Mike, c'mon. You handled yourself like a true professional. I was impressed.'

'He called me a stupid grease monkey.'

'Coming from him, you should probably take that as a compliment.' Henry put his hand on Mike's shoulder. 'But listen, if it happens again, maybe you should try something different. To calm him down a bit.'

'Duct tape?'

'No, I was thinking of something a little more subtle.'

'Such as?'

'I don't know.' He paused and began rubbing his jaw again. 'Did you ever consider offering him a foot massage?'

Mike's mouth opened.

Sometimes he absolutely hated his brother's guts.

*   *   *

Jake Blansen arrived a little after four to pick up the truck, and after settling the account in the office, he made his way toward Mike.

'The keys are in the ignition,' Mike said. 'And just to let you know, I adjusted the brakes so they're not so loose. Just be ready for it. Other than that, it's good to go.'

Jake Blansen nodded. The consummate workingman, Jake was beer bellied and broad shouldered, with a toothpick wedged between his teeth and a NASCAR logo on his baseball cap. Wide swaths of sweat had soaked through his shirt, leaving circular stains beneath his arms. His jeans and boots were coated in concrete dust.

'I'll let 'em know,' Jake said. 'Though to be honest, I don't know why I got stuck with all this anyway. Maintenance was supposed to be handling all the vehicle stuff. But I guess you know how it goes. The bosses over there have everything screwed up.'

Mike nodded in Henry's direction. 'I know what you mean. That guy over there can be a real pain sometimes, too. But I heard he has to take Viagra, so I guess I can't blame him. Must be hard to know that he's only half a man.'

Jake laughed. He liked that.

Mike smiled as well, feeling at least partially avenged. 'So how many guys you got out there these days?'

'I don't even know. A couple hundred, maybe. Why? You looking for a job?'

'No—I'm a mechanic. It's just that I met one of the engineers who consults on the bridge.'

'Which one?'

'Richard Franklin. Do you know him?'

Holding Mike's gaze, Jake removed the toothpick from his mouth. 'Yeah, I know him,' he said.

'Nice guy?'

'What do you think?' he asked.

The wariness in his tone made Mike hesitate. 'I take it the answer's no.'

Jake seemed to evaluate his answer.

'So what's it to you?' he finally asked. 'You his friend?'

'No—like I said, I only met him once.'

110

'Keep it that way. You don't want to know him.'

'Why?'

After a long moment Jake shook his head, and though Mike tried to find out more, he said nothing. Instead, he turned the conversation back to the truck and left the shop a few minutes later, leaving Mike wondering what it was that Jake hadn't told him and why that suddenly seemed more important than the things he had said.

His thoughts, though, were interrupted when Singer came trotting in.

*   *   *

'Hey, big guy!' Mike called out.

When Singer got close, he jumped up, balancing on two legs, his front paws pressing against Mike's chest as if they were dancing at the prom. Singer squeaked low in his throat, sounding excited.

'What are you doing here?' Mike asked.

Singer dropped back to all fours again, then turned and started toward Mike's locker.

'I don't have any food,' Mike said, following him. 'But I know Henry has some in his office. Let's go clean him out.'

Singer led the way. After opening the bottom drawer of Henry's desk, Mike pulled out Henry's favorites—the miniature powdered sugar doughnuts and chocolate-chip cookies—and dropped into Henry's chair. He tossed them one by one, and Singer caught them in the air, gobbling them down like a frog catching flies. Though it probably wasn't good for him, his tail wagged in approval the whole time. Even better, Henry was going to be really annoyed when he realized his

111

stash was gone. Sort of like getting two for the price of one.

*　　　*　　　*

With her last customer of the day on her way out, Julie glanced around the salon. 'Have you seen Singer?' she asked Mabel.

'I let him out a while ago,' Mabel said. 'He was standing at the door.'

'How long ago was that?'

'I guess about an hour.'

Julie glanced at her watch. Singer was never gone this long.

'And he hasn't come back?'

'I think I saw him heading toward Mike's.'

*　　　*　　　*

Singer was curled up on an old blanket, snoring off the sugary treats as Mike adjusted the transmission of a Pontiac Sunbird.

'Hey, Mike,' Julie called out. 'You still here?'

Mike looked up at the sound of her voice and moved out into the bay. 'Back here,' he called out. Singer raised his head, his eyes groggy.

'Have you seen Singer?'

'Yeah, he's right here.' He nodded off to the side and grabbed a rag. As he wiped his hands, Singer rose and started toward her.

'There you are,' she said. When Singer reached her, she scratched his back as he circled her body. 'I was beginning to get worried about you.'

Mike smiled, thankful that Singer hadn't gone back.

112

She looked up. 'What's going on?'

'Nothing much. How are you?'

'I'm okay.'

'Just okay?'

'It's one of those days,' she said. 'You know how it is.'

'Yeah, I suppose I do,' he said, nodding. 'Especially today. Benny came in for starters, and then Henry almost died.'

'Wait—Henry almost died?'

'Died . . . killed . . . whatever. I stopped myself at the last minute. Couldn't stand the thought of what our parents would say to me once I was behind bars. But let me tell you—it was close.'

'Was he giving you a hard time today?'

'When doesn't he give me a hard time?'

'Poor thing,' she said. 'Remind me to cry you a river tonight.'

'I knew I could count on you,' he said.

Julie laughed. Sometimes he was so darn cute, especially with that dimple. 'So what did he do? Cut a hole in the back of your coveralls again?'

'No. That one got old after a while. And besides, the last time he did it, I covered a wrench with Krazy Glue and then asked him to hold it while I checked something out. He couldn't get the wrench off until the next morning. Had to sleep with the thing.'

'I remember that.' Julie giggled. 'He wouldn't take anything you offered him for weeks after that.'

'Yeah,' Mike said, waxing nostalgic. It was, in his opinion, one of his better moments. 'I should do things like that more often, but I just don't think that way.'

'No matter what you do, he'll always give you a

hard time. But just remember—he does those things because he's jealous.'

'You think so?'

'I know so. He's losing his hair, and he's got Dunlops disease.'

'Dunlops?'

'Yeah, his belly done lopped right over his belt.'

Mike laughed. 'Yeah, must be tough getting old like that.'

'So . . . you didn't answer my question. What was it today?'

Mike didn't, couldn't, explain Henry's comment. Instead, he motioned toward the soda machine and reached in his pocket for some change. 'Oh—you know,' he said casually. 'The same old stuff.'

Her hands went to her hips. 'Must have been good if you won't tell me.'

'I'll never tell,' he said. Then he stood straighter, and his voice took on a serious tone. 'But sometimes,' he said, 'I can't help but think that you live vicariously through his antics, and I must say that it hurts me.'

He handed Julie a Diet Coke, then got himself a Dr Pepper. No need to ask what she wanted; he already knew.

'Hurts you,' she said, taking the can.

'Like a knife.'

'Do I have to cry *two* rivers tonight?'

'Two would be nice. But make it three and I'll definitely forgive you.'

When he grinned, Julie realized how much she'd missed talking to him lately. 'So aside from Henry, anything else exciting happen today?'

Mike paused. *A guy named Jake Blansen came in and said some cryptic things about Richard. Want to*

114

hear about that?

No, now was not the time.

He shook his head. 'Not really. How about you?'

'Nothing.' She glanced toward Singer. 'Except for this guy running away. For a little while there, I actually got scared that something had happened to him.'

'Singer? No car would stand a chance if it hit him. It would be crushed like a bug.'

'It still had me worried.'

'That's because you're a woman. Men like me— we don't worry. We're trained not to panic.'

Julie smiled. 'That's good to know. When the hurricane hits, you'll be the first one I call to board up the house.'

'You do that anyway. Don't you remember? You even bought me my own special hammer.'

'Well, you can't expect me to do it. I might panic or something.'

Mike chuckled, and for a moment silence settled in. Now what? he thought. Except for the obvious.

'So how're things going with Richard?' he asked, trying to sound casual.

Julie hesitated. Yes, she wondered, how are they going?

'Okay,' she answered. 'The weekend was all right, but . . .' She trailed off, thinking, How much do I really want to say to Mike?

'But?'

'It's not important.'

He studied her. 'You sure?'

'Yeah, I'm sure.' She flashed a quick, forced smile. 'Like I said, it's nothing.'

Mike sensed her discomfort but let it go. She didn't want to talk about Richard, he didn't want to

115

talk about him. He had no problem with that.

'Well, listen, if you find that you need to talk about anything, I'm here, okay?'

'Okay.'

'I'm serious,' he said. 'I'm always around.'

'I know you are.' She put a friendly hand on his shoulder, trying to defuse the tension. 'Part of me thinks you should get out more. See the world, take exotic trips.'

'What? And ruin my streak of consecutive nights watching *Baywatch* reruns?'

'Exactly,' she said. 'Anything's better than television. But if travel's not your thing, you might consider something else. Like taking up a musical instrument or something.'

Mike pressed his lips together. 'Now that, my dear, was a low blow.'

Her eyes gleamed. 'As good as Henry's?'

He thought about it. 'No,' he said. 'Henry's was better.'

'Rats.'

'What can I say? You're just a rookie.'

She smiled, then leaned back a little, as if taking a moment to evaluate him. 'You're pretty easy to get along with, you know?'

'Because I'm easy to tease?'

'No, because you're such a good sport about it.'

Mike took a moment to scrape a bit of grease from his fingernails. 'That's funny,' he said.

'What?'

'Those words you used. Andrea said exactly the same thing to me just the other day.'

'Andrea?' Julie repeated, wondering if she'd heard him right.

'Yeah, this weekend. When we went out on our

116

date. Which reminds me—I'm supposed to pick her up in a few minutes.'

He glanced toward his watch, then his locker.

'But . . . wait . . . Andrea?' Julie couldn't mask her bewilderment.

'Yeah—she's great. We had a good time. But listen, I've got to run . . .'

Julie reached for his arm. 'But . . . ,' she said. 'You and *Andrea?*'

Mike stared at her solemnly for a couple of beats, then winked. 'Had you going, didn't I?'

Julie crossed her arms. 'No,' she snapped.

'C'mon. Just a little?'

'No.'

'Admit it.'

'Okay, fine. I admit it.'

Mike gave her a look of satisfaction. 'Good. Now we're even.'

Eleven

Julie let the door swing closed behind her, still relishing her conversation with Mike. Mabel looked up from the desk.

'Were you supposed to meet Richard tonight?' she asked.

'No. Why?'

'He came by and asked for you. Didn't you see him?'

'I was over at the garage with Mike.'

'You didn't see Richard on your way back?'

'No.'

'That's strange,' she said. 'You should have seen

117

him on the street. I mean, he just left a couple of minutes ago and I thought he went looking for you.'

'I guess not.' Julie glanced at the door. 'Did he say what he wanted?'

'Not really. Just that he was looking for you. You still might be able to catch him if you hurry.'

Mabel turned on the answering machine and finished straightening up the desk, watching Julie debate whether or not to go. When the moment passed—thus making the decision for her—she went on as if she hadn't suggested it.

'I don't know about you,' she said, 'but I'm bushed. Everyone I worked on complained today. If it wasn't about their hair, it was their kids or their husbands or the new preacher or barking dogs or how crazy the drivers are from up north. Sometimes you just want to tell them to grow up. Know what I mean?'

Julie was still thinking of Richard.

'Must be a full moon,' she muttered. 'Everyone was a little off today.'

'Even Mike?'

'No, not Mike.' Julie waved a hand in relief. 'Mike's always the same.'

Mabel pulled open the bottom drawer of her desk and removed a flask. 'Well, it's about time to shake off the cobwebs,' she announced. 'Join me?'

Mabel enjoyed shaking off the cobwebs regularly and, as a result, had fewer cobwebs than anyone Julie knew.

'Yeah, I'll join you. I'll lock the door.'

Mabel removed two plastic glasses from the bottom drawer and made herself comfortable on the couch. By the time Julie joined her, Mabel had

118

kicked off her shoes, propped her feet on the table, and already taken a drink. With her eyes closed and her head leaned back, it seemed almost as if she believed she was sitting in a chaise longue on a distant beach, basking beneath a tropical sun.

'So what's Mike up to these days?' she asked, her eyes still closed. 'He hasn't come around here much lately.'

'Nothing too exciting. Working, feuding with Henry, the usual. Other than that, not much.' She paused and her face brightened. 'Oh, did you hear that he'll be playing at the Clipper in a few weeks?'

'Oh . . . hurray.' The lack of enthusiasm was palpable.

Julie laughed. 'Be nice. And actually, it's a pretty good band this time.'

'It won't help.'

'He's not *that* bad.'

Mabel smiled before sitting up. 'Oh, honey, I know he's your friend, but he's like kin to me. I watched him running around in diapers, and trust me when I say that he is definitely *that* bad. I know it drives him crazy, too, since that's all he ever really wanted to do. But like the good book says, "Suffer not the terrible singers, for they shall ruin the ears."'

'The good book doesn't say that.'

'It should. And it probably would, if Mike had been around back then.'

'Oh well, he loves it. If performing makes him happy, then I'm happy for him.'

Mabel smiled. 'You are truly a kind and special gal, Julie. I don't care what everyone else says about you—I *like* you.' She held up her glass in toast.

119

'Likewise,' Julie said, clinking cups.

'So what's up with you and Richard?' Mabel asked. 'After he came by today, you hardly mentioned him at all.'

'It's going okay, I guess.'

Mabel's chin rose. 'You guess? As in, I *guess* I don't see the iceberg, Captain?'

'It's going okay,' she repeated.

Mabel searched Julie's face for a moment. 'So why didn't you try to catch him a few minutes ago when I suggested it?'

'No reason,' Julie answered. 'It's just that I already saw him today.'

'Ah,' Mabel said, dragging the word out. '*I guess* that makes sense.'

Julie took a drink, feeling the burn at the back of her throat. Though she couldn't talk to Mike about Richard, Mabel was different. Mabel, she thought, would help her sort through her feelings about him.

'Do you remember the locket he got me?' she asked.

'How could I forget, J.B. ?'

'Well,' Julie said, 'the problem was that I didn't wear it today.'

'So?'

'That's what I thought. But I think Richard was offended.'

'If that offended him, remind me never to serve him my meat loaf.' When Julie didn't respond, she waved her cup before going on. 'So he got offended. So what? Men have their quirks, and maybe that's one of his. And there are worse things—believe me. But I think you have to judge what happened today against everything else. You've been on what—three dates now?'

120

'Four, really. If you count last weekend as two.'

'And you said he's been nice, right?'

'Yeah. So far.'

'Then maybe he was just having a bad day. You told me he works odd hours, right? Maybe he had to go in on Sunday and work late. Who knows?'

Julie drummed her fingers against the cup. 'Maybe.'

Mabel swirled the bourbon. 'Don't worry about it too much,' she said evenly. 'As long as he didn't go overboard, it's no big deal.'

'So just let it go?'

'Not exactly. You shouldn't completely ignore it, either.'

Julie looked up, and Mabel met her eyes.

'Take it from a lady who's had too many dates and met too many men over the years,' Mabel said. 'Everyone—you included—is on her best behavior in the beginning of a relationship. Sometimes little quirks turn out to be big ones, and the big advantage that women have—sometimes the only advantage—is their intuition.'

'But I thought you just said not to worry.'

'I did. But never ignore your intuition, either.'

'So you *do* think it's a problem?'

'Honey, I don't know what to think, just like you don't. There's no book of magic answers out there. I'm just telling you not to simply shrug it off if it bothered you so much, but don't let it ruin a good thing, either. That's what dating is for, you know— to find out about a person. To find out if the two of you click. I'm just throwing a little good old common sense into the mixture, that's all.'

Julie was quiet for a moment. 'I guess you're right,' she said.

The phone started ringing, and Mabel turned toward the sound. A moment later, the answering machine picked up. After listening to see who it was, she faced Julie again.

'So, four dates, huh?'

Julie nodded.

'Will there be a fifth?'

'He hasn't asked, but I think he probably will.'

'That's a strange way of answering the question.'

'What do you mean?'

'You didn't say what *you* were going to say if he asked.'

Julie glanced away.

'No,' she said, 'I suppose I didn't.'

*   *   *

Richard was waiting for her when she got home.

His car was parked on the street in front of her house, and he was leaning against it, his arms crossed and one leg over the other, watching as she turned into the driveway.

After pulling to a stop, Julie looked toward Singer and unhooked her seat belt.

'Just stay in the Jeep until I say so, okay?'

Singer pricked his ears up.

'And behave,' she added as she stepped out. By then, Richard was standing in the drive.

'Hello, Julie,' he said.

'Hi, Richard,' she said neutrally. 'What are you doing here?'

He shifted his weight from one foot to the other. 'I had a few minutes and thought I'd drop by. I tried to catch you at the salon, but I guess you'd taken off.'

122

'I had to go get Singer. He was over at the garage.'

Richard nodded. 'That's what Mabel said. I couldn't wait, though—I had some blueprints I had to drop off before the office closed, and actually, I have to get back as soon as I'm done here. But I just wanted to say I'm sorry about this morning. I got to thinking about how I acted, and I think I went a little overboard.'

He smiled, looking contrite, a kid with his hand caught in the cookie jar.

'Well,' she began, 'now that you mention it . . .'

Richard held up his hands to stop her. 'I know, I know. No excuses. I just wanted to say I'm sorry.'

Julie brushed away a strand of hair that had fallen in her face. 'Were you really that upset that I didn't wear the locket?'

'No,' he said. 'Trust me—it wasn't about that.'

'Then what was it?'

Richard glanced away. His voice was so soft, she could barely hear it.

'It's just that I had such a good time on the weekend, and when I saw that you didn't have it on, I sort of thought that you didn't feel the same way. I guess I felt like I'd let you down somehow. I mean . . . you don't know how much I've enjoyed the time we've spent together. Can you understand what I'm trying to say?'

Julie thought for a moment before nodding.

'Yeah,' she said.

'I knew you'd understand,' he said. He glanced around, as if suddenly nervous in her presence. 'Well, listen—like I said. I gotta head back into work.'

'Okay,' Julie said simply. She forced a smile.

A moment later, this time without trying to kiss her, he was gone.

Twelve

In the darkness, under a sliver of moon, Richard approached the front door of the rented Victorian he temporarily called home. It was on the outskirts of town, surrounded by farmland, set a hundred yards back from the main road.

The house was pale in the light, half the height of the shadowed pines that surrounded it. Though somewhat neglected, it still retained an old-fashioned charm, with trim and wainscoting that brought to mind a lace-trimmed invitation to a party at the home of the governor. The property needed attention; what had once been a well-kept garden had become overgrown with weeds and kudzu, but the overgrowth didn't bother him. There was beauty in the randomness of nature, he thought, in the curved and crooked lines of shadows at night, in the varying colors and shapes of branches and leaves in daylight.

Inside, however, he preferred order. Randomness ended at the door, and as he pushed his way inside, he flipped on the lights. The rented furniture—not much, but enough to make the home presentable—was not to his taste, but in a small town like Swansboro, choices were limited. In a world of cheap products and polyester-jacketed salesmen, he'd chosen the least offensive items he'd been able to find: tan corduroy couches and oak-laminated end tables, plastic lamps with fake brass.

Tonight, however, he didn't notice the decor. Tonight, there was only Julie. And the locket. And the way she'd looked at him only moments before.

Again, he'd pushed too hard, and again, she had called him on it. She was becoming a challenge, but he liked that. He respected that, for what he despised above all was weakness.

Why on earth was she living in a small town like this?

Julie, he thought, belonged in the city, a place of crowded sidewalks and flashing signs, quick insults and snappy comebacks. She was too sharp, too stylish, for a place like this. There was no energy here for her to draw on, nothing to sustain her in the long run. Strength, if unused, wasted away, and if Julie stayed, he knew she would grow weak, just as his mother had grown weak. And in time, there would be nothing to respect.

Just like his mother. The victim. Always the victim.

He closed his eyes, retreating to the past. It was 1974, and the image was always the same.

With her left eye swollen shut and her cheek purple, his mother was loading a suitcase into the trunk, trying to move quickly. The suitcase held clothes for both of them. In her purse, she had $37 in assorted change. It had taken almost a year to save that much; Vernon handled the finances and gave her just enough to do the shopping. She wasn't allowed to touch the checkbook and didn't even know what bank he used to cash his paychecks. The little money that she possessed had been collected from the sofa cushions, coins that had fallen from his pockets as he dozed in front of the television. She'd hidden the coins in a box of laundry detergent on the top shelf in the pantry, and every time he went that way, her heart had hammered in her chest.

She told herself she was leaving for good this time. This time, he wouldn't talk her into coming back. She told herself she wouldn't believe him, no matter how sweet he was to her, no matter how sincere his promises were. She told herself that if she stayed again, he would kill her. Maybe not this month or the next, but he would kill her. And then he would kill their son. She told herself all these things and repeated them almost like a mantra, as if the words would give her the strength to go.

Richard thought of his mother on that day. How she had kept him home from school, how she'd told him to run inside and grab the loaf of bread and peanut butter, because they were going on a picnic. How she'd told him that he should bring a jacket, too, in case the temperature dropped. He was six years old and did as his mother told him, even though he knew she was lying.

He'd heard his mother screaming and crying the night before as he lay in bed. Heard the sharp crack as his father's hand connected with her cheek, heard his mother crash into the thin wall that separated his room from theirs, heard her moaning and pleading for him to stop, that she was sorry, that she'd been planning to do the laundry but had to take their son to the doctor instead. He'd listened as Vernon called his mother names and made the same accusations he always did when he was drinking. 'He doesn't look like me!' his father had screamed. 'He's not mine!'

Lying in his bed, listening to the screams, he'd

prayed that it was true. He didn't want the monster to be his father. He hated him. Hated the greasy shine in his hair when he got home from the chemical factory, the boozy way he smelled at night. Hated the fact that while other kids in the neighborhood got bikes and roller skates for Christmas, he'd been given a baseball bat with no glove or ball. Hated the way he beat his mother when the house wasn't clean enough or if he couldn't find something his mother had put away. Hated the way they always kept the curtains drawn, and how no one had ever been allowed to visit.

'Hurry,' his mother said, motioning with her arm, 'we want to find a good table at the park.'

He ran into the house.

His father would be coming home for lunch in an hour, as he did every day. Though he walked to work, he took the car keys with him, a ringed jumble connected to his belt with a chain. His mother had removed one of the keys this morning as his father smoked and read the paper and ate the bacon and eggs that his wife had cooked.

They should have left right away, right after his father had disappeared over the hill on his way to the plant. Even at six he knew that, but instead his mother had sat at the table for hours, smoking one cigarette after the next, her hands shaking. She'd neither spoken nor moved from the seat until just a few minutes earlier.

But now they were running out of time. She was frantic at the thought that they weren't going to make it. Again.

He came bursting through the door, carrying the bread and peanut butter and his jacket, and ran toward the car. Even as he ran, he could see that

127

the white of his mother's left eye was red with blood. He closed the door to the Pontiac with a slam, and she tried to put the key into the ignition but missed. Her hands were shaking. She took a deep breath and tried again. This time the engine turned over, and she tried to smile. Her lip was swollen and it came out crooked; with her face and bloody eye, there was something terrifying in that smile. She put the car into reverse and backed out of the garage. In the road they idled for a moment, and she glanced at the dashboard.

She gasped. The gas gauge showed that the tank was nearly empty.

So they stayed. Again. As always.

That night, he heard his mother and father in the bedroom, but they weren't sounds of anger. Instead, he heard them laughing and kissing; later he heard his mother breathing hard and calling out his father's name. When he got out of bed the next morning, his father and mother were holding each other in the kitchen. His father winked, and he watched him lower his hands until they rested on his mother's skirt.

He saw his mother blush.

Richard opened his eyes. No, he thought, Julie couldn't stay here. Not if she wanted to lead the life she was meant to, the life she deserved. He would take her away from all this.

It was stupid of him to have said anything to her about the locket. Stupid. He wouldn't let it happen again.

Lost in thought, he barely heard the ringing of the phone, but he rose in time to answer before the machine picked it up.

Pausing for a moment, he recognized the

Daytona area code on the caller ID and took a deep breath before he answered.

Thirteen

In the darkness of her bedroom, with an allergy headache raging, Julie threw her spare pillow at Singer.

'Would you please shut up!' she moaned.

Singer ignored the pillow. Instead, he stood near the bedroom door, panting and growling, obviously wanting Julie to get up and let him outside so he could—as only dogs can—'investigate things.' He'd been pacing through the house for the last hour, from the bedroom to the living room and back again, and more than once he'd pressed his wet nose against her, making her jump.

She pulled the pillow over her head, but it wasn't enough to block out the sound, and the compression only made her head feel worse.

'There's nothing out there,' she muttered. 'It's the middle of the night and my head hurts. I'm not getting out of bed.'

Singer continued growling. Not a sinister growl, not a snarl, not the sound he made when men came to check the electric meter or—God forbid!—tried to deliver the mail. Just a pain-in-the-neck rumbling too loud to ignore.

She threw her last pillow at him. Singer retaliated by crossing the room silently and pushing his nose into her ear.

She sat up, wiping at her ear with her finger.

'That's it! That does it!'

Singer wagged his tail, looking satisfied. *Now we're getting somewhere. C'mon!* He trotted out of the room, leading the way.

'Fine! You want me to prove there's nothing out there, you crazy dog?'

After rubbing her temples with a groan, Julie got out of bed and staggered toward the living room. Singer was already at the front windows; he'd pushed aside the curtains with his nose and was looking from side to side.

Julie peeked out as well, seeing nothing.

'See? Nothing. Just like I told you.'

Singer wasn't placated. He moved to the door and stood before it.

'If you go out, don't expect me to wait up for you. Once you're out, you're out. I'm going back to bed. My head really hurts—not that you care.'

Singer didn't seem to care.

'Fine,' she said. 'Have it your way.'

She opened the door. Though she expected Singer to bolt toward the woods, he didn't. Instead, he moved onto the porch and barked twice before lowering his nose to sniff. As he did so, Julie crossed her arms and looked around.

Nothing. No sign that anyone had been there at all. With the exception of frogs and crickets, it was quiet. The leaves were still; the street was empty.

Satisfied, Singer turned and headed back inside.

'That's it? You got me out of bed for that?'

Singer looked up at her. *The coast is clear*, he seemed to say. *No reason to be worried. You can go ahead and go back to sleep now.*

Julie scowled at him before heading back to the bedroom. Singer didn't follow. Instead, as she squinted over her shoulder on her way back to bed,

130

she saw him sitting by the window again, the curtains pushed aside.

'Whatever,' she mumbled.

In the bathroom, her head still pounding, she took some Tylenol PM to help her sleep.

When he started snarling and barking again an hour later, this time in earnest, Julie—who'd closed the bedroom door and turned on the bathroom fan—didn't hear it.

*   *   *

The next morning, standing in the driveway beneath a balled-up sun and sky so blue that it looked artificial, Julie wore sunglasses. Remnants of her headache still lingered, though it wasn't nearly as blinding as it had been the night before. Singer stood beside her as she read the note tucked beneath the windshield wiper of her Jeep.

> *Julie,*
> *I was called out of town for an emergency, so I won't be able to see you for a couple of days. I'll call as soon as I can. I won't stop thinking about you.*
> *Richard*

Julie glanced at Singer.

'So that's what all the noise was about?' she asked, holding the note in her hands. 'Richard?'

Singer looked smug as only he could. *See, I told you someone was here.*

The Tylenol had left her feeling groggy and lethargic, with an acidic taste in her mouth, and she wasn't in the mood for his superior attitude. 'Don't give me that. You kept me up for hours. And it's not like you don't know him, so get over it.'

Singer snorted and jumped into the Jeep.

'He didn't even come to the door.'

Julie closed the back and slid into the front seat. In the rearview mirror, she saw Singer circle once, then sit with his back to her.

'Yeah, well, I'm mad at you, too.'

On the way to work, as she glanced in the mirror again, Singer still hadn't turned around, nor did he lean his head over the side, letting the wind flap his tongue and ears as he usually did. As soon as she parked the car, Singer hopped out. Even though she called to him, he continued on his way, crossing the street and heading toward the garage.

Dogs.

Sometimes, she thought, they were as childish as men.

*   *   *

Mabel was on the phone, canceling Andrea's appointments. Andrea wouldn't be coming in, since she was taking another 'personal day.' At least she called this time, Mabel thought. No doubt Andrea would come in with some wild story. On her last personal day, she claimed to have seen Bruce Springsteen walking through the Food Lion parking lot and had followed him around all day before realizing it wasn't him. The question of why Bruce Springsteen would have been at the Swansboro Food Lion had never seemed to enter her mind.

When she heard the door jingle behind her, Mabel turned and saw Julie. As she reached for the

132

box of Milk-Bone biscuits she kept on hand for Singer, she noticed that Julie had come in alone.

'Where's Singer?' Mabel asked.

Julie set her purse on a shelf beside her station. 'I guess he went to visit Mike.'

'Again?'

'We had a fight.'

She said it exactly the way she used to after having an argument with Jim, and Mabel smiled. Only Julie didn't seem to understand how ridiculous it sounded to other people.

'A fight, huh?' Mabel said.

'Yeah—so I guess he's off pouting now. Like he's punishing me for having the nerve to yell at him. But he deserved it.'

'Ah,' Mabel said. 'So what happened?'

Julie told Mabel about the night before.

'He left a note to apologize?' Mabel asked.

'No, he did that yesterday when I got home. The note was just to let me know he'd be out of town for a couple days.'

Though Mabel wanted to ask how the apology had gone, it was obvious that Julie wasn't in the mood to talk about it. Mabel put the Milk-Bone box back in the cabinet and glanced toward Singer's blanket in the corner.

'It looks sort of empty here without him,' she said. 'Kind of like someone removed a couch or something.'

'Oh, he'll be back in a little while. You know how he is.'

To their surprise, however, eight hours later, Singer still hadn't returned.

*   *   *

133

'I tried to bring him back a couple of times,' Mike said, looking as perplexed as Julie felt. 'But he wouldn't follow me out, no matter how much I called. I even tried bribing him with some beef jerky, but he wouldn't leave the garage. I considered dragging him, but to be honest, I didn't think he'd let me.'

Julie looked at Singer. He was sitting beside Mike, watching Julie, his head tilted to the side.

'You still mad at me, Singer?' she asked. 'Is that what this is about?'

'Why would he be mad at you?'

'We had a fight.'

'Oh,' he said.

'You just going to sit there, or are you going to come over?' she asked.

Singer licked his lips but didn't move.

'Singer—come,' she commanded.

Singer stayed where he was.

'Heel.'

Though she'd never given him that particular command, she didn't know what else to say, and just when it seemed that she was beginning to get upset, Mike flipped his hand.

'Go on, Singer. Before you get in bigger trouble.'

At Mike's command, Singer stood and, reluctantly, it seemed, went to Julie's side. She put her hands on her hips.

'So you're listening to Mike now?'

'Don't blame me,' Mike said, trying to sound innocent. 'I didn't do anything.'

'I'm not blaming you. I just don't know what's gotten into him lately.' Singer sat beside her and looked up. 'So what did he do here all day?'

134

'Snoozed, stole my turkey sandwich when I got up to get a drink, went around back to do his business. It's sort of like he just moved in for the day.'

'Did he seem strange to you?'

'No. Not at all. Aside from being here, he seemed fine.'

'He wasn't angry?'

Mike scratched his head, knowing that she viewed it as a serious question. 'Well, to be honest, he didn't mention anything, not to me, anyway. Want me to go ask Henry? Maybe they talked while I was out or something.'

'Are you making fun of me?'

'No, never. You know I'd never do something like that.'

'Good. After almost losing my dog to someone else, I'm not exactly in the mood for joking right now.'

'You didn't almost lose him. He was with me.'

'Yeah. And now he likes you better.'

'Maybe he just misses me. I'm quite addictive, you know.'

For the first time since she'd arrived, Julie smiled. 'You are, huh?'

'What can I say? It's a curse.'

Julie laughed. 'It must be tough being you.'

Mike shook his head, thinking how beautiful Julie looked.

'You have no idea.'

*   *   *

An hour later, Julie was standing over the sink in her kitchen, gamely holding on to the dish towels she'd hastily wrapped around the broken faucet,

135

doing her best to stem the flow of water that had exploded toward the ceiling like a domestic geyser. She grabbed another towel, adding it to the others, then tightened her grip, which reduced the spray somewhat. Unfortunately, it also routed some of the water her way.

'Could you get me the phone?' she shouted, holding her chin high to keep the water from hitting her face.

Singer traipsed to the living room; a moment later, with her free hand, Julie took the portable phone from his mouth. She hit the first number on her speed dial.

* * *

Mike was on the couch, munching on Doritos, his fingers frosted with orange powder, a can of beer wedged between his legs. Along with the Big Mac he'd picked up (and finished) on the way home, this was dinner. On the couch beside him was his guitar, and as always, once he'd finished playing, he closed his eyes and leaned back, imagining Katie Couric describing the scene to a national television audience:

'It's the most anticipated concert event of the year,' Katie gushes. 'With a single album, Michael Harris has set the music world on fire. His first album alone has already sold more than the Beatles and Elvis Presley did in their entire careers combined, and the televised concert is expected to have the largest viewing audience in history. It's being broadcast simultaneously around the globe to an estimated three billion people, and the live

crowd is estimated to be approaching two million. This is history in the making, folks.'

Smiling, Mike slipped another Doritos into his mouth. Oh, yeah, he thought. Oh, yeah.

'You can hear the crowd behind me, chanting his name. It's amazing how many people he's affected. People have been coming up to me all day telling me that Michael Harris has changed their lives with his music . . . and here he comes now!'

Katie's voice is drowned out as the crowd surges forward and erupts in deafening applause. Mike walks on stage, holding his guitar.

He scans the crowd. The audience goes insane; the sound is ear-shattering. He is showered with flowers as he moves toward the microphone. Women and children are overcome at the sight of him. Men, fighting their jealousy, wish they could be him. Katie nearly passes out.

Mike taps the microphone, signaling he's almost ready to begin, and suddenly the audience quiets. They are waiting for him, but he doesn't start playing right away. Seconds pass, then more seconds, and by now the audience is shaking with fevered expectation, but still he lets the anticipation build.

And it does until it's almost unbearable. The audience feels it, Katie feels it. Billions of people watching their televisions feel it.

Mike did, too.

On the couch, he let the adoration wash over him, his hand on the bag of Doritos.

Oh, *yeah* . . .

When the phone on the table beside him suddenly blared like an alarm, Mike was ripped from the fantasy and he jumped; his hand jerked upward, sending a volcanic eruption of Doritos in all directions and spilling the beer into his lap. Acting on instinct, he tried to brush off the beer, but it didn't do much except leave orange streaks on his crotch.

'Crap,' he said, setting aside the empty can and bag. He reached for the phone with one hand while trying to brush at the beer stain. More streaks. 'C'mon,' he said, 'stop that.' The phone rang again before he picked it up.

'Hello?'

'Hey, Mike,' Julie said, sounding stressed. 'You busy?'

The beer kept soaking through the fabric, and he shifted slightly in the hopes of getting more comfortable. This did no good—instead, the beer worked its way around to the seat of his pants. Now there, he thought, was a squishy feeling he could do without.

'Not really.'

'You sound distracted.'

'Sorry about that. Just had a little accident here involving my dinner.'

'Excuse me?'

Mike reached for the bag and started picking the Doritos off his guitar. 'It's nothing serious,' he said. 'I'll be okay. So what's up?'

'I need you.'

'You do?' As his ego inflated, he momentarily forgot about the mess he was sitting in.

'My faucet exploded.'

'Oh,' he said, his ego deflating just as quickly. 'How'd that happen?'

'How should I know?'

'Did you jerk it or something?'

'No. I just tried to use it.'

'Was it loose before?'

'I really don't know—but can you come over or not?'

He made an instant decision. 'I'd have to change my pants first.'

'Excuse me?'

'Never mind. I'll be there in a few minutes—I have to swing by the hardware store to get you a new faucet.'

'You won't be long, will you? I'm stuck holding a rag here, and I've got to go to the bathroom. If I cross my legs any harder, I'm going to snap my knees.'

'I'm on my way.'

In his haste to get dressed and out the door, coupled with the prospect of seeing Julie, he fell only once as he pulled on his pants.

It seemed pretty reasonable to him under the circumstances.

Fourteen

'Julie?' Mike called out as he entered the house.

Julie craned her neck, loosening her grip slightly on the rags.

'In here, Mike. I think something happened, though. It doesn't seem to be leaking anymore.'

'I just shut off the water with the valve out front.

It should be fine now.'

Mike poked his head into the kitchen, and one word came immediately to mind: *breasts*. Julie, soaked to the point that he could clearly see the outlines of her breasts, looked as though she'd been targeted during spring break by rowdy boys, the kind who consider drinking gallons of beer and wet T-shirt contests the high point of their existence.

'You have no idea how much I appreciate you coming over like this,' Julie said. She shook the excess water from her hands and unwrapped the faucet.

Mike barely heard her. Don't stare at her breasts, he told himself, whatever you do, don't stare at her breasts. A *gentleman* wouldn't stare. A *friend* wouldn't stare. Squatting, he opened his toolbox. Singer sat beside him and sniffed the box, as if looking for goodies.

'No problem,' he mumbled.

Julie began to wring out the rags one at a time. 'I mean it. I hope I didn't drag you away from anything important.'

'Don't worry about it.'

Julie pulled her T-shirt away from her skin and looked at him. 'Are you okay?' she asked.

Mike began fishing around for the basin wrench—a long, thin plumbing tool used to reach bolts in difficult places.

'I'm fine. Why?'

'You're kind of acting like you're upset.'

'I'm not upset.'

'You won't even look at me.'

'I'm not staring.'

'That's what I just said.'

'Oh.'

'Mike?'

'Here it is!' he said suddenly, thanking God for the opportunity to change the subject. 'I was hoping I put this in here.'

Julie kept staring at him, puzzled. 'I think I'm going to go change,' she said finally.

'I think that's probably a good idea,' Mike muttered.

*   *   *

The job at hand gave Mike something to focus on, and he took to it immediately, if only to clear Julie's image from his mind.

He spread around some towels he'd grabbed from the linen closet and soaked up most of the thin film spread across the floor, then emptied the cupboard below the sink, stacking the bottles of various cleansers on either side of the doors. By the time Julie got back, he was already working to replace the faucet—only his torso and lower body were readily visible. Both his legs were sticking out; despite the towels, there were wet circles on either knee where he'd had to kneel. Singer was lying beside him, his head pushed into the darkened space beneath.

'Would you stop panting?' Mike complained.

Singer ignored the comment, and Mike exhaled, making a point to breathe through his mouth.

'I'm serious. Your breath stinks.'

Singer's tail vibrated up and down.

'And give me some room, will you? You're in the way.'

Julie saw him push—or rather try to push—

Singer without much effect. Chilled, she'd slipped into a pair of jeans and a light sweat-shirt. Her hair was still wet, though she'd brushed it back, away from her face.

'How's it going under there?' she asked.

At the sound of her voice, Mike raised his head, bumping it on the sink trap. Singer's breath was hot on his cheeks, the odor making his eyes water.

'Good. I've just about got it done.'

'Already?'

'It's not that hard—just have to remove a couple of nuts and the faucet pops off. I didn't know what kind of faucet you wanted, so I just grabbed one that looks like your old one. I hope that's okay.'

She glanced at it. 'It's fine.'

'Because I could go get a different one. It's no big deal.'

'No—as long as it works, it's perfect.'

She saw his arms start to crank the wrench again, and to her surprise, she caught herself eyeing the wiry muscles of his forearms as he worked. A moment later, she heard a *plink* as something dropped beneath the cabinet.

'Got it,' he said.

He slid out from under the sink and, seeing that she'd changed, felt himself relax. It was easier this way. Less threatening. Less breasty. He stood and lifted the old faucet free, then handed it to her.

'You really destroyed that thing,' he said, pointing to the gaping hole at the top. 'What did you use to turn it on, a hammer?'

'No. Dynamite.'

'You might want to use a little less next time.'

She smiled. 'Can you tell what went wrong with it?'

'Just old, I guess. It's probably original with the house. It's the one thing I haven't had to replace around here, but I probably should have looked at it the last time I fixed your disposal.'

'So you're saying it was your mistake?'

'If you say so,' he said. 'I mean, if it makes you feel better and all. But give me another minute here and I'll have everything up and running, okay?'

'Sure.'

He put the new faucet in place, crawled back underneath, and hooked it up. Then, excusing himself from the kitchen, he vanished out the door for a moment, Singer trailing close behind. After turning the water valve back on, he came back in and tried the faucet, making sure it wasn't leaking.

'Looks like you're good to go.'

'I still think you made that look too easy,' she said. 'Before you got here, I was wondering which plumber to call if you couldn't get it done.'

Mike feigned offense. 'I can't believe that after all this time you would even think of such a thing.'

Julie laughed as he squatted to start putting the cleansers back.

'Oh, no, you don't—let me get that,' she said, kneeling next to him. 'I can do *something*.'

As they were putting things away, Julie more than once felt his arm brush against her and wondered why she even noticed it at all. A minute later, the cupboard was closed and the towels were bundled up, still dripping. She left the kitchen for a moment to throw them in the laundry room while Mike put his tools away. When she came back, she headed straight for the refrigerator.

'I don't know about you, but I need a beer after

143

all the excitement this evening. Do you want one?'

'I'd love one.'

Julie grabbed two bottles of Coors Light and handed one to Mike. After twisting off the cap, she clinked her bottle against his.

'Thanks for coming over. I know I said it already, but I had to say it again.'

'Hey,' Mike responded, 'that's what friends are for, right?'

'C'mon,' Julie said, waving the bottle, 'let's sit on the porch with these. It's too nice to stay inside.'

She started toward the door, then suddenly stopped. 'Wait—did you say you've already eaten dinner? When I called you earlier, I mean?'

'Why?'

'Because I'm starved. In all the commotion, I didn't get a chance to eat. You up for sharing a pizza?'

Mike smiled. 'That sounds great.'

Julie started toward the phone, and as she moved away, Mike wondered if the evening would somehow end up breaking his heart.

'Ham and pineapple okay?' she called out.

Mike swallowed. 'Whatever you want is fine with me.'

*　　　*　　　*

They sat in rockers on the porch, the heat of their skin escaping into the cool evening, cicadas humming and mosquitoes circling just outside the screen. The sun had finally dipped from sight, the last rays of light reflected from the horizon shining between the trees.

Julie's home, which sat on half an acre, was

bordered on the back and sides by vacant wooded lots, and when she wanted to be alone, this was the place she went. It was also the reason she and Jim had bought the home in the first place. Both of them had always dreamed of owning an older home with graceful, wraparound porches. Though the house desperately needed work, they'd put in their offer the same day they'd walked through it.

Singer was dozing on the porch near the steps, one eye popping open every now and then, as if to make sure he wasn't missing anything. In the waning light, Julie's features took on a pale glow.

'This reminds me of the first time we met,' Mike said, smiling. 'Do you remember that? When Mabel invited all of us over to her place so we'd have a chance to meet you?'

'How could I forget? It was one of the most terrifying moments of my life.'

'But we're such nice people.'

'I didn't know that. Back then, you were all strangers to me. I had no idea what to expect.'

'Even with Jim?'

'Especially with Jim. It took me a long time to realize why he did what he did for me. I mean, I'd never known anyone like him, and I had a hard time believing that there were people out there who were just . . . good. I don't think I said a single word to him that night.'

'You didn't. The next day, Jim mentioned that to me.'

'He did?'

'Not in a bad way. And anyway, he told us beforehand not to expect you to say much. Said you were kind of timid.'

'He did not.'

'He called you mousy.'

She laughed. 'I've been called a lot of things, but mousy isn't one of them.'

'Well, I think he said that just so we'd give you a chance. Not that we really needed an excuse. The fact that both he and Mabel liked you was enough for us.'

Julie paused for a long moment, looking almost forlorn. 'It's still hard for me to believe that I'm here sometimes,' she said.

'Why?'

'Just the way things worked out. I mean, I'd never even heard of Swansboro until Jim mentioned it, and here I am, twelve years later, still hanging around.'

Mike looked at her over his bottle. 'You sound like you want to leave.'

Julie tucked one leg beneath her. 'No. Not at all. I like it here. I mean, there was a while there after Jim died that I thought I should start over someplace new, but I just never got around to it. And besides, where would I go? It's not like I wanted to live near my mom again.'

'Have you talked to her lately?'

'Not for a few months. She called me on Christmas and said she wanted to come up and visit, but I haven't heard from her since. I think she said that so I'd offer to send her money for the flight or something, but I wasn't about to do that. It would just open old wounds.'

'I know that's got to be hard.'

'It is sometimes. Or it used to be, anyway. But I don't really allow myself to think about it much anymore. When I first started going out with Jim, I wanted to make contact with her, if only to let her know that everything had worked out for me. I guess I wanted her approval, you know? It's strange that I cared about that, but as disappointing as she was as a mother, it was still important.'

'But not anymore?'

'Not so much. She didn't show up for the wedding, she didn't show up for the funeral. After that, I just sort of gave up. I mean, I'm not rude when she calls, but there's not much feeling there. I may as well be talking to a stranger.'

As she spoke, Mike stared toward the darkening shadows near the trees. In the distance, small bats appeared and disappeared in blinks, as if they'd never been there at all.

'Henry drives me nuts half the time, and my parents are just as wacky as he is, but it's nice to know they're around for support. I don't know what I'd do without them. I don't know if I could make it on my own like you have.'

She looked at him. 'You'd make it. Besides, I'm not totally alone. I've got Singer here, and I've got my friends. That's enough for now.'

Mike wanted to ask where Richard fit into that equation but decided not to. He didn't want to ruin the mood. Nor did he want to ruin the light, easy feeling he had now that his beer was almost finished.

'Can I ask you a question?' Julie said.

'Sure.'

'Whatever happened with Sarah? I thought you two had something special going, and then all of a sudden, you weren't seeing each other anymore.'

Mike adjusted himself in the chair. 'Oh, you know . . .'

'No, not really. You've never told me why it

147

ended.'

'There wasn't much to tell.'

'That's what you always say. But what's the real story?'

Mike was quiet for a long moment before shaking his head. 'You don't want to know.'

'What'd she do? Cheat on you?'

When Mike didn't answer, Julie suddenly knew her guess was correct.

'Oh, Mike. I'm sorry.'

'Yeah, me too. Or I was, anyway. It was some guy from work. His car was at her house when I went by one morning.'

'What did you do?'

'You mean did I get angry? Of course. But to be honest, it wasn't entirely her fault. I hadn't exactly been the most attentive boyfriend at the end. I guess she felt neglected.' He sighed, rubbing a hand over his face. 'I don't know—I guess part of me knew it wasn't going to last, so maybe I stopped trying. And then something was bound to happen.'

Neither said anything for a moment, and noticing he was almost empty, Julie pointed to his bottle.

'Need another one?'

'Probably,' he said.

'You got it.'

She rose and Mike scooted the rocker back a little to make room for her, watching as the door slapped shut behind her. He couldn't help but notice how good she looked in jeans.

He shook his head, forcing the thought away. Now was not the time for that. If they were having wine and lobster, maybe, but pizza and beer? No, this was just a casual night. The ways things used to be—before he'd done something as crazy as

148

allowing himself to fall in love with her.

He still wasn't sure exactly when it had happened. After Jim had been gone for a while, he knew that. But he couldn't pin it down any more than that. It wasn't as if a light had suddenly blinked on; it was more like a sunrise, where the sky grows lighter and lighter, almost imperceptibly, before you realized it was morning.

When Julie came back out, she handed him the bottle and took her seat again.

'Jim used to say that, too, you know?'

'What?'

' "Probably." When I asked him if he wanted another beer. Did he get that from you?'

'Probably.'

She laughed. 'Do you still think about him?'

Mike nodded. 'All the time.'

'I do, too.'

'I'm sure. He was a good guy—a great guy. You couldn't have done any better. And he used to tell me that he couldn't have done any better, either.'

She leaned back in her seat, thinking how much she liked what he said. 'You're a good guy, too.'

'Yeah. Me and about a million others. I'm not like Jim was.'

'Sure you are. You're from the same small town, you had the same friends, you liked to do the same things. For the most part, you two seemed more like brothers than you and Henry. Except, of course, for the fact that Jim could never have fixed that faucet. He couldn't fix anything.'

'Well, Henry couldn't have fixed it, either.'

'Really?'

'No. Henry could have fixed it. But he wouldn't have. He hates getting his hands dirty.'

149

'That's funny, considering you two own a garage.'

'Tell me about it. But I don't mind. To be honest, I like what I do a whole lot more than his part of the job. I'm not a big fan of paperwork.'

'So I guess being a loan officer is out, huh?'

'Like Jim was? No way. Even if I could somehow con my way into getting the job, I wouldn't last more than a week. I'd approve everybody who walked in the door. I'm not real good at saying no when someone really needs something.'

She reached over, touching his arm. 'Gee, really?'

He smiled, suddenly at a loss for words, wishing with all his heart that the touch would last forever.

*   *   *

The pizza arrived a few minutes later. A pimply teenager wearing glasses with thick black frames examined the ticket for an inordinately long time before stammering out the total.

Mike was reaching for his wallet when Julie nudged him out of the way, holding her pocketbook.

'Not a chance. This one's on me.'

'But I'll eat more.'

'You can eat the whole thing if you want. But I'm still paying.'

Before he could object again, Julie handed the delivery boy the money, telling him to keep the change, then carried the box back to the kitchen.

'Paper plates okay?'

'I eat off paper plates all the time.'

'I know,' she said, winking. 'And I can't tell you how sorry I am for you.'

150

*　　　*　　　*

For the next hour they ate together, talking quietly in the familiar way they always did. They talked about Jim and things they remembered, and eventually the subject changed to happenings around town and the people they knew. From time to time, Singer would whine, looking as if he felt ignored, and Mike would toss a piece of crust his way without a break in the conversation.

As the evening slowly wound down, Julie found herself holding Mike's gaze a little longer than usual. It surprised her. It wasn't as if he'd done or said anything out of the ordinary since he'd come over; it wasn't even that they were sitting alone on the porch and sharing dinner almost as if the evening had been planned in advance.

No, there was no reason for her to feel differently tonight, but she didn't seem able to control it. Nor, she realized, did she really want the feeling to stop, though that didn't make sense, either. In his sneakers and jeans, his legs propped up on the railing, his hair mussed, he was cute in an everyday guy kind of way. But then, she'd always known that, even before she'd started dating Jim.

Spending time with Mike, she reflected, wasn't like the dates she'd recently been on, including the past weekend with Richard. There was no pretension here, no hidden meanings in the phrases they spoke, no elaborate plans designed to impress the other. Though it had always been easy to spend time with Mike, she suddenly realized that in the whirlwind of the past couple of weeks, she'd almost forgotten how much she enjoyed it.

It was what she'd most enjoyed about being

151

married to Jim. It wasn't only the heady flush of emotions when they'd made love that had enthralled her; more than that, it was the lazy mornings they'd spent reading the newspaper in bed while drinking coffee, or the cold December mornings they'd planted bulbs in the garden, or the hours they'd spent traipsing through various stores, picking out bedroom furniture, debating the merits of cherry or maple. Those were the moments she'd felt most content, when she finally allowed herself to believe in the impossible. Those were the moments when all seemed right with the world.

Remembering those things, Julie watched Mike eat, the corners of her mouth upturned slightly. He was fighting long strings of cheese that ran from his mouth back to the slice, making it look more difficult than it was. After taking a bite, he would sometimes sit up suddenly and fumble with the piece, using his fingers to keep the toppings from sliding off or the tomato sauce from dripping. Then, laughing at himself, he would swipe at his face with a napkin, mumbling something along the lines of 'Almost ruined my shirt with that one.' That he didn't take himself too seriously, or mind when she didn't, either, made her warm toward him in a way that reminded her of how she imagined old couples felt as they sat on park benches, holding hands. It was still on her mind a few minutes later when she followed him into the kitchen, both of them carrying the remains from dinner, and watched him find the cellophane in the drawer by the oven without having to ask where it was. As he took it upon himself to wrap the pizza and place it in the refrigerator, then automatically reach for the garbage when he noticed it was full, there was a

152

moment, just a moment, when the scene seemed as if it weren't happening now, but as if it were taking place sometime in the future, just an ordinary evening in a long procession of evenings together.

*   *   *

'I think we just about got it all,' Mike said, looking around the kitchen.

The sound of his voice brought Julie back, and she felt her cheeks redden slightly.

'Looks that way,' she agreed. 'Thanks for helping to pick up around here.'

For a long moment neither of them spoke, and Julie suddenly heard the refrain she'd lived with the last couple of years start up, as if a recording had been switched on. *A relationship with Mike? No way. Not a chance.*

Mike brought his hands together, interrupting the thought before it went any further.

'I should probably get going. I have an early day tomorrow.'

She nodded. 'I figured. I should probably get to bed soon, too. Singer kept me up last night for hours.'

'What was he doing?'

'Whining, growling, barking, pacing . . . pretty much whatever he could do to bug me.'

'Singer? What's going on?'

'Oh, Richard came by last night. You know how Singer gets around new people.'

It was the first time that Richard's name had come up all evening, and Mike suddenly felt his throat catch, as if someone were pressing a thumb to it.

153

'Richard was here last night?' he asked.

'No—not that way. We weren't on a date or anything. He just came by to leave a note on my car to let me know he'd be out of town.'

'Oh,' Mike said.

'It was nothing,' Julie added, suddenly feeling the urge to clarify.

'So what time was this?' Mike asked.

Julie turned to the clock on the wall, as if she needed to see the position of the hands to remember.

'I guess around two or so. That's when Singer started, anyway, but like I said, it went on for a while. Why?'

Mike pressed his lips together, thinking, And Singer growled the whole time?

'I guess I was just wondering why he didn't leave the note before he left in the morning,' he said.

Julie shrugged. 'I have no idea. Maybe he didn't have time.'

Mike nodded, wondering whether to say more, then finally decided not to. Instead, he reached for his toolbox and the faucet he'd replaced, not wanting the evening to end with something that might come across the wrong way. He took a small step backward.

'Listen . . .'

Julie ran a hand through her hair, noticing for the first time a small mole on his cheek that looked almost ornamental, as if it had been dotted there by a makeup artist looking for exactly the right effect. Why, she wondered, did she see that now?

'I know—you've got to go,' she said, cutting off the thought.

Mike shifted from one foot to the other. Not

knowing what else to say, he held up the faucet.

'Well, thanks for calling me about this. Believe it or not, I'm glad you did. I had a great time tonight.'

Their eyes met and held for a moment before Mike glanced away. Julie felt herself exhale—she didn't even realize she'd been holding her breath—and despite herself, she found her eyes sweeping over Mike as he walked ahead of her to the door. The jeans fit snugly around his rear, and she felt her cheeks redden again, the blood rushing to the surface like silt stirred from the bottom of a country pond.

Her eyes jerked upward as Mike turned the door handle. For a moment, she felt as if she'd been watching someone at a party from across a crowded room, someone she'd never seen before. In any other situation, at any other time, she would have laughed at the absurdity of it all.

But strangely, she couldn't.

After saying good-bye, she stood in the doorway watching as Mike went to his truck. In the moment before he closed the door, with the dome light above him glowing like a filtered halo, he waved.

Julie returned the wave and then watched as the red tail-lights of his truck receded into the distance. For almost a minute, she stood on the porch, trying to make sense of her feelings. Mike, she thought again, *Mike*.

Why was she even bothering to think about it? It wouldn't happen. Crossing her arms, she laughed to herself. Mike? Sure, he was nice; sure, he was easy to talk to; and yes, he was cute. But *Mike?*

The whole thing, she suddenly decided, was preposterous. A bunch of nonsense.

Julie turned to go in. Wasn't it?

Fifteen

In his office the following morning, Henry set the Styrofoam cup of coffee on his desk. 'So that's it?' he asked.

Mike scratched the back of his head. 'That's it.'

'You just left? Like that?'

'Yeah.'

Henry's index fingers came together, forming a triangle that he rested under his chin. Though normally he would have ridden Mike about the fact that he hadn't taken the opportunity to ask Julie out, it wasn't the time for that.

'So let me make sure I've got this straight. You hear a bunch of cryptic stuff from this Jake Blansen about Richard which might or might not mean anything but is definitely a little weird sounding, especially since he wouldn't say any more about it. *Then* you find out that Richard is coming around her place in the middle of the night and hanging around for God knows how long and you decide not to tell her that it sounds a little weird to you? Or even mention the fact that there might be something to be concerned about?'

'She's the one who told me that Richard came by. It's not like she doesn't know he was there.'

'That's not the point, and you know it.'

Mike shook his head. 'Nothing happened, Henry.'

'You still should have said something.'

'How?'

Henry leaned back in his seat. 'The same way I just did. Just tell her what you're thinking.'

156

'You can say it that way, but I can't,' he said, meeting his brother's eyes. 'She might have thought I was just saying it because of how I feel about her.'

'Look, Mike,' Henry said, sounding more like a parent than a brother. 'You're her friend and you'll always be her friend, whether or not anything ever happens between you two. The same goes for me, too, okay? And I don't like the thought of this guy hanging around her place in the middle of the night. That's creepy no matter what reason the guy comes up with. He could have left the note in the morning, he could have called her on the phone, he could have left a message at work . . . What kind of guy gets dressed, hops in his car, and heads across town to leave a note at two A.M.? And didn't you say that Singer kept her up for hours? What if that meant he was skulking around the whole time Singer was acting up? And what if Blansen was trying to warn you somehow? Didn't you think about any of those things?'

'Of course I did. I didn't like it, either.'

'Then you should have said something.'

Mike closed his eyes. It had been such a great evening up until that point.

'You weren't there, Henry,' he said. 'And besides, she didn't seem to think it was odd at all, so don't make this into something bigger than it might be. All he did was leave a note.'

'How do you know that was all he was doing?'

Mike started to say something, but the expression on Henry's face made him stop.

'Look,' Henry said, 'I'm usually more than willing to let you do your own thing even when you screw up, but there's a time and place for everything. This isn't the time to start keeping secrets from

157

her, especially about stuff like this. Does that make sense?'

After a moment, Mike's chin dropped to his chest.

'Yeah,' he said, 'that makes sense.'

*   *   *

'Well, it sounds like you two had a good time,' Mabel said.

'We did,' Julie replied. 'You know how he is. He's always a lot of fun.'

Mabel swiveled in the empty seat as they were talking; no customers were scheduled for another few minutes, and they had the place to themselves.

'And your faucet's good to go?'

Julie was busy setting up her station, and she nodded. 'He put a new one in.'

'Did he make it look easy? Like you wondered why you had to call him in the first place?'

'Yep.'

'Don't you hate that?'

'Every single time.'

Mabel laughed. 'He sure is something, isn't he?'

Julie hesitated. From the corner of her eye, she saw Singer sitting by the front door and staring out the window, as if wanting to be let out.

Though Mabel's question didn't require a response, there was an element of seriousness to the possible answer, one that she hadn't stopped thinking about since the night before. She wasn't sure why the evening lingered in her mind. It wasn't exciting; it wasn't even all that memorable. But the night before, with the moonlight streaming through her window and moths beating

158

against the windowpane, Mike had been not only the person she'd been imagining before she trailed off to sleep, but also the first one she'd thought about as her eyes fluttered open this morning.

Julie's reply came effortlessly as she moved toward the door to let Singer out.

'Yes,' she said, 'he is.'

* * *

'Mike,' Henry called out, 'you've got company.'

Mike poked his head out of the supply room. 'Who is it?'

'Take a wild guess.'

Before he could answer, Singer trotted up beside him.

* * *

It was late afternoon by the time Julie marched over to the garage. Hands on her hips, she glared at Singer.

'If I didn't know better, I'd think this was all sort of a plan to make sure I'd come over here,' she said.

As soon as she said it, Mike did his best to project his thanks to Singer telepathically.

'Maybe he's trying to tell you something.'

'Like what?'

'I don't know. Maybe that he hasn't been getting enough attention lately.'

'Oh, he gets plenty of attention. Don't let him fool you. He's spoiled rotten.'

Singer, sitting on his haunches, began scratching

with his back leg, as if demonstrating his indifference to what either of them was saying. Mike was unfastening the snaps of his coveralls as they were talking.

'I hope you don't mind,' he said, 'but this thing is driving me crazy. I got some transmission fluid on it and I've been breathing the fumes all day.'

'So you've got a little buzz going, huh?'

'No, just a headache. I'm not that lucky.'

Julie watched as he pulled the coveralls down and slipped them off, balancing first on one leg, then the other, before balling them up and tossing them into the corner. In jeans and a red T-shirt, she thought he looked younger than he actually was.

'So what's on your agenda tonight?' she asked.

'Just the usual. Saving the world, feeding the hungry, fostering world peace.'

'It's amazing how much a person can do in a night if he puts his mind to it.'

'So true.' Mike gave a boyish grin. But as Julie ran a hand through her hair, he was suddenly struck by the same nervousness he'd felt the night before, when he'd first walked into the kitchen.

'How about you? Anything exciting planned?'

'No. I have a little cleaning to do at home and a few bills to pay. Unlike you, I have to take care of the little things before I set out to perfect the universe.'

Mike caught sight of Henry leaning against the doorjamb as he studied the stack of papers he was holding, pretending not to notice Mike and Julie, but making sure his presence was known, so that Mike wouldn't forget what he'd said earlier. Mike pushed his hands into his pockets. He didn't want to do this. He knew he had to, but he didn't want to. He took a deep breath.

'Hey, do you have a few minutes?' he asked. 'There's something I'd like to talk to you about.'

'Sure. What's up?'

'Would you mind going somewhere else? I think I need a beer first.'

Though puzzled by his sudden seriousness, Julie couldn't deny that she was pleased he'd asked.

'A beer sounds great,' she said.

*   *   *

A short walk up the street near the edge of downtown, Tizzy's was sandwiched between a pet shop and a dry cleaner's; like the Sailing Clipper, it was neither clean nor particularly comfortable. A television blared in the corner of the bar, the windows were chalky with dirt, and the air was filled with smoke that curled above the tables like the contents of a lava lamp. For those who visited Tizzy's regularly, none of those things were important, and there were half a dozen people who practically lived in the place. According to Tizzy Welborn, the owner, his bar was popular because 'it had character.' By character, Mike assumed he meant cheap booze.

On the plus side, Tizzy wasn't a real stickler for rules. Customers needed neither shoes nor shirts to get service, nor did he care what customers brought with them. Over the years, everything from samurai swords to inflatable dates had been dragged through the doors; despite Julie's rigorous denials, it was in this category that Singer also fell. As Mike and Julie settled onto a pair of stools at the far end of the bar, Singer circled once before lying down.

161

Tizzy took their order before setting two beers in front of them. Though not as chilled as they could be, they weren't warm, and Mike was thankful for that. In this place, a customer couldn't count on much.

Julie looked around. 'This place is such a dive. I always feel like I'll catch something contagious if I stay for more than an hour.'

'But it's got character,' Mike said.

'Sure it does, big spender. So what's so important that you felt the need to drag me here?'

Mike wrapped both hands around the bottle. 'It's something that Henry said I should do.'

'Henry?'

'Yeah.' He paused. 'He thought I should have said something yesterday. To you, I mean.'

'About what?'

'About Richard.'

'What about Richard?'

Mike sat up straighter in his seat. 'About him dropping off that note the other night.'

'What about it?'

'Henry thought it sounded a little weird. You know, him coming by in the middle of the night to do it.'

Julie looked at him skeptically. 'Henry was worried about that?'

'Yeah. Henry.'

'Mmm . . . but you weren't.'

'No,' Mike said.

Julie took a drink of her beer. 'Why was Henry so worried? It's not as if Richard were peeking in the windows. Singer would have gone through the glass if that happened. And the note did say there was an emergency, so maybe he left right away.'

'Well . . . there was something else that happened, too. The other day, someone from the bridge crew came into the garage and he said something kind of weird.'

'Like what?'

While running his fingernails through the carved grooves in the bar, Mike told her what Jake Blansen had said and went into a bit more detail about Henry's comments. When he'd finished, Julie put her hand on Mike's shoulder, her lips curling slowly into a smile.

'Oh, that's so sweet of Henry to worry about me like that.'

It took a moment for Mike to digest her response.

'Wait—you're not mad?'

'Of course I'm not mad. It makes me feel good to know that I've got friends like him who watch out for me.'

'But . . .'

'But what?'

'Well . . . uh . . .'

Julie laughed, gently nudging Mike's shoulder. 'C'mon, admit it—you were worried, too. It wasn't just Henry, was it?'

Mike swallowed. 'No.'

'Then why didn't you just say that at the beginning? Why put it all on Henry?'

'I didn't want you to be mad at me.'

'Why do you think I'd be mad at you?'

'Because . . . well, you know . . . you're dating the guy.'

'And?'

'I didn't want you to think . . . well, I wasn't sure you'd . . .'

Mike trailed off, not wanting to say it.

'You didn't want me to think that you were just saying it so I'd stop seeing him?' Julie asked.

'Yeah.'

Julie seemed to study him. 'Do you really have that little faith in our friendship? That I'd just ignore the last twelve years?'

Mike didn't answer.

'You know me better than anyone, and you're my best friend. I don't think there's anything you could say to me that would lead me to believe that you're doing it just to hurt me. If there's one thing I've come to know about you, it's that you're not even capable of something like that. Why do you think I like spending time with you so much? Because you're a good guy. A nice guy.'

Mike turned away, thinking she might as well have called him a eunuch.

'Nice guys finish last. Isn't that what people say?'

Julie used her finger to rotate his face back to hers and met his eyes. 'Some people. Not me, though.'

'And what about Richard?'

'What about him?'

'You've been spending a lot of time with him lately.'

She leaned back on her stool, as if trying to bring him into better focus.

'Why, if I didn't know better, I'd say you sound jealous about that,' she teased.

Mike took a drink of his beer, ignoring her comment.

'Don't be jealous. We went out on a few dates and had a few laughs. So what? It's no big deal. It's not like I'm planning on marrying the guy.'

164

'You're not?'

Julie snorted. 'You're kidding, right?' She paused, but Mike's expression made her answer her own question. 'You're not kidding, are you,' she said. 'What—did you think I was in love with him?'

'I had no idea.'

'Oh,' she said. 'Well, I'm not. I'm not even sure I'd go out with him again. And it's not because of what you just told me, either. Last weekend was great, it was fun, but it just wasn't there, you know? And then Monday, he just seemed a little off somehow, and I decided it wasn't worth it.'

'Really?'

She smiled. 'Really.'

'Wow.' It was all Mike could think to say.

'Yeah, wow.'

Tizzy walked past and turned the channel on the television to ESPN before checking to see if they wanted another drink. Both Julie and Mike shook their heads.

'So what's next, then?' Mike asked. 'Gonna see good old Bob again?'

'I hope I don't have to.'

Mike nodded. In the dinginess of the surroundings Julie was luminescent, and he felt his throat go dry. He took another drink of his beer.

'Well, maybe someone else will come along,' he offered.

'Maybe.' Julie rested her chin in her hand, holding his gaze.

'It won't take long. I'm sure there are a dozen guys just waiting for their chance to ask you out.'

'I only need one.' She smiled broadly.

'He's out there,' Mike declared. 'I wouldn't worry about it.'

165

'I'm not worried. I think I've got a pretty good handle now on what I'm looking for in a guy. Now that I've been out a few times, things are a little clearer. I want to find a good guy. A nice guy.'

'Well, you deserve one, that's for sure.'

Mike, Julie couldn't help but think, was sometimes as dense as marbles. She tried another tack.

'So what about you? You ever going to find someone special?'

'Who knows.'

'You will. If you look, that is. Sometimes they're right under your nose.'

Mike tugged at the front of his shirt. He hadn't realized how hot it was, but he felt as if he might start sweating if he didn't get out of here in a few minutes. 'I hope you're right,' he said.

Again they were silent.

'So,' she said, willing him to say something.

'So,' he said, glancing around the room.

Julie finally exhaled. I guess this is going to be up to me, she thought. If I wait for this Casanova, I'll be so old that he'll have to escort me in my walker.

'So what are you doing tomorrow night?' she asked.

'I haven't thought about it.'

'I was thinking we might go out.'

'Go out?'

'Yeah. There's a place on the island that's really nice. It's right on the beach, and I hear the food's pretty good.'

'Should I find out if Henry and Emma want to come?'

She brought her finger to her chin. 'Mmm . . . how about if it's just the two of us?'

166

'You and me?' He could feel his heart thumping beneath his ribs.

'Sure. Why not? Unless you don't want to, of course.'

'No, I want to,' he said a little too quickly, then immediately regretted it. Taking a deep breath, he forced him-self to calm down. Be cool, he thought. He gave her his James Dean look. 'I mean, I think I'll be able to work that out.'

Julie stifled a laugh.

'Gee,' she said, 'I appreciate that.'

*   *   *

'So you asked her out, huh?' Henry said.

Mike was leaning like a cowboy in an old western, one knee bent, his foot pressed against the wall, head angled downward. He was studying his fingernails, as if the whole thing were no big deal.

'It was time.' Mike gave an elaborate shrug.

'Well . . . good. And you're sure it's a date?'

Mike raised his eyes as if Henry's question tried his patience. 'Oh yeah. It's definitely a date.'

'So how did you do it? I mean, did it just come up?'

'I just worked into it. Slow-like. I just let the conversation go that way, and when the time was right, it happened.'

'Just like that, huh?'

'Just like that.'

'Mmm,' Henry said. He knew Mike was lying somehow, but he couldn't quite put his finger on it. It did, after all, *sound* as if they were going out on a date.

'So what did she say about Richard?'

Mike brushed his fingernails against his shirt and examined them. 'I think that's pretty much over now.'

'Did she say that?'

'Oh, yeah.'

'Huh,' Henry said. He was drawing a temporary blank as to what to say next. Couldn't tease him, couldn't offer advice, couldn't do anything without first figuring out why the whole sequence of events sounded a little fishy.

'Well, I guess all I can say is that I'm proud of you. It's about time that you two got the ball rolling.'

'Thanks, Henry.'

'No problem.' He motioned over his shoulder. 'Listen—I've got a little work left in the office, and I want to get home at a decent hour, so let me get back to it.'

'You got it.' Feeling just about as good as he'd ever felt in his life, Mike lowered his foot to the floor and headed back to the garage a moment later. Henry watched him go, then walked into his office, closing his door behind him. He picked up the telephone, dialed, and a moment later heard Emma's voice on the other end.

'You're never gonna believe what I just heard,' he said.

'What?'

Henry filled her in.

'Well, it's about time,' she crowed.

'I know. I said the same thing. But listen—do you think you could get Julie's side of the story?'

'I thought you said Mike told you all about it.'

'He did. But he's leaving something out.'

Emma paused. 'You're not planning anything, are

168

you? To sabotage this?'

'No, not at all. I just want to know how it really happened.'

'Why? So you can tease him?'

'Of course not.'

'Henry . . .'

'C'mon, sweetie. You know me. I wouldn't do anything like that. I just want to know where Julie's coming from, you know? Mike's taking this pretty seriously, and I don't want him to get hurt.'

Emma was quiet, and he knew she was wondering whether or not to believe him.

'Well, I haven't had lunch with her in a while.'

Henry nodded, thinking, That's my girl.

*　　　*　　　*

Julie unlocked the front door, carrying a bag of groceries and the mail, and staggered in the direction of the kitchen. Out of practically everything, she'd stopped at the store in hopes of picking up something healthy, but she'd grabbed a single serving of microwave lasagna instead.

Singer hadn't followed her in; he'd hopped out of the Jeep after it had stopped and taken off through the wooded lots that stretched to the Intracoastal Waterway. He wouldn't be back for a few minutes.

Julie popped the lasagna in the oven, changed into shorts and a T-shirt in her bedroom, then headed back to the kitchen. She thumbed through the mail—bills, assorted coupon mailers, a couple of mail-order catalogs—then set the whole stack off to the side. She wasn't in the mood to deal with those things right now.

She was going out with Mike, she thought. Mike.

She whispered his name aloud, checking to see if it sounded as unbelievable as it felt right now.

Yep.

As she was thinking, her eyes flashed to the answering machine and she noticed the blinking light. She hit play and Emma's voice came on, asking if she'd like to go to lunch on Friday. 'If you can't make it, give me a call. Otherwise, let's meet at the deli, okay?'

Sounds good to me, Julie thought. A moment later, the machine beeped and she heard Richard's voice come through. He sounded tired, as if he'd been swinging hammers all day.

'Hey, Julie. Just calling to check in, but I guess you're not around, huh? I'll be out most of the evening, but I'll be home tomorrow.' He paused, and she could hear him take a long breath. 'You can't believe how much I miss you right now.'

Julie heard the click as he hung up the phone. On the windowsill, she saw a finch hop twice before flying away.

Oh, boy, she suddenly thought, why do I get the feeling he's not going to take this very well?

Sixteen

Mike swung by Julie's the following evening a little before seven, dressed in Dockers and a white linen shirt. After turning off the truck engine, he slipped his keys into his pocket, grabbed the box of chocolates, and started up the walk, rehearsing what he was going to say. Even though she wanted him to be himself, he couldn't shake the desire to impress her, to dazzle her, really, starting with his opening line. After hours of contemplation, he'd decided on 'What a great idea to go to the beach. It's beautiful tonight,' not only because it sounded natural, but because it wouldn't sound as if he were coming on too strong. This was his chance, maybe his only chance, and he didn't want to go down in flames.

Julie stepped outside just as Mike was approaching the door and said something friendly, probably a greeting of some sort, but her voice, coupled with the staggering realization that *the date was actually happening!*, ruined his train of thought, and he forgot what he'd intended to say. In fact, he pretty much forgot about everything.

There were pretty women everywhere, he thought as he looked at her. There were women who made men turn their heads even if they had a date on their arm, there were women who could get off with a warning when a trooper pulled them over for speeding simply by batting their eyelashes.

And then there was Julie.

Most people would consider her attractive. There were flaws, of course—a nose that upturned slightly, a few too many freckles, hair that more often than not seemed to do as it pleased. But as Mike watched her start down the steps, her sundress billowing slightly in the spring breeze, he knew he'd never seen anyone more beautiful.

'Mike?' Julie said.

Okay, he thought, this is my chance. Don't blow it. I know exactly what to say. Just stay calm and let the words flow naturally.

'Mike?' Julie said again.

Her voice brought him back. Everything except

171

the opening line.

'Are you okay?' she asked. 'You look a little pale.'

Mike's mouth opened for a moment, then closed when he realized he didn't remember what he'd intended to say. Don't panic, he thought, beginning to panic. Whatever you do, *don't panic!* He decided to just trust himself and took a deep breath.

'I brought chocolate,' he finally said, holding out the box.

Julie looked at him. 'I see that. Thank you.'

'I brought chocolate'? That's all I could come up with?

'Hello?' Julie sang. 'Anyone there?'

The opening line . . . the opening line . . . Mike concentrated and felt the line beginning to take form in bits and pieces. Julie, however, was waiting for him to say something, anything.

'You're beautiful at the beach tonight,' he finally blurted out.

Julie studied him a moment, then smiled. 'Thank you. But we're not there yet.'

Mike shoved his hands into his pockets. Idiot!

'I'm sorry,' he said, not knowing what else to do.

'About what?'

'Not knowing what to say.'

'What are you talking about?'

Her expression was a curious blend of confusion and patience, and it was that, above all, that finally enabled Mike to figure out the right thing to say.

'Nothing,' he said. 'I guess I'm just glad to be here.'

Julie sensed the sincerity of his words.

'So am I,' she said.

Mike recovered slightly with that. He smiled but looked off into the distance, as if beginning a protracted, scholarly study of the neighborhood. He said nothing right away, unsure where to go from here.

'Well, you ready to go?' he asked at last.

'Whenever you are.'

As he turned and started toward the truck, Mike heard Singer bark from inside the house, and he looked over his shoulder.

'Singer's not coming?'

'I wasn't sure you'd want him along.'

Mike stopped. Singer, he thought, might ease his nerves by reducing expectations on both their parts. Kind of like a chaperon. 'He can come if you want. We'll be at the beach, and he'd love it.'

When she looked toward the house, Singer barked again. His face was in the window. She wanted him to come since he went practically everywhere with her, but then again, it was supposed to be a date. With Richard—or any of the other men she'd dated, for that matter—she'd hadn't even considered it.

'You sure you wouldn't mind?'

'Not at all.'

She smiled. 'Give me just a second to go open the door, okay?'

A couple of minutes later, as they were driving over the bridge that led to Bogue Banks, Singer barked again. He was in the bed of the pickup, his lips and tongue flapping in the wind, looking as pleased as a dog could look.

*   *   *

Singer curled up in the warmth of the sand in front of the restaurant as Julie and Mike took their seats

173

at a small table on the second-floor patio. Low-slung clouds were thinning out in the slowly darkening sky. The ocean breeze, always stronger on the island, made the flaps of the table umbrella move in steady rhythm, and Julie tucked her hair behind her ears to keep the strands from blowing into her face. The beach itself was largely empty—the crowds didn't start until after Memorial Day—and the waves rolled over the smooth swells of sand near the water's edge.

The restaurant itself was casual and pleasant, and because of its location right on the beach, most of the other tables were occupied. When the waiter came by, Julie ordered a glass of wine; Mike opted for a bottle of beer.

During the short ride over, they'd talked a little about what they'd done earlier that day; as usual, they touched on Mabel and Andrea, Henry and Emma. While they chatted, Mike tried to gather himself. He couldn't get over the fact that he'd mangled a full day's worth of planning when he'd botched the opening line, but somehow it had worked out anyway. He wanted to attribute it to his natural charm, but deep down he knew that Julie hadn't noticed simply because she didn't find it out of the ordinary. There was something disheartening about that, but on the plus side, at least she hadn't teased him about it.

During their first few minutes at the restaurant, Mike found it difficult to concentrate. After all, he'd thought of this moment pretty much every single day for the last couple of years. And he kept returning to the thought that—if he played this right—there was a chance he might kiss Julie later. When she lifted the wineglass and took a sip, puckering her lips as she did so, Mike knew it was one of the most sensual things he'd ever seen.

Through their drinks, he kept up a stream of conversation and even made her laugh a couple of times, but by the time dinner came, his nerves were so jangled that he couldn't remember much of anything that was said.

Get a hold of yourself, he thought.

*   *   *

Mike was not being himself.

Julie wasn't surprised. She knew it would take a while for him to loosen up. Still, she hoped it would happen a little sooner rather than later. She wasn't completely comfortable, either, and he wasn't exactly making it easy on her. The way his eyes kept boggling every time she touched her glass made her want to ask if he'd ever seen anyone drink wine before. The first time it happened, she thought he was trying to warn her that she was on the verge of swallowing a bug that had landed in her drink.

Tonight was different from the night he'd come over to fix her faucet, but she hadn't anticipated how awkward it might feel when she'd asked him out at Tizzy's yesterday. After all, Mike was not only a potential part of her future, he was a fixture in her past as well. And, of course, Jim's.

She'd thought about Jim more than once as they were eating and found herself comparing the two. What surprised her was that Mike, even while making this harder than it should be, was holding up fairly well. Mike would never be like Jim, but there was something about the way she felt when

175

she was with him that reminded her of the good times in her marriage. And she felt sure, as she had with Jim, that not only did Mike love her now, but there would never come a day when he wouldn't. There was only a brief moment during dinner when the feeling of betrayal forced its way to the forefront of her thoughts, leaving her with the impression that Jim was somehow watching over them, but it passed as quickly as it came. And for the first time, in its wake, she was left with a warm sensation, one that reassured her that Jim wouldn't be upset at all.

By the time they finished their dinner, the moon had risen, leaving a fan of white over the darkened water.

'Would you like to take a walk?' Mike suggested.

'That sounds great,' she said, putting her glass on the table.

Mike stood. Julie straightened her dress, then adjusted the strap that had fallen over her shoulder. Moving to the railing, Mike squeezed past her, and through the smell of salt and brine came the odor of his cologne, reminding her how much had suddenly changed. Mike leaned over, looking for Singer, his face passing through a shadow, but when he turned his head, the moonlight seemed to catch and hold the rough texture of his skin, giving him the appearance of someone she barely knew. His fingers, perched on wrought iron, were stained with grease, and she realized once again how different he was from the man who'd once walked her down the aisle.

No, she thought, I'm not in love with Mike.

Julie felt herself begin to smile. Not yet, anyway.

*   *   *

'You got kind of quiet there toward the end of dinner,' Mike said.

They were walking along the water's edge; they had taken off their shoes, and Mike had rolled up his pants legs to midshin. Singer wandered ahead of them, his nose to the ground, in search of crabs.

'Just thinking,' Julie murmured.

Mike nodded. 'About Jim?'

She glanced at him. 'How did you know?'

'I've seen that expression lots of times. You'd make a terrible poker player.' He tapped the side of his head. 'Nothing gets by me, you know.'

'Yeah? So what was I thinking, exactly?'

'You were thinking . . . that you were glad you married him.'

'Oh, now that's going out on a limb.'

'Was I right, though?'

'No.'

'So what were you thinking about?'

'It's not important. Besides, you don't want to know.'

'Why? Is it bad?'

'No.'

'Then tell me.'

'All right. I was thinking about his fingers.'

'His fingers?'

'Yeah. You have grease on your fingers. I was thinking that in all the time I was married to Jim, I never saw his fingers look like yours.'

Mike self-consciously moved his hands behind his back.

'Oh, I didn't mean it in a bad way,' she said. 'I know you're a mechanic. Your hands should

177

be dirty.'

'They're not dirty. I wash 'em all the time. They're just stained.'

'Don't be so defensive. You know what I mean. Besides, I kind of like it.'

'You do?'

'I guess I kind of have to. They come with the package.'

Mike's chest puffed out as they walked in silence for a few steps. 'So, do you think you'd like to go out tomorrow night? Maybe we could head into Beaufort.'

'That sounds like fun.'

'We might have to leave Singer this time,' he added.

'That's okay. He's a big boy. He can handle it.'

'Is there any place in particular you like to go?'

'It's your turn to pick. I've done my duty.'

'And you did it well.' Mike sneaked a look at her, reaching for her hand. 'What a great idea to go to the beach. It's beautiful tonight.'

Julie smiled as his fingers interlocked with hers. 'Yes, it is,' she agreed.

*   *   *

They left the beach a few minutes later when Julie started getting chilled. Mike was reluctant to let go of her hand, even when they reached his truck, but he didn't have a choice. He considered taking it again once he was in the car, but she'd put both hands in her lap and was staring out the side window.

Neither of them said much on the way home, and when he walked her to the door, he realized that he had no idea what she was thinking. He knew exactly what he was thinking, however—he hoped she would hesitate on the porch, right before they said their good-byes, giving him the chance to make sure his pucker was just right. Didn't want to blow this, either.

'I had a great time tonight,' he said.

'Me too. What time should I be ready tomorrow?'

'Seven o'clock?'

'Sounds great.'

Mike nodded, feeling like a teenager. This was it, he thought, the big moment. It all comes down to this.

'So,' he said, playing it cool.

Julie smiled, reading his thoughts. She reached for his hand and squeezed it before letting go.

'Good night, Mike. I'll see you tomorrow?'

It took a second to process the rejection, and he shifted his balance from one foot to the other, then back again. 'Tomorrow?' he asked uncertainly.

She opened her purse and began searching for the keys. 'Yeah. Our date, remember?'

She found the keys and slipped one into the lock, then looked up at him again. By then, Singer had joined them and she opened the door, letting him inside.

'And thanks again for a nice evening.'

She waved before following Singer into the house. When the door closed behind her, Mike simply stared before he realized she wasn't coming back out. A few seconds later, he left the porch, kicking at the gravel as he made his way to the truck.

*   *   *

Knowing she wouldn't be able to fall asleep, Julie began flipping through the pages of a catalog as she sat on the couch, replaying the evening. She was glad she hadn't kissed Mike on the porch, though she wasn't sure why. Maybe she just needed more time to adjust to her newfound feelings toward him.

Or maybe she just wanted to see him squirm. When he squirmed, he was cute in a way that only Mike could be. And Henry was right, he was fun to tease.

She picked up the remote and turned on the television. It was still early—not even ten o'clock yet—and she settled on a CBS drama about a small-town sheriff who feels compelled to risk his life to rescue people.

Twenty minutes later, just as the sheriff was about to save a youngster trapped in a burning car, she heard a knock at the door.

Singer rose quickly, bounding through the living room. He poked his head out the curtains, and she assumed that Mike had come back.

Then Singer started growling.

Seventeen

'Richard,' Julie said.

'Hey, Julie.' He held out a bouquet of roses. 'I picked these up at the airport on the way home. Sorry they're not as fresh as they should be, but there wasn't much of a selection.'

Julie stood in the doorway, Singer by her side. He'd stopped growling as soon as she'd opened the door, and Richard offered an open palm. He sniffed before looking up, making sure the face matched the familiar scent, then he turned away. *Oh, him*, he seemed to say. *Not thrilled with this, but okay*.

It wasn't so easy for Julie. She hesitated before taking the flowers, wishing he hadn't brought them.

'Thank you,' she said.

'I'm sorry for coming by so late, but I wanted to say hi before heading back to my place.'

'It's okay,' she said.

'I called earlier to let you know, but I guess you weren't in.'

'Did you leave a message?'

'No. I didn't have time. They were announcing final boarding and my seat wasn't confirmed. You know how it goes. I left you one yesterday, though.'

'Yeah'—she nodded—'I got that one.'

Richard brought his hands together in front of him. 'So, were you in?' he asked. 'Earlier, I mean?'

She felt her shoulders give a little. She didn't want to do this now.

'I was out with a friend,' she said.

'A friend?'

'You remember Mike? We grabbed a quick dinner.'

'Oh, yeah. From the bar that night, right?' he said. 'The guy who works in the garage?'

'That's the one.'

'Oh,' he said. He nodded. 'Have fun?'

'I haven't seen a lot of him lately, so it was nice to be able to catch up.'

'Good.' He glanced off to the side of the porch, then down at his feet, then at her again. 'Can I come in? I was hoping we might be able to talk for a few minutes.'

'I don't know,' she hedged. 'It's kind of late. I was just getting ready for bed.'

'Oh,' he said, 'that's fine. I understand. Can I see you tomorrow, then? Maybe we can have dinner.'

In the shadows his features seemed darker, but he smiled, as if he knew what her answer was going to be.

Julie blinked, holding her eyes closed for an extra instant. I hate that I have to do this, she thought, I hate it, I hate it, I hate it. Bob, at least, probably had the suspicion that the end was coming. Not Richard.

'I'm sorry,' she said, 'but I can't. I already made plans.'

'With Mike again?'

She nodded.

Richard absently scratched the side of his cheek, continuing to hold her gaze. 'So that's it, then? For us, I mean?'

Her expression answered for her.

'Did I do something wrong?' he asked.

'No,' she protested, 'it's not that.'

'Then . . . what is it? Didn't you have fun when we went out?'

'Yes, I had fun.'

'Then what is it?'

Julie hesitated. 'It's not about you at all, really. It's about Mike and me. We just seem . . . Well, I don't know how to explain it. What can I say?'

As she struggled for words, his jaw began to tighten and she could see the muscle flexing in his cheek. For a long moment, he said nothing.

'Must have been an exciting few days while I was gone, huh?' he said.

'Look, I'm sorry . . .'

'For what? For going behind my back as soon as I left? For using me to make Mike jealous?'

It took a moment for his words to register. 'What are you talking about?'

'You heard me.'

'I didn't use you . . .'

Richard ignored her, his tone becoming angrier. 'No? Then why are you ending this when we're still getting to know each other? And how did Mike suddenly get so interesting? I mean, I leave town for a few days, and the next thing I know, it's over between us and Mike has taken my place.' He stared at her, his lips beginning to turn white at the edges. 'It sure as hell sounds to me like you planned this all along.'

His outburst was so startling, so unexpected, that the words came out before she could stop them. 'You're a jerk.'

Richard continued to look at her for a long moment before finally glancing away. His anger suddenly gave way to an expression of hurt.

'This isn't fair,' he said softly. 'Please, I just want to talk for a minute, okay?' he pleaded.

When Julie looked at him, she was amazed to see tears forming in his eyes. The man was an absolute

183

roller coaster of emotions, she decided. Up, down, all around. 'Look, I'm sorry, Richard. I shouldn't have said what I did. And I didn't mean for you to get hurt. Really.' She paused, making sure he was listening. 'But it's late and we're both tired. I think I better head in before either of us says anything else. Okay?'

When Richard didn't respond, she took a step backward and began to close the door. Richard suddenly thrust his hand out, stopping her.

'Julie! Wait!' he said. 'I'm sorry. Please . . . I really need to talk to you.'

In the future, when she remembered this moment, she would always recall with shock how quickly Singer moved. Before she had time to process the fact that Richard had taken hold of the door, Singer had launched himself toward the hand, as if trying to catch a Frisbee in flight. Singer's jaw found its target, and Richard howled in pain as he tumbled over the threshold.

'Singer!' Julie screamed.

Richard fell to his knees, one arm extended as Singer shook his head from side to side, snarling.

'Stop him!' Richard screamed. 'Get him off me!'

Julie lunged toward Singer, grabbed his collar, and tugged hard. 'Let him go!' she commanded. 'Let him go, now!'

Despite the fury of the moment, Singer fell back immediately and Richard drew his hand instinctively to his chest, wrapping his other hand around it. Singer stood by Julie's side, fangs showing, the hair on his back standing up.

'Singer, *no!*' she cried, still stunned by the dog's ferocity. 'Is your hand okay?'

Richard moved his fingers, wincing. 'I don't think

anything's broken.'

Julie's hand traveled to Singer. His muscles were rigid, his eyes locked on Richard.

'I didn't even see him coming,' Richard said quietly. 'Remind me not to hold your door again when your dog's around.'

Though he spoke as if the incident were somewhat comedic, Julie didn't reply. Singer had acted instinctively to protect her, and she wasn't about to punish him for that.

Richard stood then, opening and closing his hand. Julie could see the indentations of Singer's teeth, though it didn't look as if he'd broken the skin. He moved a step farther away from her.

'I'm sorry,' he said. 'I shouldn't have tried to stop you from going inside. That was wrong of me.'

You got that right, she thought.

'And I shouldn't have gotten angry with you earlier, either.' He sighed. 'It's just that this came at the end of a really hard week. That's the reason I wanted to come by. I know it's no excuse, but . . .'

He sounded both sincere and contrite, but she held up her hands to stop him.

'Richard . . . ,' she said.

Her tone made it plain she didn't want to go into it again. Richard's eyes darted to the side. He stared, seemingly at nothing, the porch light flickering on his face, and Julie saw that she hadn't been mistaken about the earlier tears. His eyes were misting again.

When he spoke again, his voice was choked up, ragged.

'My mother died this week,' he whispered. 'I just came from her funeral.'

'That's why I had to leave the note on your Jeep that night,' Richard explained. 'The doctor said that I'd better catch the first flight I could because he wasn't even sure she'd last another day. I caught the first flight out of Raleigh on Tuesday morning, and with all the new security, I had to leave in the middle of the night to get there in time.'

A few minutes had passed, and Richard was sitting on Julie's couch, staring at the ground, still fighting the tears. It had taken a moment to register what he'd said, but once she did, she couldn't help but feel a jolt of sympathy for him. After she'd stammered out the usual—'I'm sorry' and 'Why didn't you tell me right away?'—Richard had broken down completely, and his tears had gotten to her. Julie had allowed him into the house after putting Singer in the bedroom. Now she was sitting across from him in the chair, listening as he spoke, thinking, Great timing, Julie. You can really pick your moments when it comes to breaking hearts, huh?

'I know it doesn't change what you told me on the porch, but I didn't want us to end with a fight. I enjoyed the time we spent too much for that.'

He cleared his throat and pressed his fingers against the lids of his eyes. 'It just seemed so sudden, you know? I wasn't prepared for what you told me.' He sighed. 'Hell, I wasn't prepared for much of anything. You can't imagine what it was like up there. Everything . . . the way she looked at the end, what the nurses were saying, the way it smelled . . .'

Both hands went to his face and she heard his

ragged breath, a series of quick intakes followed by a long exhale.

'I just needed to talk to someone. Someone I knew would listen.'

Oh . . . boy, Julie thought. Could this have possibly been any worse?

She forced a wan smile.

'We can talk,' she said. 'We're still friends, aren't we?'

*   *   *

Richard rambled on for a couple of hours, bouncing from subject to subject: his memories of his mother, what he was thinking when he first walked into the hospital room, how it felt the following morning to know he was holding her hand for the last time. After he'd been talking for a while, Julie offered him a beer; as the evening went on, he finished three without seeming to notice. Every now and then he'd pause and stare off to the side of the room, a dazed expression on his face, as if he'd forgotten what he was trying to say; other times he spoke as though he'd just downed a double espresso, the words running together. Throughout it all, Julie listened. She asked an occasional question when it seemed appropriate, but that was all. She saw tears more than once, but when they welled up, Richard would pinch the bridge of his nose to stop them.

Midnight came and went. The hands of the clock on the mantelpiece rolled past one, then began edging toward two. By then, the beer and emotional exhaustion had taken their toll. Richard had begun to repeat himself, and his words had

187

begun to slur. When Julie went to the kitchen for a glass of water for herself, she noticed that Richard's eyes had closed. Wedged into the corner of the couch, his head was angled against the back cushion, his mouth open. His breaths were coming in steady rhythm.

Holding the glass of water, she stood in place, thinking, Oh, this is just *great*. So what do I do now?

She wanted to wake him but didn't think he was sober enough to drive. She wasn't comfortable having him stay, but then again, he was already asleep, and if she woke him again, he might want to talk some more. Despite her willingness to listen if he needed her to, she was exhausted.

'Richard,' she whispered. 'You awake?'

Nothing.

A moment later, she tried again with the same result. She figured she could shout or nudge him awake, but considering the options, it seemed like more trouble than it was worth.

It's no big deal, she finally decided, he's out.

Julie turned out the lights and, leaving him where he was, headed back into the bedroom, closing and locking the door behind her. Singer was on the bed. He raised his head, watching as she slipped into her pajamas.

'It's only for tonight,' she explained, as if trying to convince herself she was doing the right thing. 'It's not like I'm changing my mind. It's just that I'm tired, you know?'

*   *   *

Julie woke at dawn, and after peeking at the clock,

188

she groaned and rolled over, trying to ward off the day. She was sluggish and felt as if she were suffering from a hangover.

After crawling out of bed, she cracked open the door to peek out; Richard still appeared to be sleeping. She hopped into the shower and dressed for work; she didn't want him to see her in her pajamas. By the time she entered the living room— with Singer moving warily beside her—Richard was sitting up on the couch, rubbing his face. His keys were perched on top of his wallet on the table in front of him.

'Oh, hey,' he said, looking embarrassed. 'I guess I conked out, huh? I'm sorry about that.'

'It was a long day,' she said.

'Yeah, it was,' he responded. He took a moment to reach for his wallet as he stood. A brief smile flickered across his face. 'Thanks for letting me stay last night. I appreciate it.'

'No problem,' she said. 'You gonna be okay?'

'I guess I have to be. Life goes on, right?'

His shirt was wrinkled, and he brushed at it with his hands. 'I'm sorry again for the way I acted last night,' he added. 'I don't know what got into me.'

Julie's hair hadn't dried completely, and she felt a drip of water soak through the fabric of her blouse.

'It's okay,' she said. 'And I know it must seem like it came out of the blue, but . . .'

He shook his head. 'No—it's fine. You don't have to explain—I understand. Mike seems like a nice guy.'

She hesitated. 'He is,' she finally said, 'but thank you.'

'I want you to be happy. That's all I ever wanted. You're a great person, and you deserve that.

Especially after listening to me drone on last night. You have no idea how much that meant to me. No hard feelings?'

'No hard feelings,' she repeated.

'Still friends?'

'Sure,' he said.

'Thanks.' Then, after a beat, he picked up his keys and started toward the door. Opening it, he looked over his shoulder.

'Mike's a lucky guy,' he called out. 'Don't forget that.' He smiled, but it carried with it a trace of melancholy. 'Good-bye, Julie.'

When he finally got in the car, Julie felt herself exhale, thankful that it had gone a lot better than she'd thought it would. Then, frowning, she changed her mind. Well, better than last night, anyway. Anything was better than that.

But at least it's over now.

Eighteen

Inside the rented Victorian, Richard made his way up the stairs to the corner room. He'd painted the walls black and covered the windows with duct tape and a light-blocking tarp; a red light dangled over a makeshift table along the far wall. His photography equipment was in the corner: four different cameras, a dozen lenses, boxes of film. He turned on the lamp and angled the shade so the light could fan out better.

Near the shallow containers of chemicals he used to develop the film was a stack of photographs that he'd taken on his date with Julie, and he reached for them.

He thumbed through the images, pausing every now and then to stare at her. She'd looked happy that weekend, he thought, as if she'd known her life had suddenly changed for the better. And lovely, too. In studying her expressions, he couldn't find anything to explain what had happened last night.

He shook his head. No, he wouldn't hold her mistake against her. Anyone who could move from anger to empathy as effortlessly as she had was a treasure, and he was lucky to have found her.

He knew quite a bit about Julie Barenson now. Her mother was a drunk with a preference for vodka who lived in a ramshackle trailer on the outskirts of Daytona. Her father was currently in Minnesota, living with another woman and surviving on a disability check for a mishap that had occurred while working construction. They'd been married two years before he'd left town suddenly; Julie was three years old at the time. Six different men had lived with Julie and her mother at one time or another, the shortest for a month, the longest for two years. Moved half a dozen times, always from one dump to the next.

A different school every other year until high school. First boyfriend at fourteen; he played football and basketball, and a picture of them together had made the yearbook. Appeared as a minor character in two school plays. Dropped out before graduation and vanished for a few months before coming here.

He had no idea what Jim had done to entice her to a place like Swansboro.

Happy marriage, bland husband. Nice, but bland.

He'd also learned about Mike from one of the

locals after he'd met him at the Clipper. Amazing how buying a few drinks at a bar can accomplish so much.

Mike was in love with Julie, but Richard had already known that. He hadn't known about the demise of his previous relationship, however, and Sarah's infidelity had intrigued him. He remembered nodding as he'd considered the possibilities that had suddenly opened up.

He'd also learned that Mike had been best man at Julie's wedding, and their relationship began to make sense to him. Mike was comfortable, a link to her past, a link to Jim. He understood Julie's desire to hold on to that, to pull away from anything that might take that away. But it was a desire born of fear—fear of ending up like her mother, fear of losing everything for which she'd worked so hard, fear of the unknown. He wasn't surprised that Singer slept in the room with her, and he suspected that she'd locked her bedroom door as well.

So careful, he thought. It was probably something she'd been doing even as a child, considering the men her mother had brought home. But there was no reason to live that way. Not anymore. She could move forward, as he had.

Their childhoods probably weren't that different after all. The drinking. The beatings. The cockroach-infested kitchen. The smell of mold and rotting drywall. The soupy well water from the tap that made him sick to his stomach. His only escape had been through the photographs in books by Ansel Adams, photographs that seemed to whisper of other places, better places. He'd discovered the books in the school library, and he'd spent long hours studying them, losing himself in the surreally beautiful landscapes. His mother had noticed his interest, and though Christmas was usually a dismal affair, she'd somehow persuaded his father to spend money on a small camera and two boxes of film when Richard was ten years old. It was the only time in his life that he could remember shedding tears of happiness.

He spent hours photographing items in the house or birds in the backyard. He took pictures at dusk and dawn because he liked the light at those hours; he became adept at moving silently, obtaining close-ups that seemed impossible. When he finished a roll of film, he would run inside and beg his father to have them developed. When the photos were ready, he would stare at them in his bedroom, trying to assess what he'd done right or wrong.

In the beginning, his father seemed amused at his interest and even glanced through the first couple of rolls. Then the comments started. 'Oh, look, another bird,' he'd say sarcastically, and, 'Gee, here's another one.' Eventually he began to resent the money being spent on his son's new hobby. 'You're just pissing it away, aren't you?' he'd snarl, but instead of suggesting that Richard do some chores around the neighborhood to pay for the developing himself, his father decided to teach him a lesson.

He'd been drinking again that night, and both Richard and his mother were trying to stay out of his way, doing their best not to be noticed. As Richard sat in the kitchen, he could hear his father ranting as he watched a football game on television. He'd bet on his favorite team—the Patriots—but had lost, and Richard heard his father's anger as he pounded down the hall. A moment later his father walked into the kitchen with the camera, and he set it on the table. In his other hand was a hammer. After making sure he had his son's attention, he smashed the camera with a single swing.

'I work all week to make a living and all you want to do is *piss it away!* Now we won't have this problem anymore!'

Later that year, his father died. The memories of that event were vivid as well: the cut of morning sunlight on the kitchen table, the vacant look on his mother's face, the steady drip of the faucet as the hours rolled toward afternoon. The officers spoke in hushed tones as they came and went; the coroner examined and removed the body.

And then, the wailing of his mother, once they were finally alone. 'What will we do without him?' she sobbed, shaking him by the shoulders. 'How could this have happened?'

This was how: His father had been drinking at O'Brien's, a dingy bar in Boston not far from their home. According to people at the bar, he'd played one game of pool and lost, then sat at the bar the rest of the night, drinking boilermakers. He'd been laid off at the plant two months earlier and had been spending most nights there, an angry man looking for pity and solace in the company of alcoholics.

By that time, Vernon was beating both of them regularly, and the night before he'd been particularly brutal.

He left the bar a little past ten, stopped at the corner market for a pack of cigarettes, and drove past the houses in the blue-collar neighborhood where he lived. A neighbor who was walking his dog saw him as he was nearing home. The garage had been left open, and Vernon pulled the car into the small space. Boxes were piled against both walls.

This was where the speculation began, however. That he had closed the garage door, there was no doubt, evidenced by the high levels of carbon monoxide. But why, the coroner wondered, hadn't he turned the engine off first? And why did he get back into the car after closing the garage door? For all intents and purposes, it looked like a suicide, though his friends at O'Brien's insisted there wasn't a chance he would have done something like that. He was a fighter, not a quitter, they said. He wouldn't have killed himself.

The officers came back to the house two days later, asking open-ended questions and looking for answers. The mother wailed incoherently; the ten-year-old offered only his steady gaze. By then, the bruises on the faces of the mother and son had begun to green at the edges, giving them both a haunted appearance. The officers left with nothing.

In the end, it was ruled an accident, and the death was attributed to alcohol.

A dozen people attended the funeral. His mother wore black and cried into a white handkerchief as he stood beside her. Three people spoke at the graveside, offering kind words for a man who was momentarily down on his luck but was otherwise a good human being, a steady provider, a loving husband and father.

The son played his part well. He kept his eyes downcast; at times, he brought his finger to his cheek as if to swipe at a tear. He slipped his arm around his mother, and nodded grimly and said thank you when others came up to offer their condolences.

The next day, however, when the crowds were gone, he returned to the grave and stood in front of the freshly turned earth.

Then, he spat on it.

In the darkroom, Richard tacked one of the photographs to the wall, reminded that the past casts long shadows. It's easy to get confused, he thought. He knew she couldn't help it, and he understood. He forgave her for what she had done.

He stared at her image. How could he not forgive her?

Nineteen

Because she was already dressed by the time Richard left, Julie had enough time to stop and grab a newspaper before she went into work. She sat at a small table outside a bagel shop, sipping coffee and reading, while Singer lounged at her feet.

Putting aside the newspaper, she watched the quiet downtown come to life. One by one, signs in store windows were flipped, doors propped open to catch the early morning breeze. The sky was cloudless, and there was a hint of dew on the windshields of cars that had been parked on the street overnight.

Julie rose, offered the newspaper to a couple at the next table, tossed her empty cup into the garbage, and started up the street toward the salon.

The garage had already been open for an hour, and thinking she still had a few minutes before she had to be at work, she decided, Why not? I'm sure he's not too busy yet. Besides, she wanted to drop in to make sure that what she'd been feeling the night before wasn't her imagination.

She didn't intend to tell Mike that Richard had ended up spending the night. Try as she might, she couldn't think of any way to tell him that wouldn't seem suspect, especially in light of what had happened with Sarah. He would always wonder about it, she felt, creating a stubborn splinter of doubt and hurt. Anyway, it wasn't important. It was over now, and that's all that mattered.

She crossed the street, Singer trotting ahead. By the time she walked past the cars waiting to be serviced, Mike was already making his way toward her, looking as though he'd just picked the winning ticket in the lottery.

'Hey, Julie,' he said. 'What a nice surprise.'

Though he had a streak of grease on his cheek and his brow was already shiny with sweat, she couldn't help but think, You look pretty darn good. And I'm definitely not imagining it.

'Yeah, I'm happy to see you, too, big guy,' Mike added, reaching toward Singer. It was while he was petting Singer that she noticed the Band-Aids.

'Hey, what happened to your fingers?'

Mike glanced at his hands. 'Oh, it's nothing. They're just a little sore this morning.'

'Why?'

'I guess I kind of scrubbed 'em too hard last night after I got home.'

She frowned. 'Because of what I said on the beach?'

197

'No,' he said. Then, shrugging, he added, 'Well, I guess that was *part* of the reason.'

'I was just teasing.'

'I know,' he said. 'But I got to wondering whether a new soap might work better.'

'So what did you use? Ajax?'

'Ajax, 409, Lysol. I pretty much tried everything.'

She put her hands on her hips and studied him. 'You know, sometimes I can't help wondering what you'll be like when you grow up.'

'I don't think there'll be much chance of that, to tell you the truth.'

She laughed, thinking, *I like this guy*. How could I not?

'Well, I just wanted to drop in to tell you I had a great time last night.'

'Me too,' he said. 'And I'm looking forward to tonight.'

'It should be fun.'

Their eyes met before Julie glanced at her watch. 'But listen, I should probably be going. I've got appointments all morning, and I'm supposed to have lunch with Emma, so I can't fall behind.'

'Say hi to Emma for me, will you?'

'Sure,' she said. 'Have fun today.'

'You too.'

She winked. 'And watch those fingers, will you? I'd hate to think you'll be bleeding all over the engines you work on.'

'Ha, ha,' he said. Not that he minded being teased. He knew this was her way of flirting with him. Real flirting, not friendly flirting.

And by God, he liked that! He liked that a lot!

They said good-bye, and a moment later Julie was crossing the street with a bounce in her step.

*   *   *

'So it looks like your date went pretty well, huh?' In his hand, Henry held a half-eaten doughnut.

Mike hooked his thumb into his coveralls and sniffed. 'Oh yeah,' he said. 'It went *real* well.'

Henry waved the doughnut and shook his head. 'Will you cut the James Dean stuff, little brother? I'm telling you—it's not you. And it can't hide the cross-eyed goofy look in your eyes, either.'

'I don't look goofy.'

'Goofy. Love-struck. Whatever.'

'Hey, I can't help it if she likes me.'

'I know you can't. You're just irresistible, aren't you?'

'I thought you'd be happy for me.'

'I am happy,' he said. 'And I'm proud of you, too.'

'Why?'

'Because somehow, whatever your plan was, it looks like it worked.'

*   *   *

'So what happened with Richard?' Emma asked. 'At the bar the other night, it looked like you two were getting along great.'

'Oh, you know how it goes . . . He was nice, but I just didn't feel anything for him.'

'I guess it was the way he looked, huh?'

'That part, I'll admit, wasn't so bad,' Julie said, and Emma laughed.

They were having salads at the deli, formerly a home in the historic district. Sunlight spread across the table in the corner, collecting in their glasses of

199

tea and making them glow amber.

'I said the same thing to Henry after I got home. I kept asking why he didn't look that way anymore.'

'What did he say?'

'He said . . .' Emma sat up in her seat and lowered her voice, mimicking Henry. '"I don't know what you're talking about, but if I wasn't sure you loved me so much, I'd think you just insulted me."'

Julie laughed. 'You sound exactly like him.'

'Honey, when you've been married as long as I've been, you'll find out that it's not all that hard to do. The only thing I'm missing is the waving doughnut.'

Julie giggled into her tea, spilling a bit on the table. 'But he still makes you happy, right? Even after all this time?'

'Most of the time he's a pretty good guy. Sometimes I want to whack him with the frying pan, but I guess that's normal, right?'

Julie's eyes took on a mischievous gleam as she leaned forward in her seat. 'Did I ever tell you I once threw a pan at Jim?'

'You did? When did that happen?'

'I can't remember. I don't even remember what we were fighting about, but I launched that pan right at him. It missed, but I had his attention after that.'

Emma's eyebrows went up and down. 'Life behind closed doors is always a mystery, isn't it?'

'I'll say.'

Emma took a sip of her tea, then started on her salad again. 'So what's this I hear about Mike?'

Julie had known this was coming. In lieu of politics or sports or the latest headlines, people in this small town thrived on the goings-on of its citizens.

'That depends on what you heard.'

'I heard he asked you out and that you went to dinner.'

'Kind of. Actually, I was the one who asked him out.'

'He couldn't do it?'

She looked over her glass. 'What do you think?'

'Mmm . . . I think he probably froze up like a shallow pond in winter.'

Julie laughed. 'Pretty much.'

'So how was it? What did you do?'

Julie recounted their date, and when she was finished, Emma leaned back in her seat.

'Sounds like it went well.'

'It did.'

She studied Julie's face for a moment. 'And, what about . . . you know . . . Did you think about . . .' She trailed off, and Julie finished for her.

'Jim?'

Emma nodded, and Julie considered it. 'Not as much as I thought I would,' she said. 'And it didn't really bother me at all by the end. Mike and I . . . we just get along so well. He makes me laugh. He makes me feel good about myself. It's been a long time since I felt that way.'

'You sound surprised.'

'I was. To be honest, I wasn't sure how it would go.'

Emma's face softened. 'That's not surprising. You and Jim were really something. We used to joke about the way you stared at each other when we went out.'

'Yeah, we were something,' she said, a touch of wistfulness entering her voice.

201

Emma paused. 'How did Mike seem?'

'Fine, I guess. He was pretty nervous, to tell you the truth, but I don't think it had much to do with Jim. I think it had more to do with the date itself.'

'Oh, gee, really?'

Julie smiled. 'Really. But I had a good time.'

'So . . . do you like him?'

'Of course I like him.'

'No. I mean, do you *like* him?'

That's what it came down to, didn't it? Julie thought. In the end, she didn't need to answer; her expression spoke volumes, and Emma reached across the table to squeeze Julie's hand.

'I'm glad. I always figured this was coming.'

'You did?'

'I think everyone did, with the exception of you and Mike. It was just a matter of time.'

'You never said anything.'

'I didn't have to. I figured that you'd recognize the same things in Mike that I do when you were good and ready.'

'Like what?'

'That he'll never let you down. That boy's got a heart the size of Kentucky, and he loves you. That's important. Take it from someone who knows. My mom used to tell me that whatever you do, marry someone who loves you more than you love him.'

'No she didn't.'

'Of course she did. And I listened to her. Why do you think Henry and I get along so well? I'm not saying that I don't love him, because I do. But if I ever left Henry or something, God forbid, ever happened to me, I don't think he'd be able to go on. And the guy would risk his life for mine in a heartbeat.'

202

'And you think Mike's that way?'
'Honey, you can bet your bottom dollar on it.'

*　　　*　　　*

Julie was still thinking about her lunch with Emma when she left the salon at the end of the day.

Thinking about a lot of things, actually. Especially Jim. No doubt that wasn't Emma's intention, and even Julie couldn't put her finger on exactly why she was feeling as she did, but it had something to do with Emma's comment about her mother. And, of course, Emma's remark about Henry not being able to go on if he ever lost her.

That afternoon, she'd missed Jim more than she had in a long time. She supposed it was because of what was happening with Mike. She was moving on, but she began to wonder if Jim would have been able to, had their positions been reversed. She thought he probably would have, but if not, did that mean he had loved her more than she'd loved him? And what will happen, she wondered, if I do fall in love with Mike? What would happen to her feelings for Jim? Her memories of Jim? Those were the questions that cycled endlessly through her mind after lunch, questions with answers she didn't want to face. Would her memories gradually diminish, she wondered, fading away like decaying photographs?

She didn't know. Nor did she know why the prospect of seeing Mike tonight left her feeling more nervous than she'd been yesterday. More nervous than she'd felt about any of her other dates, for that matter. Why now?

Maybe, she thought, answering her own question, it's because I know this one is different.

Julie reached the Jeep and got in; Singer hopped into the back, and Julie started the engine. She didn't head toward home. Instead, she followed the main street for a few blocks and took a left, heading toward the outskirts of town. A few minutes later, after another turn, she reached Brookview Cemetery.

Jim's headstone was a short walk away, just over the rise and off the main path, in the shade of a hickory tree. Julie made her way up the path. When she got close, Singer stopped, refusing to follow any farther. He never had. In the beginning, she wasn't sure why Singer always stayed back, but over time she came to think that somehow he knew she wanted to be alone here.

She reached the gravesite and stood over it, not knowing what she would feel today. She took a deep breath, waiting for the tears to come, but they didn't. Nor did she feel the heaviness she always had in the past. She pictured Jim in her mind, recalling the happy times, and though a faint feeling of sadness and loss came with the memories, it was like hearing a clock tower chime in the distance, echoing softly before finally fading away. In its place, there was a numbness; she wasn't sure what it meant until she saw the winged angel etched above his name, the one that always reminded her of the letter that had come with Singer.

It would break my heart if I thought you'd never be happy again . . . Find someone who makes you happy . . . The world is a better place when you smile.

Standing by his grave, she suddenly realized that maybe *this* was what he'd meant by those words. And as she had the night before, she suddenly knew Jim would be happy for her.

No, she thought, I won't forget you. Ever. And neither will Mike.

That's what makes him different, too.

She stayed until the mosquitoes began to circle. One landed on her arm and she slapped it away, glad she'd come but knowing she should probably be going. Mike was going to pick her up in less than an hour, and she wanted to be ready.

A breath of wind shook the leaves above, sounding like the faint rattle of shaken pebbles in a jar. After a moment it stopped, as if someone had muted the sound. But then it wasn't quiet anymore; from the road she heard a passing car, the sound of the engine rising and falling, before disappearing. A child's voice carried from the distant houses. There was a faint brushing sound, something scraping the bark of a nearby tree. A cardinal broke from the branches, and glancing over her shoulder, Julie saw Singer swivel his head, his ears twitching. He remained rooted in place, however, and Julie saw nothing. She frowned slightly and crossed her arms. Turning from the headstone, she tucked her head down and began walking toward the car, goose pimples lifting the hairs on her arms.

Twenty

Mike appeared right on time, and Julie stepped out, closing the door behind her before Singer had the chance to get out. Noticing that he was wearing a jacket and slacks, she smiled.

'Wow,' she said, 'that's two nights in a row that you're looking pretty spiffy. This is going to take a little while to get used to.'

Julie could have been talking about herself. Like the night before, tonight she was wearing a sundress that accentuated her figure. Small gold hoops dangled from each ear, and Mike caught the slightest trace of perfume.

'Too much?' he asked.

'Not at all,' she reassured him. She touched his lapel. 'I like this—is it new?'

'No, I've had it for a while. I just don't wear it that much.'

'You should,' she said. 'It looks good on you.'

Mike rolled his shoulders and motioned toward the truck before she could dwell any further on it.

'So—you ready to go?'

'Whenever you are.'

As he began to turn, Julie reached for his arm. 'Where are the Band-Aids?'

'I took 'em off. My fingers are better now.'

'Already?'

'What can I say? I'm a quick healer.'

Standing on the porch, she held out her hand like a teacher requesting that a student spit out his gum, and Mike held them out.

'They still look red to me.' She paused before

looking up with a curious expression. 'How hard did you scrub? It looks like a couple of them were bleeding.'

'It stopped,' he said.

'Goodness,' she said. 'If I had known what you'd do, I wouldn't have said anything. But I think I've got something that'll make them feel better.'

'Like what?'

Julie held his eyes as she raised his hand to her mouth and kissed his fingertips.

'There. How's that?' she asked, smiling.

Mike cleared his throat. Like I was holding on to a live electric wire, he thought. Or standing in a wind tunnel. Or flying down a mountain on skis.

'Better,' he managed to answer.

*   *   *

They ate dinner at the Landing, a waterfront restaurant in downtown Beaufort. As on the night before, they opted to sit at a table on the patio, from which they could watch the boats pulling into and out of their slips. On the planked boardwalk, couples and families passed by holding ice-cream cones or bags filled with tourist mementos.

Julie put her napkin in her lap and leaned forward.

'Good choice, Mike,' she said. 'I love this place.'

'I'm glad,' he said, relieved. 'I like it, too, but I usually come for lunch. I haven't had dinner here in a while. I'd feel funny coming by myself for dinner.'

'You could always come with Henry.'

'I could,' he said, nodding. 'Or not.'

'You don't like going out with Henry?'

207

'I spend all day with him. It would be like you going out with Mabel.'

'I like going out with Mabel.'

'Mabel doesn't insult you.'

Julie laughed, and Mike put his napkin in his lap. Julie appeared relaxed and radiant to him, completely at ease in her surroundings.

'How'd your lunch go with Emma?' he asked.

'Oh, it was fun. She's easy to talk to.'

'Like me?'

'No, not like you. You're easy, too, but in a different way. I can talk to her about things that we don't.'

'Like me?' he said again.

She gave him a sly wink. 'Of course. What good is going out with somebody if you can't tell people about it?'

'What did you say? Good stuff, I hope.'

'Don't worry. It was all good.'

Mike smiled as he reached for the menu. 'So would you like to start with a bottle of wine? Perhaps a Chardonnay? I was thinking the Kendall-Jackson might be nice. It's not too heavy, and I think the oak flavor is just about right.'

'Wow,' she said, 'I'm impressed. I didn't realize you knew so much about wine.'

'I am a man of many talents,' he admitted, and Julie laughed as she picked up her menu.

They lingered over wine and dinner, talking and laughing, barely noticing the waiter scurrying about the table, collecting their plates. By the time they were ready to go, the sky was filled with stars.

The boardwalk was still bustling, but the crowd was younger now; people in their twenties and thirties leaned against the railings that overlooked the water and milled around the bars. A few steps down the boardwalk there were two patio restaurants, and in each, an entertainer was setting up his equipment and making the final adjustments to his guitar. More boats had arrived than the slips could hold, and in the spirit of Friday night, the late arrivals tied up to the boat nearest to them until a few dozen of varying shapes and sizes were clustered together like a floating shantytown. Beers and cigarettes were exchanged freely, boats rocking as people used them like bobbing sidewalks, and strangers were forced to become chummy with people they'd probably never see again, all in the name of having a good time.

As they left the restaurant, Mike offered his hand. Julie took it, and as they began to stroll the boardwalk, their shoes clicking against the wood like the clip-clop of tethered carriage horses, Mike felt the warmth of her hand radiate up his arm, right toward the center of his chest.

* * *

They spent another hour in Beaufort, watching and talking until Julie felt any last traces of nervousness evaporate completely. Mike still held her hand, his thumb sometimes tracing the back of hers. They stopped for a piece of fudge and walked shoeless through the grassy park before finding a place to sit and enjoy it. The moon had risen and the stars had shifted by the time they returned to the still-lively boardwalk. Lazy waves slapped against the seawall, and the white glow of the reflected moon slipped across the water. They stopped once more to sit at a weathered table beneath the rotating blades of a

209

creaky ceiling fan. The singer at the restaurant nodded toward Mike—it was obvious they knew each other—and Mike ordered another beer while Julie sipped a Diet Coke.

As they listened, Julie could feel Mike's eyes on her, and she marveled at how much had changed in the past couple of days. How much she had changed. And how much, she thought, was about to change from this point on.

It was funny that you could know someone for years but still discover something you never noticed before. Despite the hazy lighting, she could see traces of gray in the hair near Mike's ears; she could see a tiny scar beneath the fold of his brow. Two days ago, she would have said he looked to be in his late twenties; now she could make out smile lines on his cheek and crow's-feet at the corners of his eyes.

The musician eased into another song, and Mike leaned toward her.

'Jim and I used to come here a lot,' he said. 'Before you moved to town. Did you know that?'

'He told me. He said that you two used to come here to meet women.'

'Did you know that we were here when he first told me about you?'

'Here?'

'Yeah. We were here the weekend after he came back from Daytona. He told me about this girl he'd met.'

'What did he tell you?'

'That he bought you breakfast a few times. And that you were pretty.'

'I looked terrible.'

'He didn't think so. He also said that he promised

you he'd find you a job and a place to live if you came up here.'

'Did you think he was crazy?'

'Without a doubt. Especially because he couldn't seem to stop talking about you.'

'So what did you think when I took him up on it?'

'I thought you were crazy, too. But after that, I got to thinking you were brave.'

'You didn't.'

'Sure I did. It takes guts to change your life like you did.'

'I didn't have any choice.'

'You always have a choice. It's just that some people make the wrong one.'

'My, aren't we feeling philosophical tonight.'

'It happens sometimes when I've had a couple of drinks.'

The music stopped then, and their conversation was interrupted when the singer put down his guitar and came over to their table to whisper something in Mike's ear.

Julie leaned forward. 'What's going on?' she asked.

The singer looked up. 'Oh, hey. Sorry for interrupting. I'm taking a break and wanted to know if Mike would like to take over for a song or two,' he said.

Mike turned toward the setup and stared before finally shaking his head.

'I would, but I'm on a date,' he said.

'Oh, go ahead,' Julie urged. 'I'll be fine.'

'You sure you wouldn't mind?'

'Not at all. Besides, it's obvious you want to.'

Mike grinned and put his bottle on the table; a minute later, the guitar strap was over one shoulder and he was plucking a couple of strings, tuning it. He glanced at Julie, then winked before strumming the first chords. It took only a moment before everyone recognized the song. First, they clapped and hooted, a couple of people whistled; and then, to Julie's surprise, people began to wave their beers in time as they sang along.

He'd chosen a crowd pleaser on boozy nights, that perennial juke-box favorite 'American Pie.'

His voice, she observed, was typically out of tune, but tonight, with this crowd, it didn't matter. They sang and swayed along in time, Julie included.

When Mike finished, he put down the guitar to a nice round of applause and started back toward the table, offering those who patted him on the back an 'it was no big deal' expression. Julie watched him with a mixture of newfound admiration and pleasure.

Mike, she thought, had just made a really nice night even better.

A little later, when they were leaving, the bartender told them that their bill had already been taken care of.

'One of your fans, I guess,' he said.

*　　　*　　　*

During the ride home, Julie felt pleasantly surprised at how much fun the evening had been. Mike walked her to the door, and when she turned to face him, she could see in his face that he was thinking about kissing her, but after what had happened the night before, he was unsure how to go about it. Julie looked up at him, giving him the official go-ahead, but instead of moving closer,

Mike missed her signal.

'Listen, I had a great time tonight—'

'Would you like to come in for a few minutes?' Julie said, cutting him off. 'There might be an old movie on that we can watch for a little while.'

'Are you sure it's not too late?'

'Not for me. But if you'd rather head on . . .'

'No, I'd love to come in.'

She unlocked the door and led him in. Singer had been waiting at the door and greeted them both before he headed outside. He pointed his nose in the air and barked once, then lowered his head to sniff the yard as if satisfied there were no critters in need of a good chase. A minute later, he'd vanished into the shadows of the trees.

Inside, Mike took off his jacket and slung it over the recliner as Julie went to the kitchen and brought back two glasses of water. Mike was still standing, and she motioned toward the couch. They sat, close but not touching, as Julie picked up the remote and started flicking through the channels. Though they didn't find a movie worth watching, they did find an old episode of *I Love Lucy*, and they laughed through that. That was followed by *The Dick Van Dyke Show*.

By the time the show ended, Singer had returned to the front door and barked again. At the same time, Julie yawned.

'I guess it's about time for me to go,' Mike said as he stood from the couch. 'Looks like you're getting tired.'

She nodded. 'Let me walk you out.'

At the door, Mike turned the handle and pulled; Singer pushed past them on his way to the living room as if he, too, knew it was time to go to bed.

213

As she watched Mike struggle into his sport coat in the open doorway, Julie flashed to the fact that he had been her friend for years and that moving forward possibly meant the end of all that. Was it worth the risk? she wondered. She wasn't sure.

And would kissing Mike be a lot like kissing her brother? If she had one, that is?

She didn't know that, either.

But like a gambler at a slot machine, hoping the next spin would change her life for the better, she closed in before she lost her nerve. Taking his hand, she pulled him toward her, near enough to feel his body against her. She looked up at him, tilting her head slightly as she leaned in. Mike, recognizing what was happening but still having trouble believing it, tilted his head and closed his eyes, their faces drawing near.

On the porch, moths were fluttering around the light, bouncing against it as if trying to break through the glass. An owl called from the nearby trees.

Mike, however, heard nothing at all. Lost in her breathlike touch, he knew only one thing for sure: In the instant their lips first met, there was a flicker of something almost electrical that made him believe the feeling would last forever.

*   *   *

That was nice, Julie thought. Actually, even better than she'd thought it would be. And it was definitely *not* like kissing her brother.

She was still thinking about it after she'd heard him crank the engine of his truck and disappear down the street. She was smiling and had reached to turn off the lamp when she caught a glimpse of Singer.

He was staring at her, his head angled and ears up, as if asking, *Did I just see what I thought I saw?*

'What?' she said. 'We kissed.' She collected the glasses from the table, still feeling Singer's eyes on her. For some reason, it felt almost as if she were a teenager who'd been caught by a parent.

'It's not like you've never seen me kiss someone before,' she continued.

Singer kept staring.

'It's no big deal,' she said, heading toward the kitchen. She put the glasses in the dishwasher and turned on the light above the faucet. When she turned, a shadow loomed and she jumped back before she recognized what it was.

Singer had entered the kitchen. He was sitting next to the counter, looking at her with the same expression. Julie put her hands on her hips.

'Would you stop staring at me like this? And quit following me around. You scared me.'

With that, Singer finally glanced away.

That's better, she thought. She picked up a rinse rag, ran the top over it, and started wiping the counter before deciding to leave the kitchen until tomorrow. Instead, she tossed the rag in the sink and headed back to the bedroom, her mind already replaying scenes from the evening. She felt herself blush a little.

All in all, she decided, Mike was a very good kisser.

Lost in thought, she barely registered the sweep of headlights as a car rolled down her normally quiet street, slowing as it passed her house.

*   *   *

'You awake!' Julie asked into the receiver the following morning.

Mike struggled with the sheet and sat up in bed as he recognized her voice. 'I am now.'

'So come on. The day's a-wastin',' she said. 'Up and at 'em, Private.'

Mike rubbed his eyes, thinking that she sounded as if she'd been up for hours. 'What are you talking about?'

'The weekend. What do you have planned?'

'Nothing, why?'

'Well, get up and get dressed. I was thinking we might head to the beach together. It's supposed to be a great day. I figured we could bring Singer and let him run around for a while. Does that sound good to you?'

*   *   *

They spent the day walking barefoot through the white sand, throwing a Frisbee for Singer, and sitting on towels as they watched foam curl atop the waves. They grabbed a pizza for lunch, stayed until the sky was purple with early dusk, and had dinner together as well. From there, they went to a movie; Mike let Julie choose the film and didn't complain when he realized that it was a chick flick. And when Julie had tears in her eyes halfway through and snuggled closer to him for the remaining hour, it more than canceled out the scathing critical review he was preparing in his mind.

It was late by the time they made it back to her

216

place, and again they kissed on the porch. It lasted a little longer this time. For Julie, that made it better; for Mike, being any better was neither possible nor necessary.

They spent Sunday at Julie's house. Mike mowed the lawn, trimmed the hedges, and helped her plant impatiens in the flower box. From there, he moved inside and began fixing those little things that tended to go undone in an older house—replacing the nails that had popped through a couple of boards in the hardwood floor, unsticking the locks, hanging the new light fixture she'd purchased for her bathroom months ago.

Julie watched him as he worked, noticing once again how good he looked in his jeans and how he was most confident when he was doing those types of things. When she kissed him once in the midst of hammering, the expression on his face told her exactly how he felt about her, and she realized that what had once been uncomfortable was now the response she craved.

When he left, she went inside and closed her eyes, leaning against the inside of the door. Wow, she thought, feeling exactly the way Mike had felt two nights before.

Twenty-one

After work the following Tuesday—an extra-busy day at the salon, since Andrea hadn't shown up and a couple of her clients had asked Julie to take care of them—Julie was pushing a cart slowly down the grocery store aisle, grabbing what she needed for dinner. Mike had promised to cook for her, and though she wasn't thrilled with the list he'd provided, she was willing to give it a shot. Despite his promises that it would be good, she couldn't imagine anything that included potato chips and sweet pickles would qualify as fine dining. But he seemed so excited about it, she didn't want to hurt his feelings.

She was just about finished before she realized she'd forgotten something. She was scanning the spice section, trying to remember whether he'd needed minced or spiced onion, when she felt the cart stop suddenly as it bumped into someone.

'Oh, excuse me,' she said automatically. 'I didn't see you . . .'

'It's okay . . . I'm fine,' he said. He turned around, and Julie's eyes widened.

'Richard?' she asked.

'Oh, hey, Julie,' he answered, his voice soft. 'How are you?'

'Fine,' she said. 'How are you doing?' Julie hadn't seen him since the morning he'd left, and he looked a little the worse for wear.

'Getting by,' he said. 'It's been hard. There's a lot I have to take care of. But you know how it goes.'

'Yeah,' she said. 'I do know. How's the hand, by the way?'

'Better. Still bruised, but nothing to worry about.' Then, as if squeezing his fingers closed brought back memories of that night, he looked down. 'Listen, I want to apologize again for what I did last week. I had no right to get so angry.'

'It's okay.'

'And I also want to thank you again for listening to me. Not a lot of people would have done what

218

you did.'

'I didn't do much.'

'Yeah,' he insisted, 'you did. I don't know what I would have done without you. I was in pretty dire straits that night.'

She shrugged.

'Well,' he said as if trying to figure out what to say next. He adjusted the grocery basket on his arm. 'Please don't take it the wrong way, but you look terrific.'

He said it as a friend would, without implications, and she smiled. 'Thank you.'

In the aisle, a woman was heading toward them, her cart full. Julie and Richard moved to the side to make room for her to pass.

'Listen, one more thing about the other night,' Richard added. 'I feel like I owe you something for being so understanding about the way I acted.'

'You don't owe me anything.'

'I'd still like to show my appreciation. Just as a way of saying thank you, I mean. Maybe I could take you out to dinner?'

She said nothing right away, and Richard, noting the hesitation, went on.

'Just dinner—nothing more than that. It won't even be an official date. I promise.'

She looked off to the side, then back at him again. 'I don't think that I can do that,' she said. 'I'm sorry.'

'It's okay,' he said, 'I just thought I'd make the offer.' He smiled. 'So no hard feelings about the other night?'

'No hard feelings,' she repeated.

'Okay.' He took a small step away from her. 'Well, I've got some things I still need to grab. See you around?'

'Sure.'

'Good-bye,' he said.

'Good-bye, Richard.'

*   *   *

'So what exactly are these called again?' Julie asked.

Mike was standing over the stove in his apartment, the ground beef in the frying pan sizzling.

'Creole burgers.'

'So it's Cajun?'

'Yep,' he said. 'Why do you think I asked for these two cans of soup? That's what gives it the authentic flavor.'

Only Mike, she thought, would consider Campbell's chicken gumbo soup authentic Cajun cuisine.

When the meat was ready, he poured in the soup, then added a bit of ketchup and mustard before beginning to stir. Julie leaned against him to look at the concoction, an expression of distaste on her face.

'Remind me never to become a bachelor.'

'Yeah, yeah. You joke now, but in a little while you'll feel like you're eating in heaven's dining room.'

'I'm sure.'

He bumped against her in feigned protest and felt her move with him.

'Did anyone ever tell you that you have an occasional tendency toward sarcasm?' he asked.

'Just a couple of times. But I think it was you that

said it.'

'I always knew I was a smart guy.'

'So did I,' she said, 'but it's your cooking I'm worried about, not your brains.'

*　　*　　*

Fifteen minutes later they were sitting at the table, Julie staring at her plate.

'This is a sloppy Joe,' she announced.

'No,' he said, picking up the sandwich, 'this is a Creole burger. Sloppy Joes have a tomato flavor.'

'While you prefer the distinctive Louisiana flavor?'

'Exactly. And don't forget to eat your pickle as you go. Sort of adds to the whole experience.'

Julie glanced around the small apartment, stalling for time. Though the major pieces of furniture were passably tasteful, there were those touches that made it clear he lived in the style of single men everywhere. Like the gym shoes in the corner of the living room near his guitar. And the pile of unfolded clothes on his bed. And the giant-screen television, with a collection of imported beer bottles lining the top. And the dartboard mounted on the front door.

She leaned across the table, getting Mike's attention. 'Love the ambiance you've created tonight. All we need is a candle and I'd feel like I'm in Paris.'

'Really? I think I've got one,' he said.

He rose from the table and opened a drawer; a moment later, a small flame flickered between them. He took his seat again.

'Better?'

221

'Just like a college dormitory.'

'In Paris?'

'Mmm . . . maybe I was wrong. It's more like . . . Omaha.'

He laughed. 'So are you going to try it, or are you scared?'

'No. I'll try it. I'm just enjoying the anticipation.'

He nodded toward her plate. 'Good. Then you can figure out a nice way to apologize to the chef.'

Julie picked up the sandwich and took a bite. Mike watched her as she seemed to study the flavor.

'Not bad,' she said after swallowing.

'Not bad?'

She stared at the sandwich, a faint look of surprise on her face. 'Actually it's kind of tasty.'

'Told you,' he said. 'It's the chicken gumbo soup that does it.'

She picked up the pickle and winked. 'I'll try to remember that.'

*　　　*　　　*

On Wednesday, it was Julie's turn to make dinner. She prepared sole stuffed with crabmeat and sautéed vegetables, accompanied by a bottle of Sauvignon Blanc. ('It's not Creole burgers, but I *guess* it'll do,' Mike teased.) On Thursday they met for lunch in Emerald Isle. Afterward, while they were walking through the fine sand, Singer jabbed her in the leg with a stick he'd found. He dropped it in front of them, and when they ignored it, he grabbed the stick again, blocking their movement with his body. He looked up at Mike. *C'mon*, he seemed to be saying, *you know the drill*.

'I think he wants you to throw it,' Julie remarked. 'He doesn't think I throw it far enough.'

'That's because you're a girl.'

She elbowed him. 'Watch it, buster. There's a feminist lurking somewhere in here that takes offense to comments like that.'

'Feminists take offense to everything that men do better.'

He pulled away before she could elbow him again and grabbed the stick. He pulled off his shoes and socks, then rolled up his pants legs. He jogged toward the water and waded in, high enough for the waves to roll in just below his knees. He held the stick out in front of him. Singer stared at it as if it were a fresh-cut steak.

'Ready?' Mike asked.

He cocked his arm and threw the stick as far as he could. Singer charged into the waves.

Julie took a seat on the sand, pulling her knees up and wrapping her arms around them. It was cool out; the sky was broken with patches of white, and the sun peeked through the clouds sporadically. Terns darted along the water's edge, looking for food, their heads bobbing like darning needles.

Singer came bounding back with the stick and shook the water from his coat, soaking Mike in the process. Mike grabbed the stick, then threw it again before turning Julie's way, his shirt plastered against his skin. From where she was sitting, she could see the muscles in his arms and the way his chest tapered to his hips. Nice, she thought, very nice.

'Let's do something tomorrow night, okay?' he called out.

Julie nodded. When Singer returned, Julie pulled her legs a little tighter and watched them start over. In the distance, a shrimp trawler eked its way over the water, long nets spread behind it. The lighthouse from Cape Lookout flashed in the distance. Julie felt the breeze on her face as she watched them, wondering why she'd ever been worried.

*   *   *

'Putt Putt?' she asked as they pulled into the lot the following evening. She was dressed in jeans, as was he; earlier in the day, he'd told her not to bother dressing up, and now she understood the reason. 'This is what you want to do tonight?'

'Not just that. There's lots of stuff to do. They've got video games, too. And batting cages.'

'Oooh,' she said. 'I'm thrilled.'

'Ha! That's just because you don't think you can beat me,' Mike said with a sniff.

'I can beat you. I'm like Tiger Woods when it comes to stuff like this.'

'Prove it,' he said.

She nodded, a gleam of challenge in her eyes. 'You're on.'

They got out of the truck, and made their way to the booth to get the clubs. 'Pink and blue,' he said, pointing out the color of the golf balls. 'You and me. Mano a womano.'

'Which one do you want?' she asked, playing innocent.

'Ha!' he snorted. 'Keep it up and I'll show you no sympathy on the course.'

'Ditto.'

224

A couple of minutes later, they reached the first hole.

'Age before beauty,' she offered, motioning to him.

Mike feigned a look of offense before putting the ball in place. The first hole required the ball to travel through a rotating windmill before it descended to a lower level where the hole was. Mike steadied himself over the ball.

'Watch and learn,' he said.

'Just get on with it.'

He hit the ball straight, and it passed through the opening in the windmill; after leaving the tube, it ended up less than a foot from the hole. 'See? It's easy.'

'Step aside. Let me show you how it's done.'

She put her ball down and hit it. It bounced off the blades of the windmill and came back to her.

'Mmm . . . so sorry,' Mike said, shaking his head. 'Too bad.'

'Just getting warmed up.'

She took a little longer before pulling back and hitting the ball again. This time it made it, and when she looked to see where it would end up, she saw it rolling toward the hole before it vanished from sight.

'Nice shot,' Mike conceded. 'Lucky, though.'

She poked him with the club. 'That's all part of the plan.'

*   *   *

In a darkened bedroom of the rented Victorian, Richard was sitting in bed, his back against the headboard. He'd pulled the drapes closed. The

225

room was illuminated only by a small candle on the nightstand, and as he rolled a piece of wax between his fingers, he thought about Julie.

She had been nice enough at the grocery store, but he knew she'd regretted running into him. He shook his head, wondering why she'd tried to hide it. It was pointless, he thought. He knew exactly who she was. In some ways, he knew her better than she knew herself. He knew, for instance, that she was with Mike tonight and that she saw in him the comfort she'd once had and hoped to find again.

She was afraid of anything new, he realized, and he wished she could see that there was so much more for her out there, so much more for the both of them. Didn't she see that if she stayed here, Mike would drag her down? That her friends would ultimately hurt her? That's what happened when you let fear govern your decisions.

He had learned that from experience. He'd despised his father, as Julie had despised the men who'd moved in and out of her life. He hated his mother for her weakness, just as Julie hated her own mother's weakness. But Julie was trying to make peace with her past by trying to relive it. Fear was leading her to the illusion of comfort, yet in the end, it would remain an illusion. She didn't have to end up the way her mother had; she didn't have to lead the life her mother had. Her life could be anything she wanted it to be. As his was.

*   *   *

'Lucky shot!' Mike cried again. Halfway through the course, the score was tied, until Julie's latest shot, which ricocheted off the wall and dropped into the cup. She swaggered over to retrieve her ball.

'How come it's always luck when I make it and skill when you do it?' she demanded.

Mike was still staring at the path the ball had taken. 'Because it is! There's no way you could have planned that!'

'You sound like you're getting nervous.'

'I'm not getting nervous.'

Mimicking his action earlier, she ran her fingernails over her chest and sniffed. 'You should be. You'd hate to let a girl beat you.'

'You won't beat me.'

'So what's the score?'

He stuffed the card and pencil into his back pocket. 'It doesn't matter. It's the score at the end that's important.'

Mike stalked toward the next hole, Julie giggling behind him.

* * *

Richard slowed his breathing, concentrating on Julie's image. Even though she was confused right now, he knew she was different from other people. She was special, better, like him.

It was that secret knowledge of his uniqueness that had sustained him in one foster home after the next. Aside from a few articles of clothing, the only items he'd brought with him were the camera he'd stolen from one of his former neighbors and the box of photographs he'd taken.

The first people who took him in seemed nice enough, but for the most part, he ignored them. He came and went as he pleased, wanting nothing more than a place to sleep and food to eat. As in many foster homes, he was not the only child, and he shared a room with two older boys. It was these two boys who stole his camera two months after he'd moved in, selling it at a pawnshop in order to buy cigarettes.

When Richard found them, they were playing in the vacant lot next door. On the ground was a baseball bat, and he reached for it. They laughed at first, since they were both taller and heavier. In the end, however, they were rushed to the hospital in a pair of ambulances, their faces crushed beyond recognition. The foster care caseworker wanted to send Richard to a juvenile detention center. She'd come to the house later that day with the police, after his foster parents had reported him. Richard was handcuffed and driven to the station. There, he'd sat on a hard wooden chair across from a burly officer named Dugan in a small mirrored room.

Dugan, with his pockmarked cheeks and bulbous nose, had a way of rasping as he spoke. Leaning forward, he told Richard how badly he'd injured the boys and that he was going to spend the next several years locked away. But Richard hadn't been afraid, just as he hadn't been afraid when the police had come to question him and his mother about his father. He'd known this was coming. He looked down, then began to cry.

'I didn't want to do it,' he said quietly. 'But they took my camera, and I told them I would report it to the caseworker. They were going to kill me. I was scared. One of them attacked me—with a knife.'

With that, Richard opened his jacket and Dugan

saw the blood.

Richard was taken to the hospital; he'd been slashed across his lower stomach. The only reason the wound wasn't more serious, Richard claimed, was that he'd managed to twist free from their grasp at the last minute. Dugan found the knife on the warehouse roof, exactly where Richard said he'd seen one of the boys throw it.

The two boys, not Richard, were sent to the juvenile detention facility, despite their pleas that neither of them had ever touched the knife, let alone slashed Richard with it. But the man at the pawnshop said he'd bought the camera from them, and no one believed their protests. They both had records, after all.

Years later, Richard saw one of the boys in the neighborhood, walking on the opposite side of the road. He was a man by then, but when he saw Richard he froze; Richard simply smiled and kept on walking, remembering with disdain the cut he'd so easily inflicted upon himself.

Richard opened his eyes. Yes, he knew from experience that all hurdles could be overcome. Julie simply needed the right person to help her. Together, they would be able to accomplish anything, but Julie had to want him to do this for her. He needed her to accept what he had to offer.

Was that too much to ask?

*   *   *

'What's the score now?' Julie asked.

They were on the final hole, Mike looking serious now. He knew he was a shot down; his first shot had gone off course and had stopped behind a protruding rock, making the next shot impossible to sink. He wiped his brow, ignoring the grin on Julie's face.

'I think you might be ahead,' he said. 'But don't choke on the final hole.'

'Okay,' she said.

'Because you might lose if you do.'

'Okay.'

'I mean, you'd hate to throw it away at the end.'

'Okay.'

'So whatever you do, make sure you don't even make the slightest mistake.'

'Mm . . . you're right, coach. Thanks for the pep talk.'

She put her ball in place and stood over it, her eyes flickering from the ball to the hole and back again. She hit her next shot, and the ball rolled steadily, coming to rest an inch from the hole. I wish I had a camera, she thought when she glanced at Mike; the expression on his face was priceless.

'Looks like the pressure's on,' she commented, rubbing it in. 'I think you have to sink this one just to tie, and from where you are, you can't make it.'

Mike was staring at her ball before he finally looked her way and shrugged. 'You're right,' he admitted. 'It's over.'

'Ha!'

He shook his head. 'I hate to admit this, but I wasn't really trying tonight,' he said. 'I let you win.'

Julie hesitated only briefly before charging him with her club raised as Mike made a halfhearted attempt to flee. She caught him, spun him around, and pulled him close.

'You lose,' she said. 'Admit it.'

'No,' he said, meeting her eyes. 'You got it wrong.

I might have lost the game, but I think I won the match.'

'How so?'

He smiled, leaning in to kiss her.

*   *   *

Richard rose from the bed and walked to the window. Peering outside, he saw shadows stretching across the property, blanketing the ground in darkness.

In time he would tell Julie everything about himself. He would tell her about his mother and father, he would tell her about the boys at the foster home, and he knew she would understand why he'd had no choice but to do what he'd done. He would tell her about Mrs Higgins, the school counselor who had taken a special interest in him in high school, once she discovered he'd been orphaned.

He remembered talking to her as she sat on the couch in her office. She may have been pretty at one time, he remembered thinking, but any glamor she'd possessed had long since vanished. Her hair was a mixture of dirty blond and gray, and when she smiled, the wrinkles made her face look dry and cracked. But he needed an ally. He needed someone to vouch for his character, to say that he wasn't a troublemaker but a victim; and Mrs Higgins was perfect. In the office, everything about her demeanor suggested a desire to appear empathetic and kind—the way she leaned forward with sad eyes, nodding steadily as he told one terrible story after another about his childhood.

More than once, Mrs Higgins had tears in

her eyes.

Within months, she came to see him as a surrogate son, and he played the part well. He gave her a card on her birthday; she bought him another camera, a 35-millimeter with a quality lens, one of the cameras he still owned today.

Richard had always been strong in math and science, but she talked to his history and English teachers and they began to go easier on him. His grade-point average took a sudden jump upward. She informed the principal that his IQ tested at the genius level and pressed for Richard to be admitted to the programs for gifted students. She suggested that he build a portfolio of his photographs to showcase his talents and paid all the costs to put one together. She wrote a letter of recommendation to the University of Massachusetts, her alma mater, professing that she'd never seen a young man overcome so much. She paid a visit to the school and met with the admissions committee, begging them to give him a chance while showing his portfolio. She did everything she could, and though she felt a deep sense of satisfaction when she learned that all her hard work had paid off, it wasn't Richard who told her.

For once he'd been accepted to the university, he never spoke to her again. She had served her purpose, and he had no more use for her.

In the same way, Mike had served his purpose for Julie, but it was over now. Mike had been a good friend, but it was time to send him on his way. Mike was shackling her, holding her back, preventing her from choosing her own future. Their future.

Twenty-two

For Julie, the days began to acquire a new rhythm. From the mornings when Mike left the garage to greet her on the street, to their lunches at out-of-the-way places, to the lazy evenings spent in long conversation, he was becoming an exciting and important part of her life.

They were still inching their way through the relationship as if both believed that a casual wave of the hand could make it vanish like smoke. Mike hadn't spent the night at Julie's, Julie hadn't spent the night at Mike's, and though there were a couple of nights when the opportunity had presented itself, neither seemed ready.

Walking Singer one day after work, Julie acknowledged that it was just a matter of time. It was Thursday, two weeks after they'd first gone out and, more important, a week and a half after their *third* date, which was, according to the magazines, the magic number when it came to twisting the night away. They'd passed that marker without acknowledging it, but that didn't surprise her. In the years since Jim had died, she'd had those moments when she felt rather . . . sensual, she liked to call it; but it had been so long since she'd been to bed with a man, she'd sort of come to accept celibacy as a permanent way of life. She'd even forgotten what it was like to *want* something like that, but lo and behold, the old hormones had kicked in big time lately and there were moments when she found herself fantasizing about Mike.

Not that she was ready to pounce on him without

warning. No, that would probably send Mike's ticker into spasms. Anyway, she'd no doubt be as terrified as he was. If kissing him the first time had been nerve-racking, what in the world was the next step going to be like? *Oh*, she imagined herself saying as she stood in front of him in the bedroom, *these bulges? Sorry, but you know we've been eating out a lot lately. Just dim the lights, sweetie.*

It was possible that the whole thing might end up a fiasco, complete with jabbing elbows and bumping heads and disappointment in the end. And then what would happen? Sex wasn't the most important thing in a relationship, but it sure wasn't number three or four, either. She figured that when it came right down to it, the stress associated with their first time together was going to make it nearly impossible to enjoy. Should I do this? Should I whisper that? It's like going on a game show with impossible questions, she thought, only the contestants have to be naked.

Okay, she chided herself, so maybe I am worrying about it too much. But that's what happens when you've been with only one person in your entire life, and that was a guy you'd been married to. This was the payback, she supposed, for leading a fairly tame life, and to be honest, she didn't want to think about it anymore. A walk with Singer was supposed to be relaxing, not a cause for clammy hands.

Up ahead, Singer wandered into the wooded lots that stretched to the Intracoastal Waterway, and Julie spotted the path most of the Realtors had been using. A month ago, signs had sprouted up all the way to the water, and she'd seen orange plastic strips marking where they intended to put the road.

In a couple of years, she'd have a neighborhood, which—though nice in the way of property values—was kind of a bummer, too. She liked the feeling of privacy the lots provided, and it was great for Singer. She really didn't want to have to start following him around with a pooper scooper, so as not to sully the newly sodded lawns. The very thought nauseated her, and she couldn't face the looks that Singer would give her. She had no doubt he'd understand what was going on. After the first few times, he'd stare at her before turning his nose, thinking something along the lines of, *I did my business by the tree—do be a darling and clean that up for me, will you?*

No way, she thought. There wasn't a chance she'd put up with that.

She walked for fifteen minutes before she reached the water and sat for a little while on a stump, watching the boats as they floated past. She couldn't see Singer but knew he was nearby; he'd come to check periodically to make sure she was following him.

He was protective of her. Just like Mike in his own way.

Mike.

Mike and her *together*. *Really* together. A moment later, Julie found her thoughts right back where she'd started, clammy hands and all.

*   *   *

As she approached the house an hour later, she heard the phone ringing. Hurrying inside, she let the screen door close with a bang behind her. Probably Emma, she thought. Emma had been calling a lot lately—she loved what was happening with Mike and couldn't wait to talk about it. And to be honest, Julie kind of liked talking about it, too. Just for perspective, of course.

She put the receiver to her ear. 'Hello?'

There was no reply on the other end, though it seemed the line was still open.

'Hello?' she said again.

Nothing. Julie put the phone back in its cradle and went to let Singer in. In her haste, she'd slammed the door in his face. But as soon as she reached the door, the phone rang again, and she went through the same routine.

Again, there was silence on the other end. Only this time, before she lowered the phone, she thought she heard a faint click as the caller hung up.

*   *   *

'So how are things going with Julie?' Henry asked.

'Good,' Mike answered, his head buried beneath a hood. Over the past week, he hadn't said much about it to his brother simply because he hadn't had the time. With summer coming, air conditioners were going on the blink as fast as they were being switched on, and people were rolling into the garage with dirty rings on the collars of their shirts. Besides, it was so much *fun* having information Henry wanted and not sharing it. Kind of made him feel he had the upper hand for once.

Henry regarded him. 'Based on how much you've been seeing her, I'd hope they're going better than that.'

'You know how it is,' Mike said, continuing to

236

work. He reached for a socket wrench and began trying to loosen the bolts that held the compressor in place.

'Actually, I don't.'

Yeah, I know!

'Like I said, it's going good. Can you hand me a rag? My hands are kind of slick.'

Henry passed it over. 'So I heard you made her dinner at your place a little bit ago.'

'Yep,' Mike said.

'And?'

'And what?'

'What happened?'

'She liked it.'

'That's it?'

'What do you want me to say, Henry?'

'How do you think she feels about you?'

'I think she likes me.'

Henry brought his hands together. Now they were getting somewhere. 'You think she likes you, huh?'

Mike took an extra few seconds to answer, knowing Henry wanted details.

'Yep.'

Under the hood, he smiled, thinking, This is great!

'Mmm,' Henry said. Oh, this guy thinks he's so slick, but there's more than one way to get answers. 'Well, listen, I was wondering if you two would like to head out on the boat next weekend with Emma and me.'

'Next weekend?'

'Yeah. I figure we'll do a little fishing, have a few beers. It'll be fun.'

'I think we might be able to work that out.'

Henry raised his eyebrows. Little brother thinks he's a big shot now, he thought. Funny what getting a girlfriend will do.

'Try not to sound so thrilled,' he grumbled.

'Hey, don't get all flustered. I just meant that I had to check with Julie first.'

'Oh,' Henry said, 'that makes sense.' And unfortunately, he thought, it did.

Henry stood beside Mike for another minute, but Mike didn't so much as bother to pull his head out of the car. Finally Henry turned and headed to his office, thinking, Okay Mike, you're in for it now. All I wanted was a little info, but no, you had to play the strong, silent type.

The only problem was, even after twenty minutes, he couldn't think of anything he could do. He loved a good zinger, but fair was fair, and he wasn't about to ruin things for his little brother.

I may be a weak man, he thought, but I'm not a mean one.

* * *

'I'm telling you, you're practically glowing these days,' Mabel said.

'I am not. I've just been in the sun lately,' Julie answered.

They were in the salon, enjoying a lull between clients. Andrea was cutting hair at her station and carrying on a conversation about politics that was doomed as soon as she mentioned that she liked the current governor because 'his hair looked nicer than the other guy's.' The 'other guy' she was referring to seemed irrelevant to her client; he hadn't come for the conversation anyway.

238

'It ain't the sun I'm talking about, and you know it.'

Julie reached for the broom and began sweeping the floor around her chair.

'Yes, Mabel, I know. You aren't exactly the most subtle person I've ever met.'

'Why be subtle? It's so much easier just to come out with it.'

'For you, maybe. We mortals are sometimes plagued by things like how we might be coming across to other people.'

'Darlin', you can't worry about stuff like that. Life's too short. Besides, you like me, don't you?'

'You're one of a kind, that's for sure.'

Mabel leaned toward her. 'Then dish up.'

*   *   *

An hour later, Andrea's latest client had finished up and left, leaving a tip big enough to cover the new Miracle Bra she'd had her eye on. In the past couple of weeks, she'd decided that her problem was that her chest wasn't quite big enough to attract the right kind of guy, but the new bra would definitely help with that.

It would also help her feel a little better about herself. For the past week and all morning long, Mabel and Julie had been whispering to each other as if they were planning to rob the bank down the street, but even Andrea understood they were talking about Julie's relationship with Mike. Not that they were willing to share anything other than the basics. So she'd kissed him? What's the big deal? Andrea had been kissing boys since second grade, but Julie seemed to believe the whole thing

239

was as romantic as the movie *Pretty Woman*.

And besides, Andrea thought, the thing with Mike was completely ridiculous. Mike or Richard? Come on, she told herself, the choice is obvious, even for a moron. Mike's a nice guy, but he wasn't Richard. Wasn't even close to Richard. Richard had it all, and Mike? The big zip as far as sex appeal went. But Julie was as blind as an albino bat when it came to men.

If anything, Andrea thought, Julie should be talking to me. I could give her some serious pointers on how to fix the situation with Richard.

Just then the bell on the door jingled, and Andrea turned her head, thinking, Well, speak of the devil . . .

*   *   *

For a long moment, the salon was silent. Mabel had slipped out for a few minutes, and Julie's client was heading out, too. Richard held the door for her as she left. He was wearing sunglasses, and when he turned back around, the reflection of her own features when he faced her left Julie with an odd, sinking feeling in her stomach. Singer sat up on the blanket.

'Richard,' Julie said.

The word came out tentatively.

'Hello, Julie. How are you?'

There was no reason to be rude, but she didn't feel like exchanging pleasantries, either. Though she didn't mind bumping into Richard now and then, since it was inevitable in a small town, she wasn't sure she wanted him to keep coming here. It was one thing for their meetings to be accidental, it was completely another to know that she'd continue seeing him regularly, and she didn't want to do anything to encourage him. She certainly didn't want a repeat of their meeting at the grocery store.

'What's up?' she asked instead.

Richard slipped off his sunglasses and smiled. When he spoke, his voice was soft. 'I was hoping that you had time to cut my hair. It's about that time again.'

Wondering if that was his only reason for coming, she scanned her appointment book, already knowing what she'd find. She began shaking her head.

'I'm sorry. I don't think I can fit it in—I'm pretty busy today. My next appointment is in a few minutes, and after that, I have a color job to do, and they can take a long time.'

'I guess I should have made an appointment, huh?' he said.

'Sometimes I can work people in, but today I just don't have the time.'

'I see.' He glanced away. 'Well, since I'm already here, maybe we could set something up. How about Monday?'

She flipped the page, again knowing what she'd find.

'I'm booked solid then, too. Mondays are always busy. That's when the regulars come in.'

'Tuesday?'

This time, she didn't need to look. 'I'm only working half a day. I've got some things to take care of in the afternoon.'

Richard closed his eyes slowly, then opened them again, as if asking, *So this is how it's going to be, huh?* However, he didn't turn to leave. Sensing the tension between them, Andrea stepped back from her chair.

'I can do it, sugar,' she said. 'I've got a little time.'

After a moment, Richard took a small step backward, still holding Julie's eyes.

'Yeah,' he said, 'that'll be fine.'

Andrea tugged at her miniskirt, glanced in the mirror, then led the way.

'C'mon, sugar. Let's go to the back. I need to wash your hair first.'

'Sure. Thank you, Andrea.'

She looked over her shoulder at him, giving him her best Christmas smile, thrilled by the way her name sounded on his lips.

*   *   *

'What was he doing there?' Mike asked. As soon as he'd seen Richard leave the salon—Mike had a tendency to stare in the salon's direction whenever he had a spare minute, if only to imagine what Julie was doing right then—he'd hurried over, and Julie went outside to meet him.

'He came in for a haircut.'

'Why?'

'Well, that's what we *do* in the salon.'

He gave her an impatient glance, and she went on. 'Oh, don't make this into something it wasn't. I barely talked to him. Andrea cut his hair, not me.'

'But he wanted you to do it, right? Even though you broke it off with him?'

'That I can't deny. But I think he got the impression that I'd rather not see him anymore, even at work. I wasn't mean about it, but I'm sure he got the message.'

'Well . . . good,' he said. He paused. 'He does realize that you're . . . you know, seeing me, right?'

Instead of answering, she reached for his hand. 'You know, you're kind of cute when you're jealous.'

'I'm not jealous.'

'Of course you are. But don't worry, I think you're cute all the time. See you tonight?'

For the first time since he'd spotted Richard, Mike felt himself relax a little. 'I'll be there,' he said.

*   *   *

When Julie went back into the shop a few minutes later, Andrea was already working again, though her face was still flushed from her time with Richard. It was the first time, Julie realized, that she'd ever seen Andrea look nervous around a man. And good for her. Andrea deserved someone employed for once, though she couldn't imagine her sticking with someone like that for long. Julie had the strange suspicion she'd get bored with it rather quickly.

She finished with her work a little after five and began closing up. Andrea had finished a half hour before and was already gone. Mabel was cleaning up in the back while Julie took care of the reception area, and it was then that she noticed the pair of sunglasses on the counter, beside the potted plant.

She saw instantly that they were Richard's, and for a second she considered calling him and letting him know they were here; then she decided not to.

Mabel or Andrea could do it. It was better that way.

*   *   *

Julie swung by the grocery store to pick up the makings for dinner and was walking in the front door when she heard the phone ringing. She put the grocery bag on the table and answered.

'Hello?'

'Hello, Julie,' Richard said. His tone was friendly, nonchalant, as if they spoke on the phone every day. 'I wasn't sure you'd be in yet, but I'm glad I caught you. I missed not being able to talk to you today.'

Julie closed her eyes, thinking, Not again. Enough is enough already.

'Hi, Richard,' she said coolly.

'How are you?'

'I'm fine, thanks.'

Hearing her tone, he paused on the other end. 'You're probably wondering why I'm calling.'

'Kind of,' she said.

'Well, I was just wondering if you happened to come across a pair of sunglasses. I think I might have left them in the shop.'

'Yeah, they're there. I left them on the desk. You can pick them up on Monday.'

'You're not open on Saturdays?'

'No. Mabel doesn't think that people should work weekends.'

'Oh.' He paused. 'Well, I was heading out of town, and it would be great if I could get them before I go. Would it be possible for you to unlock the door for me tonight? It won't take but a few

244

minutes of your time. Once I get them, I can be on my way.'

Julie held the phone to her ear without answering, thinking, You've got to be kidding. I know you left them on purpose just to have a reason to call.

'Julie? You there?'

She exhaled, knowing he could hear it on the other end, but not really caring anymore. 'I think this has gone far enough, okay?' she said, no trace of sympathy or kindness in her tone. 'I know what you're doing, and I've tried to be nice to you, but I think it's time to stop, okay?'

'What are you talking about? I just want my glasses.'

'Richard. I'm serious about this. I'm seeing someone else now. It's over. You can pick up your glasses on Monday.'

'Julie . . . wait—'

Julie pushed the button to cut off the call.

Twenty-three

An hour later, Mike opened Julie's front door and poked his head in. 'Hey, I'm here,' he called out.

Julie was in the bathroom blow-drying her hair, and as soon as Singer heard Mike's voice, he trotted out to greet him.

'You decent?' Mike called out. He heard the dryer click off.

'Yeah,' Julie answered, 'come on back.'

Mike walked through the bedroom and peeked in the bathroom door. 'You showered?'

245

'Yeah. I was feeling kind of grungy,' she said. She wound the cord around the dryer and put it in the drawer. 'When it's busy like today, I feel like I'm coated in other people's hair by the time I'm through. I'll be done in a few minutes.'

'Do you mind if I stay?'

'Not at all.'

Mike leaned against the counter as Julie reached for her eye shadow, and he watched as she applied it in short strokes, framing her eyes. Next came the mascara, and she brushed her lashes with the same practiced moves, the top first and then the bottom, leaning toward the mirror as she did so.

There was something sensual about a woman when she was doing those things, something that spoke of her desire to be considered attractive, Mike thought as he watched. He noticed the subtle differences as she changed before his eyes. Because they were staying in, this evening's performance was meant just for him, an idea he found undeniably erotic.

He knew he was in love with Julie. The past couple of weeks they'd been together made that clear, but it was different from the way he'd felt before they'd started dating. She wasn't a fantasy anymore, but something real, something he couldn't imagine living without, and he crossed his arms, as if bracing himself against the possibility that all this might still slip away.

She put on a pair of earrings, smiling briefly, wondering what he found so interesting, yet feeling warmed by his appreciation nonetheless. She reached for the perfume, spritzing a little on her neck and on her wrists, then rubbed her wrists together, this time holding his gaze.

'Better?' she asked.

'You look beautiful,' he said. 'As always.'

Julie squeezed by Mike on her way out, her body brushing against his, and Mike followed, his eyes drawn to the gentle sway of her hips and the smooth curve of her bottom. In bare feet and faded jeans, she seemed the picture of grace, though Mike knew she was moving no differently than she always did.

'I thought we'd do steaks tonight,' she said. 'Does that sound okay?'

'Sounds great, but I'm not all that hungry yet. I had a late lunch at the garage. But a beer sounds good.'

Julie reached for a wineglass from the cupboard. As she stood on her tiptoes, her blouse lifted enough to show her belly, and Mike turned away, forcing himself to think about baseball. A moment later, standing before him, she held out the glass and Mike poured the wine, then grabbed a beer for himself. He opened it and took a long drink.

Then he took another.

'Do you want to sit outside for a while?' she asked.

'Sure.'

They went to the porch, and Julie held open the screen door so Singer could head to the yard. Her blouse was sleeveless. Mike noticed the thin muscles of her upper arm and the swell of her chest and couldn't help but imagine what she might look like naked.

He closed his eyes and took a deep breath. Please, he thought, don't let me make a fool of myself. Please.

He took another long drink, nearly finishing

the can.

This, he thought, was going to be one hell of a long night.

* * *

It wasn't nearly as bad as he'd thought it would be. As usual, they settled into a lighthearted conversation while the evening breeze kicked in; Mike fired up the grill an hour later and cooked the steaks while Julie went inside to throw a salad together.

In the kitchen, Julie reflected that Mike had the look of a nymphomaniac who'd been stranded on a desert island for years. The poor guy had been staring at her all night, and though he tried to be circumspect, she knew exactly what he was thinking, because frankly, she was thinking the same thing. Her hands were so clammy, she could barely hold the vegetables.

She diced cucumbers and tomatoes and added them to the bowl, then set the table with her good china and flatware. Standing back to admire the effect, she realized that something was missing. She found two candles, put them in the center, and lit them. After turning off the overhead light, she nodded, satisfied.

She went to the living room and slipped an Ella Fitzgerald CD into the stereo and was putting the wine on the table when Mike came in, holding the steaks. He stopped just inside the door when he saw what she'd done.

'You like it?' she asked.

'It looks . . . wonderful,' Mike said.

She noticed that he was looking directly at her as

he spoke, and for a long moment, they simply stared at each other. Finally, Mike looked away and set the steaks on the table. Instead of sitting, however, he moved toward Julie and she felt her stomach tighten. Oh Lord, she thought, am I really ready for this?

Standing before her, Mike brought one hand up to her face, his palm open, as if asking permission to go on. In the background, the music played softly; the aroma of dinner filled the small kitchen. Julie was vaguely aware of it all. Mike seemed to fill the entire room.

It was at that moment that Julie knew she'd fallen in love with him.

Mike gazed at her as if reading her mind, and Julie gave in. She pressed her face against his hand, closing her eyes and letting his touch become part of her. Mike moved closer until she could feel his chest against hers and the strength in his arms as he slipped them around her.

Mike kissed her then. It was soft, almost like the movement of air beneath a hummingbird's wings, and though they'd kissed many times, this one seemed more real than any before. He kissed her again, and as their tongues met, Julie embraced Mike, certain in the knowledge that their years of friendship had been moving both of them steadily toward this moment.

When they pulled apart, Mike took Julie's hand and led her from the kitchen to the bedroom. They kissed again as Mike slowly began undoing the buttons on her blouse. She felt his fingers against her skin, then felt his hand move to the snap on her jeans. He kissed her neck, burying his hands in her hair.

'I love you,' Mike whispered.

The room seemed to be nothing but shadows and the echo of Mike's words. Julie sighed.

'Oh, Mike,' she said, feeling his breath play over her skin. 'I love you, too.'

*   *   *

They made love, and though it wasn't as embarrassing as Julie had feared it would be, they didn't exactly set the world on fire. More than anything, Mike wanted to please Julie and Julie wanted to please Mike and there was way too much thinking on both their parts for either to simply enjoy what was happening.

When they were finished, they lay in bed next to each other, breathing hard and staring at the ceiling, both of them thinking, I am *really* out of practice. I hope Julie (Mike) didn't notice.

Unlike some couples, though, they were comfortable holding each other afterward, their initial feelings of urgency now replaced by tenderness. Again, Mike told Julie he loved her; she said the words, too. And an hour later, when they made love a second time, it was perfect.

*   *   *

It was past midnight and they were still in bed. Julie was watching as Mike made small circular motions on her belly with his fingers. When she couldn't take it anymore, she wiggled and laughed, reaching to stop his hand.

'That tickles,' she protested.

He kissed her hand and looked at her. 'You were

250

great, by the way.'

'Oh, are we stooping to that level now? Like I'm some one-night stand and you want to pad my ego so you don't feel guilty for taking advantage of me?'

'No, I mean it. You were great. The best ever. I never knew it could be this way.'

She laughed. 'Clichés, clichés.'

'You don't believe me?'

'Of course I do. I was *great*,' she said. 'The best ever. You never knew—'

Mike started tickling her before she could finish, and Julie squealed as she writhed away from his grip. Then, lying on his stomach, Mike propped himself up on his elbows.

'And by the way,' he said, 'I didn't take advantage of you.'

Julie rolled on her side to see him better, then tugged at the sheet.

'Oh, no? All I knew is that one minute I was getting ready to have dinner, and the next minute our clothes were flying all over the bedroom.'

'I was pretty seductive, wasn't I?'

'You were very seductive.' She reached down and ran a finger over his cheek. 'I do love you, you know.'

'Yeah, I know.'

She pushed him away. 'And here I was trying to be serious for a change,' she said. 'The least you can do is tell me, too.'

'Again? How many times do you want me to say it?'

'How many times do you want to say it?'

Mike looked at her, then reached for her hand again and kissed each fingertip. 'If I had my way,' he said, 'I'd say it every day for the rest of my life.'

Ah, that was sweet.

'Well, since you love me so much, would you mind getting us something to eat? I'm starved.'

'Sure.'

As he leaned over to grab his pants, the phone started ringing on the end table beside him.

Once. Twice. On the third ring, Mike answered it.

'Hello?' he said. He paused. 'Hello?'

Julie closed her eyes, hoping he wouldn't say the word again.

'Hello?'

He hung up the phone. 'No one was there,' he said. 'I guess it was a wrong number or something.' He looked at her. 'You okay?'

She forced herself to smile. 'Yeah,' she said. 'I'm fine.'

The phone rang again. This time, Mike glanced at her with a look of puzzlement before answering.

The same thing happened again.

Julie crossed her arms. Though she told herself it probably meant nothing, she couldn't shake the sense of déjà vu that suddenly washed over her, the same feeling she'd had when she'd visited Jim's grave.

Someone, she thought, was watching her.

Twenty-four

The changes in Julie's life began that night.

Most of them were wonderful. Mike spent Saturday with Julie and they made love once in the morning and again before they went to sleep. On

252

Sunday, she and Mike went to the mall in Jacksonville and she bought a new bathing suit, as well as some new shorts and sandals. When she modeled the bikini for him after she got home, Mike stared with boggling eyes, then bolted from the couch to chase her. She ran through the house, laughing and screaming, before Mike caught her in the bedroom. They tumbled to the bed, giggling, only to find themselves buried in the sheets a few minutes later.

Other than being naked a lot, she was surprised—and thankful—that making love hadn't altered the friendship between them. Mike still joked and made her laugh, she still teased him, he still held her hand as they watched movies on the couch.

But as much as she wanted to deny it, what would stand out most in her mind in thinking back on that week were the phone calls. The two calls late on Friday night. On Saturday, there were two more. On Sunday, the phone rang four times, and on Monday it was five, but on those two days, Mike had stepped out of the house for a moment and she'd been the one to answer. On Tuesday, after she'd gone to bed—Mike had gone back to his place for the night—there were four calls before she'd finally unplugged the phone. And on Wednesday, when she stepped into the kitchen after a day at work, she noticed her answering machine was full.

She remembered hitting the button for the first call, then skipping to the next message. Then the next. One right after another, the calls had come. The recorder had noted the time; each new call had been placed the moment the previous call had been disconnected. On the fourth message, her breath quickened; by the ninth, her eyes had begun to well with tears. By the twelfth, she was hitting the delete button almost as fast as she was hitting the play button, in an almost frantic attempt to stop what was happening.

When she'd finished, she sat at the table trembling.

All in all, twenty calls had been made to her machine that day, each lasting two minutes.

In none of them did the caller say anything.

And on Thursday and Friday, there were no calls at all.

Twenty-five

'It sounds to me like everything's going great,' Emma said on Saturday.

Earlier that day, Mike and Julie had met Henry and Emma at the boat launch on Harker's Island. They'd loaded the boat with coolers of food and beer, sunscreen, towels and hats, tubs of ice, and enough fishing gear to hook anything that might happen to cross the stern, including Moby Dick, Orca, and Jaws himself. By midmorning, in the sound near Cape Lookout, Mike and Henry were standing next to each other, reels in hand, engaged in a competition that could only be described as profoundly juvenile. Every time either one of them caught a fish, he'd get to shake a bottle of beer and point it at the other. One of the tubs was already filled with enough mackerel and flounder to feed a waddling army of starving seals, and both men had removed their beer-soaked shirts and hung them on the rail to dry.

Julie and Emma were sitting in small lawn chairs near the cabin, acting a little more grown-up. The sun beat down on them steadily. Because it wasn't yet summer, the humidity was bearable, though their cans of beer were coated in condensation.

'It is,' Julie agreed. 'Better than great, actually. This last week makes me wonder what I was so afraid of all this time.'

The way she said it made Emma pause.

'But?'

'But what?'

'There's something bothering you, isn't there?'

'Is it that obvious?'

'No. But it doesn't need to be obvious. I've known you long enough to recognize the signs. So what is it? Something to do with Mike?'

'No. Not at all.'

'Do you love him?'

'Yeah, I do.'

'Then what is it?'

Julie cautiously set her beer on the deck. 'I've been getting some strange phone calls lately.'

'From whom?'

'I don't know. No one ever says anything on the other end.'

'Heavy breathers?'

'No, not even that. No sound at all.'

'And you don't know who they're from?'

'No. When I dialed star sixty-nine, the recording said it was a private number, so I called the phone company. All they can tell me is that the calls are coming from a cellular phone. But the number isn't registered, so they can't trace it.'

'How is that possible?'

'I have no idea. They explained it, but I wasn't really listening. After they said they couldn't help me, I sort of tuned out.'

'Do you have an idea who they might be from?'

Julie turned and watched Mike cast his line again. 'I think it might be Richard. I can't prove it, but it's just a feeling I get.'

'Why?'

'The timing, I guess. I mean, I can't think of anyone else it could be. I haven't met anyone new besides him and . . . I don't know . . . I just think he's the one. The way he acted when I told him it was over, the way he keeps popping into my life.'

'What do you mean?'

'It's just little things. I bumped into him in the grocery store, then he came into the salon for another haircut. And whenever we do see each other, it's like he's trying to find out how he can have another chance with me.'

Emma looked at her. 'What does Mike think?'

'I don't know. I haven't told him yet.'

'Why not?'

Julie shrugged. 'What's he going to do? Go after the guy? Like I said, I don't even know for sure that Richard's the one who's calling.'

'Well, how many calls have there been?'

Julie closed her eyes for a moment. 'On Wednesday, there were twenty messages on the machine.'

Emma sat up. 'Oh, my God. Have you told the police about this?'

'No,' Julie said. 'It wasn't until then that I even admitted what was happening. I guess I was just hoping that it was a mistake of some kind, like

256

some sort of computer malfunction with the phone company. I was just hoping it would stop. And maybe it has. My phone hasn't rung at all the last two days.'

Emma reached for Julie's hand. 'People like that don't stop. You read about this kind of stuff in the papers all the time: Ex-boyfriend wanders in and settles the score. This is stalker kind of stuff. Don't you realize that?'

'Of course I do. And I've thought about it. But, again, what am I going to say to the police? I can't prove it's Richard calling and neither can the phone company. He hasn't threatened me. I haven't seen his car parked on my street or near the salon. He hasn't been anything but polite when we do run into each other, and even then, there have always been other people around. All he'd have to do is deny it.' She made the points like a lawyer summing up a case. 'And besides,' she said, 'like I told you, I don't know for sure that it's him. It could be Bob for all I know. Or someone I don't even know.'

Emma watched her before squeezing her hand.

'But you're ninety-nine percent certain it was Richard.'

After a moment, Julie nodded.

'And no calls last night? Or the night before? When Mike was there?'

'No. It was quiet. I guess he stopped.'

Emma frowned, thinking about it.

Or wanted her to believe that he'd stopped?

She wasn't about to say that. 'Strange,' she said instead. 'And kind of scary. It gives me the creeps just thinking about it.'

'Me too.'

'So what are you going to do?'

Julie shook her head. 'I have no idea.'

*   *   *

An hour later, Julie was standing at the bow when she felt Mike slip his arms around her and nuzzle her neck. She leaned into his grip, feeling strangely comforted as he moved to stand beside her.

'Hey there,' she said.

'Hi. You looked lonely up here.'

'No. Just enjoying the breeze. I was getting kind of hot in the sun.'

'Me too. I think I got sunburned. The beer must have washed off my sunscreen.'

'So did you win?'

'I don't want to brag, but let's just say he got a lot more sun than I did.'

She smiled. 'So what's Henry doing now?'

'Probably pouting.'

She glanced behind her. Henry was leaning over the side, beer can in hand, filling it with seawater. When he saw Julie looking, he stood and brought a finger to his lips, begging for silence.

'So, are you ready for tonight?' she asked. 'At the Clipper?'

'Yeah. I knew most of the songs already.'

'What are you gonna wear?'

'Probably just jeans this time. I think I'm getting a little old to dress like a kid.'

'And you're just realizing this now?'

'Sometimes it takes me a while.'

She leaned into him. 'Like with me?'

'Yeah, like with you, too.'

In the distance, assorted boats had dropped

anchor near the beach at Cape Lookout. On the first warm weekend of the year, it was crowded with families. Kids splashed and shrieked in the water, parents sprawled on towels. Behind the crowd, the lighthouse rose eighty feet into the air; painted white with black diamonds, it looked like a folded checkerboard stood on end.

'You've been kind of quiet today,' Mike said, squeezing her.

'Just thinking.'

'About something Emma said?'

'No. Just the opposite. It's something I mentioned to her.'

Mike could feel the wisps of her hair as they feathered his face. 'Do you want to talk about it?'

Julie took a deep breath before recounting the things she'd told Emma. As he listened, Mike's expression shifted from confusion to concern, then finally to anger. When she was finished, he reached for her hand and turned her around.

'So you think it was him when I answered the phone that night?'

'I don't know.'

'Why didn't you tell me about this before?'

'There wasn't anything to tell. Not until a couple of days ago, anyway.'

Mike glanced away, frowning, then looked back at Julie. 'Well, if it happens again, I'm gonna put a stop to it.'

Julie seemed to study him, then slowly broke into a smile. 'You have that sexy look in your eyes again.'

'Don't try to change the subject,' he said. 'This is serious. Remember what we talked about in Tizzy's?'

'Yeah,' she said, 'I remember.' Her voice was flat. 'It's just the way I deal with things when I'm upset. Try to joke my way out of things. Old habit, you know?'

After a long moment, Mike put his arms around her again. 'Don't worry,' he said. 'I'm not going to let anything happen to you.'

*   *   *

Lunch was an informal affair—sandwiches and chips and a deli container of potato salad. Having told Mike and Emma, and with a full stomach, Julie felt a little better. She drew some comfort from the fact that both had taken what was happening as seriously as she did.

She even began to relax and let herself have fun. Though she could see in Mike's face that he hadn't forgotten what she'd said, Mike was Mike, and he could stay serious for only so long, especially with Henry egging him on. At one point, Henry offered Mike the beer he'd filled earlier and Mike took a drink before choking in midswallow and spraying it overboard. Henry roared, Emma giggled, and after Mike wiped his chin, he laughed as well. But he didn't forget. Later, he grabbed a flounder and used it to flavor one of Henry's sandwiches by running the fish over the bread.

Henry turned green as he gagged, then threw the sandwich at Mike. Mike retaliated by launching a spoonful of potato salad at his brother.

While all this was going on, Emma leaned close to Julie. 'Imbeciles,' she whispered into Julie's ear. 'Never forget that men are imbeciles.'

It was because of the phone calls, however, that

260

Julie had one beer more than she usually did. It was exactly what she needed today, she thought, and with the hazy logic of someone whose world is slightly spinning, she tried to force her fears away. Maybe the calls were Richard's version of a temper tantrum. Maybe he was mad because of the way she'd talked to him when he'd called about his sunglasses. She remembered that she had been pretty rough on him. Granted, he'd deserved it, but it couldn't have been easy for him to hear. But because he hadn't shown up yet to pick them up from the salon, she guessed she'd been right in thinking that the whole thing had been a ruse to see her again. The phone calls were his way of letting her know he was upset that his plan hadn't worked out.

And, she reminded herself again, the calls had stopped two days ago. Not a long hiatus, but then they hadn't been going on that long in the first place. It was probably over, she thought, as if trying to reassure herself. Despite what Emma might think, she *was* taking this seriously. Being homeless as a teenager, however briefly, had left her with a healthy sense of paranoia. Until she was certain the calls had really stopped, she wasn't going to do anything stupid: no late evening walks alone, she'd keep the doors locked, she'd keep Singer in the bedroom with her on those nights that Mike wasn't there. She'd be careful.

Julie crossed her arms and listened to the water as it rushed beneath the bow.

No, it wouldn't get any worse, she told herself. There was no chance of that at all.

*   *   *

By midafternoon, Emma had slipped in a Jimmy Buffet CD and the music was playing loud; they'd lifted anchor and were passing Cape Lookout as they headed back toward Harker's Island. The boat was moving in rhythm with the gentle swells, and Emma was cuddling up with Henry as he steered, nibbling occasionally at his ear.

Mike was cleaning up at the stern, putting the tackle back in the box and making sure the reels were secured. Julie stood near the bow again, feeling the wind move her hair. Like Mike, she'd burned a little, and the skin on her shoulders was tender to the touch. So were the various other parts she'd missed when applying the sunscreen: the top of her left ear, her forehead near the hairline, a swath along her thigh, and another on her shin. Amazing, she thought, how the sun had found those spots and taken its revenge. I look like a pink-spotted cheetah.

Though the weather remained glorious, it was time to head home. Emma and Henry had faced a small mutiny earlier that morning, complete with tears and screams, because their kids couldn't understand why they weren't invited. Feeling somewhat guilty, they'd promised to take them out later for pizza and a movie. Mike had to be at the Clipper by eight to start setting up with the band. Julie didn't plan on heading in to see him play until around ten or so, and she wanted to take a nap before then. She was bushed. The beer and sun had made her woozy.

She went to her gear bag and threw on a shirt. It was as she was pulling on her shorts and glancing toward the beach that her eyes registered something wrong. Even a closer look wasn't enough to make it obvious right away. Shielding her eyes from the sun, she scanned the boats, then the water's edge, then the people on the shore.

It was there. Somewhere, it was there.

And whatever it was, it didn't fit.

Frowning, Julie looked closer still, then finally realized what had snagged her attention. And she was right. It didn't fit, not on a hot day at the beach.

She lowered her hand, puzzled.

Someone wearing jeans and a dark blue shirt was standing near the dunes, holding . . . what? Binoculars? A telescope? She couldn't tell, but whatever it was, it was definitely focused on the boat.

On *her*.

Julie felt suddenly heavy as the man lowered whatever it was he was holding, and for an instant, she almost convinced herself that she was mistaken. But then, as if knowing exactly what she was thinking, the person waved, his arm moving slowly back and forth like the pendulum of a grandfather clock. *I'm here*, he seemed to be saying, *I'm always here*.

Richard.

She felt the blood drain from her face, and she inhaled sharply, stifling part but not all of the sound with the back of her hand.

But when she blinked, Richard was gone. She moved to the bow and leaned forward. Nothing. No sign of him anywhere. It was as if he'd never been there at all.

Mike had heard her and reached her side a moment later.

'What is it?' he asked.

Julie was still staring toward the beach. Mike's eyes followed hers, and after finding no sign of Richard, no sign of anything unusual, Julie curled beneath his arm. 'I don't know,' she said.

It had to be an illusion, she thought. It couldn't have been real. No one could move that fast.

No one.

*   *   *

Mike brought Julie home and was still in the driveway unloading her things when she went inside. Singer followed her, and when she put her purse on the kitchen counter, he balanced on his two back legs to greet her. She was trying to fend off his lapping tongue when she noticed the answering machine blinking with a single message.

She pushed Singer away and his feet met the floor; he padded toward the living room and out the door, probably to visit with Mike. In the kitchen, the refrigerator was humming. A fly was flailing against the window, buzzing in anger. She heard none of it. Nor could she hear Mike or Singer, or even the sounds of her own breathing. Instead, in the kitchen, the only thing she noticed was the machine. The blinking was ominous, hypnotic.

Play me, it seemed to be saying. *Play me* . . .

For an instant, the floor seemed unsteady, and Julie found herself on the boat again, looking toward the beach. He'd waved at her, she thought. He'd been watching her, and now he'd called to tell her about it.

She shook her head. No, that wasn't it. He wasn't

there. He was never there. It had been a mirage. Her eyes had been playing tricks, a product of one too many beers and a case of the jitters.

In the kitchen, the machine kept blinking.

C'mon, Julie thought, get a hold of yourself. Anyone could have left a message, so what's the big deal? That's the reason I have the machine in the first place, so just head over there and press the button. As soon as I do, I'll find out Mabel or another friend has called, or it's someone calling for an appointment, or someone wanting me to subscribe to one magazine or another, or to support the local United Way. Just press the button and see how ridiculous this is.

Yet moving to the phone was almost impossible. Her stomach was knotted up; her legs were stiff. She reached the machine and brought her hand up, then hesitated, her finger resting on the button.

Play me . . .

She closed her eyes, thinking, I can do this.

Breathing hard, she couldn't deny that as brave and logical as she'd tried to be, as much as she'd tried to convince herself that she was blowing this out of proportion, fear was getting the best of her. Please, she thought, let there be no messages filled with nothing. Let me hear a voice. Any voice but his.

With a trembling hand, she pressed the button.

At first there was nothing but silence, and she found herself holding her breath. Then, faintly, came the sound of someone whispering, a whisper impossible to identify, and she leaned closer to the machine to make out the voice. She listened, concentrating hard, and just as she was reaching for the delete button to erase it, she recognized the message itself. Her eyes grew wide as she heard the chorus of a song, a tune she knew by heart.

A tune from her evening in Beaufort with Mike two weeks ago.

'Bye, bye, Miss American Pie . . .'

Twenty-six

Julie's cries brought Mike running inside.

She stood beside the machine, her face white as she hit the delete button over and over.

'What happened?' Mike demanded. 'Are you okay?'

Julie barely heard the words. She was trembling as images raced through her mind, one right after the next, leaving her nauseated. Richard *had* been at the beach today—she was sure of that now. It *was* Richard who'd been making the calls—there wasn't the slightest doubt about it. And Richard, she suddenly knew, hadn't stopped at just those things. He'd also been watching them in Beaufort. He'd stayed out of sight while she and Mike had dinner, he'd seen them take the walk in the park, and he'd been close by, close enough to know the song that Mike had sung for her. For all she knew, he'd been the one who'd bought their drinks afterward. He'd also called the night Mike stayed over. And she knew with sinking certainty that he'd been watching her in the cemetery.

He'd been *everywhere*.

This can't be happening, she thought as her throat constricted, but it *was*. Everything seemed suddenly, terribly wrong. The kitchen was too bright, the curtains were open, the windows looked over the wooded lots where anyone could hide. Where *he* could hide. Shadows stretched into darkness, and as clouds began to roll overhead, the world took on a grayness, like an old horror movie filmed in black and white. If he'd been watching her today, if he'd been watching her *always*, he was probably watching her now.

In the yard, Singer lifted his nose and barked.

Julie jumped, feeling her heart begin to hammer, and she turned into Mike, burying her face in his chest just as the tears started to come.

People like that don't stop, Emma had said.

'Julie? C'mon . . . tell me what happened,' Mike pleaded. 'What's going on?'

Her voice was cracked and faint when she finally answered. 'I'm scared,' she said.

*   *   *

Julie was still shaking when she got in the car with Mike a few minutes later. A nap was out of the question now, of course; there wasn't a chance she was going to sleep. And there wasn't the remotest possibility that she was going to stay at her house alone while Mike went to the Clipper. Mike had offered to back out of the show, but she didn't want him to, sure that they would just sit around home rehashing the fear all night long. No need to relive the suffocating terror.

No, what she needed was an escape. A night on the town, some loud music, and a few more beers and she'd be good as new. Back to the same old me, she thought.

As if that's going to be possible, the little voice

inside her said skeptically.

Julie frowned. Okay, so it probably wasn't going to work, but obsessing about it *certainly* wouldn't work. And she was *not* going to stay home. And she was not going to think about it, she told herself, other than to figure out just what she was going to do from here on.

She'd always believed that people come in two varieties: those who look out the windshield and those who stare in the rearview mirror. She'd always been the windshield type: Gotta focus on the future, not the past, because that's the only part that's still up for grabs. Mom throws me out? *Gotta get some food and find a place to sleep.* Husband dies? *Gotta keep working, or I'll end up going crazy.* Got some guy stalking me? *Gotta figure out a way to stop it.*

In the car with Mike, she steeled herself. Julie Barenson, she thought, a take-charge kind of gal.

The puffing up worked for a moment before her shoulders sagged. Yeah, right, she thought. It wasn't going to be that easy this time, because this little scenario wasn't finished yet, and the future's kind of hard to concentrate on when the past isn't quite done. Right now, she was stuck in the present, and it wasn't a good feeling at all. Despite the brave act she was putting on, she *was* scared, even more scared than when she'd been living on the streets. There, she'd been able to find a way to stay invisible—survival by hiding, she'd called it, which was pretty much the opposite of what was happening with Richard. The problem now was that she was too visible, and she couldn't do a thing about it.

When Mike parked on the street in front of his

268

place, she found herself looking over her shoulder and straining to hear anything out of the ordinary. The darkened spaces between the houses didn't do much for her nerves; nor did the rustling, which turned out to be a stray cat poking through the garbage.

And the *questions* that plagued her—oh, those were doozies for the nerves, weren't they? What did he want? What was he going to do next? For a moment she imagined herself lying in bed at night with the room black and, when her eyes adjusted to the darkness, realizing he was there, in the room with her. He'd be standing beside the bed, his eyes the only thing visible through the mask, something in his hand as he approached her . . .

Julie shook that last image from her mind. Let's not get carried away. That's not going to happen. She was not going to let that happen. Mike wasn't going to let that happen. No way. Not a chance.

But what to do?

She wished she hadn't deleted the message. In fact, she wished she hadn't deleted any of the messages, since they were the only proof she had that something was actually happening. The police might have been able to do something with them.

But they could do something anyway, couldn't they?

Julie thought about that, coming to the same conclusion she'd shared with Emma. Oh, she could try, of course, but even with the new stalking laws, without proof there was nothing the police could do. She'd end up sitting across from some pudgy, overworked officer who would tap his pencil against the pad, waiting for her to provide concrete evidence.

What did he say on the first messages? *Nothing.*

Has he ever threatened you? *No.*

Have you ever seen him following you? *No, except at the beach.*

But you couldn't be sure it was him. *He was too far away.*

If the person was whispering on the last message, how do you know it was Richard? *I can't prove it, but I know it was him.*

Long pause. Uh-huh. Well, is there anything else? *No. Except that I've got a major case of the willies and I'd like to be able to take a shower without imagining Norman Bates on the other side of the curtain.*

Another tap of the pencil. Uh-huh.

Even to her, it sounded far-fetched. Thinking it was him didn't make it him. But it was Richard! She was absolutely sure of it.

Wasn't she?

*   *   *

At the Clipper, Julie took a seat at the bar alongside a few other men who'd come earlier to watch a baseball game.

Julie ordered a beer and was nursing it slowly as eight o'clock came and went. The television was turned off and the people at the bar left; after the band had checked the amplifiers and tuned their instruments, they went backstage to relax. Mike joined Julie. They made a point of not talking about what had happened, which was, she thought, a lot like talking about it, when it got right down to it. But Julie could see the anger in Mike's eyes when he finally told her that he was needed

270

on stage.

'I'll be watching,' he said.

By that point, a few people had wandered up to the bar, others had seated themselves at tables, and still others had congregated in small groups. By nine-thirty, when the music started, even more people had arrived and there was a steady stream coming in the door. People were crowding the bar to order drinks, but Julie ignored them, thankful that the noise and atmosphere were at least partially drowning out the endless questions. Still, she turned reflexively toward the door whenever it opened, afraid of seeing Richard.

Dozens of people entered, but Richard didn't.

The hours passed in steady rhythm—first ten, then eleven, then midnight—and for the first time since that afternoon, Julie felt herself regaining a bit of control. And like Mike, with that feeling came anger. More than anything, she wanted to give Richard a verbal lashing in public, the kind of high-volume tirade that included pointed forefingers being poked into his chest. *Just who do you think you are?* she imagined herself screaming at him. *Do you honestly think I'm going to put up with this crap for another minute?* (Poke.) *I've put up with too much in my life—I've survived too much in my life—to let you get the better of me. I will not, repeat,* will not, *let you ruin my life.* (Poke, poke.) *Do you think I'm some patsy?* (Poke.) *Some wimpy little thing who's gonna sit on the couch and tremble, just waiting for you to make the next move? Hell, no!* (Poke, poke.) *It's time to get on with your life, Mr Richard Franklin. The best man won, and so sorry, pal, but you weren't him. As a matter of fact, you'll never be him.* (Poke, poke,

271

poke, followed by cheering as dozens of women spontaneously jumped up, applauding.)

While she was envisioning her revenge, a group of young men wedged in next to her, ordering drinks for themselves and others in their group who couldn't get close enough. Their order took a few minutes, and when they left, she glanced off to the side.

Halfway down the bar, she saw a familiar figure leaning toward the bartender to order a drink.

Richard.

His image was like a blow to the solar plexus, and all those devastating comebacks were forgotten.

He was here.

He'd followed her.

Again.

*   *   *

Mike had seen Richard come in a minute earlier and wanted to jump off the stage to head him off, but he forced himself to keep playing.

Richard had seen Mike as well. He nodded to him with a smirk before making his way to the middle of the bar, pretending not to notice that Julie was there.

You can shove that nod where the half-moons meet, Mike thought, feeling the adrenaline kick in again. One wrong move and this guitar will be rammed up there as well.

*   *   *

Julie could see him, she could *feel* him, the sensation like heavy breaths inside a crowded elevator.

He did nothing. He neither looked her way nor made any move toward her. Instead, he stood with his back to the bar, scanning the crowd with a drink in hand, looking just like any of the other men in the place. As if he honestly believed she'd think this whole thing were a coincidence.

Screw you, Julie thought. You can't scare me.

The band started another song, and she glanced toward Mike. His face was tight, his eyes flashing a warning. He mouthed the words *I'm almost done*, and she nodded, suddenly in dire need of a drink. A real drink, something served straight up and swallowed in a single motion.

In the dim light, Richard's profile was shadowed. One leg crossed over the other, and for an instant, she thought she saw his mouth form an amused smile, as if he knew she was watching him. Her mouth, she realized, had gone dry.

Who am I kidding? she suddenly thought. He scares the hell out of me.

But it was time to end this.

Without knowing where she found the guts to do what came next, Julie rose and started toward him. Richard turned when she was close, his expression opening up as if he were pleasantly surprised to see her.

'Julie,' he said, 'I didn't know you'd be here. How are you?'

'What are you doing here, Richard?'

He shrugged. 'Just having a couple of drinks.'

'Cut it out, will you?'

She said it loud enough for others nearby to turn.

'Excuse me?' he asked.

'You know exactly what I'm talking about!'

273

'No, I don't . . .'

'You followed me here!'

'What?'

By now, even more people had turned to watch, and Julie felt the words she'd rehearsed coming back to her. From the stage, Mike was watching with frantic intensity, and the moment the song ended, he started toward them, letting his guitar fall to the stage.

'You think you can just follow me around and I'm just going to take it?' Julie demanded, her voice rising.

Richard held up his hands. 'Julie . . . hold on. Hold on. I don't know what you're talking about.'

'You picked the wrong girl to try to scare, and if you keep this up, I'll call the police and get a restraining order. I'll have you locked up. You think you can call my house and leave messages like you did—'

'I didn't leave any messages—'

Julie was screaming now, and people were looking from her to Richard and back again as the words sparked between them. By now, a half-circle had formed around them and they'd moved a step back, as if expecting fists to fly.

Julie, meanwhile, was on a roll. Living the fantasy, she realized, was even better than imagining it. *(That's right! You* go, *girl!)*

'—and get away with it? Did you think I wouldn't notice you watching me today?'

Richard took a step backward. 'This is the first time I've seen you. I was at the site all day.'

Lost in her emotions, Julie didn't register his denials.

'I'm not going to put up with this!'

'Put up with what?'

'*Just stop!* I want you to *just stop!*'

Richard looked toward the faces surrounding them, shrugging as if trying to enlist their sympathy.

'Look—I don't know what's going on here, but maybe I should just leave—'

'It's *over*. Do you *understand that!*'

Mike pushed his way through the crowd at that moment. Julie's face was red, but she looked scared, and for an instant, Richard's eyes met Mike's. In the briefest of flashes, invisible unless one was looking for it, Mike recognized the same smirk on Richard's face that he'd seen when he'd first walked into the bar—a look of challenge and defiance, as if daring Mike to do something about this.

That was all it took.

The fury that had been building since the afternoon exploded. Richard was standing when Mike plowed into him, driving his head into Richard's chest like a football player making an open field tackle. The momentum momentarily lifted Richard from the floor and sent his upper torso crashing onto the bar. Bottles and glasses shattered on the ground, and screams broke out in the crowd.

Mike grabbed Richard by the collar and cocked his arm, and though Richard's hands went up, he was off balance, which allowed Mike's first punch to connect with his cheek. Richard crashed into the bar again and was holding on to it to keep from falling. When his head came up—more slowly this time—there was a gash beneath his eye. Mike hit him again. Richard's head whipped sideways. It looked almost as if the events were happening in slow motion as Richard hit a stool and bounced off, tumbling until he hit the floor. When he rolled over, blood was streaming from his mouth. Mike was set to lunge again when a few men reached out to restrain him from behind.

The fight had lasted less than fifteen seconds. Mike struggled to free himself before he realized the people behind him were holding him not so that Richard could have his chance, but because they were worried Richard might be hurt even further. As soon as they let him go, Julie took his hand and led him out the door.

Even the band members knew enough not to try to stop them.

Twenty-seven

Once outside, Mike leaned against the tailgate, trying to collect himself.

'Give me just a minute,' he said.

'You okay?' Julie asked.

Mike brought his hands to his face and exhaled, speaking through his fingers. 'I'm fine. Just crashing a little.'

Julie moved closer, tugging at his shirt. 'That's a side of you that I haven't seen before. But you should know that I was handling it okay on my own.'

'I could see that. But the look he gave me really set me off.'

'What look?'

Mike described it, and Julie shivered. 'I didn't see

that,' she said.

'I don't think you were meant to. But I guess it's finally over now.'

For a long moment, neither of them spoke. Behind them, a few people had stepped outside and were staring in their direction. Julie's thoughts, however, were elsewhere. What was it that Richard had said? That he'd been working? That he'd been at the site all day? She hadn't listened when he'd said them, but the words were coming back now.

'I hope so,' she said.

'It's over,' Mike said again.

Julie smiled briefly, but she was clearly distracted. 'He said he wasn't the one watching me today,' she said. 'Or making the calls. He said he didn't know what I was talking about.'

'You didn't really expect him to admit it, did you?'

'I don't know. I guess I didn't expect him to say anything.'

'You're still sure it was him, though, aren't you?'

'Yeah, I'm sure.' She paused. 'At least I think I'm sure.'

He reached for her hand. 'It was him. I saw it in his face.'

Julie stared at the ground. 'Okay,' she said.

Mike squeezed her hand. 'C'mon, Julie. You don't want me to start worrying that I just beat up a guy for nothing, do you? He's the one. Trust me. And if he does anything else, we'll go to the police and tell them everything that's happened. We'll get a restraining order, we'll press charges. We'll do whatever it takes. Besides, if he wasn't the one, what was he doing there tonight? And why did he get so close without saying hello? You were only a few feet away.'

Julie closed her eyes. He's right, she thought. He's absolutely right. Richard wouldn't have gone there. Hadn't he said he didn't like it? No, he was there because he'd seen them go in. He'd known they would be there because he'd watched them. And of course he would lie about it. If he'd done everything else just this side of pyschoville, why should she expect him to tell the truth?

But why had he let himself be seen this time? And what did that mean?

Despite the warmth of the air, Julie felt suddenly chilled.

'Maybe I should go to the police anyway. Just to get a report filed.'

'It might not be a bad idea.'

'Will you go with me?'

'Of course.' Mike reached up and touched her face. 'So, you feeling better?'

'A little. Still scared, but better now.'

Mike ran his finger over her cheek before leaning in to kiss her.

'I told you I wasn't going to let anything happen to you, and I'm not. Okay?'

His touch made her skin tingle. 'Okay.'

*   *   *

In the bar, Richard was finally able to get to his feet. Among the first to reach him was Andrea.

She had seen Mike jump from the stage and begin pushing his way through the crowd. The guy she was dancing with—another winner, she acknowledged, though the neck scar was kind of sexy—grabbed her hand and said, 'C'mon . . . fight.'

278

They followed the path Mike had taken, and though they were too late to see the fight start or end, she did see Julie leading Mike away by the hand while Richard used the lower rungs of the stool to pull himself up. He was being helped by others, and as spectators rehashed what had happened, she caught the gist of what went on.

'He just attacked the guy . . .'

'This guy was minding his own business when this lady started screaming at him, and then this other dude barged in . . .'

'He wasn't doing anything . . .'

Andrea saw the gash on his cheek, the blood at the corner of his mouth, and stopped chewing her gum. She couldn't believe it. She'd never heard Mike so much as raise his voice, let alone attack someone. Pout, maybe, head off to stew, maybe, but never something violent like this. But the proof was right here in front of her. Richard was right in front of her, and as he staggered to his feet, her next move registered at once. *He's hurt! He needs me!* She cast off the guy she'd been dancing with and practically lunged toward Richard.

'Oh, my God . . . are you okay?'

Richard looked at her without answering, and when he wobbled, Andrea reached out, slipping her arm around him. Not an ounce of fat on him, she noticed.

'What happened?' she asked, feeling flushed.

'He came up and hit me,' Richard said.

'But why?'

'I don't know.'

He wobbled again, and Andrea felt him lean on her.

His arm slipped over her shoulder. Muscles

there, too, she noted.

'You need to sit down for a minute. Here—let me help.'

They took a tentative step, and the crowd started to part. Andrea liked that. It seemed almost as if they were in the final scene of a movie, just before the credits roll. She had just begun batting her eyes for effect when Leaning Joe, hobbling on his prosthetic leg, suddenly showed up to help Richard as well.

'C'mon,' he barked. 'I'm the owner here. We need to talk.'

He began leading Richard to the table, and when he suddenly changed direction, Andrea was jostled to the side and forced to let go. A minute later, Leaning Joe and Richard were talking over a small table.

From across the bar, her moment ruined, Andrea pouted as she watched them. By the time her date came back to her side, she'd already decided what she had to do.

*   *   *

All in all, it was a day that Julie would rather not relive.

Sure, it was good to test the engines, so to speak. She'd pretty much gone through every emotion possible since she'd crawled out of bed that morning, and every single one seemed to be in fine working order. Overall, she thought, if she were ranking the days, this one would have been number one in fright (bypassing the first night she'd slept beneath a highway overpass in Daytona), number three in despondency (the day Jim died and the funeral still occupied the first two slots in that sorry category), and number one in overall exhaustion. Throw in a smattering of love, anger, tears, laughter, surprise, relief, and the day-long push and pull of worry when imagining what would come next, and it was definitely a day she'd remember for a long, long time.

In the kitchen, Mike was tapping decaffeinated coffee grounds into the filter. He'd been quiet in the car and was still quiet now; he'd asked for aspirin as soon as they got home and had chewed four tablets before filling a glass of water to wash them down. Julie sat at the table. Singer chose that moment to lean against her until she gave him the attention that, no doubt in his mind, had been in relatively short supply lately.

Mike was definitely right. The whole thing must have been planned, and not only that, Richard had anticipated how she would react. He must have. His answers, his lies, had come too quickly, too naturally, too *smoothly*, for it to be otherwise.

And Richard had put up no fight at all.

Those things still bothered her. Especially, she decided, the last one.

Something didn't quite make sense there. Even if Mike had had the element of surprise, it hadn't been that *much* surprise. She'd seen Mike coming and had time to move out of the way, but not only hadn't Richard fought, he hadn't moved at all. If Richard had known what she would do, wouldn't he also have known how Mike would react? Or at least have had an inkling? So why hadn't he cared?

And why did it feel as if he'd planned that part, too?

'You sure you're not dizzy? That's a nasty bump,' Leaning Joe said.

He and Richard were standing just inside the door of the Clipper. Richard shook his head. 'I just want to go home.'

'I'd be happy to call an ambulance for you,' he offered. To Richard, it seemed as if he were really saying, *Please don't sue me*.

'It's okay,' Richard said, tired of the old man. He pushed through the door and stepped into the darkness. Scanning the parking lot, he noted that the police had already left. The rest of the parking lot was quiet as well, and he started making his way to his car.

As he approached, he realized someone was leaning against it.

'Hi, Richard,' she said.

Richard hesitated before answering. 'Hello, Andrea.'

Andrea raised her chin slightly and met his eyes. 'You feeling any better?'

Richard shrugged.

After a moment, Andrea cleared her throat. 'I know this might sound odd considering what happened tonight, but would you mind giving me a lift home?'

Richard glanced around. Again, he saw no one.

'What about your date?'

She nodded toward the Clipper. 'He's still inside. I told him I was going to the bathroom.'

Richard raised an eyebrow, saying nothing.

In the silence, Andrea took a step toward him. When she was close, she slowly raised her hand and touched the bruise on his cheek, her eyes never leaving his.

'Please?' she whispered.

'How about we go someplace else instead?'

She tilted her head, as if wondering what he meant.

He smiled. 'Trust me.'

*   *   *

In Julie's kitchen, the coffeemaker was gurgling as Mike sat at the table.

'What are you thinking?' he asked.

That everything that happened tonight seems wrong somehow, she thought. Knowing that Mike would do his best to convince her she'd misinterpreted it, however, she kept her answer vague. 'Just going through it all again. It keeps replaying in my mind, you know?'

'Yeah, for me, too.'

The coffeemaker beeped, and Mike got up from the table and poured two cups. Singer's ears lifted, and Julie watched as he made his way through the living room. In their haste to leave earlier, she hadn't drawn the shades, and she knew a car was coming down the street. There wasn't that much traffic at this time of night, and she watched to see if she recognized one of the neighbors coming home after an evening on the town.

Singer went toward the window as the light began to intensify. But instead of watching the sky fade to black again as the car whizzed by, she saw the beams from the headlights solidify. Moths and insects, drawn toward the glow, made the beams look as if they were composed of swirling fingers.

Singer barked and began growling; the glow of headlights remained steady.

The car, she could tell, was idling in the road, and she sat up in the chair. She heard the engine rev, and suddenly the lights switched off. A car door slammed.

He was here, Julie thought. Richard had come to the house.

Mike looked toward the window.

Singer's growls grew louder, and the hair on the back of his neck stood up. Mike put a hand on Julie's shoulder and took a tentative step toward the door. Singer was barking and growling steadily now as Mike moved forward.

Singer went wild then, and in the fury came something unexpected. The sound was at once normal and startling, and Mike paused, as if trying to decide that what he'd heard was real.

Then it came again. Someone, they realized, was knocking on the door. Mike turned toward Julie as if asking, *Huh*?

He peeked out the window, and Julie saw his shoulders drop; when he glanced at her again, there was a look of relief on his face. He patted Singer's back and said, 'Shh, it's okay,' and Singer stopped growling. He followed Mike, however, as Mike reached for the door handle.

A moment later, Julie saw two police officers standing on the porch.

*   *   *

Officer Jennifer Romanello was new in town, new on the job, and looking forward to the day she'd have her own squad car, if only to get away from

284

the guy she was working with. After doing the majority of her police training in Jacksonville, she'd moved to Swansboro less than a month earlier. She'd been riding with Pete Gandy for two weeks now and had four weeks to go—all rookies had to work with an experienced officer during their first six weeks on the job to complete their training— and if she heard him mention 'the ropes' again, she thought she'd strangle him.

Pete Gandy turned the key, shutting off the ignition, and glanced over at her.

'Let me handle this,' he said. 'You're still learning the ropes.'

I'm really going to kill him, she thought.

'Should I wait in the car?'

Though she had said it in jest, Pete missed the tone, and she could see him flexing his arm. Pete took his biceps very seriously. He also liked to look at himself in the rearview mirror before he went into action.

'No. Come on up. Just let me do the talking. And make sure to keep your eyes open, kid.'

He said this as though he were old enough to be her father. In reality, he'd been on the force only two years, and despite the fact that Swansboro wasn't exactly a hotbed of high-profile criminal activity, Pete had developed a theory that the Mafia had started infiltrating the town, and darned if he wasn't going to be the one to handle it. Pete's all-time favorite movie was *Serpico*. It was the reason he'd joined the force.

Jennifer closed her eyes. Why of all the idiots did I get stuck with this guy?

'Whatever you say.'

'Mike Harris?' Officer Gandy said.

Pete Gandy had put on the 'I know the uniform intimidates you' pose, and Jennifer fought the urge to slap the back of his head. She knew that Pete had been acquainted with both Mike and Julie for years—in the car, he mentioned that Mike serviced his car, and he got his hair cut at the salon. He hadn't even needed to look up Julie's address. Life in a small town, she sighed. For a gal who grew up in the Bronx, this was a whole new world, and she was still getting used to it.

'Oh, hey Pete,' Mike said. 'What can I do for you?'

'Can we come in for a minute? We need to talk to you.'

'Sure,' Mike said.

They hesitated, and Mike glanced down at Singer. 'Don't worry about him. He'll be fine.'

The officers stepped into the living room, and Mike motioned over his shoulder with his thumb. 'Can I get you some coffee? I just made a pot.'

'No, thank you. We're not allowed to drink on the job.'

Jennifer rolled her eyes, thinking, That only goes for booze, you putz.

By then, Julie had come out from the kitchen and was standing a few feet back, her arms crossed. Singer went to her side and sat.

'What's this all about, Pete?' she asked.

Officer Pete Gandy didn't like being called Pete while wearing the uniform, and for a moment, he wasn't sure how to react to the familiarity. He cleared his throat.

'Were you at the Sailing Clipper this evening, Mike?'

'Yeah. I played with the Ocracoke Inlet.'

Pete glanced toward Jennifer, as if showing her how it was done. Oooh, big scoop, she thought. Only a million people verified that fact already.

'And were you involved in an altercation with one Mr Richard Franklin?'

Before Mike could answer, Julie stepped into the living room.

'What's going on?' she asked.

Pete Gandy lived for this moment. Next to pulling his gun, this was far and away the best part of the job, even if he was doing this to someone he knew. Duty was duty, after all, and if he let the little things slide, before he knew it, Swansboro would be the murder capital of the world. In the last month alone, he'd issued a dozen tickets for jaywalking and another dozen for littering.

'Well, sir, I hate to do this to you, but I've got a number of witnesses who say you attacked Mr Franklin without provocation. That's assault, and it's against the law.'

Two minutes later, Mike was being led away to the squad car.

Twenty-eight

'They took him to jail?' Mabel asked in disbelief.

It was Monday morning, and because Mabel had been visiting her brother in Atlanta, she hadn't heard anything until she'd walked in that morning. For the past ten minutes, Julie had filled Mabel in on everything that had happened. Andrea was busy mangling a gentleman's hair as she strained to listen in. She hadn't smiled since Julie had started talking, and the more she heard, the more she wanted to tell Julie that she didn't know what she was talking about.

Richard wasn't dangerous! Mike attacked *him!* Besides, Richard wasn't even interested in Julie anymore. Richard, she felt sure, had finally seen the light. And talk about romantic! He'd taken her to the beach and they'd talked! For hours! And he hadn't even made a pass at her! No guy had ever treated her with that kind of respect. And he was sweet, too. He'd asked her not to tell Julie because he didn't want to hurt her feelings. Did that sound like a stalker? Of course not! Even though he'd refused her offer to come inside when he'd finally dropped her off at her house, she'd been glowing since she woke up yesterday morning.

Julie shrugged. Her face was drawn and pale, as if she hadn't slept much.

'Pete Gandy questioned him for an hour, and he was there until Henry bailed him out.'

Mabel looked baffled. 'Pete Gandy? What was he thinking? Didn't he listen to what Mike was saying?'

'Not that I could tell. He kept trying to write this off as some sort of jealous spat. Kept wanting to know the real reason he attacked Richard.'

'Did you tell him what's been going on?'

'I tried, but he didn't think it was relevant. Not to the assault charge.'

Mabel tossed her purse onto the magazine-covered table. 'He's an idiot. But he's always been an idiot. How he ended up on the force, I'll

288

never know.'

'That may be true, but it doesn't help Mike. It doesn't help me, either, for that matter.'

'So what's next for Mike? Is he going to be charged?'

'I have no idea. We'll find out today, I guess. He has an appointment with Steve Sides later.'

Steven Sides was a local defense attorney; Mabel had known his family for years.

'That's a smart choice. Have you ever met him?'

'No, but Henry has. Hopefully, he'll be able to work out something with the prosecutor.'

'So what are you going to do? About Richard?'

'I'm changing my phone number today.'

'That's it?'

'I don't know what else I can do. Pete wouldn't listen to me, other than to say that if it kept happening, I should report it.'

'Did he call again on Sunday?'

'No. Thank God.'

'And you didn't see him?'

'No.'

Across the salon, Andrea frowned, thinking, That's because he was still thinking about me. Now quit bad-mouthing him.

'So you think he set that whole thing up, don't you?'

'I think he's been setting everything up, including Saturday night. Including me. I think he considers this whole thing a game.'

Mabel met her eyes. 'It's not a game, Julie,' she said.

It took a while for Julie to respond.

'I know,' she said.

'So what was he like?' Henry asked. 'During the interview?'

They were seated in Henry's office, the door closed behind them. Mike exhaled in disgust.

'It's hard to explain.'

'What do you mean?'

'It's like he already had an idea in his head as to how it all came about, and nothing I said could change his mind.'

'He didn't care about the phone calls? Or the fact he was watching you guys earlier?'

'No. He said it sounded like she was blowing it out of proportion. People shop, he said, they get haircuts. No big deal.'

'And how was the other cop? The lady?'

'Pete wouldn't let her say anything, so I have no idea.'

Henry reached for his coffee and took a sip. 'Well, you really did it this time,' he said. 'Not that I blame you. I would have done the same thing had I been there.'

'So what do you think will happen?'

'Well, I don't think you'll end up in jail, if that's what you're asking.'

'That's not what I'm talking about.'

Henry looked at him. 'You mean with Richard?'

Mike nodded.

Henry put the cup of coffee back on his desk. 'I wish I could tell you, little brother,' he said.

*   *   *

Officer Jennifer had just about had her fill of

Officer Pete, and they'd been working together for only an hour that morning. She'd had to come in early to finish up the reports from Sunday that Officer Pete hadn't quite gotten around to, because, as he said, 'I'm too busy trying to protect the streets to be tied down at a desk my whole shift. And besides, it'll help you learn the ropes.'

In the two weeks she'd been working with him, she hadn't learned anything about the job, other than the fact that Pete was more than happy to slough off the busywork so he could have more time to devote to curling weights in front of the mirror. The man, she decided, was an absolute moron when it came to interviewing people.

The other night was a prime example.

She didn't need to be a Nobel Prize winner to see that Mike and Julie were scared, and not because Mike was being hauled off for questioning in the middle of the night. No, they were scared of Richard Franklin, and if what they were saying was true, Jennifer figured they had every right to be. Pete Gandy might have the instincts of a wooden post, but Jennifer's were well honed, in spite of the fact that she'd just finished her training. But then, she'd grown up hearing about this kind of stuff.

Jennifer came from a long line of cops; her father was a cop, her grandfather was a cop, and both brothers were cops, though all were still living in New York. How she'd ended up in coastal North Carolina was a long story, involving college, an ex-boyfriend, the need to make her own mark in the world, and the desire to see another part of the country. It all sort of collided about six months earlier, when she'd applied for the police academy on a whim and surprised herself by actually being accepted for a job opening in Swansboro. Her father, though proud she was 'joining up with the good guys,' was aghast that she was doing it in North Carolina. 'They all chew tobacco and eat grits and call every woman darlin'. How's a nice Italian girl like you going to fit in down there?'

Only she had fit in, oddly enough. It was much better than she'd expected so far, especially the people, who—get this—were so friendly that they waved to strangers while driving. Everyone was great, in fact, except for Pete Gandy. Out of the corner of her eye, she could see him flexing that arm again, making his muscle bulge, and whenever he passed another car, he nodded to the other driver, as if saying, *Keep the speed down, buddy*.

'So what did you think of Mike Harris's story the other night?' Jennifer finally asked.

Since he was caught up in his nodding, it took a moment for Pete to realize she was speaking.

'Oh, well, uh . . . he was making excuses,' he said. 'If I've seen it once, I've seen it a hundred times. Everybody who's charged blames the other guy. No criminal is ever guilty, and if he is, there's a very reasonable explanation. Once you've been through the ropes, you'll get used to that pretty quick.'

'But didn't you say you knew him and that he always seemed like a laid-back guy?'

'Doesn't matter. The law's the law, same for everybody.'

She knew he was trying to sound wise and worldly and above all fair, but in the two weeks she'd been partnered with Pete, none of those adjectives seemed to apply. Wise and worldly? The man considered professional wrestling a real sport, and fairness didn't even seem to be in the man's vocabulary. One of his jaywalking tickets had gone to a lady hobbling across the street in a walker, for heaven's sake, and the other night, when she'd opened her mouth to ask Mike Harris a question, Pete had waved her off, commenting that 'the little lady is still learning the ropes about interrogation. Don't mind her.'

Had they been anywhere but the station, she would have put him in his place for that one. She'd almost done it anyway. Little lady? Once she was out of training, she vowed she'd make Pete Gandy pay for it. Somehow, some way, he'd pay.

Anyway, since she was still technically in training, albeit the last stages, what could she do but seethe? Besides, that wasn't the point. Mike Harris and Richard Franklin were what this was all about. And Julie Barenson, of course. Because of what Mike and Julie had said and the 'too smooth to be anything but squirrelly' way Richard had acted when they'd talked to him, she hadn't slept well after getting off her shift.

Richard, she had the feeling, was not the innocent victim in this. And neither Julie nor Mike struck her as liars.

'Don't you think we should at least look into it, though? What if they were telling the truth?'

Pete sighed as if the topic bored him. 'Then they should have come down to the station to file a report. But they didn't. And they admitted they had no evidence. She didn't even know for sure that it was Franklin who was calling. So what does that tell you?'

'But—'

'It tells you that they were probably making it up. Look, it was a good collar, and we've got him dead to rights.'

Jennifer tried again. 'But what about her? Julie Barenson. She looked scared, don't you think?'

'Of course she was scared. Her little honey was just locked up. You'd probably be scared, too. Anyone would be.'

'In New York, the police—'

Pete Gandy raised his hand. 'No more New York stories, okay? Things are different down here. Blood runs a little hot in these parts. Once you learn the ropes, you'll realize that nearly every altercation has something to do with a feud or vendetta of some sort, and the law doesn't much like to get involved with those unless they cross the line, like this one. Besides, before you came in this morning, I was talking to the chief, and he said that he's had a call from the lawyer and that they're trying to work out something, so I think for the most part, this is pretty much over. At least where we're concerned. Unless it goes to court.'

Jennifer looked at him. 'What are you talking about?'

Pete shrugged. 'That's all he said.'

Another thing she couldn't stand about Officer Gandy was the fact that he kept information from her about the cases they worked on. Pete Gandy liked to be in control of things, and this was his little way of letting her know that he was in charge.

When Jennifer didn't say anything, Pete went back to his nodding routine again.

Jennifer shook her head. Imbecile.

In the silence, her thoughts returned to Mike and Julie, and she wondered if maybe she should talk to them again, preferably when Pete wasn't around.

Henry was standing beside Mike in the office, listening in on the phone conversation to his lawyer. 'You've got to be kidding me' was followed by 'You're not serious' and 'I can't believe this!' Mike paced the small office, his heavy strides punctuated by looks of disbelief, and he kept repeating those statements. At last, his jaw setting, he began answering in monosyllables, then finally hung up the phone.

He neither moved nor said a word to Henry. Instead, he stared at the phone, skimming his tongue over his teeth.

'What was that all about?' Henry asked.

To Henry, it looked as if his question rolled through a complex filter, translated from English into something else, then back again. His face had taken on the 'from bad to worse' look.

'He says he just heard from Richard Franklin's attorney,' he said.

'And?'

Mike couldn't look at Henry. He was angled toward the door, though his eyes didn't seem to be focusing. 'He said they intend to file a temporary restraining order against me until the case gets sorted out. He says that Richard Franklin considers me a menace.'

'You?'

'He also says they intend to file a civil suit against me.'

'You're kidding.'

'That's what I said. But according to the other lawyer, Richard is still dizzy from the other night. Supposedly, he thought he was okay and was able

295

to make it home Saturday night. But by Sunday morning, his vision was blurry and he was so dizzy that he had to call a cab to bring him to the hospital. His lawyer is claiming that I gave him a concussion.'

Henry rocked back slightly. 'Did you tell him that Richard is lying? I mean, nothing against you, and I'm sure it was a good shot, but c'mon, a concussion?'

Mike shrugged, still trying to process everything, wondering how this had suddenly spun so out of control. Two days ago he'd just wanted Richard to stop bothering Julie. Three days ago he hadn't been thinking about the guy, period. And now he was considered a criminal because he'd done what he was supposed to do.

Officer Pete Gandy, he decided, was definitely off the Christmas party list. Not that he had a Christmas party, but if he ever did, Pete Gandy wasn't going to be invited. Had he listened, had he even tried to understand Mike's reasoning, none of this would be happening now.

Mike stood from the chair. 'I've got to talk to Julie,' he announced, slamming the door on his way out.

*   *   *

By the time he reached the salon, Julie needed only a glance to surmise that Mike was just about as upset as she'd ever seen him.

'It's ridiculous,' he repeated. 'I mean, what good are the police if they won't do anything about him? I'm not the damn problem here, he is.'

'I know,' Julie said soothingly.

'Don't they know I wouldn't make up the stuff I tried to tell him? Don't they know I wouldn't have come after him unless he'd deserved it? What the hell good is keeping on the right side of the law if they're not going to believe anything you say? Now I'm the one who has to defend myself. I'm the one who's out on bail. I'm the one who has to hire lawyers. What does that say about the criminal justice system? This guy can do whatever he wants, but I can't do a damn thing.'

Julie didn't answer right away, nor did Mike seem to need a response. Finally, she reached for his hand and tugged on it until he relented.

'You're right, it doesn't make any sense,' she said. 'And I'm sorry.'

Though her touch seemed to calm him, Mike couldn't meet her eyes. 'I am, too,' he said.

'Why are you sorry?'

'Because I screwed things up with the police. That's what I'm really worried about. I can handle whatever happens to me, but what about you? Because of me, the police don't believe your story. And what if they don't believe me or you in the future, either?'

Julie didn't want to think about that anymore. She'd been thinking about it all morning. The whole thing had worked out just the way Richard wanted. She was more certain than ever that he had planned it all.

'It just doesn't seem fair,' Mike said.

'Did the lawyer say anything else?'

Mike shrugged. 'Just the usual stuff. That there's no reason to worry just yet.'

'Easy for him to say.'

Mike let go of Julie and took a deep breath.

'Yeah.' It came out sounding tired, defeated, and Julie looked up at him.

'You still coming over to my place tonight?'

'If you want me to. If you're not too mad at me.'

'I'm not mad at you. But I would be if you didn't come. I really don't want to be alone tonight.'

*　　　*　　　*

Steven Sides's office was located near the courthouse. Once inside, Mike was led to a paneled room dominated by a large rectangular table and shelves filled with law books. He took a seat as the attorney pushed open the door.

Steven Sides was fifty, with a round face and black hair that was turning gray at the temples. His suit was expensive—one of those silk numbers imported from Italy—but it looked rumpled, as if he hadn't hung it up after wearing it last. There was a puffiness to his skin and the tip of his nose that suggested the habit of a few too many after-hours cocktails, but there was a steadiness to his demeanor that gave Mike confidence. Sides spoke slowly, carefully, with every word measured for effect. He let Mike rant for a few minutes, before guiding him into the story with a series of questions. It didn't take long for Mike to tell him everything.

When he was finished, Steven Sides set his pencil on his legal pad and leaned back.

'Like I said on the phone, I wouldn't worry about the altercation on Saturday night right now. For one thing, I'm not sure the district attorney is going to push for prosecution, for various reasons.' He began to tick them off, one by one. 'Your clean

298

record, your good standing in the community, and the fact that he's well aware that you'd be able to bring in dozens of character witnesses make it unlikely that he'd find a jury who would convict you. And once I tell him what led you to this point makes prosecution that much more doubtful, even if there is no proof of the stalking. It could still play well to a jury, and he knows it.'

'But what about the civil case?'

'That's a different matter, but it's not something that would happen right away, if it happens at all. If the district attorney doesn't prosecute, that won't be good for Franklin's case. If the district attorney prosecutes and loses the case, that won't look good, either. In all likelihood, they won't go to court unless he wins at trial, and like I said, I just don't see that happening. You thought Julie was in trouble and you reacted; for better or worse, most people would find that perfectly reasonable. And the restraining order is just for show. I'll assume you have no problem staying away from Richard Franklin.'

'Not at all. I never wanted to be around the guy in the first place.'

'Good. But let me handle the prosecutor, okay? And don't go talking to the police again. Just refer them to me and I'll handle it.'

Mike nodded. 'So you really don't think I should worry about this?'

'Not yet, anyway. Let me talk to a few people, and I'll let you know where we are in a couple of days. If you're going to worry about anything, worry about Richard Franklin.'

Sides leaned forward, his face serious. 'What I'm going to tell you is just for you, okay? And I'm only doing this because you seem like a decent guy. If you say that I'm the one who told you what I'm about to say, I'll deny it.'

After a moment, Mike nodded.

The lawyer waited, making sure he had Mike's complete attention.

'There's one thing you should understand about the police. The police are great when there's a burglary or a murder. That's what the system was set up for—to catch people after the fact. Even with the stalking laws on the books, there's still nothing that the police can really do if someone targets you and he's been careful not to leave evidence that gets him locked up first. If a person is hell-bent on doing you harm and he doesn't care about the possible consequences, then you're pretty much on your own. You'll be the one who has to deal with this.'

'So you think Richard Franklin might want to hurt Julie?'

'That's not the right question to ask. The question is, do you believe that? If you do, you'll have to be ready to deal with it. Because if it gets worse from here, no one's going to be able to help you.'

* * *

The conversation left Mike feeling off-kilter. Sides was obviously a smart guy, and though Mike was feeling better about his legal prospects, his relief was offset by Sides's warning.

Was it over with Richard now?

Mike paused outside his truck and thought about it. He pictured Richard's face in the bar again. He saw the smirk, and with that, the answer came to him.

This wasn't going to stop, he knew. Richard was just getting started.

And as he crawled into the truck, he heard Sides's voice again.

No one's going to be able to help you.

* * *

That evening, Mike and Julie did their best to have as normal a night as possible. They grabbed a pizza on the way home, then watched a movie, but neither bothered to hide the fact that whenever a car drove up the street, they both stiffened until it had passed. They kept the curtains drawn and kept Singer inside. Even Singer picked up on their nervousness. Pacing the house as if on patrol, he neither barked nor growled. When he closed his eyes to doze, he did so with one ear cocked forward.

The only thing unusual about the night was that it seemed too quiet. Because Julie's phone had been switched to an unlisted number, it hadn't rung. She had decided to give the number to only a few select people, and she'd told Mabel not to offer it to clients. *If Richard can't call,* she thought, *maybe he'll get the message.*

Julie shifted on the couch. Maybe.

After dinner, she'd asked Mike about his meeting with the lawyer, and Mike had told her what Sides had said—namely, that he didn't think Mike had all that much to worry about. But to Julie's vigilant eye, Mike's demeanor suggested that Sides had said a good deal more than that.

Across town, Richard stood above the tray of chemicals in his darkroom, his face glowing red, watching as the image on the photographic paper slowly took form. The process still struck him as mysterious—ghosts and shadows, darkening, becoming real. Becoming Julie.

Her eyes shimmered back at him in the shallow pan, shimmered all around him.

Always, he returned to the photography, the single constant in his life. Staring at the beauty of reflected light and shadows on the images brought a sense of purpose, reminding him that he controlled his own destiny.

He was still exhilarated from the other night. Julie's imagination was running wild, no doubt. Even now, she was probably wondering where he was, what he was thinking, what he would do next. As if he were some kind of monster, the bogeyman of childhood nightmares. He wanted to laugh. How could such a terrible thing make him feel so good?

And Mike, charging in like the cavalry at the bar. So utterly predictable. He'd almost wanted to laugh then, too. No challenge with that one. Julie, though . . .

So emotional. So brave.

So *alive*.

Studying the photograph in front of him, he again took note of the similarities between Julie and Jessica. Same eyes. Same hair. Same air of innocence. From the moment he'd walked into the salon, he'd thought they could be sisters.

Richard shook his head, feeling the memory of Jessica pull at him.

They had rented a house in Bermuda for their honeymoon, not far from large resorts. It was quiet and romantic, with ceiling fans and white wicker furniture and a porch that faced the ocean. There was a private beach where they could spend hours in the sun alone, just the two of them.

Oh, how he'd been looking forward to that! He'd taken dozens of photographs of her during the first couple of days.

He loved her skin; it was soft and unlined, burnished in its coat of oil. By the third day, her skin had darkened to bronze, and in her white cotton dress, she was dazzling. That night, he'd wanted nothing more than to take her in his arms and slowly peel the dress from her body and make love to her beneath the sky.

But she'd wanted to go dancing. At the resort.

No, he'd said, *let's stay here. It's our honeymoon.*

Please, she'd said. *For me. Will you do this for me?*

They went, and it was loud and filled with drunks, and Jessica was loud and kept on drinking. Her words began to slur, and later she swayed as she made her way to the rest room. She bumped into a young man and nearly spilled his drink. The young man touched her arm and laughed. Jessica laughed with him.

Richard seethed as he watched it happen. It embarrassed him. It angered him. But he would forgive her, he told himself. She was young and immature. He would forgive her, because he was her husband and he loved her. But she would have to promise not to do it again.

But that evening, when they were back at the house, he tried to talk to her and she wouldn't listen.

I was just having fun, she'd said. *You could have tried to have fun, too.*

How could I, with my new wife flirting with strangers?

I wasn't flirting.

I saw you.

Stop acting crazy.

What did you say to me? What did you say?

Ow . . . let me go . . . you're hurting me . . .

What did you say?

Ow . . . please . . . Ow!

What did you say?

In the end, she'd disappointed him, Richard thought. And Julie had disappointed him, too. The grocery store, the salon, the way she'd hung up on him. He was beginning to lose faith, but she'd redeemed herself at the bar. She hadn't been able to ignore him, she hadn't been able to simply walk away. No, he thought, she'd *had* to talk to him, and though her words were spiteful, he knew what she was really feeling. Yes, he knew, she cared for him, for weren't anger and love opposite sides of the same coin? Great anger wasn't possible without great love . . . and she'd been so angry.

The thought made him soar.

Richard left the darkroom and made his way to the bedroom. On the bed, amid the clutter of the cameras and lenses, he reached for the cell phone. His home phone, he knew, would leave a traceable record, but he had to hear her voice tonight, even if it was only on the machine. When he heard her voice, he could see the two of them at the theater again, tears in her eyes, he could hear her breath speed up as the Phantom decided whether to let his lover leave him or whether both of them should die.

He dialed the number, then closed his eyes in anticipation. But instead of Julie's familiar voice, there was a recording from the phone company. He ended the call and dialed again, more carefully this time, but got the same recorded message.

Richard stared at the phone. Oh, Julie, he wondered, why? *Why?*

Twenty-nine

After the tumult of the past month, the next week of Julie's life was startlingly quiet. She didn't see Richard anywhere during the week or on the following weekend, Monday had been equally uneventful, and she kept her fingers crossed that today would be no different.

It seemed as if it would. Her phone was evidence to the fact that unlisted, unforwarded numbers were an effective way to stop unwanted calls, and though it was a welcome relief not to worry about it, she'd begun thinking that she might as well bury the phone in the backyard, since it was obvious that no one was ever going to give her a ring just to shoot the breeze, ever again, for the rest of her life.

Only four people—Mabel, Mike, Henry, and Emma—knew the number, and since she spent all day with Mabel and all night with Mike, neither one of them had reason to give her a jingle. Henry had never called in all the years she'd known him, which pretty much left Emma as the only person who might even consider calling. But after hearing how the calls had rattled Julie, Emma was apparently giving her a break, not wanting to be responsible for peeling Julie off the ceiling.

Okay, she admitted, it wasn't so bad at first. It was kind of nice being able to cook or shower or thumb through a magazine or cuddle with Mike and know that she wouldn't be disturbed, but after a week, it got kind of irritating. Sure, she could call out and she did, but that wasn't the same. Because no one called, because no one *could* call, it sort of began to feel as if she'd been transported back to the pioneer days.

Funny what a quiet week will do to a person's perspective.

But it *had* been quiet, that was the thing. Really quiet. *Normally* quiet. She hadn't so much as seen anyone who might be Richard, even from a distance, and she *was* watching for him practically every minute. And so, of course, were Mike and Mabel and Henry. She'd peek out the windows of the salon in both directions a dozen times a day. When she was driving, she would sometimes turn suddenly onto a different road and stop, staring in the rearview mirror to see if anyone was following her. She scanned parking lots with a professional eye and faced the door when she stood in line at the post office or the supermarket. When she got home, Singer would head toward the woods and she would call him back so he could check out the house. She would wait outside, her hand on the container of pepper spray she'd picked up at Wal-Mart, while Singer scoured the rooms. But within minutes, Singer would come back, tail wagging and drool dripping, looking as happy as a kid at a birthday party.

What are you still doing on the porch? he seemed

to ask. *Don't you want to come in?*

Even the dog noticed she was acting a little paranoid. But as the old cliché went, better safe than sorry.

And then there was Mike. Mike hadn't so much as let her out of his sight for more than a few minutes except when she was at work. Although having him around was great, there were moments when it got a little suffocating. Some things, she thought, were better done without Mike *right there*.

On the legal front, there was mixed activity. Officer Romanello had come by the week before and talked to both of them; she got their story and said not to hesitate to call her if anything out of the ordinary happened again. That made Julie feel better; Mike felt better for it, too, but so far, they hadn't had reason to call. On another front, the district attorney had declined to press charges, and though he held open the possibility that they might be reinstated at a later date, Mike was off the hook for the time being. He'd done this, he said, not because he felt Mike was justified, but because Richard hadn't shown up to give his formal statement. Nor had they been able to contact him.

Strange, she thought when she heard about it.

But eight days of nothing, absolutely nothing, had emboldened Julie. Not that she was dumb enough to forget the possible risk—I will *never* be one of those abused guests on morning talk shows that everyone in the audience considered an idiot for not *seeing it coming*, she told herself—but a subtle change *had* taken place, without her particularly being aware of it. The week before, she'd *expected* to see Richard. She'd expected to see him lurking everywhere, and she'd been prepared for it. What she'd do exactly depended on the circumstances, of course, but she had no qualms about screaming or running or setting Singer loose on the guy if she had to. I'm ready for anything, she repeated to herself, just make your move. Any inkling of trouble and you'll be sorry, Mr Franklin.

But a thousand moments of looking and listening and not finding a trace of him had slowly nicked away at her resolve. Now, though she still felt a heightened sense of wariness, she'd reached the point where she *didn't* expect to see him. So when Mike mentioned that Steven Sides had left a message, asking him to swing by for a brief meeting after work, Julie told him that she was tired and was going to head on home alone.

'Just come on over when you're done,' she said. 'And if you're going to be late, give me a call, okay?'

*   *   *

Singer bounded out of the Jeep as soon as she parked and circled the yard, moving farther and farther from her, his nose to the ground, when she called for him. Raising his head, he looked at her from across the yard.

Aw, c'mon, he seemed to be saying. *You haven't taken me for a walk in ages.*

Julie got out of the car.

'No, we can't go now,' she said. 'Maybe later, when Mike gets here.'

Singer stayed where he was.

'I'm sorry, but I don't really want to head out there, you know?'

Even from a distance, she saw his ears droop.

308

Aw, c'mon.

Julie crossed her arms and glanced around. She didn't see Richard's car, nor had she seen it while she was driving. Unless he was planning to hike in a couple of miles, he wasn't here. The only car parked on her street bore the name of the realty company that was offering the lots for sale, along with the name of the lady who was selling them, Edna Farley.

Edna was a regular at the shop. Though Mabel did her hair, over the years Julie had gotten to know Edna. Plump and middle-aged, she was nice in the way that all Realtors were—cheerful and enthusiastic, with a tendency to leave her business cards around the salon—but also a little scatterbrained. When she was excited, which was practically all the time, she seemed to miss the obvious and was always one step behind in the conversation. While others had moved on to other subjects, Edna would continue to discuss the previous one. Occasionally Julie found it annoying, but she tolerated her in an 'I'm glad it's Mabel and not me' kind of way.

Singer's tail moved back and forth, like a wave. *Pleeeease?*

Julie didn't want to go, but she hadn't taken Singer for a walk in ages.

She looked up the street again. Nothing.

Would he walk a couple of miles on the off chance she'd take her dog for a walk?

No, she decided, he wouldn't. Besides, Singer was with her, and Singer wasn't a Chihuahua. All she had to do was yelp and he would come charging like a Samurai warrior on steroids.

But she still didn't like it. The woods scared her

309

now. There were too many places to hide. Too many places to watch and be watched. Too many opportunities for Richard to hide behind a tree and wait until she'd passed and then creep up behind her, twigs cracking beneath his weight . . .

Julie felt panic clawing at her again, and she forced it away. Nothing was going to happen, she repeated. Not with Singer nearby, not with Edna pacing the lots. Not without his car in the area. Richard wasn't here.

So why not take the dog for a walk?

Singer barked as if to get her attention. *Well?*

'Okay,' she finally said. 'But we can't stay long. It looks like there might be a storm coming.'

Even before she finished speaking, Singer had turned and wandered into the woods, vanishing behind a clump of trees.

*   *   *

It took five minutes before she realized she was whispering to herself.

'Nothing is going to happen,' she was saying. 'It's perfectly safe out here.'

And it was, she thought, it had to be, but let's go over the reasons again, shall we? Because this just doesn't *feel* right for some reason. So she did and again came up with the logical conclusion that Richard wasn't lurking nearby. But it still didn't help. She began to hyperventilate.

So much for a relaxing walk in the woods.

Julie crept along the trail, pushing at overgrown branches. The foliage had thickened since she'd last been out here, or at least it seemed that way. In the past, she could see tendrils of light breaking

310

through the cover, but because the sun was low and the clouds above were charcoal gray, the woods seemed unusually dark.

This was stupid. Stupid, stupid, stupid. If they had her phone number, those morning talk shows would probably be calling tomorrow.

Why weren't you more careful? the host would ask.

Because, she would answer, dabbing at her eyes, *I'm a twit.*

She stopped to listen; she heard nothing except the faraway chirping of a magpie. She turned from side to side, looked up and down the trail, and saw nothing unusual. Nothing. 'Of course it's safe,' she whispered.

Okay, girl, she thought, you got yourself into this, and let's stay calm here. I may not see Singer, but he's around. I'll just let Singer wander, and in a few minutes we'll head back home and everything will be back to normal. Might take a glass of wine to restore order, but hey, I'm only human. And Singer loves this, after all . . .

In the distance she heard Singer bark, and her heart hammered in her chest with enough force to make her eyes go black at the corners. All righty, then, she thought, changing her mind, I think that's a pretty clear message . . .

'Singer! C'mon,' she shouted. 'Let's go back! Time to go!'

She waited and listened, but Singer didn't come. Instead, he barked again, but it wasn't an angry bark. It sounded like a bark of greeting, a friendly bark.

Julie took a step in the direction of the sound and stopped. Don't go, she thought, until she recognized another sound. A voice. Someone was

311

talking to Singer, and when she recognized it, she heaved a sigh of relief. Edna Farley . . .

She walked quickly then, following the curving path until she could see the water of the Intracoastal. Here, the forest cleared and she saw Edna patting Singer on the head. He was sitting on his haunches, his mouth open. When he heard Julie enter the clearing, he turned his head.

This is the life, he seemed to be saying. *A little walk, a little love . . . What could be better?*

Edna, too, had turned.

'Julie!' she called out. 'I thought you might be heading this way. How are you?'

Julie started toward her. 'Hey, Edna. I'm fine. Just taking a walk.'

'It's a nice day for it. Or it was when we got out here. But now it looks like it might start to rain in a little while.'

By then, Julie had drawn near.

'We?' she asked.

'Yeah, my client is looking over a couple of the far lots. They've been on the market for a while, but he seems pretty interested, so keep your fingers crossed for me.'

It was as she was speaking that Singer suddenly stood and moved to Julie's side, the hair on the back of his neck bristling. He started to growl. Julie felt her heart begin to pound as she turned in the direction in which Singer was staring. Her eyes took a moment to adjust, and she drew a labored breath. In the background, she could hear Edna going on.

'Oh, here he is now,' Edna was saying.

Before Julie could move, before she could think to do anything other than stare, Richard was standing beside Edna. He wiped his brow and smiled at her, making Edna flush a little.

'You were right,' Richard said. 'Those lots were nice, too, but I think I like the ones on this side a little better.'

'Oh, yes. You're absolutely right,' Edna said. 'And the view of the water on this side is priceless. They're not making any more waterfront, you know. It's a wonderful investment.' She laughed, but neither one of them was listening to Edna now. 'Oh, where are my manners? I'd like you to meet a friend of mine . . .'

'Hello, Julie,' Richard said. 'What a nice surprise.'

Julie said nothing; it was all she could do to remain standing. Singer continued to growl, his lips curling up to reveal his teeth. Edna stopped in midsentence. 'Oh, you two know each other?' she inquired.

'You could say that,' Richard said. 'Isn't that right, Julie?'

Julie tried to steady herself. You . . . bastard, she thought. How did you know I'd be here? How did you *know?*

'Hey, Julie, what's with Singer?' Edna asked. 'Why's he acting so upset?'

Before she could answer, Richard glanced toward Edna.

'Edna—did you bring the information about the dimensions of the lots like I asked? And the prices? I think I should take a look at the prospectus while I'm out here.'

At the word *prices*, Edna's eyes lit up.

'Of course I did. It's all in the car,' she said. 'Let me go get it. I'm sure you'll be pleased—they're very reasonably priced. I'll be back in just a few minutes.'

'Take your time,' he said, shrugging. 'I'm in no hurry.'

A moment later she was tottering toward the path, like a bowling pin about to fall. When she was gone, Richard turned his smile on Julie.

'You look wonderful,' he said. 'I've missed you. How've you been?'

It was then that Julie realized with a sudden, sinking urgency that they were alone, and the realization was enough to jolt her to her senses. She took a step backward, thanking God in heaven that Singer was between them.

'What are you doing here, Richard?'

Richard shrugged, as if he'd known she would ask. 'It's a great investment. I'm thinking that this might be a good place for me to put down some roots. A man needs a place to call home, and this way, we could be neighbors.'

Julie paled.

He smiled. 'Would you like that, Julie? Me living right next to you? . . . No? Then maybe I just wanted to talk to you. You changed your phone number, you won't go anywhere alone. What else could I do?'

She backed away another step; Singer stayed in place, as if daring Richard to approach her, his rear legs shaking as if ready to pounce.

'I don't want to talk to you,' she said, hating her plaintive tone. 'Why can't you get that through your head?'

'Don't you remember our dates?' Richard said, his voice soft. He looked almost wistful, and the whole scene suddenly struck Julie as surreal. 'Our time together was special. Why don't you want to admit that?'

'There's nothing to admit.' She took another step away.

'Why are you acting this way?' He sounded wounded, puzzled. 'Mike's not here now—it's just us.'

Julie's eyes darted sideways, to the entrance of the path. Time to get out of here.

'If you make one move toward me or try to follow me, I'll scream—and this time, I won't pull Singer off.'

He offered a gentle smile, as if patiently trying to explain something to a child.

'There's no reason to be scared. You know I'd never hurt you. I love you.'

She blinked. He loves me?

'What the hell are you talking about?' she finally said, the words coming out with more force than she'd anticipated.

'I love you,' he said again. 'And we can start over now. We'll go to the theater again—I know you liked that. Or if you don't want to do that, we can go anywhere you want. It doesn't matter. And we'll just chalk up this infatuation with Mike as a mistake, okay? I forgive you.'

As he spoke, Julie continued backing away, her eyes growing wider with every word. But it wasn't simply his words that scared her, it was the look of utter sincerity on his face.

He gave a sly smile. 'I'll bet that you haven't even told him that you let me spend the night at your house. How do you think he'd feel about that?'

His words struck her with almost physical force. Richard saw her reaction and, seeing that he was

315

right, held out his hand.

'Now come on, let's go someplace quiet and get a bite to eat.'

Julie backed away, stumbling on an exposed root and almost losing her balance. 'I'm not going anywhere with you,' she hissed.

'Don't be this way. Please. I'll make you happy, Jessica.'

For a second, Julie wondered if she had heard Richard correctly, but she knew she had.

'You . . . are . . . insane,' she sputtered.

This time, her words stopped him.

'You shouldn't say that,' Richard said, his voice acquiring an ugly edge. 'You shouldn't say things you don't mean.'

From the corner of her eye, Julie saw Edna reentering the clearing again.

'I'm coming,' she called out cheerfully. 'I'm coming . . .'

Richard was still staring at Julie when Edna reached them. She looked from one to the other.

'Something wrong?' she asked.

Richard finally turned away from Julie's gaze. 'No,' he said, 'not at all. We were just trying to figure out how many homes there might eventually be. I think Julie likes her privacy.'

Julie barely heard him answer. 'I've got to go,' she said suddenly, starting to back away again.

Richard smiled. 'Bye, Julie. See you around.'

Julie turned and started out of the clearing. Singer stayed for a moment as if making sure Richard wouldn't follow, then went after her.

Once out of their sight, she started to run, then began running faster. She crashed through branches along the path, her breath heavy and fast.

She fell once and got up quickly, ignoring the pain in her knee. Hearing noise, she glanced behind her; there was no sign of Richard behind her. She started to run again, forcing her legs to keep moving, feeling the branches sting her face as she plowed ahead. Almost there, she prayed, almost there . . .

Minutes later, she was choking back tears when Mike entered the house. He held her while she cried. After telling him what had happened, she finally gathered her senses enough to ask why he was home so soon.

Mike's face had gone white. When he spoke, his voice was a whisper.

'My lawyer wasn't the one who left the message.'

Thirty

Officer Jennifer Romanello was seated at the kitchen table half an hour later, her eyes on Julie as she recounted her story.

It hadn't taken long for Julie to tell her everything. Though the words were important, it was the look on Julie's face that confirmed she was telling the truth. Despite the outer calm she was trying to maintain, it was clear she was pretty much a wreck. Even Jennifer got a major case of the willies; goose pimples rose on her skin when Julie recounted how Richard had called her Jessica.

'I don't like the sound of this,' she said when Julie was finished.

Though she knew it was an understatement worthy of someone with Pete Gandy's intelligence, what else was she supposed to say? *Holy cow! Buy a gun and lock the doors—this guy's a nut!* Mike and Julie were so shaken, they needed someone to keep her cool. Besides, it's exactly what her dad would have said. Her dad was the master at keeping people calm in tense situations. He always said it was the single most important thing an officer could do if he wanted to live long enough to draw a pension.

'What do we do?' Mike asked.

'I'm not sure yet,' Jennifer said. 'But can I go over a couple of things again, just to make certain I have them right?'

Julie was vacantly chewing on her nails, thinking about the one part of the story she'd left out.

I'll bet that you haven't even told him that you let me spend the night at your house. How do you think he'd feel about that?

Mike probably wouldn't care, since nothing happened. It wasn't anything like Sarah had done to him. And it wasn't important to the story, right? So why couldn't she say it?

Lost in thought, she didn't realize at first that Jennifer had just asked a question.

'Do you have any idea how he knew you were out there?' Jennifer repeated.

'No,' she said.

'But he was there before you were?'

'I guess he rode with Edna. I don't know how long he was there, but he definitely arrived before I got there. I saw her car by the side of the road, and I didn't see them walking in.'

Jennifer turned to Mike. 'And you thought you had a meeting with your lawyer?' she asked.

'There was a message at the garage that I was

318

supposed to meet him at five. One of the other guys at the garage took the message, but when I got to the lawyer's office, he didn't seem to know anything about a meeting, so I came straight to Julie's.'

Mike looked almost sick. And angry.

Jennifer turned to Julie again. 'Can I ask why you went out there in the first place?'

'I'm a twit,' Julie mumbled.

'Excuse me?'

'Nothing.' She took a deep breath. 'I hadn't seen or heard from Richard in a week, and I guess I hoped it was over.'

'I don't think that you should do that in the future. Public places are fine, but try to avoid places where he might find you alone, okay?'

Julie snorted. 'I don't think you have to worry about that anymore.'

'And what do you know about Jessica?'

'Nothing, really. He said he was married to her for a few years and that it didn't work out. He didn't say any more than that. We never talked about her.'

'And he's from Denver?'

'That's what he told me.'

'And again, he didn't threaten you specifically?'

'No. But he didn't have to say anything. He's crazy.'

No argument there, Jennifer thought. Sounds crazy to me.

'And he's never suggested what he might do next?' Jennifer asked.

Julie shook her head. I've had all sorts of fantasies, she thought, want to hear about those? Instead, she closed her eyes. 'I just want it to stop,' she whispered.

'Are you going to arrest him?' Mike asked. 'Or bring him in for questioning?'

It took a moment for Jennifer to respond. 'I'll do what I can,' she said.

She didn't need to say anything else. Mike and Julie turned away.

'So where does that leave us?' Julie asked.

'Look, I know you're worried. I know you're scared. And believe me, I'm on your side, so don't think I'm going to leave here and forget about this. I'm going to look into Richard Franklin's past to see what I can come up with, and I'm sure I'll be talking to him at some point. But remember, I have to work with Officer Gandy on this . . .'

'Oh, great.'

Jennifer reached across the table and squeezed Julie's hand.

'But I give you my word,' she said, 'that we will look into this. And we're going to do everything we can to help you. Trust me, okay?'

It was the kind of rah-rah speech that everyone wanted to hear at a time like this.

Not surprisingly, it went over with a thud.

* * *

Andrea was watching *The Jerry Springer Show* when she heard the phone ring. Reaching for it absently, she kept her eyes on the screen as she mumbled a hello.

A moment later, her eyes lit up.

'Oh, hi!' she said. 'I was hoping you would call . . .'

320

Jennifer could barely concentrate on the drive home. Instead, all she could focus on was the queasy feeling in her stomach and the screaming case of the willies that the hum of the engine couldn't seem to drown out. The whole thing scared her on a number of levels. As a police officer, she knew how dangerous stalkers could be. However, as a woman, she also found herself empathizing with Julie in a more personal way. All she had to do was close her eyes and she was right there with Julie, feeling her helplessness. There was nothing worse. Most people lived under the illusion that they were in control of their lives, but that wasn't completely true. Yeah, you could decide what to have for breakfast and what to wear and all those little things, but as soon as you stepped out into the world, you were pretty much at the mercy of everyone else around you, and all you could do was hope that if they were having a bad day, they wouldn't decide to take it out on you.

She knew it was kind of a glum outlook on things, but that's exactly what she saw happening now. Julie's illusion of security had been shattered, and now she wanted Jennifer—someone, *anyone*, really—to put it back together. What had she said? *I just want it to stop*. Yeah, who wouldn't want that? What she really meant was that she wanted things to go back to the way they were. Back to when the world felt safe.

It wouldn't be that easy. Part of the problem was that Jennifer was feeling kind of helpless herself. *They* had called *her* for help, after all, but she couldn't even talk to Richard on her own in an official capacity yet. And Pete Gandy, though he'd probably do what she asked if she acted all coquettish, would probably screw everything up as soon as he opened his mouth.

But she could investigate the guy on her own. And just as she'd promised Mike and Julie, that's exactly what she intended to do.

*   *   *

An hour after Jennifer Romanello had left, Julie and Mike were still sitting at the table. Mike was sipping on a beer, but Julie hadn't joined him. She couldn't stomach the glass of wine she'd poured earlier and had dumped it in the sink. She just stared ahead vacantly, saying little, and though she looked tired, Mike knew better than to suggest that she go to bed, since sleep was an impossibility for both of them.

'You hungry?' he finally asked.

'No.'

'You want to rent a movie?'

'Not really.'

'Well, I have an idea,' Mike said. 'Let's just sit around and stare at each other for a while. And maybe we can worry a little, just to break up the monotony. I mean, we need to find something to do to pass the time.'

With that, Julie finally smiled.

'You're right,' she said. She reached for his beer and took a sip. 'I'm getting kind of tired of it, anyway. Doesn't seem to be doing me any good.'

'So what do you want to do?'

'Would you just hold me?' she asked as she stood and walked over to him.

Mike got up and put his arms around her. He pulled her close, absorbing the warmth of her body. In the circle of his arms, Julie leaned her head against his chest.

'I'm glad you're here,' she whispered. 'I don't know what I'd do without you.'

Before Mike could say anything, the phone rang. Both he and Julie tensed at the sound. They continued to hold each other as it rang a second time.

Then a third.

Mike let go of her.

'Don't,' Julie cried, fear in her eyes.

It rang a fourth time.

Mike ignored her. He went to the living room and picked up the phone. He held it facedown for a moment, then raised it slowly to his ear.

'Hello?' he said.

'Oh, hi. For a second there, I wasn't sure you were in,' said the voice on the other end, and Mike's face relaxed.

'Oh, hey, Emma,' he said, breaking into a smile. 'How are you?'

'I'm fine,' Emma said, her voice full of energy. 'But listen, I'm in Morehead City, and you're not going to believe who I just saw.'

Julie moved into the living room next to Mike, and he held the phone away from his ear so she could hear as well.

'Who?'

'Andrea. And you'll never believe who she was with.'

'Who?'

'She was with Richard. And get this, I just saw him kiss her.'

'I have no idea what it means,' Julie said. 'I mean, it doesn't make sense.'

Mike had hung up the phone and they were sitting on the couch, a single lamp shining behind them. Singer was sleeping by the front door.

'Did she mention anything in the shop this week? About seeing him, I mean?'

Julie shook her head. 'Nothing. Not a single word. I know she cut his hair, but that's all I knew about.'

'Didn't she hear the things you were saying about him?'

'She must have.'

'But she didn't care?'

'Either that or she didn't believe them.'

'Why wouldn't she believe you?'

'Who knows. But I'll talk to her tomorrow. Maybe I can talk some sense into her.'

*   *   *

Later, Richard brought Andrea to his house and they stood on the porch, staring toward the sky. Pressed against her, he wrapped his arms around her belly, moving his hands toward her breasts. Andrea leaned her head against him and sighed.

'For a while there, I wasn't sure you were going to call.'

Richard kissed her neck, and the warmth of his lips made her shiver. The moon cast a silver shimmer on the trees.

'It's so beautiful out here,' she said. 'So quiet.'

324

'Shh. Don't say anything. Just listen.'

He didn't want to hear her voice, because it reminded him that she wasn't Julie. He was with another woman, a woman who meant nothing to him, but her body was soft and warm, and she desired him.

'And the moon . . .'

'Shhh,' he said again.

An hour later, when they were in bed together, Andrea moaned and dug her fingers into his back, but Richard had told her not to make any other sounds. No whispers, no talking. He had insisted on total darkness in the room as well.

He moved above her, feeling her breath on his skin. *Julie*, he wanted to whisper. *You can't keep running from me. Don't you see what we have? Don't you crave the completion that our union will bring?*

But then he remembered their meeting in the woods, the look of horror in her eyes. He saw her revulsion, heard her words of rejection. He felt her hatred. The memory wounded him, an assault on his senses. *Julie*, he wanted to whisper, *you were cruel to me today. You ignored my profession of love. You treated me as if I meant nothing . . .*

'Ow,' he heard in the darkness, 'not so hard . . . you're hurting me . . . Ow!'

The sound brought him back.

'Shh,' he whispered, but he didn't relax his hands. In the dim light from the window, he could just make out a shadow of fear in Andrea's eyes. He felt a surge of desire.

Thirty-one

Though her shift started at eight, Jennifer was seated at the computer by six on Wednesday morning, the copy of the original arrest report on Mike Harris beside her. At the top of the report were the basics: Richard Franklin's name, address, phone number, place of work, and so forth, and she skimmed that part before reading the description of the altercation itself. As she'd suspected, there was nothing helpful there about Richard's background, but it felt like the right thing to do. She needed something to help get the ball rolling.

Her father, thank God, had been helpful the night before. After getting home, she'd called him to get his impressions, and when she had finished, her father had pretty much confirmed her thoughts, vague though they were, as to what might happen in the future. 'It could go either way,' her father said, 'so you gotta find out whether he's really nuts or just acting that way.'

She still wasn't sure where to begin, since the information on Richard Franklin was sketchy and the hours she had to look into him weren't exactly standard business hours. The personnel department at the bridge project didn't open until later, and though that seemed the most obvious place to begin, her father had suggested she start with the landlord instead. 'They're used to evening calls, so it's okay to call after hours. Maybe you can pull up a Social Security number and driver's license number, as well as references. They usually require those on rental applications.'

326

And that was exactly what she had done. After getting the name of the owner of the property through an acquaintance who worked for the county, she spoke to the owner, a man who sounded no older than thirty. The house, she learned, had been owned by his grandparents; the rent was always paid on time through his corporation, and Richard Franklin had put up both a security deposit and the first and last months' rent in advance. The owner himself had never met Richard; he hadn't even visited the property in over a year. A local real estate company was in charge of management, and he gave her that number.

Next, she had called the manager, and after a bit of cajoling, he'd faxed over the rental application. His references listed his local employer and the head of personnel; no one from Ohio or Colorado. She did manage to get his Social Security and driver's license numbers, and as she sat at Pete Gandy's desk, she typed those into the computer.

She spent the next hour searching for information, beginning with North Carolina. Richard Franklin apparently had no criminal record in the state, nor had he been arrested. Though his driver's license had been issued in Ohio, it was too early to check with the Department of Motor Vehicles there. Ditto with Colorado.

Then, using her laptop, she plugged into the high-speed phone line and checked the Internet. Using standard search engines, she found about a zillion references to his name and quite a few personal Web pages on Richard Franklin, but not the Richard Franklin she wanted.

After that, she started running into roadblocks.

To get information in Colorado and Ohio concerning a possible record would take at least a day and the cooperation of another department, since police records were maintained locally. Not so hard if she was an officer, but not really kosher for someone in training. Besides, they would have to call her back, and if they rang while she was out—which no doubt she would be, since she was riding with Pete Gandy today—she'd have to explain to the chief why she had a call in to the Denver and Columbus Police Departments, and she might be off the case entirely, if not out of a job.

Then again, she wondered whether his past was what he claimed it was.

Was he really from Denver originally? Julie thought so, but who really knew? Her father had said as much last night: 'New in town and kind of psycho? I don't know that I'd put a lot of stock in anything he said to this lady. If he's been good at skirting the law so far, I'm sure he's just as good at skirting the truth about his past.'

Though it was illegal, Jennifer decided to check his credit record. She knew there were three major credit-reporting agencies, and most offered a free report annually. Using the rental application as a guideline, she typed in the information required—no doubt the same information that the management company had used when renting him the home. Name, Social Security number, latest address, previous address, bank account number—she hit paydirt.

Richard Franklin's records were spelled out in plain detail over a number of pages.

The only recent inquiry had been made by the

328

management company for the house rental—no surprise there—but what struck her was that none of the records seemed to make much sense. Especially for a gainfully employed engineer.

There were no credit cards currently registered or in use, no open auto loan, no personal credit lines. A quick scroll through the record showed that every account on the credit report had been closed.

Studying the record in more detail, she saw that there was one major default from a bank in Denver, four years earlier. It was listed under real estate, and from the size of it, she assumed it was a mortgage on a home.

There were a series of other late payments around that time. Visa. MasterCard. American Express. Phone bill. Electric bill. Water bill. Sears Card. All were registered as delinquent for a year but were eventually paid off.

Afterward, he'd closed the Visa and MasterCard accounts, as well as the American Express and Sears accounts.

Jennifer leaned back in her chair, thinking about it. Okay, she knew he'd lived in Denver at one point, and it seemed as if he'd run into some sort of financial trouble four years ago. Could be any number of explanations for that—lots of people weren't too good at managing money—and he'd mentioned to Julie that he'd been divorced. Maybe that had something to do with it.

She stared at the screen. But why weren't there any more recent entries?

He was probably using the corporation to pay his bills, just as he was doing with his rental, she thought. She made a note to check on it.

What else? Without a doubt, she knew she also had to find out more about Jessica. But without further information, there was absolutely nothing to go on.

Jennifer unplugged her laptop and stowed it in its padded case, wondering what to do next. Her best bet, she decided, was to wait until the personnel office opened so she could talk to the people there. Richard was a consulting engineer on a major project and working with a major company, so undoubtedly they had other references. Maybe one of them could shed light on what had happened four years ago. But that meant another hour of waiting.

Not knowing what else to do, she scanned the arrest report again before finally focusing on his address and thinking, Why not? She wasn't even sure what she was looking for, exactly; she just wanted to see where he lived in the hope that it might give her more of an impression of the man. Her computer tucked under her arm, she grabbed a cup of coffee on her way out the door and got into her car.

Because she was still learning her way around, she checked the map in the glove compartment before following the main road out of town, into the rural area of the county.

Ten minutes later, Jennifer turned onto the gravel road where Richard Franklin lived. She slowed the car as she approached the mailbox, looking for a number, trying to estimate where she was. After finding it, she picked up speed again, seeing she had a ways to go.

She was struck by how remote these homes were. Most sat on multiple acres, and she wondered why an engineer from a major city would choose to live out this way. It was convenient neither to town nor to his job, nor to anything else, for that matter. And the road kept getting worse.

As she drove farther, the homes grew older and more run-down. More than one looked abandoned. She passed the ruins of an old tobacco barn. The sides had toppled when the roof caved in and kudzu blanketed the structure, weaving through the boards. Behind it sat the remains of a tractor, rusting in the weeds.

Another few minutes, another mailbox number. She was getting close now.

Jennifer slowed the car. His house, she assumed, was the next one on the right, and she spotted it through the trees. Set back from the road, the home was two stories, not as neglected as the others, but the yard was horribly overgrown.

Still . . .

People who lived out this way probably did so because it was family property or because they had no other choice. Why would he have chosen a place like this?

Because he wanted to hide?

Or was hiding something?

She didn't stop the car; instead she drove past and made a U-turn half a mile up the road. The same questions cycled through her mind as she passed the house again and made her way back to the station.

*   *   *

Richard Franklin drew back from the curtains, frowning slightly.

He had a visitor, but he didn't recognize the car. It wasn't Mike or Julie, he knew. Neither of them owned a Honda, and he was certain they wouldn't have come to look for him here. Nor was it anyone who lived out this way. The road ended a couple of miles up, and none of his neighbors owned a Honda.

But someone had come. He'd watched them creep up the road, driving way too slowly, knowing they were looking for something. The U-turn had confirmed his suspicions. If it had been a wrong turn or someone lost, they wouldn't have slowed in front of his house—and only his house—then sped up again.

No, someone had come to see where he lived.

'What are you staring at?' Andrea asked.

Richard let the curtain fall back in place and turned. 'Nothing,' he said.

The sheet had slipped down, exposing her breasts. He moved toward the bed and sat beside her. On her arms he could see bruises, and he ran a tender finger over them.

'Good morning,' he said. 'Did you sleep well?'

In the morning light, wearing only jeans, Richard looked exotic. Sensual. So what if he got a little rough last night?

Andrea pushed aside a loose strand of hair that had fallen across her cheek. 'When we finally got around to sleeping, I did.'

'Are you hungry?'

'A little. But I have to go to the bathroom first. Where is it again? I was kind of tipsy last night.'

'It's the last door on the right.'

Andrea scooted from the bed, taking the sheet as she went. Her legs felt wobbly as she moved out of the room. Richard watched her go, wishing she'd left the night before, then turned to the window again.

Someone had come to see where he lived.

Not Henry or Mabel, either. He knew their cars as well. Who was it, then? He rubbed his forehead.

The police? Yes, he could imagine Julie calling them. She'd been completely irrational yesterday. Scared and angry. And now she was trying to take control by changing the rules of the game.

But which officer had she called? Not Pete Gandy. He was sure of that. But how about the other one, the new one? What had Gandy said about her? That her father was a police officer in New York?

He thought about it.

Officer Romanello hadn't believed his account about the altercation in the bar. He could read that in her eyes, in the way she'd watched him. And she was a woman.

Yes, he decided, it must have been her. But would Gandy be supporting her in this? No, not yet, he thought. And he would take care to make sure that Gandy wouldn't. Officer Gandy was an idiot. He would be as easy to handle as Officer Dugan had been.

One part of the problem solved. Now, as for Julie . . .

Richard's thoughts were interrupted by a scream coming from Andrea's direction. When he went into the hallway, Andrea was standing still, staring with wide eyes, her hand over her mouth.

She hadn't opened the door on the right, the one that led to the bathroom. She was staring into the room on the left.

The darkroom.

She turned to look at Richard as if seeing him for the first time.

'Oh my God,' she said. 'Oh my God . . .'

Richard brought his finger to his lips, his eyes locked on her. 'Shh . . .'

When she saw the look on his face, Andrea took a step backward.

'You shouldn't have opened that door,' Richard said. 'I told you where the bathroom was, but you didn't listen.'

'Richard? The pictures . . .'

He took a step toward her. 'This is so . . . *disappointing.*'

'Richard?' she whispered again, backing away.

*   *   *

Jennifer made it back with a few minutes to spare. Thankfully, Pete Gandy hadn't arrived yet, and she went to his desk, knowing she didn't have much time. She jotted the number of the main office for the bridge project on a scrap of paper, then put the arrest record back in the file where it belonged. No need for Pete to see what she'd been up to just yet.

She dialed the number, and a secretary answered; after Jennifer explained who she was, she asked to speak to Jake Blansen and was put on hold.

It was the man Mike had mentioned before.

As she was waiting, Jennifer reminded herself to tread carefully; the last thing she wanted was for Richard to find out what she was doing. Nor did she want Mr Blansen to call and complain to her chief or tell her she'd need a subpoena to get this type of information. Neither of those were options,

334

so instead she decided to stretch the truth just a bit, under the ruse of verifying the arrest report.

Jake Blansen came on the line, his voice husky and southern cured, as if he had smoked unfiltered cigarettes for fifty years. Jennifer identified herself as an officer in Swansboro, went through the customary small talk, and then segued into a brief recap of the incident.

'I can't believe I misplaced the information regarding the arrest, and since I'm just starting, I don't want to get into any more trouble than I'm already in. Nor do I want Mr Franklin to think that we don't have our act together. We want to have the record complete, in case he comes back in.'

She played the sheepish officer to the hilt, and though it was a shaky house of cards at best, Mr Blansen didn't seem to notice or care.

'I don't know how much I can help you,' he said without hesitating, the words coming out in a slow drawl. 'I'm just the foreman. You probably need to talk to corporate. They're the ones that have that kind of information on the consultants. They're in Ohio, but the secretary can get you the number.'

'Oh, I see. Well, maybe you can help me.'

'I don't see how.'

'You worked with Richard Franklin, didn't you? What's he like?'

For a long moment, Jake Blansen was silent. Then:

'Is this for real?'

'Excuse me?'

'You. This. Losing the incident report. Being with the police. All of it.'

'Yes, of course. If you'd like, I can give you my extension and you can call me back. Or I could

335

come out there.'

Jake Blansen drew a deep breath. 'He's dangerous,' he said in a low voice. 'The company hired him because he keeps costs down, but he does it by scrimping on safety. I've had men hurt out here because of him.'

'How so?'

'He puts off maintenance, things break, people get hurt. OSHA would have a field day here. One week, it was one of the cranes. The next week, it's a boiler in one of the barges. I even reported it to corporate, and they promised to look into it. But I guess he found out and he came after me.'

'He attacked you?'

'No . . . but he threatened me. In an indirect way. He started off like we were buddies, you know? Asking about the wife and the kids, things like that. And then he told me how disappointed he was that I didn't trust him, and that if I wasn't more careful, he'd have to let me go. Like all of this was my fault, and he was doing me a big favor by trying to protect me. And he puts his arm over my shoulders and sort of mumbles that it would be a shame if there were any more accidents . . . The way he said it gave me the feeling he was talking about me and my family specifically. He gave me the creeps, and to be honest, I was thrilled to see him go. I danced a jig the rest of the day. So did everyone else on the project.'

'Wait . . . he left?'

'Yeah. He quit. Had some out-of-town emergency, and when he got back to town, he let us know he needed to take some time off for personal reasons. Haven't seen him since.'

A minute later, after being transferred back to

336

the secretary and getting the number in Ohio she needed, Jennifer hung up the phone and called the corporate headquarters. She got passed from one person to the next before she was finally told that the person who could help was out temporarily but would be back later that afternoon.

Jennifer jotted down the name of the man she should call—Casey Ferguson—and leaned back in her chair.

Richard was dangerous, he'd said. All right, but she already knew that. What else? Richard had quit his job a month ago; he'd told her and Pete something different. It wasn't something that would normally matter, but the timing didn't escape her.

He'd quit after coming back from the emergency. He'd quit after Julie had told him she didn't want to see him anymore.

A *connection?*

Across the room, she saw Pete Gandy walk through the door. He hadn't seen her sitting at his desk, and she was glad of that. She needed just a moment more.

Definitely too coincidental, she decided, especially after learning what she had earlier this morning about his past. But Julie, by her own admission, had seen Richard only a few times, and though he'd called her on numerous occasions, he'd never stayed on the phone long.

Jennifer glanced out the window, wondering.

What else had he been doing with his time since then?

*   *   *

Mike pulled his truck to a stop at the garage. The fog was finally beginning to thin. Julie was looking toward the floor of the truck, and he followed her gaze, coming to rest on the tips of her shoes. They were coated with a layer of dew from her lawn, and when Julie realized what she was looking at, she gave a halfhearted shrug as if to say, *I guess we'll see what happens today.*

Neither had slept well, and both had spent the morning moving sluggishly. The night before, Mike couldn't seem to get comfortable and he got up four times to get a glass of water. While he was up, he found himself drawn to the front window, where he stood for a long time, looking out. Julie, on the other hand, had spent the night dreaming. Though she couldn't remember any dreams in detail, she woke with a feeling of dread. That feeling lingered and returned in waves as she dressed and ate breakfast.

When Julie got out of the car, she felt no more in control than she'd felt earlier. Mike hugged and kissed her and offered to walk her across the street to the salon, but Julie declined. Singer, meanwhile, bounded down and headed toward the salon in search of his biscuit.

'I'll be fine,' Julie reassured him. She sounded doubtful and knew it.

'I know,' he said, sounding equally unsure. 'I'll swing by in a little bit to see how you're doing, okay?'

'Okay.'

As Mike headed into the garage, Julie took a deep breath and crossed the street. Downtown wasn't busy yet—the fog seemed to have set back everyone's clocks just a little—but halfway across she imagined that a car was suddenly speeding toward her, and she broke into a jog, trying to dart out of the way.

Nothing was there.

As soon as she reached the sidewalk, she adjusted her purse and looked again, trying to collect herself. Coffee, she thought, another cup of coffee and I'll be fine.

She swung into the diner. The waitress filled her cup from the pot on the warming burners. She added cream and sugar, spilling a bit on the counter, and as she reached for a napkin to wipe it up, she had the strange sensation that she was being watched by someone in the corner. Her stomach knotted as she turned in that direction, scanning a series of booths, some cluttered with the remains from earlier breakfasts.

But no one was there.

She closed her eyes, on the verge of tears. She left the diner without saying good-bye.

It was early—the salon wouldn't be open for another hour or so, but she was sure Mabel was already in. Wednesdays were her days for taking inventory and placing orders, and when Julie pushed open the door, she saw Mabel dutifully scanning the shelves of shampoos and conditioners. When Mabel glanced over her shoulder at Julie, her face assumed a look of concern. She set aside the clipboard.

'What happened?' were the first words she said.

'I look that bad, huh?'

'Richard again?'

Julie bit her lip in answer, and Mabel immediately crossed the room and put her arms around her, squeezing tight.

Julie inhaled sharply, fighting for control. She didn't want to break down; aside from feeling scared, crying seemed to be the only thing she'd been doing lately.

And she was exhausted. So despite her efforts she felt tears prick the backs of her eyes, making them sting—and a moment later she was sobbing in Mabel's arms, her body shaking, her arms and legs so weak that she felt she would fall over if Mabel let go.

'There, there,' Mabel murmured. 'Shh . . . you're going to be okay. . . .'

Julie had no idea how long she cried, but by the end her nose was red and her mascara had run. When Mabel finally let her go, Julie sniffed and reached for a tissue.

She told Mabel about seeing Richard near her house. She told her everything he'd said and the way he'd looked; she recounted her call to Officer Romanello and their conversation in the kitchen.

Mabel's face expressed the depth of her concern and sympathy, but she said nothing. When Julie told her about Emma's phone call, Mabel shivered.

'I'll go give Andrea a call,' Mabel offered quickly.

Julie watched Mabel cross the room and pick up the receiver. She offered a tentative smile that gradually gave way to a look of concern when it became obvious that Andrea wasn't answering.

'I'm sure she's already on her way in,' Mabel said. 'She'll probably be here in just a couple of minutes. Or maybe she's decided to take one of her personal days. You know how she is. Wednesdays are usually fairly slow, anyway.'

To Julie, it sounded almost as if Mabel were trying to convince herself.

Jennifer spent part of the morning—when she was supposed to be finishing Pete's reports—surreptitiously making calls to utility companies. Her suspicions were confirmed. Each bill had been paid through Richard's corporation, RPF Industrial, Inc. All had been paid on time.

From there, she called the secretary of state's office in Denver, Colorado, and learned there was no company presently incorporated in that name, though there had been an RPF Industries, Inc. It had gone out of business a little more than three years ago. Acting on a hunch, she called the secretary of state's office in Columbus, Ohio, and she learned that Richard's Ohio corporation had been incorporated a little more than a month before he began working with J. D. Blanchard Engineering and only a week after RPF Industries had gone out of business in Colorado.

Calls to the bank where his corporation had its accounts in Columbus provided little information, except for the fact that Richard Franklin did not have a personal checking or savings account registered there.

At the desk, Jennifer pondered this new information. To her, it seemed obvious that Richard Franklin had folded one business only to start another with a similar name in another state and that afterwards he had made the decision to live his life with the lowest-possible profile he could. Both decisions had been made at least three years earlier. Strange, she thought. Not criminal, but strange.

341

Though she'd first assumed that it might have been because he'd been in trouble with the law—who else would go through this type of trouble to hide, and with all that was going on with Julie, it seemed obvious—she dismissed the notion. Low profile was one thing, invisible was another, and Richard Franklin could be found relatively easily by anyone willing to look for him, including the police. Simply look up his credit report and the address was right there. So why all the cloak-and-dagger stuff?

It didn't make sense.

Jennifer checked the clock, hoping her call to J. D. Blanchard would shed some light on the subject.

Unfortunately, she still had another couple of hours to wait.

*   *   *

Pete Gandy entered the gym on his lunch break and saw Richard Franklin on the bench press. Richard worked through six reps—not as much weight as Pete Gandy could do, but not bad—then put the weight back on the bench.

When Richard sat up, it took him just a moment to recognize Pete Gandy.

'Hey, Officer, how are you? Richard Franklin.'

Pete Gandy approached him. 'I'm fine. How are you feeling?'

'Getting better.' Richard smiled. 'I didn't know you worked out here.'

'I've been a member for years.'

'I was thinking of joining. I got a trial membership today.' He paused. 'You want to work in a set while I recover?'

342

'If you don't mind.'

'Not at all.'

A chance meeting, followed by small talk.

Then, a few minutes later: 'Hey, Officer Gandy . . .'

'Call me Pete.'

'Pete,' Richard said. 'I just realized there was something I forgot to tell you the other night, and you probably know about it. Just in case.'

'Yeah?'

Richard explained. Then, as he was finishing: 'Like I said, I wanted you to know. Just in case.'

Walking away, he thought of Officer Dugan and his expression when Richard had opened his jacket. Idiot.

Thirty-two

Julie would always remember it as the last normal day she would know.

And that was in the general sense of the word, since nothing had seemed normal for weeks. Singer was strangely nervous at the shop; he paced restlessly between the chairs as Mabel and Julie worked. Customers came in, but none seemed particularly chatty. Julie supposed it was due to the fact that she didn't want to be there (she didn't want to be anywhere else, either, for that matter, unless it was someplace far, far away) and assumed her clients picked up on that, especially the women.

After the fog burned off the temperature soared, and to make things worse, halfway through the morning, the air conditioner stopped working, which only added to the oppressive feel of the place. Mabel propped the door open with a brick, but because there wasn't so much as a slight breeze, it didn't seem to do much, other than let the heat in. The ceiling fan was inadequate, and as the afternoon wore on, Julie was on the verge of breaking into a serious sweat. Her face had taken on a shiny glow, and she tugged irritably at the front of her blouse to fan her skin.

She hadn't cried since Mabel had held her, and by the time Mike stopped by, she'd composed herself enough to hide the fact that she'd broken down again. She hated that she'd succumbed this morning; she liked to imagine that she'd been handling this with a quiet dignity. It was one thing to show Mike what she was really feeling, it was another thing to let everyone else know, even if they were friends. Since the morning, Mabel had been casting furtive glances her way, as if ready on a moment's notice to charge across the room with arms held wide in case she needed to be held again. It was sweet, but in the end, all it did was remind her of why she was so upset in the first place.

And Andrea. She still hadn't shown up. After checking the appointment book, Mabel noticed that she had no appointments scheduled until later in the morning, so there were a couple of hours where she could still convince herself that Andrea was just taking the morning off.

But as the hours passed and Andrea's customers began to show up, Julie's worries grew.

Though she and Andrea weren't really friends, she hoped Andrea was okay. And she prayed she wasn't with Richard. She debated calling the police, but what would she say? That Andrea hadn't come in? She knew that the first question they would ask was whether her absence was unusual. And Andrea had always been flighty about coming to work.

When did Richard and Andrea get to know each other, anyway? During the haircut? There'd obviously been some sort of attraction on Andrea's part, but from what Julie observed, Richard hadn't seemed to respond. No, she thought, his eyes had kept angling toward me while I worked. He looked at me then the same way he looked at me as soon as Edna had walked away.

Andrea was with Richard, Emma had told Mike. *I just saw him kiss her.*

It wasn't more than a few hours after she'd seen him in the woods that Emma had called. Moreover, if they were together in Morehead City—a half-hour drive from Swansboro—he must have gone from their little *visit* to meet Andrea. And he did this, she thought, right after he told me that he loved me.

It made no sense at all.

Had Richard known that Emma was nearby? Though they'd met only once, she had no doubt that Richard would recognize Emma again, and she wondered if it was intended as some sort of message for Emma to report back. But if it was a message, she couldn't figure out what it might be. If he'd done it to lull her into a false sense of security, he was barking up the wrong tree. She wasn't about to fall for that one again.

No way, nohow. There was nothing he could do to surprise her anymore.

At least, that's what she thought.

345

On the phone with Casey Ferguson of J. D. Blanchard, Jennifer held her pen over her pad.

'Yes, of course,' Ferguson said, continuing to stall, 'but we're not supposed to release this information. Personnel files are confidential.'

'I understand that,' Jennifer said, shifting in her chair, doing her best to sound as serious as possible. 'But as I said, we're in the middle of an investigation.'

'We have strict confidentiality agreements. The states require them for us when we contract with them.'

'I understand,' Jennifer said again, 'but if we have to, we'll subpoena the files. I just didn't want your company to be accused of obstructing an investigation.'

'Is that a threat?'

'No, of course not,' Jennifer said, but she knew she'd overplayed her hand when Ferguson spoke again.

'I'm sorry I can't help,' Casey Ferguson finally said. 'If there is a subpoena, then of course we'll be happy to cooperate.'

A moment later, he clicked off and Jennifer swore under her breath as she hung up the phone, wondering what she was going to do next.

*   *   *

That night at Julie's, Mike took her hand and led her to the bedroom.

They hadn't made love since the night before they'd encountered Richard in the bar. Despite

346

that, neither of them felt any sense of urgency. Their lovemaking was slow and tender, filled with gentle kisses. Afterward Mike held Julie close for a long time, his lips brushing against the skin between her shoulder blades. Julie drifted off until Mike's movement roused her from sleep. It was dark but early, not yet ten, and Mike was pulling on his jeans.

'Where are you going?'

'I have to take Singer out. I think he's gotta go.'

Julie stretched. 'How long did I sleep?'

'Not long—an hour or so.'

'Sorry.'

'I liked it. It was nice listening to the way you were breathing. You must have been really tired.'

Julie smiled. 'I still am. But I'm going to grab a bite to eat. Do you want anything?'

'Just an apple.'

'That's it? No cheese or crackers or anything?'

'No. I'm not all that hungry tonight. Just beat.'

He slipped out of the room as Julie sat up and turned on the lamp, squinting as her eyes adjusted to the light. She rose and went to the chest of drawers to pull out a long T-shirt. Pulling the shirt over her head, she walked down the hall.

Mike was standing in the doorway, waiting for Singer, and he glanced at her as she passed him on the way to the kitchen. She opened the refrigerator and pulled out a yogurt and a couple of chocolate-chip cookies, then grabbed an apple on her way back out.

It was while passing through the living room that she saw the locket, and she froze. It was on the desk near her calendar, partially hidden by a stack of catalogs, and the sight of it made her suddenly

347

queasy. The locket brought with it images of Richard: how he'd looked as he'd given it to her, Richard suddenly grabbing for the door, Richard in the woods, waiting for her. She didn't want it in the house, but in all that had happened, she'd forgotten it was there.

Now it was on the desk, and she'd spotted it easily, without looking for it. Without wanting to see it. Why hadn't she seen it before now?

Behind her, she could hear the clock ticking. From the corner of her eye, she could see Mike leaning against the door. The locket was reflecting the light from the lamp on the end table, its glow somehow sinister. She realized her hands were shaking.

The mail, she suddenly thought. Yes, that's it. When I put the stack of mail on the desk, it must have moved the locket somehow. She swallowed. Right?

She didn't know. All she knew was that she didn't want it in the house anymore. As ridiculous as she knew it was, it seemed evil to her now, as if touching it would somehow make Richard appear. But she had no choice.

Forcing herself to move toward it, she reached over and slid it out from under the catalogs. It's just a locket, she told herself. Nothing more. She considered throwing it in the garbage, but instead she decided to stash it in her drawers and sell it at one of the local pawnshops later, when all this was settled. It wouldn't be worth much with her initials inside, but she'd get something for it, and she'd put that money into the church basket on Sunday. She wasn't about to profit from the thing, and the money would go to a good cause.

348

She carried it with her to the bedroom and glanced at it as she was opening the drawer. The floral designs on the outside looked as if they'd taken weeks to craft by someone who obviously cared a great deal about his work.

Too bad, she thought. She'd be lucky if she got $50 for the thing.

As she began moving her clothes to the side, she found her eyes drawn back to it again. The locket itself was the same, but something was different. Something . . .

Her breath caught in her throat.

No, she thought. Please . . . no . . .

She unclasped the chain, knowing it was the only way to be certain. Moving toward the mirror in the bathroom, she drew both ends around the back of her neck, holding it in place where it would clasp.

Then, looking into the mirror, she tried to steel herself for what was already obvious. The locket, which once nestled between the upper part of her breasts, now rested two inches higher on her chest.

I'll get you a shorter chain, he'd said. *That way you can wear it whenever you want.*

Julie suddenly felt dizzy, and she backed away from the mirror, letting go of the chain as if it had scalded her fingers. The locket tumbled down her blouse before bouncing against the tile floor with a metallic ping.

Still, she hadn't screamed.

No, the scream didn't come for another couple of seconds, when she looked down at the locket.

It had popped open in the fall.

And from both sides, in pictures he'd chosen especially for her, Richard was smiling back at her.

This time, Jennifer Romanello wasn't alone when she came to Julie's home. Officer Pete Gandy was sitting at the kitchen table, looking across at them, not bothering to hide the dubious expression on his face. The locket was on the table, and Pete reached out to pick it up.

'So let me get this straight,' he said while opening the locket, 'you beat the guy up, and as payback, he gives Julie a couple of pictures of himself. I don't get it.'

Mike clenched his hands beneath the table to keep from exploding.

'I told you already. He's been stalking her.'

Pete nodded but kept staring at the pictures. 'Yeah, I know. You keep saying that, but I'm just trying to see if there are any other possible angles here.'

'Possible angles?' Mike asked. 'Can't you see that this is proof right here? That he's been in the house? That's breaking and entering.'

'But nothing seems to be missing. There were no signs of a break-in. All the doors were locked when you got home and the windows were closed. You said so yourself.'

'We're not saying he took anything! And I don't know how he did it, but he did. All you have to do is open your eyes!'

Pete held up his hands. 'Now take it easy, Mike. No reason to get upset. I'm just trying to get to the bottom of this.'

Both Jennifer and Julie were as steamed as Mike, but Pete had told Jennifer that he was going to handle this once and for all and that she shouldn't say a word. Her expression was a mixture of horror and morbid fascination, especially after her own investigation this morning. Was it possible he could be this blind?

'Get to the bottom of this?'

'Yeah,' Pete said. He leaned forward and put the locket on the table again. 'Now I'm not saying that this doesn't seem a little fishy, because it does. And if Julie's telling the truth, then Richard Franklin has a little problem that's gonna require a visit from me.'

Mike's face tightened. 'She's telling the truth,' he said through gritted teeth.

Pete ignored the comment and looked across the table at Julie. 'Are you sure about everything? You're certain that the only way Richard could have put these pictures in here is by breaking into your house?'

She nodded.

'And you said you hadn't so much as touched this necklace in the last few weeks?'

'No,' she said. 'It was buried under some magazines on the desk.'

'C'mon, Pete,' Mike cut in, 'what's that got to do with anything?'

Pete ignored the comment, his skeptical gaze still focused on Julie.

'There's no other time that he could possibly have put those pictures in there?' he persisted. 'No other time at all?'

In the aftermath of his questions, the kitchen was strangely silent. Pete continued to stare, and under his knowing gaze, Julie finally realized what he knew. She felt her stomach clench.

'When did he tell you?' she asked.

'Tell him what?' Mike asked. When Julie finally answered, her voice was quiet but filled with loathing.

'Did he give you a call and tell you he forgot to mention something?' she asked. 'Is that it? Or did he happen to run into you somewhere and bring it up then?'

Pete said nothing, but he didn't have to. A sudden, almost imperceptible jerk of his head told her one of her guesses had been correct. Probably the latter, she thought. Richard would have wanted to tell him in person, so Pete could see him. So Pete could be fooled.

Mike, meanwhile, was looking back and forth between Pete and Julie, trying to figure out what she was talking about. They had some sort of hidden communication going, one that left him feeling as if the whole situation were spinning out of control.

'Could you please just answer the question?' Pete persisted.

But Julie didn't answer right away. She continued to lock eyes with Pete.

'She did answer the question!' Mike finally interjected. 'No, there's no way—'

Julie barely heard him. Instead, she turned toward the window, staring blankly at the drawn curtains.

'Yes,' she said flatly. 'There was one time he could have done it.'

Pete leaned back in his chair, his eyebrows raised. 'When he spent the night, you mean,' he said.

'What?' Jennifer cried, her jaw dropping.

'What?' Mike echoed.

Julie turned to face him.

'Nothing happened between us, Mike,' she said evenly. 'Nothing at all. His mom had died and he was upset, and we talked. Just talked. He fell asleep on the couch. That's what Pete is talking about.'

Though everything she had said was absolutely true, when she looked at Pete again, his expression confirmed that Richard had already implied something different.

And Mike, Julie noticed, saw it, too.

*　　　*　　　*

Richard lowered the camera. Equipped with a telephoto lens, the camera served as a makeshift set of binoculars, and he'd been watching Mike and Julie since they'd come home that evening. Or rather, what he could see of them through the gauzy curtains. During the day, it was impossible to make out anything, but at night, when the lights blazed from inside, he could make out shadows, and that was all he needed.

This was the night she would find it. He'd had to move the locket into better position after his meeting with Pete Gandy, of course, but he'd known she would see it on the desk.

It would be nasty business, he knew, but there was no other way. It was time to end her little infatuation with Mike once and for all.

*　　　*　　　*

After Mike had closed the door behind the officers, he leaned against it using both hands for support, as if he were about to be frisked. His head was

353

bowed, and Julie could hear his long, deep breaths. Singer stood off to the side, gazing at him curiously, as if wondering whether this were some new type of game. Mike couldn't meet her eyes.

'Why didn't you tell me?' he said, raising his chin.

Still standing in the kitchen, Julie looked away. 'I knew you'd be mad . . .'

Mike snorted, but she went on as if she hadn't heard him.

'But more than that, I knew it would hurt your feelings, and there was no reason to do that. I swear to you—nothing happened at all. All he did was talk.'

Mike stood up straighter, then finally turned around, his expression angry. Hard.

'That was the night of our first date, wasn't it?' It was also, he remembered, the night he'd first tried to kiss her but she hadn't let him.

Julie nodded. 'Nice timing, huh?'

It wasn't the time for jokes, and she regretted it immediately. She took a step forward. 'I didn't know he was going to stop by. I was just thinking of heading to bed when he came to the door.'

'And what? You just let him in?'

'It wasn't like that. We had an argument because I told him I didn't want to see him anymore. It got kind of heated, and then Singer . . .'

She paused. She didn't want to go into this. She didn't want to go into this at all, because it seemed so pointless.

'Singer what?'

Julie crossed her arms and shrugged. 'Singer bit him. When I tried to close the door, he stopped it with his hand and Singer went after him.'

Mike stared at her. 'And you didn't think any of

this was important enough to tell me? Even after everything that's happened?'

'That's just it,' she pleaded. 'It wasn't important. I told him I didn't want to see him and he got upset.'

Mike crossed his arms. 'So let me get this straight,' he said. 'He comes to the door, you have a fight, Singer goes after him, and then you invite him in to spend the night. Correct me if I'm wrong, but your story doesn't seem to make a lot of sense.'

'Don't be like this, Mike. Please . . .'

'Be like what? Someone who's a little upset that you lied to me?'

'I didn't lie to you.'

'No? Then what do you call it?'

'I didn't tell you because it didn't matter. It meant nothing, and nothing happened. It's not like all this is happening because of that night.'

'How do you know? Maybe that's what set him off in this direction.'

'But I didn't do anything but listen to him!'

Mike said nothing, and Julie saw the accusation in his eyes.

'You don't believe me?' she asked. 'What? Do you think I slept with him?'

Mike let the question hang for a long moment. 'I don't know what to think anymore.'

Julie flinched. Part of her wanted to lash out immediately, to scream at him or demand that he leave, but she resisted those instincts, Richard's words echoing through her mind.

I'll bet that you haven't even told him that you let me spend the night at your house. How do you think he'd feel about that?

She suddenly knew that this, too, was part of Richard's plan. He was playing them, just as he'd played Pete Gandy. The way he had at the Clipper. She took a deep breath, forcing herself to keep her voice steady, without anger.

'Is that what you think of me, Mike? That I'd sleep with a man I barely know on the same day I told him I didn't want to see him anymore? After I'd told you that I didn't even *like* the guy? After all the years you've known me, do you really believe I'd do something like that?'

Mike stared at Julie. 'I don't know.'

The words stung, and Julie felt her eyes tear. 'I didn't sleep with him.'

'Maybe not,' Mike finally said. He reached for the door. 'But it still hurts to think you didn't trust me with this. Especially after all this stuff started happening.'

'I do trust you. But I didn't want to hurt you.'

'You just did, Julie,' he said. 'You just did.'

With that, he reached for the door and opened it, and for the first time, Julie realized that he was going to leave.

'Wait—where are you going?'

Mike raised his hands. 'I need some time with this, okay?'

'Please,' she said. 'Don't go. I don't want to be alone tonight.'

Mike paused and took a deep breath. But a moment later, with a shake of his head, he was gone.

*   *   *

Richard watched Mike make his way down the walk and slam the door as he got in his truck.

He smiled, knowing that Julie would finally

356

understand the truth about Mike. That she couldn't rely on him. That Mike was a person who acted on impulse and emotion, not reason. That Mike wasn't worthy of her, nor ever was. That she deserved someone stronger, smarter, someone equal to her love.

In the tree, Richard couldn't wait for the moment until he led her out of this house, this town, this life she had let herself become trapped in. Raising the camera again, he watched Julie's shadow through the curtains in the living room.

Even her shadow was beautiful.

Thirty-three

'She did what?' Henry asked.

'You heard me,' Mike answered. 'She let him spend the night.'

In the fifteen minutes it took to reach Henry's house, Mike had only grown angrier. They were standing in the front yard. Emma had opened the door once to ask what was going on, but Mike had stopped in midsentence and stared at her, certain that she already knew what Julie had done. Henry raised his hand.

'Just give me a second, will you, Em? Mike's pretty upset right now.'

Before going back into the house, Emma gave Henry a look that clearly said, *I'll close the door, but I expect a full report later.* Henry turned back to his brother.

'She told you that?' Henry asked.

'Yeah, when the police were there. . . .'

357

'Hold on,' Henry said, 'the police were there?'

'They just left.'

'Why were the police there?'

'Because of the locket. Richard put his pictures in there. What the hell am I supposed to do now?'

Henry tried to follow along but was only getting more and more confused. He finally reached for Mike's arm.

'Now calm down, Mike. Maybe you better start from the beginning.'

*　　　*　　　*

'So how long are you going to keep up the silent treatment?' Pete Gandy asked.

They were cruising slowly through downtown in the squad car, and Jennifer Romanello hadn't said a word to him since they'd left Julie's house.

Jennifer turned toward the window at the sound of his voice.

'You still mad about that Mike Harris thing?' he asked. 'Because if you are, you gotta learn to get over stuff like that. Our job isn't always easy.'

Jennifer glanced at him with an expression of distaste. 'It might not be easy,' she said, 'but you don't have to be a jerk, either.'

'What are you talking about? I wasn't being a jerk.'

'No? Then what was with that little comment you made in front of Mike? There was no reason to do that.'

'You mean about Richard staying over?'

She didn't answer, but she didn't have to. Even Pete knew that was what was bothering her.

'Why're you so upset about that? It was true,

358

wasn't it?'

She decided she absolutely despised this guy.

'But you didn't have to say it in front of Mike,' she said. 'You could have taken Julie aside and asked her about it. Then she could have explained it to Mike.'

'What's the difference?'

'The difference is that you caught both of them off guard, and you probably started a major argument in the process.'

'So? It's not my business if they're not honest with each other. I was just trying to get to the bottom of things.'

'Yeah'—Jennifer nodded—'and that's another thing. Just how did you find out that he'd spent the night? Did you talk to Richard or something?'

'Yeah, as a matter of fact I did. I bumped into him at the gym. He seems like a nice guy.'

'A *nice* guy.'

'Yeah,' Pete said, sounding defensive. 'He's not going to press charges, for one thing, and that says something, right? He wants to put the whole thing behind him and forget about it. He's not going ahead with the civil suit, either.'

'And just when were you going to share this with me?'

'What's to share? Like I said, the case got dropped, and besides, it's not your concern. You're still learning the ropes.'

Jennifer closed her eyes. 'The problem is that Richard is stalking Julie and she's scared to death. Why can't you see that?'

Pete shook his head. 'Look, Richard told me about the locket, okay? He mentioned it in case something like this came up, and he told me that he put the pictures in there when he spent the night with her. And remember, even Julie admitted she hadn't looked at it since then, so who's to say he was lying?'

'And you don't care about anything else she's mentioned? About him following her? You don't think all this is a little too coincidental?'

'Hey,' Pete protested, 'I've talked to the guy a couple of times now—'

He was interrupted by the radio crackling to life. Still glaring at Pete, Jennifer reached for the radio and picked up the mike.

Sylvia, a dispatcher who'd been with the department twenty years and knew just about everyone in town, spoke as though she weren't sure what to make of things.

'We just got a call in from a trucker heading down the highway. He said he saw something strange in a ditch and thought we might want to send a car over.'

'What did he think it was?'

'He didn't say. I think he was in a rush and didn't want to stick around to answer questions. It's just off Highway 24, about a quarter mile past the Amoco station on the north side of the road.'

'We'll check it out,' Jennifer responded, thankful for something to make Pete shut up.

*　　　*　　　*

Mike had been gone for half an hour, and the house was eerily quiet. Julie went through the house, making sure the windows and doors were locked, then paced around the living room, Singer at her side. Outside, she could hear the sound of

360

crickets chirping and a light breeze moving the leaves.

Julie crossed her arms and looked toward the door. Singer sat beside her, his head resting against her leg. After a moment he whined, and Julie began to pet him. As if knowing what was going on, he hadn't left her side since Mike had walked out.

She was certain that Richard hadn't put the photos in the locket on the night he'd stayed over. He'd just come from a funeral, for God's sake. And was it plausible that he just happened to be carrying two little pictures of himself on the off chance that he'd be able to put them in the locket while she was in the other room sleeping?

Not a chance.

No, he'd been there. Inside her house. Looking around, opening drawers, rummaging through her things. Which meant he knew how to get inside.

And could do so again.

Julie's throat constricted at the thought, and she hurried into the kitchen, grabbed a chair from the table, and wedged it beneath the front-door knob.

How could Mike have left her? With Andrea missing and Richard stalking her? How on earth could he have left her alone *tonight?*

So she hadn't told him about Richard. So what? Nothing happened!

But Mike hadn't believed her. She was angry with him for that, and hurt as well. But of all the nights to desert someone . . .

Moving toward the couch, Julie began to cry.

*   *   *

'Do you believe her?' Henry asked.

Mike glanced down the street and drew a long breath. 'I don't know.'

Henry stared at him. 'Sure you do.'

'No, I don't,' Mike snapped. 'How can I know if I wasn't even there?'

'Because you know Julie,' Henry offered. 'You know her better than anyone.'

After a long moment, Mike's shoulders relaxed slightly. 'No,' he finally said, 'I don't think she slept with him.'

Henry waited a moment before responding. 'Then what's this all about, then?'

'She lied to me.'

'No, she didn't. She just didn't tell you.'

'It's the same thing.'

'No, it's not. Do you think I tell Emma everything? Especially things that don't matter?'

'This mattered, Henry.'

'Not to her, Mike.'

'How could it not matter? After all that's been going on?'

He had a point, Henry thought. She probably should have said something, but there was no reason to argue that now.

'So what are you going to do?'

Mike took a long time before answering. 'I don't know.'

*   *   *

Richard could see Julie's shadowed image as she sat on the couch. He knew she was crying, and he wanted to hold her, to comfort her, to take her pain away. He brought his finger to his lips, as if trying to hush a small child. Her emotions had become his, and he felt it all: her loneliness and fear, her heartbreak. He'd never been moved by the sight of someone else's tears before.

He hadn't felt this way after watching his mother cry in the months following his father's funeral, he remembered. But then again, by the end, he'd come to hate her.

*　　*　　*

Mike left Henry's, heading for home, his head still spinning.

The road was a blur; images he didn't seem to recognize passed on either side of him.

Julie should have told him, he thought again. Yes, he would have been upset, but he would have gotten over it. He loved her, and what was love without trust or honesty?

He was angry at Henry, too, for skimming over what had happened. Maybe he'd feel differently if Emma had cheated on him, the way Sarah had to him a few years back. Once bitten, twice shy, the old saying went.

Except that Julie hadn't cheated on him. He knew she wasn't lying about that.

But still, she hadn't trusted him. That's what this was really all about, he knew. Trust. He had no doubt she would have told Jim, so why hadn't she told him?

Was their relationship so different from what she and Jim had shared? Didn't she trust him in the same way she'd trusted Jim?

Didn't she love him?

*　　*　　*

In the tree, Richard continued to think about his mother.

He'd hoped that she would be better, stronger, after his father's funeral. But instead, she'd begun to drink heavily, and the kitchen was wreathed in a perpetual haze from the cigarettes she chain-smoked. Then she'd become violent, as if choosing to remember her husband by assuming his actions. The first time it happened, he'd been sleeping in his bed when he woke to a staggering pain, as if a match were being held against him.

His mother stood wild-eyed above the bed, his father's belt dangling from her hand. She'd used the buckle end of the belt against his skin.

'It was your fault!' she screamed at him. 'You were always making him angry!'

She swung again and again. He cowered at each strike, pleading with her to stop and trying to cover himself, but she continued to wield the belt until her arms were too exhausted to move.

The following night she'd done it again, but this time he'd expected her and accepted the beatings with the same quiet rage he had in the past with his father. He knew then that he hated her, but that there was nothing he could do to stop her right away. Not with the police suspicious about the way his father had died.

Nine months later, his back and legs scarred, he ground his mother's sleeping pills and slipped the contents into her vodka. After going to sleep, she never woke up.

In the morning, as he stood over the bed staring at her, he thought about how limited her intelligence had been. Though she'd suspected that he'd had something to do with his father's death, she couldn't bring herself to believe that the same thing could happen to her. She should have known that he was strong enough to do what he had to do. Julie, too, had been strong enough to change her life. Julie was a fighter.

He admired that about her. He loved that about her.

Of course, it was time for the fighting to end. Richard was certain that Julie would realize this now. Maybe not consciously, but subconsciously. Now that the charade with Mike was over, there was no point in delaying the inevitable.

Slowly, Richard began climbing down from the tree.

* * *

Officers Jennifer Romanello and Pete Gandy drove past the Amoco station and pulled the squad car to the side of the highway. After retrieving their flashlights, they emerged from the car.

A short distance away, Jennifer could see the lights from the gas station, saw cars being filled at the pumps. On the highway, cars whizzed past. The side of the road was bathed in swirling blue and red lights, alerting motorists to their presence.

'You go that way,' Pete said, pointing toward the station. 'I'll head this way.'

Jennifer turned on her flashlight and started her search.

* * *

Julie was still crying on the couch when she heard

the sound of movement outside her door. Singer's ears went up as he ran toward the window, growling. Her heart hammering, Julie looked around for a weapon.

When Singer barked, she jumped up from the couch with wide eyes, before she realized his tail was wagging.

'Julie?' she heard him call through the door. 'It's me, Mike.'

She moved toward the door and quickly removed the chair, relief surging through her. As soon as she opened it, Mike looked at her before glancing toward the ground.

'I know you didn't sleep with him,' he said.

Julie nodded. 'Thank you.'

'I'd like to talk to you about it, though.'

'Okay.'

He didn't say anything right away. Instead, he pushed his hands into his pockets and took a deep breath.

'Would you have told Jim?' he finally asked.

Julie blinked. It wasn't a question she'd ever considered.

'Yes,' she said. 'I would have.'

Mike nodded again. 'I thought so.'

'We were married, Mike. You have to understand that.'

'I know.'

'It has nothing to do with the way I feel about you. If you'd asked whether I would have told him while we were dating, the answer would have been no.'

'Really?'

'Really. I didn't want to hurt you. I love you. And had I known all this would have spiraled out of control the way it has, I would have told you then. I should have told you anyway. I'm sorry.'

'I'm sorry, too. For saying what I did.'

Julie stepped forward tentatively, and when Mike didn't back away, she came closer and leaned into him. She felt his arms wrap around her.

'I'd like to stay tonight,' he said, 'if that's okay.'

Julie closed her eyes. 'I was hoping you'd say that.'

*   *   *

Richard had reversed course as soon as he saw Mike pull up in front of the house, and he climbed back into the tree. Now he was watching them, his face growing hard.

No, Richard thought. No, no, *no* . . .

As if living a nightmare, he saw her go into Mike's arms; he saw her fold into him . . . No, this was not happening, this couldn't be *happening*.

Mike was back, and they were holding each other. As if they *loved* each other.

Richard forced himself to calm down, to regain control. Closing his eyes, he visualized his photographs of Jessica, of Julie, his photographs of birds; he recited lessons on how to set the proper f-stop on a camera. On lenses and their capabilities. On the proper angle of the flash, the properties of light . . .

His breathing steadied as he opened his eyes. He was in control again, but he could still feel anger coursing through him.

Why, he wondered, did she insist on repeating her mistakes?

He'd tried to be nice. He'd tried to be fair. He'd

367

been very patient with her and her little friend. More than patient.

His eyes narrowed. Didn't she have any idea what she was forcing him to do?

*   *   *

Jennifer swiveled the flashlight from side to side, looking for whatever it was the trucker had seen.

The moon hung low in the sky, below the tree line. Thousands of stars dotted the sky above. The air carried the heavy scent of blown exhaust. She moved forward slowly, scanning the embankment. Nothing.

Less than thirty feet from the road, loblolly pines stood clustered together. The underbrush surrounding them was thick with bushes and tall grass, impossible for her light to penetrate.

Cars continued to pass, but she barely registered them. She was watching the ground, moving slowly. Carefully. Jennifer took another step when she heard movement off to the side.

Raising the light, she saw two eyes reflected back at her. She stiffened in surprise before the deer suddenly broke and ran.

Exhaling, she bowed her head and continued. The gas station was closer now, and she wondered again what she was supposed to be looking for.

She stepped around a discarded garbage bag, saw aluminum cans and napkins collecting in the embankment. She was beginning to wonder if she should turn around and help Pete look in the opposite direction when the flashlight illuminated something that her mind at first refused to identify.

When it finally did, she screamed.

Pete Gandy turned at the sound and started running toward Jennifer. He reached her in less than a minute, and it was then he saw Jennifer hovering over a body. He froze, suddenly unable to move.

'Get an ambulance here *now!*' Jennifer screamed, and Pete turned and raced to the squad car.

Stifling her panic, Jennifer focused on the body below her. The face of the young woman was bloodied and misshapen. There was a sickening ring of purple around her neck. One of her hands lay at an odd angle, the wrist clearly broken. Jennifer had believed her dead until she'd reached down and registered a faint pulse.

When Pete returned, he squatted beside Jennifer.

A moment later, when he recognized the victim, he vomited on the side of the road.

Thirty-four

When Julie arrived for work on Thursday morning, she found Officers Gandy and Romanello waiting for her. By the expressions on their faces, she knew at once why they were there.

'It's Andrea, isn't it?'

Mabel was standing behind them, her eyes red and swollen. 'Oh, honey,' she said, crossing the room and going into Julie's arms. 'Mike and Henry are already on their way . . .' She began to wail, her body shaking uncontrollably.

'What happened?'

'He beat her,' Mabel choked out. 'He almost killed her . . . She's in a coma . . . They don't know if she's going to make it . . . They had to fly her to Wilmington last night . . .'

Julie's knees seemed to weaken before steadying. A moment later, Mike and Henry burst through the door. Mike saw Julie and Mabel before he locked eyes with the officers.

'What did he do to Andrea?' Mike demanded.

Jennifer hesitated. How do you describe a beating like that? The blood, the broken bones . . .

'It was bad,' Pete finally offered. 'I've never seen anything like it.'

Mabel broke into sobs again as Julie struggled with her own. Henry seemed unable to move, but Mike met Jennifer's eyes.

'Have you arrested Richard yet?' Mike demanded.

'No,' Jennifer answered.

'Why the hell not?'

'Because we don't know if he's the one responsible.'

'Of course he did it! Who the hell else would do something like that?'

Jennifer held up her hands, trying to keep control of the situation. 'Look, I know you're all upset . . .'

'Of course we're upset!' Mike shouted. 'How else should we be acting? He's still out on the streets while you two are wasting your time here!'

'Now hold on,' Pete said quickly, and Mike turned on him.

'Hold on? You're the one who screwed this up in the first place! If you weren't so damn stupid, none of this would have happened! I told you the guy was dangerous! We begged you to do something about it! But you were too busy playing tough cop to see what was happening.'

'Take it easy . . .'

Mike moved toward him. 'Don't tell me what to do! This is your fault!'

Pete's mouth straightened into a line, and he stepped toward Mike. Jennifer jumped between them.

'This isn't helping Andrea!' she shouted. 'Now both of you back off!'

Mike and Pete eyed each other, their bodies still tense. Jennifer went on quickly.

'Look—we didn't know about Richard,' she said, looking at Mike and Julie. 'Neither one of you mentioned anything about Andrea being seen with him, and we found Andrea *after* we left your place last night. She was already in a coma, and there was no way for us to know who'd done this to her. Pete and I were at the scene until almost dawn, and we came in this morning because this is where Andrea worked, not because we suspected anything. Mabel just told us about him and Andrea less than five minutes ago. Do you understand?'

Mike and Pete continued to stare at each other until Mike finally glanced away. He drew a long breath.

'Yeah, I got it,' Mike said. 'I'm just upset. I'm sorry.'

Pete continued to glare at Mike. A moment later, Jennifer turned to Julie.

'Mabel said that Emma had seen Richard and Andrea together in Morehead City, right?'

'Yes,' Julie answered. 'A couple of days ago. The day I saw him in the woods.'

371

'And none of you knew he'd been seeing her? If they were dating?'

'No,' Julie said. 'She didn't say anything to me about it. The first I heard about it was when Emma called.'

'Mabel?'

'No. Not to me, either.'

'And she didn't come in yesterday?'

'No.'

'Didn't that strike you as odd? If you knew she'd been seen with Richard, I mean?'

'Of course we were worried, but you have to understand Andrea,' Mabel offered. 'It wasn't the first time she hadn't shown up for work. She's like that.'

'Didn't she usually call, though?'

'Sometimes. Not all the time.'

Jennifer turned to Julie again. 'Why didn't you say anything about Andrea and Richard last night when Officer Gandy and I came over?'

'I didn't think about it. I was too upset about the locket, and then, after what Pete said . . .'

Jennifer nodded, knowing exactly what Julie was talking about. 'Would it be possible for Emma to come down here? I'd like to hear what she has to say.'

'No problem,' Henry said. 'Let me give her a call.'

Wanting to be certain she had everything straight, Jennifer went through the sequence of events again, then moved on to the more general questions—where Andrea liked to socialize, who her friends were, any other possibilities as to who might be involved. It was standard procedure, because she knew the lack of investigation into

372

other possible suspects could be used by the defense to claim police bias in court.

Julie found it hard to concentrate as Jennifer ran through the remaining questions. As upset as she was by what had happened to Andrea, she couldn't escape the thought that Richard had been following her for weeks. That he'd been in her house. And that she might be next.

Emma finally arrived, her eyes red from crying. Jennifer went through the same questions with her.

Emma didn't know anything other than what Julie and Mabel had already told them, though she did mention where she'd seen them—outside a bar called Mosquito Grove, just off the waterfront.

After questioning Emma, Jennifer glanced off to the side. 'Do you mind if I check Andrea's station?' she asked. 'She might have left something that'll give us an idea of when she started seeing Richard or if this was the first time.'

'No, go ahead,' Mabel offered.

Jennifer spent a minute opening drawers and sorting through them. She closed the drawers and spotted a picture of Andrea tucked into the mirror.

'Can I borrow this? In case we need it?'

'Sure.' Mabel nodded.

Jennifer studied the photograph of Andrea before looking up. 'Okay,' she said, 'that's it for now.'

Everyone seemed to nod in unison. Jennifer knew she should probably leave, but instead she moved toward Mike and Julie. After the hours she'd spent in their kitchen, she'd come to regard them almost as friends.

'I want you both to know,' she said, 'that if it is Richard who did this, then he's capable of

373

anything. It's the worst beating I've ever seen. It's almost beyond words. He's psychotic. I just wanted to make sure you understand that.'

Mike swallowed through the thickness in his throat.

'Do what you have to do to stay safe,' Jennifer said. 'Both of you.'

*   *   *

On the way out, Jennifer walked alongside Pete, neither of them saying anything. She had to give him credit, not only for letting her handle the questioning inside, but because of the new resolve she noted in his grim expression.

After getting into the car, he slipped the keys into the ignition but leaned back in his seat without starting the engine. He stared through the windshield.

'She cuts my hair,' Pete finally offered.

'Andrea?'

'Yeah. That's how I knew who it was last night.'

Jennifer stayed silent, watching as Pete closed his eyes.

'She didn't deserve what happened to her,' he said. 'No one deserves that.'

Jennifer put a hand on his shoulder. 'I'm sorry,' she said.

He nodded, as if trying to forget what he'd seen the night before. He started the engine.

'I think it's time that we pay Richard Franklin a little visit at work,' he said quietly. 'I'd rather catch him off guard if I can. I don't want to give him time to make up a story. If he's the one, then I want him to pay. Bad.'

Jennifer brought her hands together in her lap. Outside the window, trees and buildings were blurry as the car headed toward the bridge.

'He's not going to be there,' she said. 'He quit a month back.'

Pete looked at her. There were dark circles under his eyes; in the shadowed interior of the car, he looked as worn as she felt.

'How do you know that?'

'I called the personnel department at J. D. Blanchard.'

Pete continued to look at her. 'You've been investigating him?'

'Not officially.'

Pete turned his eyes to the road again and pulled over, bringing the car to a halt in the shade of a towering magnolia. 'Why don't you start from the beginning and let me know what you've been doing.' He reached for the cup of coffee he'd bought earlier that morning. 'And don't worry about getting in trouble—this will be just between you and me.'

Jennifer took a deep breath and began.

*   *   *

In the salon, Henry was staring vacantly, Mike was pale, and Mabel was dabbing at her tears. Emma looked faint as she sat curled beneath Henry's arm. Julie crossed her arms and rocked slowly back and forth on the couch.

'I can't believe it,' Emma whispered. 'I just can't believe it. How could he have done this to her?'

None of them said anything; Mabel looked down. 'I think I'm going to head down and see her today.

I don't know what else to do.'

'It's my fault,' Julie said. 'I should have warned her to stay away from him after she cut his hair. I could see she was attracted to him.'

'It's not your fault,' Mike protested. 'You couldn't have done anything to stop this. If it wasn't her, it would have been someone else.'

Like me.

Mike moved closer to her. 'She's going to be okay.'

Julie shook her head. 'You don't *know* that, Mike. You can't *promise* something like that.'

She sounded more impatient than she intended, and Mike turned away. No, he thought, I can't.

'I just don't understand it,' Julie said. 'Why here? Why did he have to come here, of all places? And why her? She didn't do anything to him.'

'He's crazy,' Mabel said. 'When they catch him, I hope they lock him up for a long, long time.'

If they catch him, Julie thought.

In the silence, Henry glanced out the window, then back to Julie.

'The police are right about doing what you have to do,' he said. 'But you can't stay here.'

Julie looked up.

'Not after what happened to Andrea,' Henry went on. 'Not with the fact that he's been in your house. It's not safe here anymore, for either of you.'

'Where should we go?'

'Anywhere. Just get out of town. Stay out of sight until they catch this guy.' He paused. 'You can use the beach house if you want. He won't find you there.'

'He's right,' Emma added. 'You've got to get out of here.'

376

'What if you're wrong?' Julie asked. 'What if he does find me?'

'He won't. The house isn't even registered in our names. It's held in trust, and he can't trace the fact that we own it. No one's been there for a couple of months, so there's no way he even knows it exists. He wouldn't even know where to look.'

'The thought of going there gives me the creeps,' she said. 'It's too quiet.'

'Do you want to stay at my place instead?' Mike offered.

'No,' she said. 'I'm sure he knows where you live, too.'

'Just go,' Mabel said. 'Henry's right. It's too dangerous here.'

'What if he follows us? What if he's watching me right now?'

Five pairs of eyes instinctively flicked to the window.

'Take my car,' Henry said. 'No, take Emma's. And leave right away. Mike and I will go check outside to see if he's around. If he isn't, just get to the highway and stay on it. It's a straight shot, and you'll know if someone's following you. Once you get to Jacksonville, make a lot of crazy turns to make sure no one's behind you. The important thing is that you get away before Richard even realizes you're gone.'

'What about the police? Shouldn't I tell them?'

'I'll handle that. Just go. And whatever you do, don't go home first.'

Moments later, Mike and Julie were gone.

*   *   *

377

It took about ten minutes for Jennifer to cover everything she'd learned—the strange credit history, the new corporation in Ohio to replace the one in Colorado, Richard's seeming desire to keep a low profile, Jake Blansen's comments about Richard being dangerous, and the fact that he no longer worked for J. D. Blanchard. Pete was tapping the steering wheel and nodding when she finished, looking as if everything she said made perfect sense.

'I knew there was something fishy about that guy,' he said. 'Even in the gym, he seemed a little too slick, you know?'

Jennifer stared at him, speechless. Despite her relief that he seemed to have seen the light—finally—and her chagrin that he needed to be pretty much smacked on the head with the obvious, at least he was on her side now.

'So I've heard,' she said finally.

Pete missed the sarcasm in her tone and tapped the steering wheel again.

'So if he's not working, where is he?' he asked.

'I don't know. We could try him at home.'

Pete nodded. 'Let's do it.'

*   *   *

Fifteen minutes later, Pete and Jennifer were pulling into the drive of the rented Victorian. Once out of the car, both of them unsnapped their holsters as they surveyed the area.

Up close, Jennifer thought the house looked seedier than it had from the road. Shades were drawn in the front windows. There was no sign of a car, though a weed-strewn drive led around to the back of the house.

The engine of their squad car ticked as it cooled. A flock of starlings broke, chirping and squawking as they exploded from the trees. A squirrel raced past, seeking safety in the upper reaches of a pine tree. Nothing else, no other sounds. No sign of movement through the windows.

'Looks like our suspect might have run,' Pete whispered.

No, Jennifer thought with sudden certainty, he's still here.

* * *

Richard watched them from behind the trees. He'd been out back, wiping down the interior of the car—he'd already scoured the house in an attempt to eliminate the most obvious signs of what had transpired the other night—when he'd heard them coming up the drive.

He'd expected them, of course, just not so soon.

* * *

Pete and Jennifer made their way carefully to the front door, the porch creaking beneath them. Standing before the peeling door, they glanced at each other before Pete knocked. Jennifer stood off to the side, hand on her holster. Her eyes flashed to the window, watching.

Then, instinctively, she drew her gun.

* * *

Richard watched the officers.

379

He took a long, deep breath, then quietly backed farther into the trees, wondering how they'd been able to connect Andrea to him so quickly.

DNA? No, he thought, that takes time, a week at least. Andrea must have said something to someone, even though he'd told her to keep her mouth shut. Either that or someone saw them together. At the bar, maybe. Or in Morehead City.

No matter. He'd already known that his time as Richard Franklin had come to an end. The situation with Andrea had only accelerated the inevitable. Despite his earlier cleaning, he knew it would be impossible to eliminate all the evidence of what he'd done to Andrea in the house. Modern forensics had improved to the point where experts could identify minute traces of blood or strands from her hair, and that was the reason he hadn't bothered to hide Andrea's body in the first place. If they somehow obtained a search warrant—which was only a matter of time, really—they would find what they needed to convict him.

Still, he wished he could have had another hour to collect his things. His cameras and lenses were inside the house, and he regretted having to part with them. And the photographs, too, especially the ones of Jessica in his briefcase. He knew that it was unlikely the police would be able to use them to find out more about Jessica—he'd been careful to destroy any photograph that even hinted of where they'd lived—but he wouldn't be able to replace them.

He'd miss the ones of Julie as well, but he wasn't as concerned about those. They'd have the rest of their lives to make up for the ones he'd left behind.

He wondered if Julie knew about Andrea yet.

Yes, probably, he thought. More than likely the police had just left her. So what would she do?

She'd run, he immediately thought. As she'd run from her mother. She'd try to hide and probably bring the fool with her. In fact, she was probably gone already.

Another reason to get away from here.

He considered the option. If they went around to check out the back of the house . . .

A gamble, but what other choice did he have? Quietly, he began moving toward the squad car.

*   *   *

'Let's head around back,' Jennifer whispered. The gun felt strangely light in her hand. 'I've got a funny feeling that he's still here.'

Pete nodded, and they left the porch. Pete headed toward the gravel drive, but when he saw Jennifer go the other way, he hesitated only briefly before following her. On this side, they had to navigate between the trees, twigs snapping beneath their feet. Tall grasses and weeds brushed their uniforms, making a scraping sound. Near the rear of the house, they paused. Jennifer was in front and, flattened against the house, she peeked around the corner.

Richard's car was parked there, the door on the passenger side open.

She held the gun to her chest, barrel raised, and nodded in that direction. Slowly Pete drew his gun.

She peeked again, scanning the yard for a glimpse of him, then nodded for Pete to follow. They crept around the back, trying to be as silent as possible.

They passed the corner windows.

381

Listening . . .

The birds had gone silent, Jennifer noticed.

Past the porch. The rear door to the house, they saw, stood open. She motioned in that direction, and Pete nodded before moving toward the house.

The car was close now. From the interior, she could hear the tinny sound of the radio, an oldies station out of Jacksonville.

Jennifer paused, looking from side to side. He's out there, she thought. And he's watching us now.

Stalking us. The way he stalked Julie.

In her mind, she saw what had been left of Andrea's face. Glancing over her shoulder, she saw Pete on the back porch, approaching the open door.

It was then that they heard the scream.

It was a piercing wail, agonizing and shrill, and Jennifer nearly pulled the trigger of her gun. She hesitated only momentarily before locking eyes with Pete.

It was coming from the front of the house.

Pete scrambled down from the porch and began running back the way they'd come. Jennifer turned to follow him. They rounded the corner and pushed through the branches, leaves and twigs slapping against them as they made their way to the front.

But when they reached the front, they saw nothing.

Everything was exactly as it had been before.

They split up then, Pete approaching the front of the house, Jennifer moving forward into the yard.

Her mouth was dry and she was breathing hard, trying to stay calm. A short distance away, she eyed a grove of low-growing trees surrounded by bushes, reminding her of a duck blind hidden for maximum effect.

She looked away, then back. She could feel the gun in her hand growing slick with perspiration.

That's where he is, she thought. He's hiding, and he wants me to come get him. Behind her, she could hear Pete moving across the gravel.

Jennifer raised the gun in front of her, just as her dad had taught her.

'Mr Franklin, this is Officer Jennifer Romanello, and my gun is drawn,' she called out slowly. 'Identify yourself and come out with your hands in the air.'

Pete turned at the sound of her voice and, seeing what she was doing, started toward her, crossing the driveway. Like her, he had drawn his gun.

From the back of the house came the sound of a car engine turning over. The engine whined as the accelerator was slammed to the floor, rocks spitting out from behind the tires. It was racing toward them from the other side of the house.

Pete stood frozen in the middle of the drive; he saw the car a moment before Jennifer did.

It wasn't slowing down.

For a moment, Pete was immobilized. He pointed the gun at the car but hesitated, and by then even Jennifer could see what was going to happen.

In the last possible second, Pete dove out of the way as the car ripped past him. He landed on his chest, like a baseball player sliding into home, and the gun flew from his grasp.

Jennifer had only a split second to take the shot, but because of Pete's dive and the broken view through the trees, she opted against it.

The car roared down the highway, veered around

the curve, and vanished from sight, leaving a trail of flying gravel in its wake.

Jennifer ran toward Pete. He was already getting up and had begun searching for his gun by the time she reached him.

Seconds passed before they found it, and they ran to the squad car without a word. Jennifer reached the passenger side and jumped in; their doors slammed simultaneously. Instinctively, Pete reached for the ignition keys.

They were gone.

It was then that Jennifer registered that the wires connecting the radio had been torn from the dash.

The sound of Richard's car had already faded.

'Damn!' Pete shouted, slamming the wheel hard.

Jennifer grabbed for her cell phone and called the station. Because it was a small town and there were only a few officers on duty, she didn't hold out much hope that they would be able to catch Richard in time. When she hung up, Pete looked at her.

'Now what do we do?'

'I'm going inside.'

'Without a warrant?'

Jennifer opened the door and stepped out. 'He tried to run you down and he's probably on his way to harm someone else. I think that qualifies as a legitimate reason for entry. Don't you?'

A moment later, Pete Gandy was behind her.

Through the rush of adrenaline and frustration, he couldn't help but notice that as far as learning the ropes, Jennifer Romanello seemed to be a rather quick study.

* * *

Jennifer was struck by the normalcy of the setting as soon as she entered.

This could be anyone's house, she observed.

The kitchen was miraculously clean, the kitchen sink gleaming in the sunlight, a washrag folded neatly over the sink. There wasn't a single pot on the stove or a used dish on the counter. Had she taken a photograph, no one would have noticed anything amiss. Though obviously old—the refrigerator looked like the models advertised in the Sears catalog right after World War II, and there was neither a dishwasher nor a microwave oven—the kitchen seemed almost homey, the kind that children remember when thinking of their grandparents.

Jennifer moved forward, passing through what was once a breakfast nook. It was surprisingly bright in this room, the morning sun riding high on the glass and sending streams of gold across the floor. A richly patterned wallpaper, light yellow and hinting of flowers, and oak crown molding gave the room a sense of richness. The table was simple, the chairs surrounding it pushed in neatly.

She moved into the living room, thinking again that there was nothing out of the ordinary. The furniture was plain, and nothing was out of place. Yet . . .

It took a moment before she realized what was wrong.

There's nothing personal here, she thought. Nothing at all. No photographs or paintings on the walls, no magazines, no newspapers stacked on the end table, no plants. No stereo system or compact discs, no television.

Just a couch, end tables, and lamps.

Jennifer looked up the stairs. Behind her, Pete came in, his gun drawn.

'Kind of empty, huh?' he offered.

'I'm going up,' she said.

Pete followed her. At the top, they peeked down the hallway before starting toward the right. Opening the door, they found the darkroom and flicked the switch. Bathed by the reddish glow, Jennifer felt suddenly weak as she realized what Richard had been doing with his time since he'd quit work.

'Lord help us,' was all she could say.

*   *   *

Not wanting to draw attention to himself, Richard slowed the car once he reached the major roads.

His heart was pounding, but he was free! Free! He'd escaped when escape seemed impossible, and he laughed aloud. He could still see the officers' faces as he tore down the driveway, and he was *soaring*.

Too bad that Pete Gandy had rolled out of the way. In his mind, he could imagine the delightful *whump* as the car crushed him, but alas, Pete would live to see another day.

He laughed again, exhilarated, and began to focus on his plan.

He had to ditch the car, but he wanted to put as much distance between Swansboro and himself as he could. He turned onto the highway that led to Jacksonville. There, he'd park the car where it wouldn't be spotted right away, and he'd begin his search for Julie.

Jessica had tried to run once, too, he remembered, and she thought she'd been careful. She took a bus halfway across the country and hoped he would simply let her go. But he'd tracked her down, and when he opened the door to the run-down motel where she was staying and found her sitting on the bed, she wasn't even surprised to see him. She'd been expecting him, and by the end, the waiting had worn her down. She didn't even have the energy to cry. When he handed her the locket, she slipped it around her neck, as if knowing she had no choice.

He helped her up from the bed, ignoring the lethargy of her movements, and put his arms around her. He buried his face in her hair, inhaling her scent, as Jessica's arms hung by her side.

You didn't think I'd let you go that easily, did you? he whispered.

Please, she whispered.

Say it.

Jessica's words came out raggedly. *No, you couldn't let me go.*

You were wrong to run, weren't you?

Jessica began to cry, as if finally recognizing what was to come.

Oh . . . please . . . don't hurt me . . . please, not again . . .

But you tried to run away, he said. *That hurt me, Jessica.*

Oh . . . God . . . please . . . no . . .

*   *   *

Standing in the doorway of the darkroom, Pete Gandy blinked a few times, his head turning from

387

side to side as he tried to take it all in.

Taped to the walls were hundreds of photographs of Julie. Julie leaving the salon and getting into her car, Julie in the woods taking Singer for a walk, Julie at dinner, Julie in the supermarket, Julie on the back porch, Julie reading the morning newspaper, Julie getting the mail. Julie on the beach. Julie on the street. Julie in her bedroom.

Julie everywhere she'd been over the last month.

Jennifer felt something collapse inside her. Even she hadn't expected this. She wanted to stay longer, she knew it was important to check the rest of the house for obvious signs that Andrea had been here. Pete was still frozen in place.

'I can't believe this guy,' he whispered as she brushed past him. In the second bedroom, Jennifer found Richard's workout equipment. He'd hung a mirror in there, surrounded by more pictures. Jennifer moved to the final door, which she assumed was his bedroom. Though she wasn't sure her actions were legal, she decided to poke around while she waited for backup to arrive.

Pushing open the door, she saw a beat-up chest of drawers that looked as if it might have been left behind by whoever had lived here before. In the closet, she found Richard's suits, hanging neatly. Against the wall, she saw the hamper; a phone sat on the floor near the head of the bed.

But it was the photo on the bedstand that held her attention.

At first, she thought it was Julie. The hair was the same, and her eyes were a similar mixture of blue and green; yet it wasn't Julie, Jennifer realized after a moment, just someone who closely resembled her. Holding a rose to her cheek, the

388

woman in the photograph was younger than Julie by a few years, her smile almost childlike.

It was as she reached for the frame that she noticed the locket around the woman's neck. The same locket that Julie had shown her in the kitchen.

The same . . .

Her foot hit something; whatever it was felt heavy, though it shifted slightly. Looking down, she saw the corner of a briefcase poking out from beneath the bed.

She slid it out and set it on the bed.

Inside were dozens of pictures of the woman in the frame, and she started sorting through them.

Pete came in behind her. 'What is it?' he asked.

Jennifer shook her head.

'More photographs,' she said.

'Of Julie?'

'No,' Jennifer said, turning toward him. 'I don't know for sure, but I think it's probably Jessica.'

Thirty-five

Within forty minutes, Richard Franklin's home was crowded with Swansboro police officers and Onslow County sheriffs. The forensics team from Jacksonville was inside collecting fingerprints and looking for evidence of Andrea's presence.

Jennifer and Pete were standing outside the home with their captain, Russell Morrison—a gruff bulldozer of a man with thinning gray hair and eyes set too close together. He had them repeat their story twice, then listened as Jennifer filled him in

389

on what she'd already learned.

When she finished, Morrison just kept shaking his head. He'd been born and raised in Swansboro and regarded himself as its protector; the night before, he'd been one of the first to arrive at the scene where Andrea had been found, even though he'd been sound asleep when he'd received the call at home.

'This is the same guy that Mike Harris assaulted in the bar? The one she claimed was stalking her?'

'Yes,' Jennifer said.

'But you don't have any concrete evidence linking him to this crime?'

'Not yet.'

'Have you talked to Andrea's neighbors to see if they've seen him around?'

'No. We came here right after the salon.'

Russell Morrison considered what he'd been told. 'Just because he ran doesn't mean he's the one who assaulted Andrea. Neither does anything you've learned about him.'

'But—'

Morrison held up his hands to cut her off. 'I'm not saying I think he's innocent. Hell, he tried to kill an officer, and that doesn't happen on my watch.' He glanced at Pete. 'You sure you're okay?'

'Yeah. Pissed off, but I'm okay.'

'Good. You're the lead on this investigation, but I'm going to put everyone on it.'

Pete nodded as they were interrupted by a shout from Fred Burris, one of the officers who'd been in the house. He was approaching them rapidly.

'Captain?' he called out.

Morrison turned toward him. 'Yeah?'

'I think we've got something,' he announced.

'What is it?'

'Blood,' he said simply.

*   *   *

Henry's beach house was on Topsail Island, a slit of land half a mile offshore, about forty minutes from Swansboro. Covered by rolling dunes speckled with sawgrass and white sand, the island was popular with families during the summer, though few people lived there year-round. During spring, visitors seemed to have the island all to themselves.

Like all homes there, the main floor of the house had been built above the garage and storage areas due to storm surges. Steps led from the back porch to the beach, and the windows along the back of the house offered an unobstructed view of the waves as they rolled in.

Julie stood at the window, staring at their ceaseless motion.

Even here, it was impossible for her to relax. Or feel safe.

She and Mike had stopped at the grocery store along the way, buying enough food to last them a week; then they swung by Wal-Mart to grab enough basic clothing to get them through the next few days. Neither of them had any idea how long they would be here, and she didn't want to go out in public unless she had to.

The drapes were drawn on every window but this one; Mike had parked Emma's car in the garage so it couldn't be seen from the road. As they were driving, he had taken Henry's advice and exited the highway three times, circling through neighborhood streets, constantly checking the rearview mirror. No one had followed them; they were sure of that. Still, Julie couldn't shake the feeling that Richard would somehow find her.

Behind her, Mike was putting the groceries away, and Julie could hear the sound of cabinets as they were opened and closed.

'Maybe they've already caught him,' Mike offered.

Julie said nothing. Singer moved beside her and nuzzled her hip. Julie's hand went automatically to his head.

'You okay?'

'No,' she said, 'not really.'

Mike nodded. Stupid question.

'I hope Andrea's okay,' he said.

When she didn't respond, Mike looked up. 'We're safe here,' he said. 'You know that, right? There's no way he could know we're here.'

'I know.'

But she wasn't so sure, and her fear was so strong that she found herself instinctively backing away from the window. At her movement, Singer's ears rose to attention.

'What is it?' Mike asked.

Julie shook her head. On the beach, she could see two couples walking near the water's edge, headed in opposite directions. Both had walked by the house without a glance only minutes before. There was no one else out there.

'Nothing,' she finally said.

'It's a beautiful view, isn't it?'

Julie lowered her gaze. To be honest, she hadn't noticed.

*   *   *

Morrison huddled with the officers outside Richard's house as he took charge, outlining what was happening and what he wanted done.

'Jacksonville police and the sheriff's department are looking for the car now to see if we can find this guy,' he said, 'but in the meantime, this is what I need you to do.'

He pointed from one man to the next as he spoke.

'Haroldson and Teeter—I need you to head down to the bridge and talk to anyone on the crew who might know some of this guy's hangouts. Where he goes, who his friends are, what he likes to do . . .

'Thomas—I need you to stay here while forensics gathers the evidence. Make sure they tag and bag everything . . . This one has to go by the book . . .

'Burris—I want you to go to Andrea's apartment and talk to the neighbors. I want to know if anyone else has seen this guy at her place . . .

'Johnson—likewise for you. I need you to head to Morehead City to find out if anyone else can verify that Andrea and Richard Franklin were together . . .

'Puck—I need you to find out who else Andrea has been seeing who might have done this. It's probable that we have the guy already, but you know how defense attorneys are. We have to look into every possible suspect . . .'

He turned to Jennifer and Pete. 'And you two—I want you to find out everything we can about this guy. Everything. And see what you can learn about Jessica, too. I want to talk to her if we can.'

'What about the subpoena for J. D. Blanchard?'

Jennifer asked.

Morrison met her eyes. 'Let me handle that.'

* * *

Like Julie and Mike, Richard Franklin stopped at the store. After pulling his car into the rear corner parking lot of the hospital—where it wouldn't draw attention by remaining parked in the same spot for a few days—he grabbed the bags from the store and walked down the block before heading into a gas station rest room. He locked the door behind him. Staring into the grimy mirror above the sink, he became his methodical self again.

In the plastic bags were items necessary for the change he'd gone through once before: a razor, scissors, hair coloring, tanning cream, and a pair of inexpensive reading glasses. Not much, but enough to alter his appearance from a distance; enough to hide in plain view for the short term. Enough to find her.

There was, however, the problem of where she'd gone. And she was gone; of that he was now certain. No one had answered the phone at the salon, and when he'd called the garage, one of Henry's flunkies had said that Mike had left as well.

So she'd run, but where? Richard smiled, knowing he'd have the answer soon. Even when people tried to be careful, they made mistakes. And her mistake, he was certain, came down to this: Someone knew exactly where she was.

Henry or Emma or Mabel probably knew. And the police would know as well. They'd want to talk to her, to tell her what they'd learned, to keep their eye on her.

One of these people, he was certain, would lead him to her doorstep.

He whistled softly under his breath as he began to alter his appearance. Thirty minutes later he emerged into the sunlight, blonder, tanner, wearing glasses, and without a mustache. A new man.

All that's left is to find another car, he thought. He headed down the street, toward the mall across from the hospital.

*   *   *

Back at the station, Jennifer's first call was to the Denver Police Department, where she was passed from person to person until finally reaching Detective Cohen. She told him who she was and about the investigation; as she spoke, she heard the detective whistle under his breath.

'Yeah,' he said, 'I'll see what I can do. I'm not at my desk, so let me call you back in a few minutes.'

After hanging up, she glanced at Pete. He was on the phone to various airlines in the Jacksonville, Raleigh, and Wilmington airports, trying to find out if Richard had indeed traveled out of town when he had told Julie he was at his mother's funeral. If so, they wanted to know where he'd gone, in the hope it would lead them to someone who could tell them about him.

Morrison was in his office, serving as the hub as information came in from the other officers. Thomas had called a few minutes earlier; he'd said that the forensics team had found evidence of semen stains on the sheets, and they were scouring the bed for additional evidence.

When Cohen called back, Jennifer picked up on the first ring.

'We've got information on a few Richard Franklins,' he said. 'It's not an unusual name, so more than one popped up in the system. Tell me about him.'

Jennifer gave him a brief description—height and weight, hair color and eyes, approximate age, race.

'Okay, give me a just a second.'

On the phone, she could hear him tapping information into the computer.

'Huh,' he finally said.

'What?'

He hesitated. 'I don't think we have any information for you.'

'Nothing? Not even an arrest?'

'Not based on what you told me. We have records of seven individuals with the name Richard Franklin. Four of those are African Americans, one is deceased, one is in his sixties.'

'What about the last one?'

'A typical druggie. He's about the same age as your guy, but nothing else about him matches up. There's not a chance he could pass for an engineer, even for a day. He's been in and out of prison for the last twenty years. And from our records, he never lived at the address you listed.'

'Is there anything else? Can you track county records? Or maybe records from other cities?'

'It's all in here,' Cohen said, sounding as disappointed as she did. 'The system was just updated a couple of years ago. We have information on anyone arrested in the state going back to 1977. If he'd been arrested anywhere in the state of Colorado, we'd know it.'

Jennifer tapped her pencil on the pad. 'Could you fax me a photograph of the last guy, anyway? Or attach it to an e-mail?'

'Sure. But I don't think he's your guy,' Cohen said, his tone dropping slightly. He paused. 'Look—if you need anything else, let me know. Sounds like a pretty bad guy. Not the kind we want walking around in public.'

After hanging up the phone, Jennifer placed a call to the Columbus Police Department, hoping for better luck.

*   *   *

Mabel had left the salon that morning and driven to the hospital. Now she was sitting beside Andrea in the intensive care unit, holding her hand and hoping that Andrea would somehow know she was there.

'You're going to be okay, sweetheart,' she whispered almost to herself. 'Your mom and dad are going to be here soon.'

The heart monitor beeped steadily in response, and Mabel eyed the phone.

She wished she knew what was going on with the investigation. For a moment, she considered calling Pete Gandy to find out. But she was still so mad at him for letting this go on as long as it had that she didn't think she could do so without screaming at him. Mike had been right. All he'd had to do was listen to Julie and none of this would have happened. Why had that been so hard? How on earth had he ever passed training?

Mabel heard the sound of footsteps approaching and looked up to see the nurse. She'd been checking in every twenty minutes to monitor any changes.

The first twenty-four hours were critical, the doctor had said. If Andrea was going to come out of a coma without brain damage, more than likely she'd show some improvement by then.

Mabel's throat tightened as she watched the nurse in action, checking vital signs and scribbling notes.

By the look on her face, Mabel knew there was no change at all.

*   *   *

Jennifer hung up with the Columbus Police Department just as Morrison came out of his office.

'Got the subpoena,' he said. 'Judge Riley signed it a few minutes ago, and it's being faxed to J. D. Blanchard right now. We should have the information shortly, unless they get their legal team involved and try to stall things.'

Jennifer nodded but was unable to hide the information in her expression.

'Still no luck?' Morrison asked.

She shook her head. 'Nothing. Not a damn thing. He hasn't so much as had a speeding ticket in either Colorado or Ohio. No arrests, no record of him even being a suspect in a crime.'

'The fax from Denver didn't help?'

'Not our guy. Not even close.' She scanned the faxed photograph anyway. 'I don't understand it. A guy like this doesn't just appear out of nowhere. I know he's done this type of thing before. There's got to be some record of it.' She ran a hand through her hair. 'Any news from the house?'

'It seems as if he did some cleaning recently. They were able to bag a few things, but we won't know for sure if any of it's of use until it's examined. Right now, we have someone running a blood sample down to Wilmington. The department there has one of the best labs in the state, and as soon as they get both samples, they'll run a comparison with Andrea's blood from the hospital. It's number one on the priority list, and hopefully, we'll get a match. Blood type checks out, though. Andrea is A positive, and so was the sample. It's not as common as O, so it seems likely that he's our guy.'

'Anything from Morehead? Or the workers at the site?'

'Not so far. Franklin seemed to keep to himself. Haroldson and Teeter couldn't find anyone who liked the guy, let alone hung out with him. Nobody even knew where he lived. They've still got a few more people to talk to, but they're not very hopeful. As for Burris and Puck, they say that no one can remember seeing Franklin anywhere near Andrea's apartment. But they're getting information on other possible suspects, just in case. She tended to associate with some pretty rough guys, and Puck is gathering their names now.'

'Richard Franklin's our guy,' Jennifer reiterated.

Morrison held up his hands as if he realized that. 'We'll know that for sure in a couple of hours,' he said. 'As for Morehead City, Johnson is showing Andrea's picture around. Good idea to grab that photo, by the way. But so far, nothing. There are a lot of bars and restaurants to cover, and they just got there a little while ago. Evening shifts in the bars and restaurants start about five, so it might

399

take a while.'

Jennifer nodded.

Morrison nodded toward the phone. 'Have you been able to track down any information on Jessica yet?'

'No,' she said. 'Not yet. That's my next step.'

* * *

Julie sat on the couch with Singer by her side, one ear cocked forward. Mike turned on the television and surfed through the channels, then turned it off. He wandered through the house, making sure the front door was locked, then looked through the window, up and down the street.

Quiet. Completely quiet.

'I think I'll give Henry a call,' he finally said. 'Just to let him know we made it.'

Julie nodded.

* * *

Pulling back her hair with both hands, Jennifer turned her attention to the photographs that had been in Richard's briefcase. Unlike Julie, Jessica appeared to have posed happily for most of them. It also seemed likely that she was indeed his wife; Jennifer noted that in a few pictures there was an engagement ring, which was later joined to a wedding band.

Unfortunately, the photographs couldn't tell her anything about Jessica herself—if indeed that was her name. None had information written on the back that might reveal a maiden name or even where they were taken. The photographs

400

themselves showed no landmarks, and after a cursory glance through them, Jennifer wondered how to find out more about her.

She searched the Internet for any mention of Jessica Franklin, looking for the obvious—anyone from Colorado or Ohio, for instance—and checked out the sites that posted a photograph. There were less than a handful of those, and none matched the woman she was looking for. It didn't surprise her. After a divorce, most women would go back to their maiden names . . .

But what if they hadn't divorced?

He'd already demonstrated how violent he could be. Jennifer looked at the phone. After hesitating for just a moment, she dialed Detective Cohen in Denver.

'No, no problem,' he said in response to her request. 'Since you called, I've been thinking about that guy. For some reason, his name sounds familiar. This shouldn't be too hard to find out. Let me check.'

She waited as he checked the records.

'No,' he finally said. 'No murder victims listed under the name of Jessica Franklin, no missing persons, either.'

'Is there any way you could find out anything about their marriage? When it took place, how long they've been married?'

'We don't have that kind of information on hand, but the county might. Your best bet is to look through property tax records, since most homes are owned in both names, and that might help you get started. But you'll need to find someone who can access the archives. And that's, of course, assuming they were married in the area.'

'Do you have the number?'

'Not offhand, but let me look it up.'

She heard him pull open a drawer, curse, then call to one of his colleagues for a book.

A moment later he recited the number, and Jennifer was jotting it down as Pete came rushing to her desk.

'Daytona,' he said. 'The son of a bitch went to Daytona when he said he went to his mother's funeral—'

'Daytona? Isn't that where Julie is from?'

'I don't remember,' Pete said quickly, 'but listen . . . if his mother died, we might be able to find some information about her in a recent obituary. I've already accessed the newspaper, and I'm printing up the information now. Pretty smart, huh?'

Jennifer said nothing as she thought about it. 'Don't you think that's odd?' she asked. 'I mean, his mother dying in the same place Julie grew up?'

'Maybe they grew up together.'

Possible, but unlikely, she thought, shaking her head. It just didn't sound right. Especially considering that there was proof he'd been in Denver four years ago and Julie certainly would have mentioned any common history they shared. But . . . why would he go to Daytona?

Suddenly she paled.

'Do you have a phone number for Julie's mother?' she asked.

Pete shook his head. 'No.'

'Get it. I think we should talk to her.'

'But what about the obituaries?'

'Forget them. We're not even sure if the story about his mother is true. Let's get his phone

402

records instead. Maybe we can find out who he called.'

I should have done that from the beginning, she realized suddenly. So much for thinking she knew everything.

'Phone records?'

'From the house, Pete. Get the phone records for Richard Franklin.'

Pete blinked, trying to keep up. 'So the obituaries don't mean anything?'

'No. He didn't go down there to see his mother. He went down there to learn about Julie. I'd bet my life on it.'

*   *   *

Henry sat with Emma at the kitchen table, his eyes absently following a fly that was bouncing against the glass.

'So they're sure no one followed them?'

Henry nodded. 'That's what Mike said when he called.'

'And do you think they're safe?'

'I hope so, but until they catch the SOB, I won't rest easy.'

'What if they don't?'

'They'll find him.'

'But what if they don't?' Emma asked again. 'How long are they going to have to hide there?'

Henry shook his head. 'As long as it takes.' He paused. 'But I should probably call and let the police know where they are.'

*   *   *

Jennifer absently twirled a strand of her hair as she finished up her conversation with Henry.

'Thanks for letting me know,' she said. 'I appreciate it. Good-bye.'

So they'd left town, she thought, hanging up. On the one hand, she probably would have done the same thing if she'd been in their situation. On the other hand, they were farther away if they needed help. Though Topsail was still in the county, it was at the southern end—at least forty minutes from Swansboro.

The archived tax records had been a dead end. The house had been listed in Richard Franklin's name only.

Without anyplace else to turn for information, Jennifer returned her focus to the photographs. Photographs, she knew, could tell her about not only the subject, but the photographer as well. And Richard had been quite good—many of the images were striking, and she found herself staring at them. Richard Franklin, she decided, wasn't simply a weekend photographer, but someone who viewed photography as art. It made sense, considering the equipment they'd found in his house.

It wasn't something she had focused on right away, but could that knowledge be helpful? And if so, how? She wasn't sure yet.

Still, the longer she looked, the more she felt that she was on the right track with this line of thinking. Though she wasn't sure exactly what the answers were yet—or even the questions, for that matter— as she stared at the photographs and wondered what they implied about Richard, she couldn't help but feel that she was getting close to something important.

Thirty-six

In Denver, Detective Larry Cohen thought about the phone calls.

Officer Romanello had wanted information on Richard Franklin, and though he'd searched the database without success, he knew he'd heard the name before. As he'd told Jennifer Romanello, the name *was* familiar.

Could have been anything, of course. A witness in one of the hundreds of cases he'd been involved with; he may even have seen the name in the newspaper at one time or another. Might even have been a stranger he'd bumped into at a party or someone he'd met in passing.

Yet he had a feeling that the name *had* something to do with police business.

If he hadn't been arrested, though, what was it?

Rising from his desk, he decided to ask around. Maybe someone else in the department would be able to clear it up for him.

* * *

An hour later, Morrison emerged from his office with both the phone records and the information from J. D. Blanchard that Richard Franklin had originally submitted. Included in the fax was his résumé and information about the previous projects on which he'd consulted.

Pete took the phone records; Jennifer put the photographs aside and began studying the information from J. D. Blanchard.

At the top of the résumé, Richard had listed an apartment in Columbus as an address; below that, however, was a gold mine. Whom he'd worked for and when, association lists, previous experience, his educational background.

'Got you,' she whispered. After calling information, she dialed Lentry Construction in Cheyenne, Wyoming, the last company he'd worked for before forming his own corporation.

After identifying herself to the receptionist, she was passed on to Clancy Edwards, the vice president, who'd been with the company almost twenty years.

'Richard Franklin? Sure I remember him,' Edwards offered almost immediately. 'He was one hell of a manager here. Really knew his stuff. I wasn't surprised when he went into business for himself.'

'When was the last time you talked to him?'

'Oh, gee . . . let me think about it. He moved to Denver, you know. I guess it must have been eight or nine years ago. We were working on . . . oh, let's see . . . that would have been in ninety-five, right? I think it was a project out in—'

'Excuse me, Mr Edwards, but do you know if he was married?'

It took a moment for Edwards to realize she'd asked another question. 'Married?'

'Yes, was he married?'

Edwards laughed under his breath. 'Not a chance. We were all pretty sure he was gay . . .'

Jennifer pushed the phone closer to her ear, wondering if she'd heard him right. 'Wait. Are you sure?'

'Well, not a hundred percent. Not that he ever

said anything about it, of course. We didn't push it, either. A man's personal business is his own as long as he can do the job. That's always been the way we work. We do a good job with affirmative action at our company. Always have.'

Jennifer barely listened as he went on.

'Wyoming's come a long way, but it's not San Francisco, if you know what I mean, and it wasn't always easy. But times are changing, even here.'

'Did he get along with everyone?' she suddenly asked, remembering what Jake Blansen had told her on the phone.

'Oh yeah, absolutely. Like I said, he really knew his stuff, and people respected him for it. And he was a nice guy, too. Bought my wife a hat for her birthday. Not that she wears it much anymore. You know how women are about—'

'How about the construction workers? Did he get along with them?'

Caught in midsentence, Clancy Edwards took another moment to catch up.

'Yeah, sure, them, too. Like I said, everyone liked him. A couple might have had a problem with his . . . well, his personal life, but everyone got along with him fine. We were all sorry to see him go.'

When Jennifer said nothing, Edwards seemed to feel the need to fill the silence.

'Can I ask what this is all about? He's not in trouble, is he? Nothing happened to him, did it?'

Jennifer was still trying to make sense of this new information.

'It's regarding an investigation. I'm sorry, but I can't say any more,' she answered. 'Do you remember if you ever received a call from an outfit called J. D. Blanchard regarding a reference?'

'I didn't, but I think the president did. We were happy to give a recommendation. Like I said, he did a real good job . . .'

Jennifer found her gaze drifting to the photographs of Jessica again. 'Do you know if he was into photography as a hobby?'

'Richard? He might have been, but if he was, he never mentioned it to me. Why?'

'No reason,' she said, suddenly running out of questions. 'I want to thank you for your time, Mr Edwards. If I need any more help, would you mind if I call you again?'

'No, not at all. You can reach me until six on most days. We have a lot of respect for law enforcement around here. My grampa used to be the sheriff for . . . oh, gee . . . I guess it must have been twenty years or so . . .'

Even as he was speaking, Jennifer was hanging up the phone, shaking her head and wondering why none of what she'd just heard seemed to make any sense.

*   *   *

'You were right,' Pete said to Jennifer a few minutes later, looking confused that she'd been right about her instincts while his had been so off base. 'There was a number listing a private investigator in Daytona.' He glanced at the note he'd scribbled. 'Richard made three calls to an outfit called Croom's Investigations. No answer when I dialed it, but I left a message. Sounds like a one-man shop. No secretary and a man's voice on the answering machine.'

'How about Julie's mother?'

408

Pete shook his head. 'Yeah, I got her number through information, but there was no answer. I'll try again in a little while. How's it going on your end?'

Jennifer briefed him on her conversation with Clancy Edwards. When she finished, Pete scratched the back of his neck.

'Gay, huh?' He nodded as if it made sense. 'I can see that.'

Jennifer reached for the résumé again, trying to ignore his comment.

'I'm going to try the next company on the list,' she said. 'It's been a long time since he's worked there, but I'm hopeful that I can talk to somebody who remembers him. After that, I guess I'll try the bank in Denver where he kept his accounts, or maybe I can get some information from some of his former neighbors. If I can locate any of them, that is.'

'That sounds like it'll take a while.'

Jennifer nodded, distracted, still thinking about the call to Edwards. 'Listen,' she said, scribbling down the basic information from the résumé, 'while I'm doing that, see if you can find out anything about his childhood. It says he was born in Seattle, so call the major hospitals and see if you can find the record of his birth certificate. Maybe we can find out more if we hunt down his family. I'll keep working on this end.'

'Sure.'

'Oh—and keep trying the detective and Julie's mother. I really want to talk to them.'

'You got it.'

*   *   *

409

It took more time than he'd imagined it would to find a car, but Richard exited the parking lot of the mall in a green 1994 Pontiac Trans Am. Turning into traffic, he headed for the highway. As far as he could tell, no one was watching him.

It was ridiculous in this day and age, he thought, that people still left their keys in the ignition. Didn't they realize that someone would take advantage of their stupidity? No, of course not. Those things could never happen to *them*. It was a world of Pete Gandys out there, blind and lazy morons who left us vulnerable to terrorists, not only with their stupidity, but with their lack of vigilance, their fat, contented ignorance. He would never be so careless, but he wasn't complaining. He needed a car, and this one would do just fine.

*   *   *

The afternoon wore on.

In the course of her calls, Jennifer had come across one dead end after another. Finding neighbors had been all but impossible—she had to convince a county worker to go through property tax records to find the owners, then find the names through information, all the while hoping they hadn't moved—and that took more time than she'd thought it would. In the course of four hours, she talked to four people, all of whom had known Richard Franklin at one time. Two were former neighbors, and two were managers who vaguely remembered Richard Franklin from the single year he'd spent working for a company in Santa Fe, New Mexico. Like Edwards, all four had said essentially the same things about Richard Franklin.

He was a nice guy who got along with everyone.

Probably gay.

If his hobby was photography, they didn't know about it.

Jennifer stood from her desk and made her way across the station to get another cup of coffee.

Who was this guy? she wondered. And why on earth did it feel as if everyone had been describing someone else entirely?

*   *   *

Halfway across the country, Detective Larry Cohen discussed the situation with a few people in the department.

Like him, they recognized the name but couldn't place it. One had gone so far as to look up the same information that Cohen had, convinced that he must have had a record, only to get exactly the same results.

Frowning, Cohen thought about it as he sat at his desk. Why was the name so familiar? Familiar not only to him, but to everyone here? If he'd never been arrested and no one could remember using him as a witness?

He bolted upright as the answer suddenly came to him. After tapping the keyboard of his computer, he scanned the basic information that came up on his screen. His hunch confirmed, he rose from his seat to find the detective he had to talk to.

*   *   *

At his desk, Pete was having more luck. He'd finished collecting the information on the early period of Richard's life, none of which was difficult to find. Feeling rather proud, he was heading over to fill Jennifer in when her phone rang. She held up a finger for Pete to wait until she was finished.

'Swansboro Police Department,' Jennifer said, 'Officer Romanello speaking.'

She heard a throat clear on the other end.

'This is Detective Cohen from Denver.'

Jennifer sat up. 'Oh . . . hey. Did you find anything?'

'Sort of. After your call, I kept thinking how familiar the name Richard Franklin sounded, so I asked around the department before it finally hit me where I'd heard it before.' He paused. 'After that, one of the other detectives here told me something rather interesting. It concerned a case he investigated four years ago about a missing person.'

Jennifer reached for her pen. 'Jessica Franklin?'

Pete glanced at Jennifer when he heard Jessica's name.

'No. Not about Jessica.'

'Then who are you talking about?'

'Richard Franklin. The guy you called me about.'

Jennifer paused. 'What are you trying to say?'

'Richard Franklin,' Detective Cohen said slowly. 'He's the missing person.'

'But he's here.'

'I understand that. But four years ago, he vanished. He didn't show up at work one day, and after a week or so, his secretary finally contacted us. I talked to the detective in charge of the investigation. From all appearances, he said it looked like the guy suddenly took off. Clothes were on the bed, and the drawers looked rifled through. Two suitcases were missing—his secretary told us they were the ones he always used on business— and his car was gone, too. He'd made a cash withdrawal from an ATM the last day that anyone saw him.'

'He ran?'

'Seemed so.'

'Why?'

'That's what the detective couldn't figure out. From the interviews with Franklin's acquaintances, no one could figure it out. They said he wasn't the type who would simply take off and leave his business behind. No one could understand it.'

'And there wasn't any legal trouble?'

'None that the detective could find. There weren't any lawsuits pending, and as I told you before, he wasn't in any trouble with us. It's like he simply decided to start over.'

It was the same thought Jennifer had had when she'd seen his credit report, she remembered.

'Why didn't his family report it?'

'Well, that's the thing. There really wasn't any family to speak of. His father was deceased, he had no siblings, and his mother was in a nursing home and suffering from dementia.'

Jennifer considered the implications. 'Do you have any information you could send me on the case?'

'Sure. I've already pulled the file. I can FedEx it tomorrow after I make copies.'

'Is there any way you could fax it over?'

'It's a thick file,' he said. 'It'll take at least an hour to get it all to you.'

'Please,' she said. 'I'm probably going to be here all night, anyway.'

'Yeah,' he said. 'I can do that. Give me your fax number again.'

*   *   *

Beyond the window above the kitchen table in Henry's beach house, the ocean was glowing orange, as if a fire had been set beneath the surface. As the last traces of the day began to vanish, the kitchen slowly grew dimmer. The overhead light buzzed with a fluorescent hum.

Mike moved close to Julie as she watched Singer on the beach. He was lying in the sand, ears up, head swiveling occasionally from side to side.

'Are you ready to eat yet?' he asked.

'I'm not hungry.'

Mike nodded. 'How's Singer doing?'

'He's fine.'

'No one's out there, you know,' Mike said. 'Singer would let us know.'

Julie nodded, then leaned into Mike as he slipped his arm around her.

*   *   *

Morrison left his office, striding toward Jennifer and Pete.

'It's Andrea Radley's blood all right. Just got off the phone with the lab and they confirmed it. No doubt about it.'

Jennifer barely heard him; instead, she was staring at the first page that had come through the fax from Denver.

'And Johnson found a witness,' Morrison went on. 'Turns out that one of the bartenders at Mosquito Grove remembered Andrea from the other night. Gave a perfect description of Richard Franklin. Said the guy was a real jerk.'

Jennifer was still staring at the first page from the fax, ignoring the other pages as they came through.

'He's not Richard Franklin,' she said quietly.

Morrison and Pete looked at her.

'What are you talking about?' Morrison asked.

'The suspect,' she said quietly. 'His name isn't Richard Franklin. The real Richard Franklin has been missing for three years. Here,' she said, handing over the first page of the fax. It was a photograph of the missing person, and despite the fuzziness of the faxed picture, the bald head and heavy features made it was clear to her that it wasn't the man they'd been looking for. 'This just came in from Denver. This is the real Richard Franklin.'

Morrison and Pete looked at the picture.

Pete blinked in confusion. 'This is Richard Franklin?' he asked.

'Yes.'

Pete continued to stare at the picture. 'But they don't look alike.'

Morrison met Jennifer's eyes. 'You're saying that this guy took over his identity?'

Jennifer nodded.

'Then who the hell are we looking for?' Morrison asked.

Jennifer glanced toward the windows at the far end of the department. 'I have no idea.'

Thirty-seven

'Thoughts?' Morrison said.

An hour later, with most of the officers present, Morrison couldn't hide his anger and frustration. With Jennifer and Pete, he'd scoured the items retrieved from the house in the hope that they might yield the suspect's true identity, but they'd turned up nothing. Neither had another examination of his phone record.

'What about fingerprints? They might help,' Burris offered.

'We're checking for a match. But unless he's been arrested in North Carolina, it won't help. I've talked to the police chief in Colorado and he's agreed to push the data through, but there's no guarantee that the suspect had even been in Denver, either.'

'But he took over Richard Franklin's identity,' Jennifer protested.

'There's no proof that he was the one responsible for the disappearance. For all we know, he stumbled across the information and took advantage of it.'

'But . . .'

Morrison raised his hands. 'Just keeping our options open. I'm not saying he wasn't involved, but we have to consider everything. Besides, that's not the issue here. The issue is Andrea Radley—what he's done, and what he's capable of doing. What do we know for sure? Romanello? You seem to have the best handle on him.'

Jennifer rattled off what she knew.

'He's educated. Most likely a degree in engineering, so that means he went to college. He likes photography and seems to have an eye for it, which means he's been doing it for some time. He had a wife named Jessica once, though we don't know anything more about her. He's probably a sociopath; he's been stalking Julie since the beginning of their acquaintance and seems to confuse her with his wife. They look a lot alike, and he's even called her by his wife's name. And because of the complexity of what he's pulled off over the past few years, I'm fairly certain he's been in trouble with the law before. I think he's probably on the run, which means he's had experience in hiding from the police.'

Morrison nodded. 'Pete? Your take?'

Pete thought for a moment. 'He's stronger than he looks. He can bench almost as much as me.'

The other officers glanced at him. 'I saw him in the gym,' he said defensively.

Morrison shook his head and exhaled, as if wondering why he'd bothered to ask. 'Okay, here's what we do. Burris—get down to Blanchard and see if they have any photographs of this guy. We don't have much time, but I want them on the evening news tonight, if possible. I'll call the station managers and explain the situation. I also want this guy's picture in the paper, so let's get a reporter down here so we can control the information. I want the rest of you trying to figure out where this guy is. Call every hotel and motel in Swansboro and Jacksonville to see if anyone matching his description checked in today. I know it's a long shot, but we can't ignore the possibility that he's right under our nose. If anything comes up, I want you to go in pairs to check it out. And after that, I need all of you here tonight after the news shows. The calls will come flooding in and we'll need everyone available to answer them. The most important thing is to find out if they've seen him today. Not yesterday, not last week. Then, try to weed out the crazies and we'll see where we are.'

Morrison looked around. 'Everyone clear?'

There were murmurs of assent all around.

'Then let's go to it.'

*   *   *

Knowing they would be searching for him in the Swansboro area, Richard had driven two hours northeast and checked into a run-down motel right off the highway, the kind of place where the customers paid in cash and no identification was required to check in.

Now he was lying in bed and staring at the ceiling. They can look, he thought, but they won't find me.

He wondered if the police had learned that he wasn't really Richard Franklin. Even if they had, he knew it didn't matter; they couldn't connect him to Franklin's disappearance or learn his former identity. The hard part had been finding the right kind of man, a man without a family, even with the computers at the various libraries he'd visited while on the run from the law. Culling the professional association lists by using the Internet had been tedious and time-consuming, but he'd stayed at it, diligent in his pursuit, looking for exactly the right man as he'd moved from one town to the next. He'd had no other choice given the circumstances, and he could still remember the sense of relief and satisfaction when he'd finally found the one he needed.

He'd driven across three states on his trip to Denver, across the Mississippi and through the badlands, then spent three weeks learning the man's routines. He'd watched the real Richard Franklin as he watched Julie now. He'd learned that Franklin was short and balding, obviously gay, and that he spent most of his time alone. Occasionally, Franklin worked late at the office, and one night he watched Franklin moving toward his car in a darkened parking lot, head down as he sorted through the keys.

Franklin didn't hear him approach, and he placed a gun to Franklin's head.

'Do exactly what I say,' he whispered, 'and I'll let you live.'

It had been a lie, of course, but the lie had served its purpose. Franklin had done everything that he had asked him to do and had answered all of his questions. Franklin had gone to the ATM and had packed a suitcase. Franklin had even allowed himself to be tied and blindfolded, in the hope that his cooperation would be rewarded.

He'd driven Franklin to the mountains and told him to lie down on the side of the road. He remembered the begging, and how Franklin's bladder had emptied in fear when he'd heard the unmistakable click of a gun being cocked.

He had almost laughed at the man's weakness, his *smallness*, thinking how different they were. The man was nothing: a tiny, inconsequential nothing. Had he been in that situation, he would have fought or tried to get away. But Franklin began to cry, and three hours later, he was buried in a grave that would never be discovered.

Without anyone pressing the search, he'd known that Franklin's file would be buried in the pile of other missing persons and quickly forgotten. As long as Richard Franklin was missing, not dead, the identity had been easy to assume. Since then, he'd trained himself not to answer to his real name or even to turn when he heard it from across the room, and when he spoke it now, it sounded foreign to him.

He'd taken care of the real Richard Franklin, just as he'd taken care of his mother and father. And the boys in the foster home. And his roommate in college. And Jessica.

His eyes narrowed.

Now it was time to take care of Mike.

*   *   *

Mabel was sitting with Andrea when her parents arrived from Boone. They'd driven through their fears and tears for six hours, and Mabel left the room so they could be alone with their daughter.

Moving to the waiting room, she thought about Mike and Julie, hoping they were safe. After seeing Andrea's wounds when the doctors had changed her bandages, she knew with certainty that Richard Franklin was a monster and that Mike and Julie were in far more danger than they realized.

Topsail wasn't far enough away. No, they had to get as far away from Swansboro as they could and stay away as long as it took. She had to convince them somehow.

420

Throughout the evening, the Swansboro Police Department was a hive of activity.

After pounding the phones, they'd come across twelve possible suspects who'd checked into hotels. With the help of the Onslow County Sheriff's Department, they investigated their leads one by one without luck.

J. D. Blanchard had a good photograph of the suspect, and Burris made copies before distributing them to the television stations. The report ran at the top of each news broadcast, making the public aware of the man suspected in the assault of Andrea Radley and letting them know that he was considered extremely dangerous. A description of the car, complete with license plate number, was also listed in the report.

As Morrison predicted, the calls flooded in within minutes of the airings.

The entire department was on hand to answer them; notes were jotted and names were taken, the crazies were weeded out.

By two A.M., the department had talked to more than two hundred people.

But none had seen the suspect that day. Nor had anyone spotted the car.

*   *   *

Exhausted, Richard thought of Jessica as he was finally trailing off to sleep.

She'd been a waitress at a restaurant he'd gone to, and though she wasn't the one who'd served him, his eyes had been drawn to her as he ate.

421

She'd seen him staring and smiled briefly, holding his gaze; he'd gone back to the restaurant as it was closing and waited for her.

It was as if she'd been expecting him; the way the streetlights played on her features as they walked the late night streets of Boston . . . how she'd stared at him across the table at dinner . . . the following weekend at Cape Cod, where they had strolled on the beach and had a picnic in the sand . . . or a picnic and a hot-air balloon ride . . . Jessica and Julie . . . so much alike . . . his thoughts of them combining into one . . . images joining together . . . Julie . . . her tears as she watched *Phantom of the Opera* . . . the sensual touch of her fingers as she cut his hair . . . her empathy when he lied about his mother dying unexpectedly . . . how proud she seemed when she introduced him to her friends at the bar . . .

God, he loved her. He would always love her.

A moment later, his breaths were deep and steady.

Thirty-eight

The following morning, a light mist hovered over the Intracoastal Waterway, burning off slowly as the sun rose above the treetops. A prism of light cut through the window of the police station, zeroing in on Jennifer's third cup of coffee of the morning.

They were looking for a ghost, she thought.

They had nothing, absolutely nothing, to go on, and the waiting was the worst part. Jennifer had come into the office after only a couple of hours of sleep, but she regretted the decision. There was nothing she could think of to do.

The fingerprints hadn't helped; though Morrison had decided to use the FBI database as well, they were backlogged with cases from around the country, and he'd been informed it could take at least a week to process.

The calls were still coming in, of course, and she was answering the phone with regularity. The news had aired again early in the morning—and was scheduled to run again at noon—but as with the night before, she wasn't getting the information she needed. Too many calls were coming in from frightened citizens who simply wanted to be reassured, or from others falsely claiming that the suspect was in their backyard. Most of the other officers had come in around the same time she had and were out investigating the claims. As the only officer still left at the station, she doubted whether any of them would pan out, but the officers had no choice but to follow up on all the leads.

It was the downside to using the media for help, she thought. Though good information was possible, bad information was guaranteed, and it siphoned off the resources needed to do the job.

Then again, what job? she wondered. The only thing they had to go on were the photographs from the briefcase, and she still couldn't figure out why she was so transfixed by them. She'd gone through them a dozen times, but as soon as she put the stack aside, she felt the urge to reach for it again.

Thumbing through, she saw the same images. Jessica in the garden. Jessica on a patio. Jessica sitting. Jessica standing. Jessica smiling. Jessica

423

looking serious.

Jennifer set aside the photos in disgust. Nothing.

A moment later, the phone rang again. After listening, Jennifer began to respond.

'Yes, ma'am. I'm sure it's safe for you to go to the hardware store . . .'

* * *

By the time Mabel left Wilmington—after staying awake most of the night—she was feeling slightly better about Andrea. Though she hadn't opened her eyes, there'd been some movement in her hand just before dawn, and the doctors reiterated to her parents what a good sign that was.

Knowing there was nothing else she could do, she got in the car and drove back to Swansboro. The morning sun made her eyes ache, and she had trouble staying focused on the road.

Her worries about Mike and Julie's safety had only intensified during the night. I'll take a nap first, she told herself, then I'll head out to the beach to talk to them.

* * *

Richard woke and showered, then hopped back into the stolen Trans Am. Two hours later, after buying a cup of coffee and a few magazines from a convenience store along the way, he pulled into Swansboro, feeling as if he'd come home.

He was dressed in Dockers and a polo shirt; with his light hair and glasses, even he didn't quite recognize himself when he peeked in the rearview mirror. He looked like any other family man heading to the beach for the weekend.

He wondered what Julie was doing at that very moment. Showering? Eating breakfast? And was she thinking of him, even as he was thinking of her? He smiled as he dropped a series of quarters into two newspaper racks out front. While the Jacksonville paper was a daily, the Swansboro paper came out twice a week.

After the convenience store, he made his way to a small park and perched on a bench near the swing sets, then opened the newspaper. He didn't want his presence in the park to alarm any parents; people were paranoid these days about adults hanging around in parks, but he supposed he understood that, even in a small town.

His picture was on the front page of the paper, and he took his time in reading the article. It offered basic information, but not much else—he had no doubt the reporter had gathered the information directly from the police department—and listed a hot line number for people to call if they had any information. When he finished reading it, he scanned the rest of the paper, looking for anything about the stolen car. Nothing. Then he settled in to read the article again, his eyes glancing up every few minutes.

He would wait all day if he had to; he knew the one he was looking for, the one who would lead him to Julie and Mike.

*   *   *

When Pete approached Jennifer's desk, she thought he looked as tired as she felt.

'Anything?' she asked.

He shook his head, stifling a yawn. 'Another false alarm. How about you?'

'Not much. There was another waitress at the Mosquito Grove who remembered seeing Andrea and Richard together. We also heard from the hospital in Wilmington. Andrea's not out of the woods yet, but the doctors are hopeful.' She paused. 'I forgot to ask this morning, but did you ever end up talking to the detective or Julie's mother?'

'Not yet.'

'Why don't you give me the numbers while you grab some coffee? I'll check 'em out.'

'Why? We already know why he went down there.'

'I don't know what else to do.'

*   *   *

Jennifer finally spoke to Julie's mother, but Pete had been right for once. The call told her nothing that she hadn't already assumed. Yes, the mother had said, a man who said he was an old friend of Julie's had come by. A week later, he'd brought a friend with him. The friend had matched the description of the suspect.

The call to the private investigator had gone unanswered again.

Still no word on fingerprints.

Without new information, she was back to where she'd been before, and she was frustrated. Was he still in town? She didn't know. What would he do next? She didn't know. Was he still after Julie? She thought so but wasn't absolutely sure. There was always the possibility that because the police were after him, he would simply leave town and start over, the way he'd done in the past.

The problem was that for all intents and purposes, he'd become Richard Franklin. There was nothing personal in the house whatsoever, with the exception of his clothing, his cameras, and the photographs. And the photographs told her nothing, except that he was a good photographer. They could have been taken anywhere, at any time, and because Richard developed them, there wasn't so much as a lab they could trace them back to . . .

Jennifer's thoughts suddenly froze as she felt the answer begin to click into place.

Anywhere, at any time?

Good at photography?

Expensive camera gear?

His own lab to develop them?

This wasn't just a hobby for him, she thought. Okay, she already knew that. What else? She stared at the stack of photos on her desk. This is something he's been doing for a long time. Years, even. Which meant . . .

He might have been using the cameras before he became the man known as Richard Franklin.

'Pete,' she suddenly called out, 'are his cameras in the evidence room, or are they still with forensics?'

'Franklin's? Yeah. We put them in yesterday . . .'

Jennifer jumped up from her chair and started toward the evidence room.

'Where are you going?'

'I think I might know a way to find out who this guy is.'

A moment later, Pete was struggling to keep up with her as she made her way through the station.

'What's going on?' Pete demanded.

Jennifer was signing out the photography gear at the counter as the officer in charge of the evidence locker watched her.

'The cameras,' she said, 'the lenses. This stuff is expensive, right? And like you said, the pictures could have been taken anytime. Even with these cameras, right?'

Pete shrugged. 'I guess so.'

'Don't you see what that means?' she asked. 'I mean, if he's had these cameras all along?'

'No, I don't get it. What?'

By then, the officer had placed a Tupperware container on the counter, and Jennifer reached for it. Too distracted to answer, she picked it up and carried it back to her desk.

A minute later, Pete Gandy watched in confused fascination as she studied the back of the camera.

'Do you have a small screwdriver?' she asked.

'What for?'

'I need to remove this piece.'

'Why?'

'I'm looking for the serial number.'

'Why?' he asked again.

Jennifer was too busy looking through her drawers to answer. 'Damn!' she said.

'They might have one in maintenance,' Pete offered, still unsure why she needed the serial numbers.

She looked up excitedly. 'You're a genius!'

'I am?'

*   *   *

428

Fifteen minutes later she had the list of serial numbers she needed. She gave half the numbers to Pete and took the other half to her desk, trying not to get her hopes up.

She called information and got the numbers for the camera manufacturers, then dialed the first one. After she explained that she needed to verify the name and address of the owner, the person on the other end typed in the number.

'It belongs to a Richard P. Franklin. . . .'

Jennifer hung up and tried the next one. Then the next. On her fourth call, however, a different name was offered.

'The camera is registered to Robert Bonham of Boston, Massachusetts. Do you need the address?'

Jennifer's hands were shaking as she jotted down the information.

*   *   *

Morrison looked it over. 'How certain are you that this is him?'

'The name was listed on four different pieces of equipment, and according to their records, it had never been reported as stolen. I'm willing to bet this is our guy.'

'What do you need from me?'

'In case there's any problem with the Boston Police Department, I'd like you to get involved.'

Morrison nodded. 'Done.'

Jennifer didn't run into any problems. The first detective she reached was able to give her the information she needed.

'Robert Bonham is wanted for questioning in the

disappearance of his wife, Jessica Bonham, four years ago,' he said.

*   *   *

Knowing that staying in one place would arouse suspicion, Richard grabbed his things and moved from one bench to another.

He wondered what she was doing inside, but then again, it didn't really matter. He'd learned long ago to be patient, and after glancing toward the windows, he raised the paper again. He'd read every article three or four times, some more than that. He knew when and where movies were playing, he knew that the community center was offering free computer classes for seniors, but the paper shielded his face from curious townspeople.

He wasn't worried about being discovered; though he knew they were looking for him, no one would think to look for him here. Even if anyone did, between the newspaper and his altered appearance, he was certain that no one would recognize him.

His car was parked around the corner, in a grocery store parking lot, and he could get to it easily if he had to. It was, he knew, only a matter of time now.

*   *   *

An hour later, with pages still coming through the fax machine from Boston regarding Jessica's disappearance, Jennifer sat at her desk, readying herself for the call she knew she had to make. After she'd dialed, a female voice picked up on the other end.

'Hello?'

'Is this Elaine Marshall?'

'Yes? Who's this?'

'This is Officer Jennifer Romanello. I'm calling from the Swansboro Police Department.'

'Swansboro?'

'It's a small town in North Carolina,' Jennifer said. 'I was wondering if you had a moment to talk.'

'I don't know anyone in North Carolina.'

'I'm calling about your sister, Jessica,' she said.

There was a long silence on the other end.

'Have you found her?' The voice was weak, as if expecting the worst.

'I'm sorry, but no, we haven't. But I was wondering if there's anything you could tell me about Robert Bonham.'

At the sound of his name, Jennifer heard Elaine Marshall draw a sharp breath.

'Why?'

'Because right now, we're looking for him.'

'Because of Jessica?'

Jennifer wondered how much to say. 'No,' she finally said. 'He's wanted in connection with something else.'

There was another long pause.

'He killed someone, didn't he?' Elaine Marshall said automatically. 'In Swansboro.'

Jennifer hesitated. 'Is there anything you can tell me about him?'

'He's insane,' she said. Her words were clipped, as if she were doing her best to stay in control. 'Everyone was afraid of him, including Jessica. He's violent and dangerous . . . and he's smart. Jessica tried to get away from him once. He used to beat her. She went to the supermarket one night for groceries and we never saw her again. Everyone knew he did it, but they never found her.'

Elaine Marshall began to cry. 'Oh, God . . . it's been so hard . . . You can't imagine what it's like not to know . . . I mean, not to be certain . . . I know she's gone, but still, there's like a tiny spark that you hold on to . . . . You try to move on, but then something happens that makes it all real again . . .'

Jennifer listened to the sobbing on the other end. 'What was he like in the beginning of their relationship?' she asked gently, after a moment.

'Why does that matter? He did whatever you think he did. He's evil . . .'

'Please,' Jennifer said. 'We just want to catch him.'

'And you think this'll help? It won't. We've been looking for him for years. We hired private investigators, we made sure the police stayed on the case. . . .' Elaine Marshall trailed off.

'He's here,' Jennifer said. 'And we want to make sure he doesn't get away. Now please. Can you tell me what was he like?'

Elaine Marshall drew a deep breath, struggling to find the right words.

'Oh, just like you'd expect—it's an old story, isn't it.' She couldn't hide the sadness in her tone. 'He was charming and handsome and pursued Jessica until she fell head over heels for him. He seemed nice at first, and we all liked him. They eloped after dating for six months, and after they were married, things changed. He got real possessive, and he didn't like it when Jessica called us. Pretty soon, she rarely left the house, but on the few occasions we did manage to see her, we saw bruises. Of course, we tried to talk some sense into her, but it took a long time before she listened to us.'

'When you say that Jessica ran away once . . .'

'She finally accepted that she had to. For a couple of days, he acted as if nothing happened. He tried to get us to tell him where she went, but of course none of us would tell him anything. We knew what was going on by then. She went to Kansas City, a place where she could start over, but he hunted her down. I have no idea how he did it, but he found her and brought her back. And she stayed with him for a couple of weeks. I can't explain it, other than to say that he had this sort of power over her when they were together. I mean, her eyes were dead when you talked to her—like she knew she could never get away—but my mom and I went over to their house and finally dragged her out of there. She moved back in with our parents, and she was trying to get her life back together. She even seemed to be doing better after a while. And then one night, she went to the supermarket and we never saw her again.'

After hanging up, Jennifer sat at the desk, thinking about the phone call, the words still ringing in her ears.

He hunted her down.

*　　　*　　　*

Mabel got out of bed and showered. Despite her exhaustion, her worry about Mike and Julie had kept her from sleeping well. She had to talk to them in person, so they knew how serious this actually was. She grabbed her car keys and had

433

headed out the door before she remembered what Julie had said in the salon right before she and Mike got in Emma's car.

What if he follows us?

Mabel froze in her driveway. What if Richard planned to follow her to the beach? What if he was watching now?

The street was clear in either direction, but Mabel wasn't so sure.

Nor was she willing to take the chance.

She turned around and headed back inside.

* * *

After sorting through the information on Robert Bonham and making a few more calls—including a second call to Elaine Marshall—Jennifer condensed the information into a couple of pages. She talked to Pete about what she wanted to do, then together they went in to see Morrison.

He looked up as Jennifer slid the pages toward him and took a moment to peruse them. When he finished, he met her eyes.

'You're sure about all this?'

'Pretty sure. We still have some calls to make, but we've verified everything that you see.'

Morrison leaned back in his chair. He sat quietly for a moment, trying to absorb the seriousness of the situation.

'What do you want to do?'

Jennifer cleared her throat. 'Until we find him, I think it's best if Pete stays out at the beach house with Mike and Julie. I don't see that we have another choice. If what we learned is true, you know what he's capable of doing, and what he's

434

likely to do next.'

Morrison fixed her with a steady gaze. 'Do you think they'll agree to something like this?'

'Yes,' Jennifer said. 'I'm sure of it. Once they know what they're up against, I mean.'

'Are you going to call them?'

'No. I think it would be best if we talked to Julie in person.'

Morrison nodded. 'If she agrees, I'll authorize it.'

A few minutes later, Jennifer and Pete got in the car.

Neither one of them noticed the stolen Trans Am when it pulled into traffic behind them.

Thirty-nine

'His name is Robert Bonham,' Jennifer began. 'The real Richard Franklin has been missing for three years.'

'I don't understand,' Julie said.

They were in the kitchen of Henry's beach house. Mike and Julie sat at the table; Pete, firmly settling into the position of the silent cop, leaned against the counter.

Mike reached for Julie's hand and squeezed it.

Jennifer knew she had to start at the beginning, since neither Mike nor Julie knew anything about the investigation. Going step by step would keep the questions to a minimum; it would also allow her to explain the gravity of the situation.

'How is that possible?' Mike asked.

'The real Richard Franklin wasn't married, and aside from his mother—who passed away in a nursing home last year—there was no one to notice if his Social Security number was back in use. And because he was considered missing—not deceased—there was nothing to raise any alarms.'

Mike stared at her. 'You think Robert Bonham killed him.' It was more a statement than a question.

Jennifer paused. 'Based on everything else we've learned about him? Yes, it seems likely.'

'Jesus . . .'

Julie looked out the window, suddenly numb. On the beach, she saw an elderly couple stop in front of the house. The man bent over and picked up a seashell, then put it in a plastic pail before moving on.

'So who's Robert Bonham?' she asked. 'And how do you know that's his real name?'

'We know his name from the serial numbers in the cameras. He'd registered them years ago. It was the only link to his past, but once we knew his name and where he was from, we were able to learn the rest fairly easily.' Jennifer glanced at her notes. 'He was raised outside Boston as an only child. His father was an alcoholic who worked at a chemical plant, his mother was a homemaker. There was more than one allegation of abuse in the home—the police had investigated half a dozen incidents over the years—until his father passed away.' After explaining the circumstances behind his father's death, Jennifer tapped the file. 'I talked to one of the officers in that case. He's retired now, but he remembered it well. He said that nobody believed Vernon Bonham had committed suicide, but because they couldn't prove anything—and knew Vernon wasn't exactly the model husband

436

and father—they let it go. But he suspected the kid had closed the garage door and turned the engine back on after Vernon had passed out.'

As she listened, Julie felt her stomach doing flip-flops. 'And the mother?' she whispered.

'Died of a drug overdose less than a year later. Again, it was ruled a suicide.'

Jennifer let the unspoken accusation hang for a moment before she went on.

'He spent the next few years in foster care, moving from one home to the next, never staying in one place too long. His juvenile records are sealed, so we can't say what else he may have done in his teens, but in college, he was suspected in the assault and battery of his former roommate. The roommate had accused him of stealing money, and Robert denied it. A few months later, the roommate was beaten with a golf club after leaving his girlfriend's place, and spent three weeks in the hospital. Though he accused Robert Bonham of it, there wasn't enough evidence to arrest him. A year later, Robert graduated with a degree in engineering.'

'They let him stay in school?' Mike asked.

'I'm not sure they had a choice, since nothing ever went to trial.' She paused. 'After that, there's no record for a few years. Either he moved to another state, or stayed out of trouble, we don't know yet. The next bit of information we have comes from 1994, when he married Jessica.'

'What happened to her?' Mike asked hesitantly, not sure if he wanted to know the answer.

'Jessica's been missing since 1998,' Jennifer said. 'She was living with her parents, and the last time anyone saw her was at the supermarket. A witness remembered seeing Robert Bonham's car in the parking lot that night, but no one saw what happened to her. He vanished the same night she did.'

'You mean he killed her,' Mike said.

'That's what her family and the police in Boston believe,' Jennifer said.

Mike and Julie leaned back in their seats, both of them pale with shock. The air seemed thick and stifling.

'I talked to Jessica's sister,' Jennifer went on slowly, 'and that's part of the reason we're here. She told me that Jessica tried to run away once. She went halfway across the country, but somehow Robert tracked her down. Actually she used the word *hunted*.'

She paused, letting the word sink in. 'I don't know if you're aware of it, but Robert Bonham— Richard—quit his job a month ago. In his house, we found pictures of you. Hundreds of pictures. From what we can tell, he's been watching you pretty much around the clock since you first started dating. And he's also been checking up on your past.'

'What do you mean?' Julie asked raggedly.

'The week he said he was with his dying mother, he went to Daytona. He went there to learn more about you. A private investigator was checking into your history—we talked to your mother about it. It seems pretty clear that he's been stalking you all along.'

Like a hunter, Julie thought, her throat constricting.

'Why me?' she finally asked. 'Why did he choose me?' The words came out plaintively, like those of a child on the verge of tears.

'I don't know with any certainty,' Jennifer said. 'But let me show you what else we found.'

More? What now?

From the file, Jennifer slid a photo across the table, the one she'd found on the bedstand. Mike and Julie looked at it, then slowly raised their eyes again.

'Uncanny, isn't it? This is Jessica. Here—I wanted you to see this, too.'

Though it made her feel as if bugs were crawling over her skin, Julie glanced at the photo again, and this time she saw what Jennifer was pointing to.

Hanging from the young woman's neck was the locket that Richard . . . Robert, whoever . . . had given Julie. She heard herself whisper her name.

'Jessica Bonham,' she said, 'J.B.'

Behind her, Julie heard Mike inhale sharply.

'I know this is hard,' Jennifer went on, 'but there's another reason we wanted to talk to you. Because of Andrea and what we believe happened with Jessica—as well as the real Richard Franklin—we'd like to have Officer Gandy stay with you two for a few days.'

'Here at the house?' Mike asked.

'If that's okay.'

Julie's eyes were almost glassy as Mike glanced toward Pete. 'Yeah,' he said, 'I think that's a good idea.'

*　　　*　　　*

Pete went out to the car and was retrieving the suitcase he'd packed when he saw Jennifer scanning the homes along the beach.

'Is it always so quiet down here?'

'I guess so,' Pete answered.

She studied the homes again. Only a few had cars parked in the driveways, the usual SUVs and Camrys and a Trans Am as well, something a teenager might drive, the car she herself had wanted in high school. Six cars altogether, but that still meant that less than a quarter of the homes were occupied. She wasn't quite comfortable with that, but no doubt it was better than staying in town.

'And you'll stay awake all night?' she asked Pete.

'Yeah,' he said, slamming the trunk. 'I'll catch a few hours of sleep in the mornings. You'll keep me up to speed on what's going on, right?'

'As soon as I find out anything, I'll give you a call.'

He nodded. Then, after a pause, he said, 'Listen, I know this is something we have to do, but do you really think he's still around? Or do you think he's on the run again?'

'Honestly? Yeah, I think he's around.'

Pete's eyes followed hers up and down the steet. 'So do I.'

*   *   *

That night, Julie couldn't sleep.

Outside, she could hear the sound of the waves as they lapped along the shore in steady rhythm. Mike was in bed beside her and had opened the window slightly; as soon as he'd fallen asleep, Julie had risen from the bed and closed it, making sure the latch was engaged.

From beneath the door, she could see a light glowing from the kitchen. Pete had been pacing the house earlier, but he seemed to have settled down in the past couple of hours.

Despite his earlier actions, she was glad he was here. Not only was he strong, more important, he carried a gun.

*   *   *

From the dune, Richard watched the yellow light glowing in the window of the beach house.

He was annoyed that Officer Gandy had decided to stay with them, but he knew the police couldn't stop him. Nor could Mike, or Singer. He and Julie were meant for each other, and he would simply overcome any obstacles to their ultimate happiness. Everything else was an inconvenience, no more challenging than changing his appearance or stealing a car. Or having to start over again.

He wondered where they would end up after leaving North Carolina. He could imagine Julie enjoying San Francisco, with its sidewalk bistros and views of the Pacific. Or New York City, where they could enjoy new theater productions every season. Or even Chicago, with its spirit and vibrancy.

It would be wonderful, he thought. Magical.

Sleep well, he thought with a smile. Sleep and dream of a new future, because tomorrow night it begins.

Forty

There was a languid feel to the night air the following evening. The breeze was steady, and the blackness of the sky was softened by cloud cover. The ocean was calm, swells rising gently. The smell of brine hung in the air like mist.

They'd finished dinner an hour earlier, and Singer was standing near the back door, his tail wagging slightly. Julie crossed the room and opened the door for him, watching as he descended the steps and vanished into the shadows a moment later.

She didn't like letting him out—despite Mike's and Pete's presence, she felt safer when Singer was beside her—but he needed to roam, and night was the best time. She didn't mind letting him out early in the morning when no one was out, but during the day, there were too many people around to let him wander without a leash.

She'd thought about going outside as well—with Pete and Mike, of course—thinking a bit of fresh air would do her good, but then she'd decided against it. No doubt Mike and Pete would have said no, even if she'd insisted. Still, it would have been nice. In theory, anyway.

Both Emma and Mabel had called her; Henry had called back later to talk to Mike. None of the phone calls had lasted more than a few minutes. None of them, it seemed, had anything much to say, except for Mabel, who'd called after speaking with Andrea's parents. Late last night, Andrea had emerged from her coma, and though she was still disoriented, it appeared she was going to be okay. Jennifer was planning to talk to her in a couple of days.

Jennifer Romanello had also called twice with updates; she'd finally been able to find the private investigator who had been snooping into Julie's past, and after the usual grousing that he couldn't ethically divulge who'd hired him, he'd knuckled under. He also offered a phone bill that confirmed a couple of calls to Richard's residence.

Unfortunately, they still hadn't found any trace of Richard. Robert. Whoever.

Julie turned from the door and walked through the living room into the kitchen, where Mike was slipping dishes into the sink. Pete was still at the table, playing solitaire. He'd played about a hundred games since noon, killing time and for the most part staying out of the way, except when he went outside to check on things.

'Perimeter is secure' had become his new favorite catchphrase.

Julie slipped her arms around Mike, and he turned his head at her touch.

'Almost done,' he said. 'Just a few more to wash. Where's Singer?'

Julie grabbed a towel and started to dry the plates. 'I let him out.'

'Again?'

'He's not used to being cooped up like this.'

'You still thinking about what Jennifer told us?'

'Thinking about that, thinking about everything. What he did in the past. What he did to Andrea. Where he is now. Why me. Whenever I heard about stalkers, there always seemed to be some twisted sort of logic to it. Like people who chase

443

movie stars. Or ex-husbands or boyfriends. But we only went out a couple of times, and we barely knew each other. So I keep thinking back and trying to figure out if it was something that I did that caused all this.'

'He's just crazy,' Mike said. 'I don't know that we'll ever understand it.'

*   *   *

From his vantage point near the dune, Richard watched Julie open the door and let Singer out. With the light glowing from behind her, she appeared like a descending angel. Richard found himself growing aroused by the thought of what was going to happen next.

Yesterday, after he'd located them, he'd pulled his car into the driveway of a home that was plastered with realty signs. Though many of the homes along the beach were still vacant this time of year, this one looked as if it had been unoccupied for a while. A quick check revealed an alarm system for the house but not for the garage, and he'd worked his way through the simple lock with a screwdriver he'd found in the glove compartment of the Trans Am. From the trunk, he'd removed the tire iron.

He'd slept on a dusty air mattress he'd found on the shelves, and in the storage area he'd found a small cooler. Though it had grown moldy, it suited his purpose, and he'd spent an hour that afternoon purchasing what he needed.

Now, all he had to do was wait until Singer wandered down the beach. He knew Julie would let him out, as she'd done last night and most probably the night before. People under stress always fell back into habits and routines, as if hoping to maintain some semblance of order in their world.

In the distance, he could no longer see Singer.

Beside him were the four hamburgers he'd picked up from Island Deli, a place he'd found near the hardware store he'd visited that afternoon.

They were still wrapped in foil, but he'd already unwrapped them once and crumbled the patties into pieces.

Taking the hamburger with him, he began crawling through the grass toward the back steps of the home.

*　　　*　　　*

'I hate this damn game,' Pete said. 'It's impossible to win.'

As Julie slipped the plates into the cupboard, she glanced toward the table. 'Put the red seven on the black eight.'

Pete Gandy blinked, still trying to see it. 'Where?'

'The final column.'

'Oh yeah. There it is.'

Lost in the game again, Pete kept his eyes focused downward.

Mike washed the last dish and pulled the plug from the drain, then looked up at the window.

With the kitchen light playing against the glass, all he could see was his own reflection.

*　　　*　　　*

Outside, Richard unwrapped the foil and scattered the crumbled beef onto the steps that led over the

445

dune and back to the house. He knew Singer would get there before Julie and Mike, so he wasn't worried about them spotting it.

He wasn't sure how much Singer weighed, so he had mixed in as much of the bitter powder as he thought he could, while preserving the aroma of beef. He didn't want Singer to sniff it a couple of times, sense that it wasn't what it appeared to be, then ignore it.

No, that wouldn't be any good at all. Singer had already bitten him once, and he didn't want to face those teeth again. Julie had stopped Singer the first time, but he was under no illusions that she would stop him again. More than that, there was something about the dog that bothered him, something he couldn't quite put his finger on. Something not . . . *doglike*, for lack of a better word. All he knew was that as long as the dog was around, Julie would remain confused and resistant.

He crept toward his hiding place again and settled in to wait.

*   *   *

Mike and Julie were sitting on the couch in the living room, watching as Pete Gandy continued to lose one game after the next.

'Did I ever tell you about the letter that I got from Jim?' Julie asked. 'The one on Christmas Eve, after he died?'

She sounded as if she were making a confession. A shadow crossed her face, and Mike could tell she wasn't sure about what she wanted to say.

'You've mentioned it, but I don't know what it said.'

Julie nodded before leaning against him, feeling his arm slip over her shoulder.

'You don't have to tell me about it if you'd rather not,' Mike offered.

'I think you should know,' she said. 'In a way, I think it was about you and me.'

Mike remained silent, waiting for her to go on. For a moment, she stared into the kitchen, then her eyes met his. Her voice was soft.

'The letter was mainly about Singer. Why he got me a Great Dane, that he didn't want me to be alone, and how since he knew I didn't have any family, he thought that a dog would help me. He was right about all that, but at the end of his letter, he said that he wanted me to be happy again. He told me to find someone who makes me happy.'

She paused, a wistful smile on her face, her first in what seemed like forever.

'That's why I think it was about you and me. I know you love me, and I love you, too, and you make me happy, Mike. Even with all this horrible stuff going on, you've still made me happy. I just wanted you to know that.'

The words sounded strangely out of place; he didn't know why she'd felt the urge to bring it up now. It almost seemed as if she were trying to find a nice way to say good-bye. Mike pulled her closer to him.

'You've made me happy, too, Julie,' he said. 'And you're right, I do love you.'

Julie put a hand on his leg. 'I'm not saying all this because I want to end things with you. Not at all. I'm saying it because I don't know how I would have handled the last few weeks without you. And because I'm sorry that I dragged you into all this.'

'There's nothing to be sorry for . . .'

'Sure there is. You were always the one who was right for me, and somehow, I think that Jim was trying to tell me that in his letter. But for a long time, I was too blind to see it. If I had listened to him, there never would have been a Richard. And I want you to know that I'm thankful not only that you put up with all that, but that you're here for me now.'

'I didn't have a choice,' he murmured.

*   *   *

Richard lay in the sawgrass, watching the steps. Minutes passed before he saw movement in the shadows near the dunes.

Singer moved into the moonlight and swung his head from side to side. The shadowed colors of his coat and his size gave him an almost ghostly appearance.

Richard watched as Singer turned again and began trotting toward the steps.

Almost there.

Singer slowed from a trot to a walk before stopping. His nose rose slightly as he seemed to study the steps, but he made no move toward them.

C'mon, Richard thought, what are you waiting for? But still Singer didn't move. Richard could feel himself beginning to tense. Eat it, he urged.

He didn't realize he was holding his breath. Along the shore, he could hear the waves rolling and turning. Sawgrass swayed in the wind. Overhead, a shooting star left a momentary streak of white.

Finally, Singer moved forward.

448

It was a hesitant step, but a step nonetheless, and his head began to stretch forward, as if he'd finally smelled it. He took another step, then a third, until he was hovering over the hamburger.

He lowered his head and sniffed, then raised his head again as if wondering whether he should.

From the distance came the faint sound of a trawler, carried by the wind.

With that, Singer lowered his head and began to eat.

* * *

In Swansboro, Officer Jennifer Romanello spent the evening learning what she could about the elusive Robert Bonham.

Earlier, the captain had called her into his office. She wasn't sure what to expect, but to her surprise, after closing the door, he'd commended her for all her work.

'We can't train instincts, but we need more of that around here. Pete Gandy might be wrong about the Mafia coming to town, but he's not wrong in thinking that Swansboro is changing along with the rest of the world,' the captain had said. 'I know we all want to believe this is a sleepy little town, and for the most part it is, but bad things happen in places like this, too.'

Jennifer had known enough not to speak as the captain looked her over. 'You knew this guy was bad from the start, and you've done a heckuva job tracking down all the information, and especially in figuring out who he was. That was all your doing.'

'Thank you,' she'd said.

Then, lest she think he'd suddenly gone soft, he

had dismissed her: His face had taken on an expression of impatience, as if wondering why she was still sitting in the office, and he'd motioned toward the door.

'Now get back to work,' he'd barked. 'I still want to know what makes this guy tick. Maybe that'll help us catch him.'

'Yes, sir,' she'd repeated, and when she'd left the office with the eyes of the other officers on her, it had taken everything she had not to break into a smile.

Now, while following the captain's orders—she was still poring over the documents from Boston and calling people who'd known Robert Bonham— she heard Burris growing animated as he was speaking on the phone, and she looked up. He was nodding furiously and jotting down information, then finally he hung up the phone. Standing up, he grabbed for the piece of paper and made his way toward her.

'We just got a call,' he said. 'His car has been located in the parking lot at Onslow Hospital in Jacksonville.'

'Is he still around there?'

'Probably not. The guard is pretty sure the car has been there for a couple of days. He goes through the lot every evening, jotting down license plates, and it's been in his book since the day you and Gandy went to talk to him at his house. But because he was working, he didn't see the information on the news until yesterday, and didn't put two and two together until now.'

That explained why no one had found the car.

'But no one has seen him?'

'Not that we know of. The Jacksonville police

450

showed the guard Robert Bonham's photograph, but he didn't recognize him. I'm heading out there now, though, to ask around. Maybe someone saw where he went. You want to come along?'

Jennifer considered it. She wasn't getting anywhere with what she was doing, but she wasn't sure where it would lead. Sure, they might find someone who saw him leave the car, but what then? What they needed to know was where he was *now*.

'No,' she said, 'I think I'll keep looking through the files. Maybe there's something that I missed.'

*   *   *

Though drapes covered most of the windows, the dining room window was open, and Richard watched for shadows. Other than the sound of the waves, he could hear nothing. The air had become still, almost as if joining him in breathless anticipation.

Julie would be heading for the back door soon; she usually didn't let Singer stay out for more than twenty minutes or so, and he wanted to see her face when she called for him. Staring toward the house, he allowed himself to hope that she would forgive him for what he had done.

He would comfort her, but there would be time for that later. After all the ugliness was over. When it was just the two of them, the way it was supposed to be.

*   *   *

Singer started up the steps to the back porch, then

451

went down the beach again to pace in circles, his tongue hanging out. He started trotting, as if trying to shake the pain from his belly.

He had already begun to pant.

*　　*　　*

Jennifer pored over the information on Jessica Bonham, wondering how he'd been able to find her.

Had he tracked her using credit cards? Doubtful, she thought. Unless he knew someone in law enforcement, that seemed unlikely. How else, then? She wondered if someone in her family had called Jessica and he'd somehow been able to track the number to where she was staying. It was possible—most people simply threw their bills away after paying them—and all he would have had to do was to call every long-distance number listed in the record. But it would have entailed sorting through garbage . . . or breaking into their house when they weren't home.

He'd done it with Julie, she thought, so maybe . . .

She wondered whether Topsail was a long-distance call from Swansboro. If so, she would have to warn Henry, Emma, and Mabel not to call Mike and Julie—and if they already had called, to burn the records as soon as they'd paid them.

Her mind wandered back to the car.

It wasn't surprising that he'd abandoned it, of course, but he had to have some way to get around. How, then? Taxi? She thought about it, then dismissed that idea. He was smart enough to know that the pickup and drop-off would have been recorded, and based on how easily he'd vanished in

452

the past, she didn't think he'd make a mistake like that.

So if he was still around, and if he was looking for Julie, how would he get around?

Tapping the phone book with her finger, she saw Captain Morrison moving through the office.

'Captain?'

He glanced at her in surprise. 'I thought you'd be heading off to the hospital to check out the car.'

'I thought about it, but . . .'

'But what?'

'Where exactly is the hospital?' Jennifer asked. 'The center of town? On the outskirts?'

'Right in the middle of town. Why?'

'What's around there? I mean, have you been in that area before?'

'Sure, many times. There's a group of doctors' offices, gas stations, the mall. Like I said, it's in the center of town.'

'How close is the mall?'

'Right across the street.' He paused. 'What's up?'

'I'm just wondering how he's getting around. Do you think it's possible that he stole a car?'

The captain's eyebrows rose. 'I'll check it out. Let me make a call.'

Jennifer nodded, her mind already going through the scenarios. She reached for the keys to the squad car.

'Where are you going?' Morrison asked.

'I think I am going to head toward the hospital to see if they found anything useful. If you hear anything about a stolen car, let me know immediately, okay?'

'You got it.'

Julie wandered to the window and put her face to the glass, scanning the beach.

'Have you heard Singer bark yet?' she asked.

Mike came up beside her. 'No, not yet. I don't think he's come back yet.'

'How long's he been outside?'

'Not that long. I'm sure he'll be back any minute.'

Julie nodded. In the distance, she could see the faint lights from a trawler off the coast. Though the beach was dark, she thought she'd be able to see Singer.

'Maybe I should go call for him.'

'Do you want me to do it?'

'No, that's okay. I need a bit of fresh air anyway.'

Pete watched her as she crossed to the door.

*   *   *

Richard leaned forward when he saw her appear in the window, her face illuminated. He knew with sudden certainty that he'd never loved anyone as much as he loved her.

Then Mike broke into the image, ruining it. Ruining everything before they both vanished from the window. He shook his head. He didn't regret what would happen to Mike.

Richard waited, knowing what she was going to do. In just a moment, he would hear her voice, echoing in the salty air. If he was lucky, she might venture down to the beach, but he wasn't counting on it. No, she'd call for Singer, but he wouldn't come.

Singer would stay exactly where he was.

Julie called for nearly three minutes, moving from the doorway to both ends of the porch, before Mike joined her.

'Not back yet?' he asked.

Julie shook her head. 'No. I can't see him, either.'

Mike looked from side to side, in both directions. 'Do you want me to go look for him? Maybe he can't hear you because of the waves.'

Julie smiled. 'Thanks.'

Mike walked down the steps. 'I'll be back in a couple of minutes.'

A minute later, she heard Mike's voice as he, too, began to call Singer's name.

Forty-one

Jennifer Romanello squinted into the oncoming headlights. Lack of sleep in the last couple of days had taken its toll, and her eyes ached. She was wondering whether to stop for a cup of coffee to help keep her awake when she heard the radio crackle to life. Recognizing the captain's voice, she reached for the mike.

'Looks like we might have something,' Morrison said. 'I just got off with the department in Jacksonville and they had a report of a stolen car from the mall parking lot on the same day Richard vanished. It's registered to a Shane Clinton, and he lives in Jacksonville.'

'Do you have an address?'

'Yeah—412 Melody Lane.'

'What kind of car was it?'

'A 1984 Pontiac Trans Am. Green.' He recited the license plate number and offered, 'We've already got an APB out on it.'

Jennifer made a mental note. 'Have you talked to him yet?'

'No, but he lives right near the hospital. Do you want his phone number?'

'Sure.'

Morrison recited it, and Jennifer committed it to memory, then decided to head that way.

*　　　*　　　*

Mike's feet sank into the sand as he moved down the beach. Glancing over his shoulder, he could see Julie standing on the porch, her image growing smaller with each step he took.

'Singer!' he bellowed again.

His eyes were gradually adjusting to the darkness, and he scanned the dunes, watching for the dog. He knew that Singer sometimes wandered over the dunes to explore in between the houses, but it was strange that he hadn't come back yet.

He was cupping his hands to call again when he noticed a shadow off to his left, near a set of stairs. He squinted, moving closer, and then recognized the shape in the sand. Turning around, he shouted in Julie's direction.

'Found him!'

He took another couple of steps forward. 'What're you doing? Come on. Let's go back inside.'

Singer's tail moved slightly, and Mike heard what

456

sounded like a low whine. The dog was panting hard, his tongue out. His chest was rising and falling rapidly.

'You look like you wore yourself out . . . ,' he started, but as Singer whined again, he paused.

'You okay?' he asked.

Still, Singer didn't move.

'Singer?' he asked again.

Mike squatted down and put a hand on the dog's chest; he could feel Singer's heart beating fast. The look in his eyes was glazed and unfocused. Singer didn't respond to his touch, and it was then that he noticed that one of Singer's rear legs was quivering.

*   *   *

Pete Gandy joined Julie on the back porch.

'What's going on?' he asked.

Julie glanced at him. 'Just waiting for Mike and Singer to get back.'

Pete nodded and they stood in silence, both of them watching the beach. Julie was just beginning to wonder where they were when she heard Mike calling her name. Even from a distance, she could hear the sound of panic in his voice. A moment later, he appeared on the sand below.

'It's Singer!' Mike shouted. 'Something's wrong! Come on!'

It took a moment for the words to register, and she blinked.

'What do you mean? What's wrong?' she shouted back.

'I don't know! Hurry!' Mike yelled.

Her chest suddenly constricting, Julie started for the steps.

'Wait,' Pete said. He tried to grab her arm to stop her, but Julie was already past him. Watching her charge down the steps, he debated whether or not to follow them.

'Shit,' he mumbled, then headed toward the beach.

* * *

Richard watched the three of them as they began to run down the beach. As they moved farther into the distance, he could feel the adrenaline race into his system. It had begun.

When they finally vanished from sight, he crept over the dune. Staying low in the shadows, he moved toward the house, tire iron in hand.

* * *

Breathing hard as she tried to keep up with Mike, Julie felt the pangs of panic begin to take hold. Behind her, she could hear Pete calling her name, pleading with her to return to the house.

A moment later, he saw where Mike was heading—and saw Singer lying in the sand.

Julie began to tremble as she ran to Singer. By the time Pete reached her, both Julie and Mike were hovering over the dog.

'What's going on?' Pete panted.

'Singer? What's wrong, baby?' Julie crooned as she stroked the fur on his back.

No response. Julie looked at Mike with a child's expression, her eyes pleading with him to tell her that she had nothing to worry about, that she was mistaken, that there was no reason to be frightened.

'Why isn't he moving?' Pete asked.

'Mike?' she asked.

'I don't know,' he mumbled. 'I just found him like this. . . .'

'Maybe he's tired,' Pete offered, but Mike's stare cut him short.

'What's wrong with him?' Julie cried. 'Help him!'

Mike gently lifted Singer's head from the sand. 'C'mon, boy, get up . . .'

Singer's neck was rigid, and his panting intensified, as if the movement had hurt him. When he whimpered, Mike lowered his head. Pete looked from Mike to Singer to Julie, wondering what to do next, feeling as confused as the others.

'We've got to do something!' Julie screamed.

It was her anguished wail that finally forced Mike into action. 'Pete—go back to the house and see if you can find an emergency veterinarian.'

'I'm not supposed to leave you alone—'

'Just go!' Mike shouted. 'And hurry!'

'But—'

'Just get going!'

'Okay, okay,' he said. A moment later he was charging into the darkness, leaving Mike and Julie with Singer.

Even as he ran, Pete could hear Julie's wails behind him.

*   *   *

Jennifer had just entered the Jacksonville city limits when she realized that something was gnawing at her. It had started a few minutes after Morrison had given her the information over the

459

radio, but she hadn't been able to put a finger on why she felt so uneasy.

She was missing something, she thought. But what?

Up ahead, only distant taillights were visible, and the road seemed to split the world in two. The engine whined as she held her foot to the accelerator. The reflectors on the highway passed beneath the tires in a rapid stutter.

It wasn't about the stolen car . . . or was it? And if so . . .

She couldn't figure it out, but she knew it was there. Something in her subconscious, something obvious, something just out of reach.

Okay, she thought, going through it again. Richard's car had been abandoned. Check. The car was stolen around the time that Richard would have arrived in Jacksonville. Check. Put those two together, and she suspected—no, she knew that Richard had taken it. Check.

What had the captain said? The make and model of the car, the person who owned it, the address where the young man lived. She thought about it. The last two meant nothing, she decided, but what about the make and model of the car?

Green Pontiac Trans Am.

The kind of car she'd wanted back in high school . . .

She frowned, wondering why that thought seemed so familiar.

*　　　*　　　*

From the porch, Richard heard Julie screaming about her dog. For a moment, he stopped to listen

460

to the wailing, feeling a twinge of sympathy. He'd known that it would be hard for her, of course, but actually hearing it—the fear and heartbreak— affected him more deeply than he'd thought it would.

He didn't want Julie to be upset, and he wished there could have been some other way. But there wasn't. He'd had to do it. Had Singer been a gentle dog, a sweet dog, he would never have hurt him. But Singer was as confused and temperamental as she was.

Julie's cries grew louder, more frantic, and the sound was terrible. He felt sorry for her and wanted to apologize, but he would save that for later, when she could see through her pain and recognize that he'd done it for the two of them.

Maybe he would get her another dog, after all this was behind them. Though he'd never wanted a dog, he realized that he could do that for her. They could pick out a dog together, and she would forget all about Singer. Maybe they'd make a special trip to the pound and get a dog who liked to fetch the way Singer did. Or they'd look through the newspaper and find someone selling puppies and pick the one they both thought was best.

Yes, he thought, that was it. Another dog. A *better* dog. That's what he would do for her when all this was over. She would like that. It would make her happy, and that's all he'd ever wanted for her. Happiness.

Now that he was feeling more in control, her cries sounded more distant to him.

On the beach, he saw a sudden movement. Knowing what it meant, Richard retreated to the corner, where he hid in the shadows.

461

Pete Gandy rushed up the steps, across the porch, and through the back door, racing for the kitchen. He tore open the drawer beneath the phone so hard that it nearly broke, and he grabbed the directory.

'C'mon, c'mon,' he said as he began flipping through the pages, looking for the nearest veterinarian.

He found the right section and began running his finger down the page, looking for someone who might be able to handle an emergency.

The nearest animal hospital was in Jacksonville, thirty minutes away, and with sudden certainty he knew that the dog wouldn't last that long.

What should I do? Pete thought. What do I do now?

He forced himself to order his frantic thoughts.

The names of the vets were listed, and he decided to call them at home, since it was too late for offices to be open. It was the only chance the dog had. But that entailed looking up phone numbers one by one.

And time was running out.

*　　　*　　　*

Jennifer had stopped at a red light in the heart of Jacksonville. Though technically she was making her way toward Melody Lane to talk with Shane Clinton, her mind was still sorting through the problem of the green Pontiac Trans Am.

The kind of car she'd wanted in high school.

462

She'd had the same thought recently, but where? At the station? No, she'd barely left her desk in the last couple of days. At her apartment? No, not there, either. Where else, then?

The light turned green and Jennifer shook her head as the car started forward again.

Have I been anywhere? Only to talk to Julie and Mike, when I dropped Pete off . . .

Her hands tightened on the wheel.

No, she thought, it couldn't be . . .

Reaching for her cell phone, she pressed the accelerator to the floor, knowing it would take at least twenty minutes to reach Topsail Beach . . . and the green Trans Am she'd seen parked up the road.

*   *   *

Pete Gandy was flipping back and forth through the phone book, running his finger down the pages, growing more and more frustrated. There were over a dozen vets listed, but most of them lived in Jacksonville, too far away to help.

There were three names left, and he turned the pages in search of the next possibility, the thin paper tearing in his fingers.

Linda Patinson was next on the list, and he turned to each section of the phone book that listed the localities. She didn't live in Jacksonville, nor did she live in Orton or Maysville. Turning to the final section, he scanned the page and found a Linda Patinson.

Her home was in Sneads Ferry, just ten minutes up the road.

He picked up the receiver and began to dial; he

hit the wrong numbers and hung up, forcing himself to take a deep breath in the process. Calm down, he told himself. If I sound crazy, she's not going to help.

He began dialing again, and the phone on the other end began to ring.

Once.

Twice.

'C'mon . . .'

Three times.

Then four.

'Be home . . .'

There was a click as someone at the other end picked up.

'Hello?'

The voice sounded young, like that of a college student.

'Hi, I'm Officer Pete Gandy with the Swansboro Police Department. I'm sorry for calling, but is this Linda Patinson the veterinarian?'

There was a moment's pause. 'Yes,' she said. Her voice sounded wary.

'I don't know what else to do. Our dog looks like he's having convulsions of some sort.'

'Well, there's an emergency vet clinic in Jacksonville.'

'I know. But I don't think he'd make it that long . . . He's shaking all over and he's breathing really fast. His heart's going and he can't even lift his head.'

Pete went on, describing Singer's condition as best he could, and when he finished, Linda Patinson hesitated. Though relatively new in practice—she'd been out of school only a few years—she knew this was serious, not only from the

464

panic in Pete's voice, but because of the symptoms he was describing.

'Has he eaten anything in the garage? Like insecticide? Or poison of some sort?'

'Not that I know of. He was fine just a little while ago.'

'What kind of dog is it?'

'A Great Dane.'

Linda Patinson hesitated. 'Is there any way you could get him into the car and bring him in? I can be in my office in ten minutes. It's just down the street . . .'

'I can find it.'

Seconds later, Pete hung up the phone and was already on the back porch. Slamming the door closed behind him, he barely noticed the shadow as it moved toward him.

*   *   *

Julie was stroking Singer lightly, her hands shaking.

'What's taking so long?' she pleaded. 'What's he doing?'

Mike didn't answer, knowing she was talking more to herself than to him. Instead, he tried to reassure her.

'He's going to be okay,' he whispered.

Singer was panting harder now, his eyes wide. His tongue was in the sand, coated with granules. With every breath came a whimper.

'Hold on, baby,' Julie pleaded. 'Please . . . oh, God . . . please . . .'

*   *   *

On the porch, Pete Gandy wasn't sure what made him turn.

The gentle scrape of shoe against wood, perhaps, or the nearly imperceptible shift of shadows thrown by the glowing yellow porch light. It wasn't simply intuition, Pete was sure. In that moment, he was thinking about poison and what it might mean; there wasn't room in his subconscious to process anything other than what he needed to do next.

But he knew, even before he saw Richard, that someone was moving toward him, and he was already beginning instinctively to duck when he felt something hard crash against his skull.

There was a flash of instant pain, then a bright light in the corners of his eyes that faded suddenly to black.

*   *   *

'Maybe I should go check on Pete,' Mike offered. 'See what's taking so long.'

Julie barely heard him, but she nodded, her lips pressed together.

Mike turned and started back toward the house.

*   *   *

Richard stared at the fallen figure of Pete Gandy. Gruesome business, yes, but necessary and, in its own way, inevitable.

Then, of course, there was the fact that Pete had a gun. Makes the rest so much easier, he thought. For a moment, after removing the gun from the holster, he considered putting a bullet into Pete Gandy's head; then he decided against it. He had

466

nothing against Pete Gandy. He was just a guy doing his job.

Richard turned and was heading for the stairs when he saw Mike coming up the beach, toward the house.

Glancing down at the body, he realized that Mike would see it immediately. His mind clicked through the problem, and he crouched down, waiting for Mike's heavy tread on the stairs.

*   *   *

As Jennifer Romanello sped to the beach house, she kept dialing the number. First the phone was busy; now no one was answering. As the phone kept ringing and ringing, she couldn't escape the feeling that something had gone terribly wrong. She reached for the radio and called for backup, but even as she relayed her concerns, she knew that no one would reach the beach house before she got there.

Forty-two

Mike looked up just as a shadowy figure launched himself from the top of the stairs.

The momentum of the attack sent him tumbling backward; his head collided with the stairs as something crashed down on him, crushing his rib cage and driving the edges of the stairs into his lower back.

The pain was staggering. Mike could see nothing, but he felt himself sliding down the stairs on his back, headfirst, each jarring motion like someone swinging a hammer against his ribs, until his head hit the sand and he suddenly stopped, his neck bent at an odd angle. Above him, he could feel someone reaching for his neck and taking hold. Feet were planted in the sand on either side of him, and a sack of what seemed like lead sat on his chest.

The hands began to tighten, and Mike fought nausea as the pain rolled through him. Even opening his eyes was difficult, but when he saw the face of Richard Franklin, his thoughts came suddenly into focus.

Julie! he wanted to scream. *Run!*

But he made no sound. Cut off from oxygen, he began to grow dizzy, his mind a jumble. As he struggled to draw breath, he reached instinctively for Richard's hands, trying to pry them off as adrenaline began to surge. But Richard's grip refused to weaken.

Mike swung wildly, connecting with Richard's face to no effect. Every cell in his body was screaming for oxygen. He thrashed his legs, trying to throw Richard off, but Richard wouldn't budge. Mike tried to whip his head back and forth, but it only served to make Richard's grip seem tighter.

And the pain . . .

Get air. It was all he could think about as he reached toward Richard's face, aiming for his eyes. Forming his hands into claws, struggling furiously, he found the target momentarily before Richard raised his head, escaping his reach.

It was then that Mike knew he was going to die.

Panicked, he reached for Richard's hands again, prying and grabbing, but this time he found a thumb and was able to latch on to it, and he jerked with every bit of strength he had left.

He felt something snap, but Richard refused to let go. As he tugged harder, the thumb was curved into an unnatural angle. Richard loosened his grip as his mouth contorted in pain. He leaned forward. That was all Mike needed. Kicking and bucking, he finally felt a wisp of air pass through his throat. He grabbed Richard's hair with his free hand and rammed his knees into Richard's back, momentum and gravity shifting the advantage. Richard went over him, landing in the sand behind him.

Gasping for breath, Mike pushed off the stairs into the sand beside Richard, but just moving to all fours left him exhausted. Though he was able to take a quick breath, his throat kept constricting, cutting it off. Richard was on his feet first and, whirling suddenly, he kicked Mike savagely in the ribs, then kicked him again. Mike toppled over onto his back, and another kick to his head followed. The pain was nearly blinding in its intensity, and again he couldn't breathe.

He thought of Julie.

Julie . . .

Staggering onto all fours, he lunged toward Richard. Richard kicked at him; Mike felt the blows but kept driving forward. A moment later, he was reaching for Richard's throat when he felt something hard wedged against his stomach and heard a pop.

At first there was nothing, but then there was fire in his belly, boiling water riding the nerves, pain shooting in all directions, climbing the spine. Mike blinked in shock, and he seemed to lose control of his tongue. His legs went still, his body weakened, and Richard shoved him off.

When Mike reached for his stomach, it was slippery, oozing. In the dim light, his blood looked like motor oil puddling beneath a car. He couldn't understand where the blood was coming from, but when Richard got to his feet, he saw the gun.

Richard stared down at him, and Mike rolled away.

Need to get up . . . have to stand . . . have to warn Julie . . .

He knew Richard would be going after her, and he had to stop that from happening. He had to save Julie. He tried to override the pain, to figure out what to do next. . . . Another kick landed on his head.

He was on his stomach again, blood pumping out beneath him. Hand to his stomach, feeling his life drain away. 'Julie!' he screamed, but the sound came out as a wheeze.

Dizzier . . . weaker . . . have to save her . . . have to protect her . . .

Another kick to his head, and then there was nothing.

*   *   *

Richard stood over Mike with eyes wide, breathing hard, energized as never before. His hands were tingling, his legs shaking, but the senses! Oh, they were so alive! It was as if he were experiencing a world he'd never known. Sight and sound were amplified, and he could feel the slightest movement of air over his skin. The effect was dizzying, intoxicating.

This was nothing like Pete. Or the real Richard Franklin. Or even Jessica. Jessica had fought, but not like this. Jessica had died at his hands, but there had been no sense of vanquishment, no victorious conquest. Just a sense of sorrow that she had forced this upon herself.

No, tonight he felt triumphant, indefatigable, unbeatable. He was on a mission, and the gods were with him.

Ignoring the pain in his thumb, Richard turned and started down the beach. On his left, the dunes were covered with grass and pocket ivy; the waves continued their endless rolls. It was a beautiful night, he thought. In the shadows ahead, he could make out Julie's form, hovering over her dog. But the dog was either gone or would be soon. We'll be alone, he thought. No more complications. No one to stop us.

He began to walk more quickly, excited by the thought of seeing her. Julie, no doubt, would be frightened when she saw him. She'd probably react the way Jessica had when she'd found him waiting in her car that night outside the supermarket. He'd tried to explain himself to her, to make her understand, but she'd struggled and dug her nails into his skin, and he'd put his hands around her throat until her eyes rolled back in her head, watching and knowing that she had forced him to do it, forced him for her own selfish reasons to let their future slip away.

But he would treat Julie with the patience she deserved. He would talk to her in quiet tones, and once she really understood the nature of his love for her, once she realized that he'd done all this for her—for them—she would acquiesce. She'd probably still be upset about Singer, but eventually he would comfort her and she would see why he'd had no other choice.

He'd want to lead her to the bedroom afterward, but he knew there wasn't enough time for that. Later tonight, once they were safely away, they would stop at a motel and make love, and they would have a lifetime together to make up for what they'd missed.

*　　　*　　　*

'He's coming, baby,' Julie whispered. 'He'll be here soon and we'll take you to the doctor, okay?'

She could barely see Singer through her tears. He was worsening with every passing minute; he had closed his eyes, and though he was still breathing rapidly, he was wheezing and there was an almost high-pitched whistle, like air escaping through a tiny hole in an air mattress, that didn't sound natural at all. It wasn't just his legs that were quivering; now it was his entire body. Beneath her hand, she could feel his muscles growing tight, as if straining to fight off death.

Singer whimpered, and Julie heard the panic in her own voice. She was running both hands through his fur, aching with him, feeling as if it were happening to her.

'You can't leave me. Please . . .'

Inside, she was screaming at Pete and Mike to hurry up, that they were running out of time. Even though it had been only a couple of minutes, it seemed an eternity, and she knew that Singer wouldn't be able to keep fighting much longer.

'Singer . . . you can make it . . . Don't give up. *Please . . .*'

She was just about to shout out for Pete and

Mike when the words caught in her throat.

At first, she refused to believe what her eyes were seeing, and she tried to blink the image away. But when she looked again, she knew she wasn't wrong.

Though his hair was a different color, though he wore glasses and the mustache was gone, she recognized him immediately.

'Hello, Julie,' Richard said.

*   *   *

Jennifer sped through traffic, whipping between cars, lights flashing.

With her eyes on the road, she gripped the steering wheel so tightly that her hands ached.

Ten minutes, she thought. All I need is ten more minutes.

*   *   *

Julie stared at Richard without breathing as everything clicked into place.

He was here. He's done something to Singer. He's done something to Pete. He's done something to Mike.

Oh, God . . .

Mike . . .

And now he was here for her.

He was walking slowly toward her.

'You . . . ,' was all she could manage to say.

A brief smile flickered across his face. *Of course,* he seemed to say, *who were you expecting?* He stopped a few feet away, and after holding her gaze for a moment or two, his eyes drifted toward Singer.

473

'I'm sorry about Singer,' he said, his voice low. 'I know how much you cared for him.'

He spoke as though he'd had nothing to do with it. A bereaved expression crossed his face, as if he were someone attending the funeral of a close friend.

Julie suddenly felt as if she were about to vomit, but she forced the bile back, trying to maintain some control. Trying to figure out what to do. Trying to understand what had happened to Mike.

Oh, God. *Mike.*

'Where's Mike?' she demanded, wanting to know but suddenly afraid to find out. It was all she could do to keep her voice steady.

Richard looked up, the same sad expression on his face. 'That's over now,' he said matter-of-factly.

His words carried an almost physical impact, and all at once she felt her hands begin to shake.

'What did you do to him?' she choked.

'It doesn't matter.'

'What did you do!?' she screamed, unable to control herself. 'Where is he?'

Richard took another step toward her, his voice still gentle. 'I didn't have a choice, Julie. You know that. He was controlling you, and I couldn't let that continue. But you're safe now. I'll take care of you.'

He took another step, and Julie suddenly slid back, away from Singer.

'He didn't love you, Julie,' he said. 'Not the way I do.'

He's going to kill me, she thought. He killed Mike and Singer and Pete, and now he's going to kill me. Julie began to stand as Richard closed in, her terror building with each step he took. She could see it in his eyes, she could see exactly what

474

he was going to do.

He's going to kill me, but he'll rape me first . . .

The realization was almost disabling, but something inside her screamed, *Run!* and Julie reacted instinctively.

She bolted, not bothering to look back, her feet slipping in the sand as she charged down the beach.

Richard didn't try to stop her. Instead he smiled, knowing there was nowhere for her to go. She would tire herself out, he knew; her panic would undo her. Instead, he hooked the gun into his belt and began to jog after her, enough to keep her in sight and close the distance when the time was right.

*   *   *

Mike was drifting in and out of consciousness. Trapped somewhere between a world of reality and dreams, his mind was finally able to latch on to the fact that he was bleeding heavily.

And that Julie needed him.

Trembling, he slowly began to rise.

*   *   *

Julie tried to keep up a fast pace as she ran toward the lights of the only beach house that seemed to be occupied. Her legs were growing weary, and she began to feel as though she were running in place. The lights looked close, but she couldn't seem to reach them.

No, she said to herself, *no!* He won't catch me. I'll make it, and they'll help me. I'll scream for help and they'll call the police and . . .

But her legs . . . her lungs were burning . . . the pounding of her heart . . .

Only terror kept her moving.

Running as hard as she could, she stole a glance over her shoulder.

Despite the darkness, she could see Richard closing in on her.

I'm not going to make it, she suddenly realized.

She was stumbling now. Her calves were cramping. It was all she could do to keep upright.

And still he was coming . . .

Where is everyone? she wanted to scream. *Help me!*

She knew with cold certainty that the sound of the waves would swallow her screams. Another few steps and she looked behind her again. Closer.

She could hear his footsteps now.

But I can't keep going . . .

She veered toward the dunes, hoping that on the other side there might be a place to hide.

*　　　　*　　　　*

Richard could see her hair rippling out behind her. He was close now, close enough to try to reach for it.

Almost there, he thought, when suddenly she turned and began to charge up the dunes. Off balance, Richard stumbled slightly but was soon on the chase again. He laughed aloud.

Such spirit! Such effort! She was every bit his equal. He almost clapped his hands in delight.

*　　　　*　　　　*

Julie could see a house towering behind the dunes, though climbing up the sand was almost too much for her; feet slipping, she had to use her hands for balance, and by the time she reached the top, her legs were buckling.

For a moment, she registered the home itself; built on pilings, it had room for cars to be parked beneath it, but little cover. The house next to it, however, was more heavily landscaped, and she turned that way.

That was when she felt Richard snare her feet like a football player making an open field tackle. Losing her balance, she tumbled down the far side of the dunes.

When Richard reached her, he bent over and took her by the arm, helping her to her feet.

'You really are a prize,' he said, grinning as he caught his breath. 'I've known it from the moment we met.'

Julie flailed in his grasp and felt his fingers dig into her arm. She struggled harder.

'Don't be this way, Julie,' he said. 'Can't you see this was always how it was going to turn out?'

Julie jerked her arm. 'Let me *go!*' she screamed.

Richard tightened his grip, making her wince. He broke into an amused grin, as if asking, *See how pointless this is?*

'We should probably be going,' he suggested calmly.

'I'm not going anywhere with you!'

She jerked again, finally breaking free from his grasp, but as she moved away from him, she felt him push her from behind, sending her to the ground again.

Staring down at her, he shook his head slightly.

'You okay?' he asked. 'I'm sorry I had to do that, but we need to talk.'

Talk? He wanted to *talk?*

Screw you, she thought. And screw this.

As soon as he began moving toward her, Julie got to her feet and tried to run, but Richard suddenly reached for her hair and jerked it hard.

She heard him give a bewildered laugh.

'Why are you making this so hard?' he asked.

* * *

On the beach, Mike was trying to stand, reaching for the stairs, fighting nausea as the pain shot through him, his thoughts random and fragmented—

Getting up . . . have to call the police . . . help Julie . . . but the pain . . . shot . . . pain . . . where am I . . . that steady roar . . . again and again . . . pain . . . coming in waves . . . waves . . . the ocean . . . Julie . . . have to help her . . .

He took a step.

Then another.

* * *

Julie swung wildly, hitting Richard on the chest and on the face. He pulled her hair again, making her scream.

'Why do you keep fighting me?' Richard asked, his voice and expression calm, as if trying to reason with a wayward child. 'Don't you understand that it's over? There's just the two of us now. There's no reason for you to act this way.'

'Let me go!' she screamed. 'Stay away from me.'

478

'Think of all we can do together,' he said. 'We're two of a kind, you know. Survivors.'

'We'll do nothing together!' she screamed. 'I hate you!'

He pulled savagely on her hair again, bringing her to her knees. 'Don't say that.'

'I hate you!' she screamed again.

'I'm serious,' he said, his voice lower, more ominous. 'I know you're upset, but I don't want to hurt you, Jessica.'

'I'm not Jessica!' she screamed.

*   *   *

Halfway up, Mike fell to his knees but dragged himself forward. With one hand holding his stomach, he reached for the railing and pulled himself up.

He was nearing the top now and could see Pete, facedown on the deck, blood pooling around his head.

Another couple of steps and he reached the deck, making his way to the door. Without the railing he was off balance, but he kept his eyes focused on the door, concentrating on what he had to do.

*   *   *

Richard stared at her, his expression curious, as if he didn't know what she meant. He blinked, and his head began tilting to the side, like a child first studying his reflection in a mirror.

'What did you say?'

'I'm not Jessica!' she screamed again.

Richard's free hand went behind his back; a

479

moment later, she saw the gun.

* * *

Mike reached the knob and turned it, feeling disembodied as the door swung open.

The phone, he thought. Have to get to the phone before it's too late.

That was when he heard something crash through the front door. Raising his eyes, he suddenly felt a surge of relief.

'Julie needs help,' he rasped out. 'Down the beach . . .'

* * *

Shocked by Mike's condition, Jennifer quickly moved to his side and helped him to the chair. Then she grabbed the phone and dialed the emergency number. When it began ringing, she handed him the phone.

'Get an ambulance!' she said. 'Can you do that?'

Mike nodded, breathing hard as he raised the phone to his ear. 'Pete . . . outside . . .'

Jennifer surged toward the door as she heard Mike requesting an ambulance. On the deck, she first believed that Pete was dead. Blood was pouring from his head, but as she bent over to check on him, he moved his arm and moaned.

'Don't move,' she said. 'Ambulance is on the way.'

She raised her eyes to the stairs. A moment later, she was charging down the steps.

* * *

Richard put the gun to her temple, and Julie instinctively stopped moving. Gone was the calm expression on his face; reality seemed to have deserted him. She could see it in the way he looked at her, in the rasping sound he made as he drew a breath.

'I love you,' he repeated. 'I've always loved you.'

Don't move, she thought. If you do, he'll kill you.

'But you're not giving me a chance to show you.' He pulled her by the hair, moving her ear closer to his mouth.

'Say it. Say you love me.'

Julie said nothing.

'*Say it!*' he screamed, and Julie flinched at the fury in his tone. It sounded raw, almost feral. She could feel the heat of his breath on the side of her face.

'I gave you a chance, and I even *forgave you* for what you've done to me! For what you forced me to do. Now *say it!*'

The fear was in her chest now, in her throat, in her limbs.

'I love you,' she whimpered, on the verge of tears.

'Say is so I can hear it. Like you mean it.'

Beginning to cry. 'I love you.'

'Again.'

Crying harder. 'I love you.'

'Say you want to come with me.'

'I want to come with you.'

'Because you love me.'

'Because I love you.'

And like a dream, from the corner of her eye she saw a vision cresting over the dune, her guardian charging through the darkness.

As the vision before her eyes took shape, Julie watched as Singer launched himself at Richard, snarling, his jaw clamping down on the arm holding the gun.

Singer didn't let go, and both Julie and Richard toppled to the side, Richard jerking at his arm, trying to free himself. Singer was tugging and shaking his head, giving it everything he had as Richard began to scream, the gun tumbling from his hand.

He was on his back now, fighting to keep Singer from his throat.

His face contorting, Richard held back Singer with one hand and began reaching for the gun. The dog didn't stop his attack, but Julie screamed, and it was the sound that gave her the strength to get up and move.

She scrambled up, knowing she didn't have much time.

Behind her, Richard's fingers curled around the handle of the gun.

It was the sound of the gun going off that made Julie suddenly freeze again. Singer yelped, his cry long and drawn out.

'*Singer!*' Julie screamed. 'Oh, God . . . *noooo!*'

Another shot and another yelp, this time weaker. Looking over her shoulder, she saw Richard maneuver Singer's body off him and get to his feet.

Julie began to tremble uncontrollably.

Singer was on his side, struggling now to get up, growling and crying at the same time, writhing in pain, blood gushing onto the sand.

In the distance came the sound of sirens.

'We have to go now,' Richard said. 'We're almost out of time.'

But all Julie could do was stare at Singer.

'*Now!*' Richard boomed. He grabbed her by the hair again and tugged. Julie fought him, kicking and screaming, when a voice called out from the top of the dune.

'*Freeze!*'

Richard and Julie saw Officer Jennifer Romanello at the same time. Richard pointed the gun toward her and fired wildly; a moment later, a choked sigh escaped him. There was a sharp, burning pain in his chest, a sound like a freight train in his ears. Suddenly the gun in his hand seemed ridiculously heavy. He fired again, missed, and felt another burning sensation in his throat, forcing him backward. He felt the blood pooling in his lungs, hearing the gurgle as he tried to draw a breath. He couldn't swallow, the sticky fluid making it impossible. He wanted to cough it up, to spit it in the officer's direction, but his strength was fading quickly. The gun slipped from his hands, and he dropped to his knees, his mind slowing. All he'd wanted for Julie was happiness, their happiness. The shapes around him were growing darker, dimming by the second. He turned toward Julie and tried to speak, but his mouth couldn't form the words.

But still, he clung to his dream, his dream of a life with Julie, the woman he loved. Julie, he thought, my sweet Jessica . . .

Richard fell forward into the sand.

Julie stared at his body, then turned toward Singer.

He was on his side, panting hard, his mouth

hanging open. Julie went to him, bending down, struggling to see him through her tears.

He whimpered as she laid her hand on his head, and his tongue flicked at it.

'Oh . . . baby,' she wept.

He was bleeding from two deep wounds, the blood soaking into the sand beneath him. Shaking, Julie put her head on his body and Singer whimpered again. His eyes were wide and scared, and when he tried to lift his head, he yelped, the sound nearly breaking her heart.

'Don't move . . . I'll get you to the vet, okay?'

She could feel his breath on her skin, rapid and shallow. He licked her again, and she kissed him.

'You're so good, sweetie. You were so brave . . . so brave . . .'

His eyes were on her. He whimpered again, and Julie stifled her cry.

'I love you, Singer,' she murmured as the muscles in his body began to relax.

'It's okay, sweetheart. No more fighting. I'm safe now, you can go to sleep . . .'

Epilogue

Julie went into the bedroom while Mike was cooking in the kitchen, the smell of spaghetti sauce filling the house. She flicked on the light.

Almost two months had passed since that awful night on the beach. Though she remembered everything that happened there, what happened later was a blur, a jumble of events that ran together. She remembered Jennifer Romanello helping her back to the house, she remembered the paramedics working on Mike and Pete, and she remembered the house filling slowly with people; after that everything went hazy, then black.

She woke up in the hospital. Pete was there as well, and Mike was in another room just down the hall. Pete was up and around in a few days, but Mike was in critical condition for a week. Once his condition stabilized and he began to improve, he stayed in the hospital for another three weeks. The entire time, Julie camped out in a chair by his bed, holding his hand, whispering to him even when he slept.

The police had more questions and also more information about Richard's past, but she found she didn't care about any of it. Richard Franklin was dead—in her mind, he would never be remembered as Robert Bonham—and that's all that mattered.

And so, of course, was Singer.

Later, she'd been told by the veterinarian that he'd been given rat poison, enough to kill six dogs within minutes. 'I don't understand it,' Linda

Patinson told Julie. 'It was a miracle he was able to move at all, let alone fight with a grown man.'

But he had, Julie thought. And he saved me.

On the day they buried Singer in Julie's backyard, a warm, soft rain fell around the small group of people who gathered to say goodbye to the Great Dane who had been Julie's companion in life and, at the end, her guardian.

*　　*　　*

Once Mike was out of the hospital, the next few weeks passed in a daze. For the most part, he had moved in. Though he still kept his apartment, he hadn't stayed there since before they'd gone to the beach house, and Julie was grateful. He had a way of knowing whether she needed to be held or wanted to be alone.

But nothing seemed right anymore; the house was too empty, left-overs were tossed in the garbage, nothing snuggled against her feet. There were times it seemed as if Singer were still around, though. From the corner of her eye, she sometimes saw movement. It was clear whenever it happened, but when she turned to see what had caused it, there was nothing at all. One time, she smelled an odor that was undeniably him. It smelled as if he were sitting beside her after playing in the ocean— but when she rose from the couch in search of the source, the odor simply vanished. And once, late at night, she felt the urge to get up and go to the living room. Though the house was dark, she heard him drinking from the water bowl in the kitchen. The sound made her freeze and her heart sped up, but again, the sound simply died away.

One night, she dreamed of both Jim and Singer. They were walking together in an open field, their backs to her, as she was running and trying to catch them. In her dream, she called to them both, and they stopped and turned around. Jim smiled; Singer barked. She wanted to go to them, but she couldn't seem to move. They stared at her with the same tilt of their heads, the same looks in their eyes, the same glow behind them. Jim put his hand on Singer's back, and Singer barked again happily, as if letting her know this was the way it was meant to be. Instead of coming toward her, they turned again and she watched them go, the outlines of their images fading slowly into one.

When she woke, she picked up her bedside picture of Singer, missing him. Her heart still ached when she looked at it, though it no longer made her cry. In the back of the frame, she'd tucked the letter that Jim had written, and now she slipped it out.

As the morning sun warmed the windows, she read it again, her eyes slowing as she reached the final paragraph.

And don't worry. From wherever I am, I'll watch out for you. I'll be your guardian angel, sweetheart. You can count on me to keep you safe.

Julie looked up, her eyes moist.
Yes, she thought, you did.

Author's Note

The genesis of a novel is always a tricky process. Often it begins with a vague idea, or in my case, a theme, and for this novel, I chose the theme of love and danger. In other words, I wanted to write a story in which two believable characters fall in love, but I wanted to add elements of suspense and peril that would ultimately put both characters in jeopardy. I can't remember where I was when I made the decision to attempt such a story, but I do remember thinking that I was going to enjoy the process of trying to write a type of novel that I hadn't written before.

Boy, was I ever wrong.

Well, let me rephrase that. While I did enjoy the process of writing the novel, the editing required was far and away the most difficult I've ever had to do. From first to final draft, the novel went through eight major revisions until my editor and I were finally satisfied that the novel accomplished what it set out to do; that is, be a love story first and foremost, and secondly—in a way that sneaks up on the reader—a compelling thriller.

In the course of my life, I've probably read a couple of thousand thrillers, and though many of them had characters fall in love within the story, I can't remember reading one where the thriller element was secondary to the relationship. The reason for this is simple—the scarier something is, the more it dominates the story. The challenge with *The Guardian*, then, was to find the right balance between the two elements and to pace the

489

story accordingly, so that the reader never lost sight of what the novel really was—a love story between two regular people who find that they've crossed paths with the wrong sort of person. Though it sounds easy, on my end it made for many sleepless nights.

I've also always wanted to write a story that included a dog. Whether it was *Old Yeller* by Fred Gipson, *Where the Red Fern Grows* by Wilson Rawls, *To Dance with the White Dog* by Terry Kay, or *My Dog Skip* by Willie Morris, I've always loved stories with dogs, and I thought that it might be nice to include a dog in this particular novel. I'm indebted to those authors for their work and the hours of enjoyment those books gave me. There was also a touching story entitled 'Delayed Delivery' by Cathy Miller in *Chicken Soup for the Pet Lover's Soul* (edited by Jack Canfield, Mark Victor Hansen, Marty Becker, and Carol Kline, HCI publishers) that inspired the prologue of *The Guardian*, and I'd like to thank her—and the editors—for bringing a tear to my eye.